KAREN HARPER

EMPTY CRADLE

MIRA

MIRA®

ISBN 0-7783-2354-4

EMPTY CRADLE

First published by the Penguin Group.

Copyright © 1998 by Karen Harper.

www.MIRABooks.com

Printed In U.S.A.

For their bravery and determination,
this novel is dedicated
to the many women and men
who become IVF heroes
in the face of great odds—
whether or not they become parents.

1

Alexis McCall's eyes glazed with tears, but she blinked them back and stared up at the white acoustical ceiling tiles she'd been studying as if she could read some answer there.

"I can get you out of here pronto if you're not still sure about this," her friend Sandra insisted. She leaned closer to Alex's high, narrow hospital bed. They whispered in the draped cubicle since nurses and at least one other patient were nearby.

"I'm *not* sure," Alex admitted, "but I'm going to do it." She squeezed Sandra's hand so hard she winced. "This is my last chance, so I have to take the risk."

"Then I'm here for you, like you were for me, *chica*." Sandra's dark brown eyes looked huge, even in a round face set in a riot of ebony curls.

"I don't know what I'd do without you, but I've never felt more alone or scared in my whole life—at least since I lost Geoff." In the silence, her stomach growled as if in protest of the coming ordeal.

"That mariachi band's in there because they told you no breakfast," Sandra said, playfully poking Alex's flat midriff. "When this is over and I get you back to your place, I'm going to scramble you some of my special *huevos rancheros.*"

"Anything but eggs today for obvious rea—" Alex began, but the swish and click of the opening curtain drowned the rest of her words. Her nurse, Beth Bradley, appeared, looking much too perky and cheerful for the early hour. She gave Alex the tranquilizing injection she'd been expecting and stayed a few moments to take her pulse. She squeezed Alex's shoulder before she walked away. The soft squeak of her crepe soles sounded incredibly loud until they were replaced by the distant drone of an airplane.

It must be high above the mountains, Alex thought, probably a jet out of Kirtland, Geoff's air force base in nearby Albuquerque. For one crazy moment it was as if from high above he sent her his strength, but from such a fathomless distance…so far away and never coming back again….

Alex panicked, lifting both hands to press them, one on top of the other, over her mouth. Sandra jumped to her feet, bending over her like a worried mother.

"I thought you were past crying over airplanes," she said, her voice rough from trying to stem her own emotions. "This is what Geoff wanted as much as you, remember. I mean, maybe not that you keep the career in high gear but the rest of it, right?"

Alex slowly lowered her hands to grip them together on her stomach. She nodded, sniffling. Sandra gave her a tissue, and she blew her nose. "Besides," Alex said, "lots of TV personalities work on air right up to the minute they deliver. Lots of women do a good job as a single parent."

Sandra nodded jerkily, then stooped to give her a quick, hard hug. Her paper scrubs crinkled. Sandra Sanchez was sweet-faced, shapely, and plump—a soft-looking woman. But her reputation in the four corners area near Albuquerque, which the TV station covered, was just the opposite. For one thing, she waved her pride in her Hispanic heritage like a bright banner. And she could be as hard and sharp as the designer acrylic nails she always sported. For KALB's top investigative reporter, the bigger and tougher the story, the better. *One phone call from Sanchez and people start looking for cliffs to jump off,* Alex had heard someone say last week.

"Alex, I know," she said, perching on the edge of the bed and emphasizing each word in her best on-air, authoritative voice, "this is going to work. In nine months you're either gonna be spending big bucks for a nanny or hauling diapers and formula to the station."

"I'm sure Mike would love that," Alex countered, referring to Mike Montgomery, their station manager. "He's already furious with me for losing control of myself on the air. I wish I could tell him the real reason I was so upset, but this whole crisis—this quest—is my personal affair—the last private thing I possess."

"I know, I know, *chica*." Sandra's gaze became distant. "Funny how we make a career of exposing other people's lives but fight like hell to protect a piece of our own." She bit her lower lip to halt the quiver of her chin. Alex knew she was recalling her own tragic loss before she tossed her head defiantly and looked back at Alex. "But I can just feel it," Sandra said as she smacked her hands together. "Just like the Holy Mother, you're gonna have an immaculate conception, but I don't want you to go over the edge trusting the man who's playing God today."

Alex forced a tight little smile. In her best moments she believed everything would be fine too. Despite terrible odds against someone with her ovulation and miscarriage problems, she had to trust the doctors and staff of this private high-tech clinic to do their brilliant best for her. And not only because her thirty-four-year-old biological clock was clanging. Frozen sperm didn't last forever, and Geoff had been dead for four years this month. But this was a time for new beginnings.

"You know," she told Sandra as she jumped back up to peek out through the drapes, "that shot I had, Versed, is an amnesiac, but I'm okay so far, I think. I want to remember all of this."

Alex sighed so hard she felt physically deflated. Maybe the drug was grabbing hold. Suddenly, she was so drowsy and limp she could barely move so much as a facial muscle. She did, however, manage a little yawn.

"On our way now," Beth told them as she whipped open the drapes. As she leaned over Alex, her warm, hazel eyes and wide, full mouth seemed to fill her heart-shaped face, framed by a chestnut pageboy with bouncy bangs. "Okay, Alexis, I'm going to test your mental reflexes," she said. "Can you tell me why it takes so many sperm to fertilize one egg?"

Alex felt so floaty that for a second she believed it was a serious question. But Sandra was grinning, so it must be a joke. She had to work harder to think because her mind was wandering.

"No, why?" she finally asked.

"Because they refuse to stop to ask for directions."

Sandra gave a muted moan, but Alex could manage only a stiff grimace. Beth adjusted the bed and pastel blanket. Pale plum, Alex thought, just like this room and the curtain—designer colors for designer babies.

Two other nurses appeared with a gurney, helped Beth lift Alex onto it, then disappeared. With Sandra trailing, Beth pushed Alex out of the prep and recovery area down a hallway lined with watercolors of flowers blooming in the desert.

"'We're off to see the wizard,'" Beth sang, "'the wonderful wizard of Oz.'"

Alex wasn't sure, but she thought she probably made that little hop-step Judy Garland did in her red sparkle shoes. Sandra laughed, but Alex only felt like Dorothy drugged in that vast field of poppies while the Wicked Witch pursued her.

She closed her eyes because the ceiling tiles and recessed lights flying by overhead made her dizzy. She tried to concentrate on Geoff's long-lost face, on his strength, but he kept fading. He was lost to her in the long corridors of passing days and the world's daring to go on without him. But that last night in bed together he had been so desperate over their continued failure to have a child.

She could hear his quick, impassioned voice now: *Alex, swear to me that even if I—I don't come back, you'll still try. Try to have our baby, a precious heritage, someone for you to love and care for...a piece of me to go on when I can't....*

He moved against her, closer in the cocooned darkness of their blanketed bed that moved and rolled with their lovemaking. *Yes, my darling,* she had vowed. *Yes, I promise you...*

"Almost to the Land of Oz," Beth said to bring her back. "Dorothy, this isn't Kansas anymore."

They passed the hall door to the embryo lab and turned into what was called the transfer room. Suddenly, the soaring sounds of Handel's majestic *Water Music* washed over Alex. Other patients had said Dr. Hale Stanhope always played classical, but his wife, Dr. Jasmine—whose nickname Alex heard was Jazz—played Basin Street's best in her lab.

The large room bathed her in dim, greenish light. She floated on her back into a watery cave under the sea. Since eggs and embryos never saw the harsh light of day inside a woman's body, soft indirect lighting, machine displays, and the doctor's high-intensity headlamp would provide the only illumination of the area during this and other in-vitro fertilization procedures.

"Why don't you just stand on her other side, Sandra?" Alex heard Beth say, and Sandra swam around the end of the gurney to get out of the way. "The doctor will be right in," she told Alex, then hid her smile by tying her mask in place.

Beth and the anesthesiologist lifted her onto the table, then bent over her. Soon she was wired to machines. By just turning her head she could watch the rise and fall of her pulse and respiration tracked in amber and green waves on instruments. Yes, it had been wavy like that on their honeymoon when they went scuba diving in the Bahamas in that deep sea cave.

Sandra jumped and looked up at the ceiling as a woman's clipped, disembodied voice filled the room: "Good morning, Alexis. Dr. Jasmine here, waiting for those lovely eggs to mix with your husband's sperm in the embryo lab next door. Then, in just two days, transfer and, hopefully, implantation. Dr. Stanhope will be right in."

Despite their shared last name, only one person at the clinic was referred to as Dr. Stanhope, so his wife went by Dr. Jasmine. The queen of the Evergreen Reproductive Health Clinic reigned only in the lab across the dividing wall from her husband's O.R. The two rooms were linked by a hatch through which harvested eggs from hormone-ripened ovaries, or sperm, or embryos could be passed to be transferred.

Yes, she was ready for this, Alex thought. She had waited too long to try IVF again without Geoff. At least now she had learned to live without him.

Beth gently lifted Alex's draped legs into stirrups and washed her with an icy disinfectant. For the crazy cost of a complete IVF cycle, couldn't they warm that stuff?

Several pricks of slightly stinging pain followed—a local anesthetic she was expecting, but it jolted her.

Even in her loggy state Alex started when the double doors to the hall opened with a resounding crack. "Good morning, Alexis," Dr. Hale Stanhope's somewhat monotone voice rang out. He was from Boston and, she thought, always sounded like those old news clips of President Kennedy. He said *potly* for *partly* and *idear* instead of *idea*.

People returned a muted good morning; Dr. Stanhope brought a reassuring presence into any room. Alex thought she said hello too, but she wasn't sure.

He bent over her, his pewter eyes framed by thick lashes and raven eyebrows that had not turned prematurely silver with his hair. Instead of pale plum scrubs like everyone else wore, his were baby blue. She hoped that the color was a good omen.

"Ready, Alexis?" he asked with a tight smile and a quick nod that seemed to answer for her. "I am, and we're going to do good work here. Ready in the lab," he ordered, instead of asked, over the piped-in music as he moved away and clicked on his headlamp. He stepped closer again, this time between her draped legs. She was grateful that he hid the long probe with its collection needle from her. Sandra must have seen it, though, because her eyes widened over her mask, and she put a shaky hand on Alex's shoulder.

"Since we have KALB-TV's noon and early evening anchorwoman and top investigative reporter in attendance," the doctor went on as Alex felt the first slight thrust of pressure, "I'll just tell everybody to watch the

TV screen, and we'll hope for some very good ratings today."

Alex turned her head to follow the Doppler ultrasound probe on the big video monitor. The black-and-silver picture shimmered like a rain-glazed window to her womb. No one looked at her now but at the image of her interior. Suddenly, this—all of it—seemed so unreal.

Watch the TV screen. The doctor's words reverberated in her head. She hoped her suspension from the station would end the mess she'd made She needed and loved that job, but the hormonal drug Pergonal had given her such wild mood swings that she had cried on the air while reporting a case of child abuse. How could anyone harm his own child, even a child he didn't want? If that bastard had been in the studio, she could have pounded his face in. By then he had been arrested, but she hoped that coverage helped make life a living hell for him from now on.

"Oh!" she cried out as she felt a deep cramp. Tears blurred the screen. Sandra gripped her shoulder harder.

"Just a little jab," Dr. Stanhope announced, his eyes riveted on the monitor, "I'm in the right ovary, first follicle," he called out, evidently loud enough so the embryo lab could hear. "See that follicle on the screen, Ms. Sanchez?" he asked Sandra, his voice a bit quieter. "That black sphere the size of a grape? The computer calculates the path for the needle to follow and draws a line on the screen. See, when I probe the follicle, it collapses and hopefully yields a ripe egg in this vial of fluid— there!"

"Yes, I see!" Sandra cried triumphantly, leaning toward Alex's prone form to get a better view of the screen.

Alex groaned as he siphoned the fluid out through the small, attached hose. She could hear but not see him splash the contents into a small, Teflon-coated bowl Beth held for him. Alex glimpsed it when she carried it past, proudly and carefully, as if it held a newborn itself. The bowl had been labeled in bold strokes of black Magic Marker: MCCALL, A. Beth passed it through the hatch as Hale Stanhope turned to his task again. Alex guessed she felt less shaky, less chicken now, as her brothers used to tease her. Which came first, she thought, the chicken or the egg?

"Here's hoping for an egg." Dr. Stanhope interrupted her scrambled thoughts. "Second follicle on the right…"

It went on in a blur—sticks and groans, terse comments. This really did hurt more than they'd led her to believe, so maybe it was worse for some patients. But pain—deep, soul-struck pain was something she had seen close up and survived.

"Egg!" Dr. Jasmine's voice boomed on the intercom. Sandra cheered; Beth patted her arm; Handel's music soared; and Dr. Stanhope hummed along. Even as that voice from the heavens called out "Egg!" three more times over the next twenty minutes, Alexis McCall lay on her back and sobbed silently in relief and joy.

Now, if only Geoff were here to lean on, to take her home.

* * *

Two huge eyes stared back at her.

Jasmine Stanhope had a habit of studying herself in the lenses of her $40,000 new Nikon electronic microscope before she pressed her face to it to peer within. The darkly mirrored reflection rested her strained eyes, but mostly it assured her that she was beautiful as well as brainy.

Her upswept, layered platinum hair haloed a classically oval face and aquamarine eyes. That, as well as her lithe model's body, always startled people when they discovered she was a doctor, an embryologist, no less. She was thirty-seven, but looked in her early thirties. And no way she would give into that damned, creeping middle-age spread, she thought, shifting on her stool. If she had to spend every spare free hour jogging or working with that *Butt Busters* video to keep the lard off her bottom, that's exactly what she'd do.

"You gonna be awhile?" Tom Anders, her young associate embryologist, asked over the roll of music—a Creole jazz band's rendition of Gershwin. "Now that we're done with this morning's harvesting, thought I'd eat my lunch outside, maybe take a quick walk down that path overlooking the ghost town," he added. Five acres of clinic property abutted ramshackle ruins that had once been a prosperous silver mine and its little, long-dead boomtown.

"Sorry, I'm going to be awhile, Tom."

"Okay. But I packed enough for two here—blue corn tortillas stuffed with sprouts, pinto beans, and chiles. A politically correct lunch, even for the Jane Fonda of the fertility world."

Not lifting her eyes from the lenses, Jasmine automatically stretched and snapped the wrists of her latex gloves. She wore her gold and diamond tennis bracelets under them, which imprinted in her flesh if she didn't shift them around. She adjusted the magnification focus knob; the egg flew into sharp relief.

"A lot of blood, a lot of cells," she observed. "But only four eggs from Alexis McCall today, and I've got to take good care of them." It went unspoken that some egg harvests went as high as twenty eggs, but this one had been really minimal. "She lost her pilot husband in Saudi Arabia during the Gulf War in that SCUD explosion in a barracks," she went on. "It's a real dicey situation to get her a viable embryo out of this with sperm there is no way to replace."

"You'll handle it, Jazz—if you're not skipping meals so you get light-headed again," he said, not budging. She could sense he was practically breathing down her neck. "I mean, Hale said you need to keep up your strength with the long, late hours you been putting in."

"Yes, Mother," she mocked gently. "And when Hale says, 'Let there be light,' all that draw breath must obey. I'll eat when I get done here," she added curtly. "In other words, I've got to get those greedy, wriggly won't-take-no-for-an-answer little tadpoles you washed and centrifuged to thrust themselves inside this lovely, waiting egg, though it looks quite happy on its own."

Even over the hum of the incubators, she could hear he finally took the hint. His lunch sack rustled, his feet scuffed the tiled floor as he walked out and closed the door.

She liked him, all the staff except one they'd assembled here these last three years, she really did, but she didn't need someone watching her closely. And she didn't want to encourage his embryonic—she smiled grimly at the pun—infatuation with her. If Hale could cope with scores of desperate women who adored him, she could handle one man. Besides, she had more important things to do.

She lost herself in the fascinating world that blossomed before her enlarged gaze. Using a micro-pipette, she swirled the egg around, marveling anew at how every one of the thousands she'd studied resembled a distinct cumulus cloud—just like unique snowflakes, no two alike. She'd never really understood how so many scientists were atheists. It was obvious to her that one ultrabrilliant mind had created the universe in definite patterns. She turned up the power of the scope again. The egg bloomed even bigger.

She moved it into a second dish, rinsed it, then added a small drop of mineral oil to it in a third dish. Her neck muscles ached as she rose to get the vial of sperm of— in this case—a dead donor whose future, if not his life, had been preserved in a glass ampule in a freezing bath of liquid nitrogen. With tweezers she removed the lab's temporary plug Tom had put on the narrow neck of the vial. She would inseminate each of the McCalls' eggs separately and pray she had four viable fertilized eggs to coddle before Hale took over again and got all the glory.

She released a tiny jet of sperm into the dish with the egg, then put it back under the microscope. She watched the battle as the writhing warriors tried to outpace each other to attack the fortress of the much bigger, thick-skinned egg. But the ranks of this army had literally met their Waterloo.

Staring into the microscope, she muttered under her breath, as if it were a magic spell, "The ultimate orgasm—the chance to beat them. And they think," she added, her voice derisive, "they're in charge of the whole big, damn world."

She shook her head in disgust if not disappointment. Before the sperm battered themselves into oblivion, she reached for her micromanipulation tools. She did a micropuncture on the egg, selected one lucky, lively sperm, and ejaculated it directly in. She might never bear Hale Stanhope a baby, but again *she* had created another potential one here.

Smiling, she rose, then knelt as if in obeisance to an invisible altar. In her daily ritual, she reached into the back corner under the counter to touch the vessel that guarded the sacrifices. Then she stood and, from the incubator on the counter, retrieved the petri dish. For one moment she rocked the fragile glass cradle with the newly harvested egg, the one nobody knew about.

2

Nick Destin was already mad as hell when his favorite big-brimmed hat blew off and went spinning across the reddish rockface like a tumbleweed. He dared not chase it so near the edge, but it snagged on a sprawling cactus growing half under a rock. He carefully retrieved it, then picked his way back across the edge of the cliff, his booted feet sending a shower of stones and gravel over the side into the gulch that held the little, long-abandoned mining town of Silver.

The owners had suddenly decided not to sell the site. Worse, he felt he was being watched. But he figured it was just his guilt at being in forbidden territory. Or maybe the uncanny, creepy aura of the site aptly named a ghost town was just getting to him. For damn sure it was not his terrible earlier disaster with Carolyn coming back to haunt him again. He was done with that and her at last.

To be sure he was alone, he surveyed the sweep of land behind him before glancing back at the ruins. Silver wasn't as large as other derelict towns in this once big mining area, but it was a ways off the beaten path, so few vandals or thieves had violated it. So he really resented that some futuristic, high-tech fertility clinic expanding here in what was the ultimate vandalism and theft of the West's precious past.

"Damn!" He scratched his hand as he dusted off his hat. He saw he'd have to pull prickers from it. He carried it, walking along the boundaries which the clinic owners had evidently set off with a barbed-wire fence since his last visit. In vaulting it at the far end he snagged the seat of his jeans and felt a barb scratch his hip. Swearing, he pulled himself free.

As he headed toward his Jeep, he skirted the back of the clinic property. Too late he saw, sitting in pine rocking chairs on the rear portico, two women staring at him.

"You're trespassing," the smaller one, dressed in paper scrubs like a nurse or a tech, shouted at him. She stood, her hands on her hips, her face frozen in dismay or anger. "You'll have to leave, or I'll call the clinic manager."

Her greeting did not improve his temper. But it wasn't that woman who drew his attention. He knew the other one. The sudden lift of her head and her surprised expression indicated she remembered him too.

"I *am* leaving," he said, "but it's fine with me if you get the manager. Tell him it's Nicholas Destin. And make it clear to him I'm walking back to *my* vehicle, which is parked on the *public* access road, by staying *off* the clinic's property line here. I checked. I know where the boundaries end."

"I'm sure your friend will be right here to pick you

up, Alexis," Nick heard the nurse say. "This intruder's obviously been down at the future annex, and the doctors don't want any liability for someone who falls there." Shooting another frown at Nick, she hurried inside.

"You'll have to forgive Beth," Alexis McCall said when the nurse banged the back door. "She's the mother hen for everyone and everything around here. How are you, Nick?"

Though he was warm from his earlier exertions and the sun, he felt his face and neck heat at her vibrant voice and steady perusal. He wished he wasn't dust-covered and sweaty with ripped jeans. All of a sudden he wished too many damn things. As he came closer, she didn't stand, but rocked slightly forward in the chair to extend her hand. His long legs took him quickly the rest of the way.

"Now I'm *really* trespassing," he told her, shaking her hand, then holding it a moment longer than he should have. He could not see but could sense her assessing stare through both pairs of their sunglasses. He could picture just what those heavily fringed, green-gold eyes looked like without any barrier between them. Instantly, he felt his own barriers go up.

Alexis McCall was a tall, slim woman who not only looked good on camera, Nick admitted, but in person. She gazed at him steadily, sure of herself. No—this close up he remembered some shadowed sorrow in her eyes and the tenseness at the corners of her full mouth as if she'd say something defiant or provocative. She seemed warm and open, but he sensed she always held something back.

She was delicate-boned, with honey blond hair the breeze lifted where she sat in the shade, while he felt as if he were under the glare of studio lights in this sun. When her hair settled again, its smooth length cupped her oval face and seemed to lift that shapely mouth into a slight smile. For once the usually vivacious woman wore very little makeup and seemed a bit wan or tired.

"Sorry to interrupt," he said. "You're doing a story here, I guess."

"Actually, no. I'm sure you get the idea they like their privacy."

"Who doesn't?" he asked, then regretted sounding so brusque.

She pulled her hand back as if surprised he still held it. "Why *are* you here anyway, Nick?"

"I thought I was in negotiations with the clinic for the land that little ghost town sits on down below, until the owners suddenly decided they're going to need it for future expansion," he explained. He put one foot on the single step and leaned forward with an arm across his knee. "But it's land down a twisting path and steep cliff from here and not good for a big structure. They've fenced it off and told me to forget it—actually, not just me. I represent a group of Santa Fe businesspeople called Living Heritage Limited, who like to preserve pieces of the past in this area."

"I never heard of that group," she said, sitting up straighter. "I certainly don't want to upset the Stanhopes, but maybe I could talk to you more about some slant for a story about Living Heritage in general."

He nodded, rotating his hand until another pricker

jabbed him. "That story you did of my shop made business boom for a while," he admitted with a taut smile. "The Pueblo artists really appreciated it. Being able to wield that much power must be something."

"Ah, the power of the media. I never think of it that way, but you're right. No, actually, I'm here for another reason and—oh, I see my friend has pulled the car up to the edge of the parking lot over there," she added, nodding in that direction.

She seemed relieved to change the subject. He realized he'd somehow inserted big boot into mouth. "I didn't mean to intrude on clinic land or your private turf," he told her. "You mind if I walk you to your friend's car?"

She rose, he thought, a bit slowly and stiffly for one so lithe. She didn't answer, but he walked along with her anyway. He saw her friend—he recognized the spitfire Hispanic reporter whose family had been in that tragedy—get out and start hesitantly toward them, but he walked all the way out and went around to open the car door for Alexis. Her friend nodded and got in the driver's side.

"Well, see you sometime," Alexis said, fastening her seat belt. He was surprised that her voice seemed to break. He felt totally annoyed that he didn't want to let her go like this.

"Yeah, sure," he replied. He closed the door, wishing he hadn't run into her today. It was the first time since he'd decided to pretty much go it alone that he wanted some serious feminine company. He leaned down to glance in. Just before the car backed away, he saw that Alex had been crying behind her sunglasses.

That hit like a fist in the pit of his stomach. She felt torn up too, but over what? If not a news story, what could a single woman be doing here at a reproductive clinic? Most of her TV audience knew she was widowed.

He stared after them a moment, even when a man came out and called his name. Clenching his fists at his sides, Nick strode back to the rear of the clinic to take him on.

"So where'd you find the Marlboro man out here?" Sandra asked as she drove out of the clinic parking lot. "He's the type I'm sure they'd love to have donate sperm, but the type who'd never do it. And he's not one of the clinic staff dressed like that."

Alex's head suddenly started to pound. Sandra talked as fast as she drove slow. They'd never get back to Albuquerque. If she hadn't felt so drained, she would have insisted on taking over the wheel.

"He was coming back from that ghost town down the cliff," she explained, massaging her temples. "Nick Destin, New Mexico Treasures—"

"I'll say he is. *¡Muy guapo!* Dark-haired with a tiny touch of silver, rugged, bronzed. He even looks kind of Hispanic until you get really close—or listen to that Southern drawl."

"He's of Greek heritage and from the South somewhere. Baton Rouge, I think. His name's really Destinapolos or something. He played football for some famous coach named Bear something-or-other at Alabama—'Bama he calls it. I interviewed him once briefly for a routine story about two years ago, that's all—"

"And just happened to remember all kinds of Trivial Pursuit stuff about him. Hey, you crying, Alex? *Madre de Dios,* you in pain? We can go right back," she said and hit the brakes on the narrow road that led to the highway.

Alex made the mistake of shaking her head, because it made it feel worse. "No, I'm fine. It's only that sitting there with Beth waiting for you, I kept wishing that I had a husband for this dream baby—someone to walk me out of there and take me home and be with me. And suddenly, it was as if that man just materialized from nowhere. He said everybody wants privacy but then walked me to the car."

"You know, when I looked into the sun, I was startled for a minute. I mean, since he was tall and broad-shouldered like—but he's dark as Geoff was blond and this Destin's a lot more solid than lanky. I remember now how you thought you were going to blush just asking him some arcane question in that short piece about Pueblo art or whatever."

"Or whatever. Look, Sandra, I'm really exhausted and working on a screamer of a headache. Would you just drive and not talk right now? Maybe I can take a nap."

"Sure. Sure," she said, her voice more thoughtful than annoyed. The car accelerated slightly again.

Alex didn't sleep or even relax. She recalled that Nick Destin was married to a stunning, auburn-haired woman who had come in the shop during the interview and stuck like glue while they did retakes. She had instinctively disliked the woman as much as she had liked Nick.

"Alex," Sandra whispered, "just one more thing."

"What?"

"You're doing a story with Destin?"

"He's heading up a Santa Fe group restoring ghost towns. If Mike okays it, that's all. And since you'll find out anyway, I'll tell you the clinic owns that town in the valley and won't sell it. Big deal. There's no story there."

"There's a story everywhere, and you know it. But right now, let's just get you home to bed."

The next morning, already running late, Alexis was on her way out the door for her sudden command performance at the station—a staff photo call and meeting with the boss—when the phone rang. Hoping it was the news she'd been waiting for, she tore to the kitchen wall phone and picked up before her answering machine kicked in.

"Alexis McCall here."

"Alexis, Dr. Stanhope."

She held her breath, listening to her heart beating as if it were on the other end of the line. She slumped against the wall. She should have asked Beth if the doctor himself called if it was good news or only if it was bad. The headache her fitful night's sleep had erased threatened to return.

"We have some reasonable progress," he went on, and she heard paper crinkling.

"Thank God." She breathed again. "But what do you mean *reasonable?*"

"The four eggs have become four viable pre-embryos. We'll transfer two tomorrow morning and freeze two in case we need a later try. I'll let you talk to the receptionist about the exact scheduling now."

"Yes, but, Doctor," she said, twisting the phone cord back and forth around her index finger, "I know four isn't many. That's what you meant by *reasonable,* isn't it?"

"With your history and age, it gives us two good tries. I take it you're still adamant about my not transferring all four at once?"

"No, I couldn't bear to do that selective removal—"

"—fetal reduction," he said, interrupting her.

"That's it. If they would all implant. I realize that—well, none of them might, but after everything, I could not bear to have any deliberately…lost."

"I understand. Tomorrow's the day, then. I'll tell Dr. Jasmine to have two ready, and I'll transfer you right now for specifics."

By the time she made the appointment and asked questions, she was really running behind. She couldn't wait to tell Sandra that she had four embryos. Pre-embryos, the doctors like to call them until they are actually implanted. Four, which—if only she could carry them, *any* of them—would become her children. No, in a very real way they were already her children.

She shivered but hugged herself for strength and whirled around once, dancing with herself. Then she leaned against the wall again. This would take a long time to sink in. At least she—and Geoff's dream—were this far. A chance to be a mother, to have a baby to bring home here to this house that was her haven from all that had happened. She grabbed a tissue to carefully blot threatening tears of joy so her blasted mascara wouldn't streak.

Then she ran upstairs to the linen closet at the end of the hall by the master bedroom. She pulled it open, knelt, and felt behind the pile of extra blankets until her hand touched hard wood.

She had promised herself she would not get this out until she knew she was pregnant, but she just had to look at it now. Her family's heirloom cedar cradle with its deeply carved decorations emerged from the darkness. It went back at least to when her mother was an infant, and her three brothers and she and Sarah had been in it once. Sarah had given it to her when she moved to Hawaii. Now, maybe, soon she could fill it with her own child.

She lifted the unwieldy cradle into her lap. Pressing her flushed cheek to the scrolled headboard, she held and rocked it as if it were a child.

En route to the station, traffic clotted, then clogged; and accident ahead blocked the freeway. Alex got off two exits early and took the side streets, trying to be careful, watching the speed limits. She didn't want anything to go wrong today.

She was shaking with excitement. Despite the cost, thank heavens she had switched to the Evergreen Clinic after her other disappointments when Geoff was still alive. Four tries for a baby—two transferred tomorrow. She'd have to do that alone because Sandra was on assignment in Taos. The Stanhopes were so kind to always allow a supporter in for these procedures. It was usually the husband, of course, or a close family member, but the way things were with her mother, though she still lived in nearby Santa Fe, she'd have to go it alone and just rely on the clinic staff more than ever.

She leaned on the horn when a van pulled out ahead of her and proceeded to go only about twenty-five miles an hour. After a week's suspension she could not be late today. But next to the chance to have a child, everything else, even Mike Montgomery's wrath and her job, paled by comparison. She would gladly scrub floors the rest of her life if she could have a family.

When she pulled into the station lot, she saw someone in an old orange Volkswagen bus had blocked the gate to staff parking. She hit the horn and motioned for him to move. From this angle, she could see no one behind the wheel.

To her amazement, then consternation that segued to disbelief, the bus backed, turned, and charged directly at her. She sat frozen before she hit the gas and yanked the wheel to try to swerve away. She hit the back fender and scraped the rear of a sleek black Lexus. The Volkswagen barely missed, careened past, then screeched to a stop.

Before she even gave a thought to the fact the driver might have a gun, she craned around to yell out the window, "You idiot!"

She gasped as the driver rolled his window down. The man—if it was a man—wore a beat-up cowboy hat and a bright red paisley bandanna over his nose and mouth like some old-time bandit.

She motioned for him to pull over but didn't get out. Neither did he. He didn't move but continued to glare at her through slitted eyes. She couldn't tell their color from where she was sitting, couldn't see his hands to know if he had a knife or gun. She agonized over whether to run inside for help or try to maneuver to block him in. She couldn't even get his license plate because mud had splattered it along with the entire back of the bus.

He gave her an obscene hand gesture and tooled away as one of their cameramen came running over. She pressed her forehead against her hands gripping the steering wheel. She had come back to work with a bang.

As soon as the station's receptionist phoned the police and summoned the station manager, Alex explained the incident to him. "Can't see using it for a story yet," Mike Montgomery mumbled as he escorted her back into the station. "All we'd have is a tight shot of two dented vehicles and an interview with you when you've supposedly been on vacation. I did cover for you with that vacation story—never used or let anyone else use the word suspension," he added as if she owed him something for that.

"I'm sure the viewers who sent in tons of sympathetic mail were glad to hear that, Mike. And the couple of hundred who made those phone calls supporting me Sandra mentioned," Alex clipped out before she realized this was no time to defy him. She bit her lower lip before she could add that vacations were usually paid days off.

"So whose car is that in the visitors spot?" Mike asked the wide-eyed receptionist as they passed her desk. "We have a guest here already this morning?"

"Not exactly," Lita said with a grimace, obviously glad she hadn't caused the mayhem and potentially bad P.R. they all feared. "It's Mr. Fanshaw's, the grocery store mogul the sales reps are trying to get to sponsor all our Lobos basketball games next year."

"Oh, no!" Alex and Mike chorused.

Alex wilted against the reception desk. "Mike, I'm telling you, if I hadn't swerved, that jerk could have killed me and himself, like some crazy kamikaze pilot. And that's exactly what I'm willing to explain to Mr. Fanshaw. My insurance will cover it, but I'm just hoping I don't need more protection than that, and I don't mean from Mr. Fanshaw."

At the bottom of the stairs, Mike stopped her with an arm on her elbow to turn her toward him. He took one step up so he could face her eye-to-eye. Though Mike was a spare short man—even standing several inches under Sandra's height—he could be intimidating until one got to know and accept him. Sandra always said he had a Napoleonic complex. He had been divorced for several years, but then, as Sandra put it— who could live with him? When he went on one of his tirades, she almost broke Alex up by smoothly sliding her hand inside her jacket in that old French dictator's pose.

Mike was red-haired, though that was muting to gray as his hairline receded to display more of his ruddy face. His hazel eyes, magnified by huge horn-rimmed glasses, could stick you to the wall. He was fiercely loyal to his mixed staff of Hispanics and Anglos who reflected their station's demographics, at least when the ratings were good.

"Has someone been harassing you with wacko calls lately?" he demanded.

"No, though I suppose there are some viewers who don't think I should have cried over a kid being disciplined by her father."

"You look pale. Maybe you should wait upstairs in my office, and we'll meet with the cops there."

"No, I'm fine, really," she protested.

"But," he added, pointing an index finger at her, "you're not leaving to look at mug shots or whatever until we get this group picture taken. We need it to advertise May sweeps."

"Mike, I can't identify the guy. Mug shots wouldn't do a bit of good," she protested as he steered her under the floating stairway for more privacy.

Alex had always felt calmed by the solidity of this building, which the station owners had recently redone to make it look more authentically pueblo. Big beams, carved corbels, and spouts to take the runoff in rare rainstorms protruded below the sturdy roofline. Large, flowering cacti seemed anchored in their beds of sand and stone just outside.

This lobby was desert earth tones—tiled floor, huge U-shaped, sand-colored leather couch, and drum-shaped coffee table. Gold and orange zinnias and scarlet geraniums in kettle-sized pots punctuated the beiges and browns. A bright red Navajo patterned carpet covered the stairway over their heads that led up to the second floor with its executive offices. The rest of the floors were terra-cotta tile. The wall behind the receptionist's desk held a mural of the panoramic view of the city's skyline against the Sandia Mountains. A wide TV screen running the station's current feed took up a good part of another wall along with the red block letters: KALB-TV ALBUQUERQUE, CHANNEL 10, YOUR PERSONAL NEWS STATION.

"Alexis," he said, his voice barely controlled, "I've had reporters who always manage to put themselves in the middle of breaking news, but never an anchorperson before. Crying over a story, almost getting hit by some lunatic on our property. You're getting yourself in trouble…"

"Mike, that isn't fair. I'll take responsibility for breaking down on the air, but I certainly didn't ask someone to try to run me down." She stood straighter though she towered above him; her bell-clear voice rose.

"All right, all right. You know I'm behind you on this, on everything," he insisted, holding up both hands in an apparent attempt to calm her with his usual line. "And before the police get here and we do that photo, I wanted to tell you to report back in tomorrow for work, so you know I'm really on your side. What? What now?" he demanded, whipping off his glasses in exasperation when she started to shake her head again.

"Mike, a week's not up until the day after tomorrow," she began, choosing her words carefully. "It's not that I'm asking for more days off, and I'm very grateful for your support to bring me back. But I have a doctor's appointment I can't break tomorrow morning." She tried to keep her voice in check; she could hear it losing pace and pitch. "And after it, I'm—supposed to rest. It's important, Mike. Please understand."

He leaned closer, punching the air between them with his glasses. "Understand exactly what? If you're under a doctor's care, have you been taking prescription medication or something? Were you on some kind of drugs last week when you flipped out?"

She opened her mouth to deny it, but actually she had been—powerful fertility drugs she refused to tell him about.

"It's not something really serious?" he asked, suddenly slack-faced and wide-eyed.

"No, not something like that," she said, but she wanted to grab him and whirl him around and scream in joy, *Yes, it's serious! I have a chance to have a baby, Geoff's baby, after all this time. These four embryos are my last hope. And when I should be so happy, so sure, inside I'm still so scared....*

"Mr. Montgomery," Lita, the receptionist, called out. "Ben called to say Mr. Fanshaw's coming downstairs to take a look at his car, and he's not too happy."

Alex's heart began to pound even harder. She took a step around Mike to glance up through the stairs. Mr. Fanshaw looked large, imposing, and furious.

"I can handle this, Mike. Let me explain to him."

"Right, like you handled me. You and I aren't done yet," he called after her. But he trusted her to face Mr. Fanshaw alone.

An hour later, having appeased Mr. Fanshaw and settled down, Alex could tell it was going to be quite a photo shoot. The on-air staff milled around in the wings, chatting in little clusters while the photographer set up chairs far enough from the backdrop so that some of them could sit and others stand behind. The buzz was about her being back early, the incident in the parking lot, and the shock that Mike was evidently not going to cover the news which happened right on their doorstep.

When Alex got Sandra off a little ways to tell her the good news about the embryo transfer tomorrow, Sandra hugged her and, luckily, stifled a whoop of joy. At least everyone would think she was just welcoming her back.

"So, did you like the tape, since you couldn't recall a thing?" Sandra asked, referring to the fact she'd made a cassette recording of what was said in the O.R. during the egg retrieval. She had hidden a tiny recorder taped between her breasts. Alex had listened last night again and again to Jasmine's voice calling out, "Egg!"

"Hale Stanhope can have his Handel, but that was music to my ears," Alex admitted with a little smile.

The photographer finally told everyone where to stand. Once they were all wedged into place, her co-anchor, Stan Jackson, kept bumping into her. He was a tall, imposing African-American, always impeccably dressed. She had to gently elbow him back before he got the message. Standing between him and the sports director, Steven Ryan, she felt flanked by brawny tackles or whatever position the biggest football team players would be. She was five ten, but the photographer made a real production out of getting a phone book for her to stand on.

Meanwhile, Mike was driving them crazy with his continued comments and commands. Sandra craned her neck and shot Alex a "Do you believe this?" look while she subtly slipped her hand under the lapel of her suit coat jacket. Alex bit her lip to keep from laughing. Even the photographer was glaring at Mike.

"Sandra, look straight ahead to get rid of that big nose shadow," Mike ordered. "Stan, too much of a gap between you and Alexis. Alexis, I know it's been a tough day, but can't you relax your face into a smile…?"

Then she realized it. Despite the squabbles and personality clashes, her co-workers had become her family. Mike was the scolding father, Sandra an indulgent but strict mother. Stan and Steve were like teasing brothers. Her producer and Lita in the lobby like sisters.

A family. It was what she desperately wanted for herself since her own was either scattered or hostile. She wanted not only a child or children, but the other part of that, a man to love and to go home to.

"Smile, everybody. Eyes right here!"

A series of strobes popped to make her see blood red spots. If the embryo transplant tomorrow didn't work out, she thought, her dreams might all be gone in a flash.

3

Men's masked faces surrounded her. Jolted awake, Alexis sat straight up in bed. She knew who the man in the VW could be.

She snapped on the bedside lamp. Trying to ignore the fact her digital clock read 3:35 and she needed her sleep for the embryo transfer, she got up and yanked on her terry-cloth robe. She hadn't watched the news coverage of him once she'd started to cry on the air, but surely that's who it was. It just had to be that bastard Hank Cordova.

As she padded barefoot downstairs, she recalled that before she'd lost control, she had read copy quoting him as saying he was proud of "smacking" his daughter: "Kids need to know who's boss. That's why society's so screwed up. I didn't want the kid in the first place, but she got no one else with her mama dead—and no one gonna take her away now or else…."

The only thing is, Cordova had been arrested for child endangerment, hadn't he? Wasn't he sitting in jail awaiting arraignment right now?

Clicking on lights downstairs, she went directly to the big Spanish mission desk in her study, which had once been Geoff's den. She had gradually taken it over, replacing his photos of fighter squadron crews with art prints. Yet his collection of antique Hopi and Zuni kachina god dolls still stood sentinel in the large, painted corner *tratero* cupboard. She had never liked their malevolent expressions, or the way their eyes seemed to follow her around the room, so she never turned on the lights that illumined them anymore. But she knew how much Geoff had valued them and had not even boxed them up.

She bent over the pile of mail addressed to her, which had come to the station the six days she'd been suspended. She had started to read some of it last night, but had been too exhausted to go on. She remembered one supportive fax had read, "Everyone's just sick to death of people hurting or even killing their own kids. That one liar let her kids drown in the family car, and there's lots of others out there like her...."

She leaned against her desk and pressed her hands to her stomach. Soon, she prayed, she'd have one or two of her own kids growing here, ones she would protect forever. She had to take care of herself for that. At least, this afternoon her friend Detective Bernice Alvarez had followed her home in a marked car after taking the police report at the TV station. In case anyone had staked out her house, they might think the police were surveilling the area.

"That's all I need," Alex muttered. "Someone besides the cops hanging around this house."

"I'll just bet, though," Bernice had assured her earlier when Alex had told her the same thing, "that perp who tried to run you down has no clue how to find your place. Otherwise, would he be stupid enough to wait in an orange VW bus at the station, for Pete's sake? I'm gonna tell your general manager that even a locked fence isn't enough security in this day and age."

"I've got a good security system on my house," Alex had assured Bernice—and herself. "We've had it for years and never had a problem." But now, what if the answer to her attacker's identity was right here in her house, in this mail?

She skimmed the short messages—e-mail and fax first—then shuffled through the letters, looking for crudely addressed envelopes. She knew she shouldn't stereotype people, but that's the way she saw Cordova, with his scruffy beard and white-trash talk. It could have been his style to hide his ugly face with that bandanna.

She found three white business envelopes in the same bold print—all upper case, no return address. She slit one open and skimmed it.

Rich TV Bitch—
Your wrong, lady, if you think you can fake cry at
what I done and get every one turned against
me—just cause they like you and stuff. Its your
fault they took my kid. But I got money and power
to you know. Enough to get out on bail—now you
will pay for foks I know and don't know saying Im
a deadbeat no count. No goverment will take her

away. That kids mine and needs smacking in line—just like you.

Not afraid to sign H. Cordova

"Out on bail. Damn. But you might just as well confess, you poor, stupid ass. I only hope," she muttered more quietly, "he doesn't know what foster family has his daughter."

She started to slit open the other two identical envelopes, then recalled—just as with letter bombs—some fingerprints could be lifted, even when several people had handled mail. Not, thank heavens, that this Cordova had the brains for handling a bomb more complicated than his old VW.

She carefully placed the three letters in a plastic Ziploc gallon bag and put it in her briefcase. After warming a glass of milk, she then sat drinking it at her desk, trying to calm herself. She'd try to call Bernice before she left for the clinic, or at least leave her a message so she could pick up that loose cannon again and get him locked away with additional charges. There was nothing worse than someone who harmed innocent kids.

But on her way out, her gaze snagged on the three rows of fierce kachina dolls glaring at her from the shadows. She walked over and turned all their faces toward the wall. Geoff had said that one of the purposes of the dolls in the pueblos was to scare children into behaving. A chill shuddered through her.

She went out and, for once, closed the door behind her.

* * *

Although she kept checking for a blur of orange in her rearview mirror and took a roundabout way out of town, the early morning drive to the clinic calmed her, especially when she got off busy I-40 and swung north on twisting 14, the old Turquoise Trail. Dawn dusted the hills, sifting gold through the tall juniper and twisted piñons that grew thick on this side of the Sandias.

She turned off the trail just past the carved sign that read EVERGREEN CLINIC. Built in the brief heyday of the little mining town, the sprawling adobe, ponderosa pine, and cedar wood building which now housed the clinic had once been a hotel. The one-floor structure, which had been added to over the early years, sprawled long and lanky above the narrow valley. When the small corporation which funded the Stanhopes had purchased the ramshackle hotel four years ago, it had had to be gutted and almost entirely rebuilt.

Alex parked and went up the tiled walk. Each lustrous, glazed deep blue tile was engraved with the name and birth date of a clinic baby. Multiple births were common with IVF, and she knew exactly where the names of seven sets of twins and two of triplets lay under her feet as she approached the *portal*. On this long front porch, cedar and pine benches and rockers, where patients sometimes waited or support groups met, were empty this year.

Inside, the spacious foyer boasted Navajo rugs on the walls alternating with hanging bunches of hot chile *ristras*. A raised adobe fireplace, unlit this morning, filled one corner of the room. Set in a series of four arched, lighted, recessed shelves called *nichos*, Alex admired anew the fine display of Pueblo painted pottery statues of the Native American figures known as storytellers.

Whereas Geoff had bought kachinas, she had collected figures like these, partly because she felt her career made her a sort of modern storyteller. And the baked, painted terra-cotta statues gave her hope. Each had a woman surrounded by many children peeping from under her arms and shawl. It was another tasteful, touching piece of this wonderful place the Stanhopes had made bloom at the edge of dry and barren land.

She turned into the peach, plum, and beige room where Alice Prettyman, the Stanhopes' official greeter and receptionist, held sway. Alice's younger sister, Dr. Joyce Prettyman—neither sister had ever married— was the clinic counselor, but she had her own fussily decorated office down the hall. But here reproductions of Mary Cassatt paintings of mothers and children graced the walls. Alex's favorite was of a blond girl in a straw hat entitled *La Jeune Fille*. She always imagined the child gave her a silent good luck nod, and she nodded back. She was certain, if she could have a daughter, she would look a lot like that.

It was so early that only four seated women waited. The fifth was ahead, checking in, a young, stylishly dressed woman who Alex overheard say she'd driven in from Taos for an initial consultation. Unless a married couples' counseling circle was going to meet, men seldom waited in this room. The ones who came to give sperm or have tests used a side entrance they obviously favored. The Stanhopes had thought of everything here, she marveled again, to make both the newly hopeful and the downright desperate as comfortable as possible.

Over the filing cabinets behind the plump, silver-haired receptionist, Alex reread the sampler the grand-motherly woman had counter-cross stitched herself: *She hath also conceived...who was called barren—St. Luke, the Physician (Luke 1:36).*

At least, she thought, her procedure today was a much quicker, easier transfer than egg harvesting. By the time Beth Bradley rolled her into the O.R. at 8:15 A.M., she was ready.

"Sometimes being married makes me feel like that," Paul Twohorses said as a Hispanic husband and wife went out, gesturing and arguing. But instead of watching the couple pass the window, Paul nodded at the silhouette of the coyote on the wall, baying at the moon. Nick hid a grin behind his coffee cup at mistakenly thinking he'd referred to the people, instead of the wolf.

"You know," Paul said, "howling crazy. But my woman, she got the gift of the gods, you know—in her hands, so I try to keep cool."

"I'm honored you've chosen my shop to be Rita's outlet in Santa Fe," Nick told Paul, the husband and business manager of Santa Cruz potter Rita Twohorses. Her art was brilliant and unique, and her reputation was growing fast in the Southwest. "And I do know what you mean about marriage," he added with a grimace.

"Yeah. Figured you would."

The two men went back to their *frittatas* in the corner window booth of the Los Lobos Cafe in Santa Fe, down the street from Nick's New Mexico Treasures. Paul didn't talk much, but then Nick was used to that in dealing with various Pueblo artists and their families. He thought Anglos talked too much anyway; it even annoyed him that the TV was on above the counter right now with the hosts of one of the morning network shows yakking away. During a commercial he heard a familiar voice and craned his neck to look around at a promo for the local news. It was her, all right—Alexis McCall.

"You'll get the real news first, up close, and personal here on KALB," she said, "so stay tuned in."

"You're frowning, man," Paul's voice cut in. "You know that lady?"

"Not real well."

"You know any woman real well?"

Nick grinned. Ironic, sometimes bitter understatement was as close as Pueblo men came to a joke. But as Nick's dark eyes met Paul's even darker ones, he saw anguish, not amusement.

"Sad but true," Nick said, deciding to go right to the heart of the matter the way these people he admired so much did—once they trusted you. "I had a real tough marriage before it ended."

Paul nodded and laid his fork down with his food half eaten. "Heard from someone who sells you goods you did. That she got—you know, real nervous."

"She had a lot of counseling, and that didn't help. A psychiatrist," he added when Paul just looked at him.

"Rita seen one too—didn't help her neither. She's gotta just quit going in circles, making it worse. But it don't hurt her artwork none," he added hastily, as if he'd overstepped. "You seen that. You know her problem, it makes her do the mothers and the little kids in her statues even better. I gotta go," he added and reached for his cowboy hat next to him. Nick had never seen a Pueblo he'd bought food for leave it before.

"Hey," Nick said, sliding quickly out of his side of the booth to shake Paul's hand, "let me know if there's anything I can do to help promote Rita's art. Let's talk more next time."

"Yeah. Thanks for the chow. I think I talked too much now, but I get like a loaded gun sometime and just blow."

Nick sat back down and watched Paul go out toward his pickup truck. He shook his head and went back to his breakfast. As long as he worked with the Pueblos, he'd probably never really get to know what they'd do next. But at least this had prodded him away from what he should not do—phone Alexis the way he'd been wanting to.

"So how are you doing today, Alexis?" Dr. Jasmine's voice came clear and crisp over the intercom in the O.R.

"Pretty well for a woman some idiot tried to hit—in my car—yesterday," Alex explained. "And then got away."

"How terrible."

"You have *no* idea who it was?" Beth piped up, patting her shoulder. "I hope you've got a good security system at home. And you be careful driving."

"It's the downside of being a public persona," she admitted with a sigh. "And, yes, I have a good security system at home, the best my husband used to say—Camelot. Their office isn't far from the house, in case I ever need them."

"I'll make a note of that name," came Jasmine's voice while Beth's concerned eyes held Alex's. "We may be needing a security system around here with unwanted interest in some of our property."

Before Alex could put in a good word for Nick Destin, Jasmine asked, "Would you like to see a baby picture while we all wait for the doctor? They're good-looking zygotes, if I do say so myself. I feel like a midwife already. There," she said as she brought the greatly magnified photo up on the TV monitor.

Alex couldn't discern what she was seeing at first, even though they hadn't given her more than a Valium for this procedure. But Beth pointed out the two embryos floating like stars in their own dark sky.

"The one on the left is a four-cell and the other a five-cell," Jasmine announced. Alex could picture her in her immaculate lab coat, with every hair in place. Dr. Jasmine sounded so sure, so strong that Alex dared to hope even more.

"Oh, yes, I see," she said, smiling at Beth. "Thanks for your part in this, Dr. Jasmine."

"Don't give it a thought," she replied. "For a woman your age, you had very good eggs. As you know, the closer a woman gets to forty, the eggs get less viable, at least as things stand right now. Hopefully, in the future there will be new ways to get around that."

Dr. Jasmine's praise about the eggs made Alex want to soar. Such a comment was to be valued more than that local Emmy award she'd won for covering the Balloon Fiesta last year. But all those thoughts lifted away when Dr. Stanhope appeared. With an almost smug smile Beth took him the catheter which Jasmine handed through the hatch. Beth held it upright, leaning close to him. In it, Alex knew, swam her two embryos waiting to be infused into her body.

"Ready, Alexis?" he asked. "This won't take long."

But it did. He tried, then withdrew it and asked Jasmine to transfer the embryos to a stiffer catheter. Beth's parade and the procedure was repeated.

"Is anything wrong?" Alex asked, lifting her head to try to see, but her draped legs blocked her view.

"Just needed a different one," he said.

The room was dim with only his headlamp throwing his monster shadow on the wall and ceiling. No need for the Doppler screen or monitors this time. No one was talking now, not even Beth, who stayed by Dr. Stanhope and quit making the short pilgrimage to comfort Alex until Alex saw his shadow bump Beth's away, so she came to stay by her side. Yet Alex had never felt more alone or scared.

She watched the minute hand on the clock jerk twenty minutes by as he tried the third catheter several times. The horrid things looked like turkey basters and had to place the embryos through the cervix near the entrance of her fallopian tubes, where the fused gametes could descend and, hopefully, implant naturally.

"Dr. Stanhope," came Dr. Jasmine's curt voice from

the ceiling to startle all of them, "please don't stress those pre-embryos. Perhaps I should baby-sit them for just a while longer."

"I hear you," he replied testily. He came around into Alex's view without the catheter, which Beth carried away, still with its point in the air.

"Didn't you do it?" Alex asked, propping herself up on her elbows. She felt deflated but angry.

"We have a little problem," he said, wiping his hands. She saw blood on the towel; her stomach cartwheeled.

"Oh, no, oh…" she began and sank back.

His stern face appeared between her and the ceiling. He gripped her arm in one latex-gloved hand. "It's nothing I can't fix—just a little delay. Alexis, it's not on your records, but are you sure you mother never took DES when she was carrying you?"

"What?" she asked, not expecting anything about her mother. Her mother didn't approve of her earlier attempts at IVF and knew nothing about this one. And she'd said when she asked her years ago that she never took DES, an anti-miscarriage drug that could cause fertility problems and worse in offspring.

"No. No DES, my mother said. Can't you put them in me? I can do this. You're not hurting me."

"I'm going to have Beth take you to recovery, and I'll come in to talk," he promised, his voice so quiet compared to her increasingly strident tones. "You've got some folded tissue in there that won't let me thread the point through to get close enough to give them a fair chance. We can put them in another way later, but I'm going to have Dr. Jasmine freeze these too."

"No, not all four frozen," she cried, grabbing his wrist. "Please—"

Beth appeared at his side to gently unwrap Alex's fingers, though he had only kindly covered her hand with his free one. "Alexis," Beth said, her voice almost scolding, "you heard the doctor say they're good ones, and he'll find another way to get them in safe and sound."

Alex felt the huge, dark weight of despair lean into her, crushing her down. She lifted both hands to cover her eyes as Beth rolled her briskly out.

"Beth." Dr. Stanhope's voice pierced Alex's tumbled thoughts as he suddenly appeared in the curtained cubicle about twenty minutes later. "I know you're busy, so you can step out while I talk to Alexis."

"She's my patient," she protested quietly as she rose from her chair she'd shoved next to the bed. "I'll be glad to stay to help."

He gave a barely perceptible jerk of his head toward the curtain. Biting her lip and looking hurt, Beth obeyed, sliding the voluminous folds carefully closed behind her.

He perched on the edge of the bed; Alex's hip rolled against his. He took her right hand in both of his. Under the starched sleeve of his monogrammed white linen coat, she glimpsed the crystal gold wafer of his watch he glanced at quickly. His hands were elegant, tapering, long-fingered—usually the workers of miracles, she thought, but not for her.

"I know you're deeply disappointed, Alexis, but what

we learned today is for the best. I can implant laparo-scopically, an amended procedure called ZIFT, if I have to. It's one of my rather rare specialties."

"Rare. It's that bad," she whispered.

"No, but you're that important, you and the clinic babies."

He'd always called them that, even in her first appointment, she recalled, as if he could envision them, just as she could. Looking into his dove gray eyes, hearing the conviction in his words, she could almost keep believing in him. But the fear of devastating failure she'd managed to ignore lately was lurking darkly just behind her last remnants of control.

Come on, Alexis, she tried to buck herself up. *You can deal with this. Pretend it's a tough story you're doing on air, someone else who needs help. Talk to this man.*

She cleared her throat. "I wonder why my previous doctor didn't have this difficulty when I had earlier IVF attempts."

"I'm wondering that too. Except perhaps the folds in your cervix have become more convoluted over the four or five years since. Or else," he said, his tone getting sharper, "he really let you down by not positioning the embryos far enough in. But there's no way to prove that now," he added quickly as he let go of her hand and stood. "It's what happens here at Evergreen that matters."

"I'll ask my mother about DES again," she said, her voice sounding listless, so unlike her. *Speak up, Alexis. Project your self-confidence,* her favorite TV journalism professor's voice jumped out at her.

"Are your parents local?" the doctor asked. One hand fumbled with his stethoscope draped around his neck, then automatically fingered the edge of the thin alligator notebook protruding from his jacket pocket. She could tell he had somewhere else to be.

"My father's dead. She's remarried but still lives in Santa Fe. I haven't seen her for—a while." She heaved a huge sigh before she could stop herself. Her lengthy estrangement from her mother was not because Alex resented her new husband, as her mother had accused last time they'd talked. Alex could simply not accept that her mother had blamed her for her inability to bear a child.

"You know," Dr. Stanhope said as he paused with one hand lifted to pull back the drapes, "not that it makes any difference on how I'll choose to proceed now, but DES used to be called by many names. Unfortunately, even in modern medicine, though we're eons away from the old days of snake oil cureralls, some things aren't what they seem. Perhaps it was just a misunderstanding between the two of you…."

"Yes, I'll find out," she said, struggling to sit up in bed. "I just wish there was something I could do now, to help with the waiting."

"Just trust me and the clinic, and I'll be in touch soon," he said as the curtain closed behind him.

4

The ornately scripted sign for Camelot Securities with the pair of crossed swords squeaked as it swung in the slight breeze. The woman's hand shook as she twisted the knob and entered the office door under it. She gripped her purse and car keys even tighter. At least they were probably used to seeing nervous people in here all the time.

"Hi, there. How can Camelot help you?" the Hispanic girl at the desk asked with a perky smile, though she kept chewing her gum.

"I'm a friend of one of your clients—Alexis McCall, the TV anchorwoman—and she recommended you—your services," she said, glancing around the small room. "Though I'd rather you don't tell her I used her name, if you know what I mean, her being well known and all. She can't seem to give endorsements."

"Oh, sure," the girl said.

The woman noted that a door evidently led to at least one other office beyond the frosted glass divider. She could see a man moving around in there, hear his muffled voice as he spoke on the phone.

"Actually," she went on, nodding at the receptionist, "I'd like not only to talk to someone who could install an alarm system for me, but the same person who put hers in. I mean, I'm really shook about some of the crimes that go on today, and I want to make sure I get one as good as Alexis has." She reminded herself not to talk to much. That was always a mistake.

"Well, sure. Just a sec." She pecked away at her computer keyboard and squinted to read her monitor. "Oh, I'm afraid hers was installed so long ago—six years, that's eons in this business, know what I mean. So there's no way the same installer's still here." She popped a muted bubble inside her mouth, and the scent of banana drifted up. "Anyhow, she doesn't really have a state-of-the-art one like we install today."

"Oh, really? What can the new ones do that hers can't?"

"How 'bout I let you talk to Gill O'Fallon? He's usually out on runs, but he's here right now. He's her rep if there's a problem, checks it twice a year and all that. So it's your lucky day, 'cause Camelot would really like to help keep you safe. You wanta talk to Gill?" she asked with another muted pop.

"That's fine with me."

It got even finer when she saw that the installer was young and seemed a bit nervous when she shook his hand and held it a bit too long in her plan to play damsel in distress. And no wedding ring. When she rolled her chair closer to his in his cubby-hole of an office, his face turned as red as his hair. Yes, as the receptionist had said, this might just be her lucky day.

* * *

Alex parked her car on a narrow side street a few blocks from the plaza and sauntered in the direction of St. Francis Cathedral, which peered above the old adobe buildings huddled around its skirts. Santa Fe was her hometown, but it hadn't seemed like home for years. Not since she'd left to attend the University of New Mexico in Albuquerque, got a job, and married Geoff, who had been stationed there. Her alienation from her mother had made it worse.

Now she walked slowly past familiar shops and restaurants spilling out onto the narrow sidewalks in the warm spring sun. She perused posted menus and looked over blankets littered with Indian jewelry and tourist trinkets. She greeted or responded in English or Spanish to waiters setting up tables and chairs for Saturday lunch. Many of them recognized and were proud of Santa Fe's hometown girl whose face and voice visited them each weekday from big, bustling "Duke City." But in this town, which prided itself in its *poco a poco* relaxed pace of life, Alex felt like a pent-up volcano.

Today, though she had come to town specifically to see her mother, she was putting it off as long as she could. But where she was going next didn't calm her either, even if for a more pleasant reason. She had butterflies in the pit of her stomach and sweaty palms.

Partway down San Francisco Street, she took a deep breath and switched her canvas bag with the three kachinas she'd carefully packed to her other hand, then lifted the heavy latch of Nick Destin's New Mexico Treasures Shop. It took a moment for her eyes to adjust to the dim interior. He was talking to several Pueblo Indians and had some pieces of pottery spread out before him.

"Alexis," he said, looking up. His voice and tanned face showed his surprise. She wondered what she'd interrupted before he smiled tautly. The others glanced slowly over, then away. "Please make yourself at home. I'll be right with you," he added.

"Take your time. I just wanted your advice about something I might want to sell."

She admired him for not leaving the others. She had often been embarrassed by people falling all over her because she was a local personality. It was even more disconcerting when they snubbed the people they'd been talking to, especially Native Americans or Hispanics. What had happened to Sandra's family made her very sensitive about that.

Alex made a slow circuit of the low-ceilinged, big-beamed gallery, which had been divided into areas by rug-draped wooden tables displaying art. It was mostly arranged by tribes or pueblos. She admired large flat baskets of the Isleta and Jemez Pueblos and double-spouted water vases with bird designs made by the San Ildefonso. While she examined the beautiful ebony pottery of the Santa Clara and Taos pots with corn motifs, she darted surreptitious glances at Nick.

She supposed he was in his early forties. He wore a light blue western shirt, boots, and black jeans with a big concha belt with chunks of turquoise set in heavy, engraved silver ovals. He had his sleeves rolled up and wore a watch with a black leather band and a Navajo ring on his right hand. His hair came just to the top of his collar, thick and black, yet etched by silver. Looking at his profile, she noted that his high-bridged nose could pass for Native American, but his chin was square instead of rounded.

He glanced at her and she looked down, moving on to a display of figurines.

Golden light poured in here, not from the front windows but from the open back door through which she could see a central courtyard called a *placita*. Big pueblo pots of fuchsia zinnias so bright they almost hurt her eyes surrounded an old, gently spouting fountain before some back buildings began. She wondered if Nick lived behind his shop.

She studied the varied storyteller statues, all with their O mouths open to tell their traditional tribal tales. Sandra had once teased that the expression showed shock at having so many kids hanging on them. Each statue had a neatly lettered card giving the name and pueblo of the artist, some Acoma, some Cochiti, and some Santa Cruz. Many of the figures were male, but those by Rita Twohorses, an artist whose work she admired and owned, were always of women tale bearers.

She jumped when Nick's voice suddenly came close behind her.

"See anything you like?"

Their eyes held as the others went out, leaving them alone in the shop. The cross-cutting light from the windows and door angled across Nick's face to highlight his firm, narrow mouth and the tiny crow's feet at the outside edges of his dark eyes.

"Oh, yes, I like almost everything. But here, my husband used to collect kachinas, and they're not really my thing. They always remind me of some sort of Star Trek aliens. I brought three of thirteen to show you today."

"Sure, I'd be glad to look them over," he said, but his eyes swept her. She felt that brief glance clear to the pit of her stomach. He took the wrapped dolls from the canvas bag she offered him and carefully unrolled them on the counter.

"It's just that I'd like to know," she said, "where you'd recommend selling these and what these samples are worth."

"A lot, Alexis." He breathed out hard through pursed lips as he examined the two-feet tall, carved and painted figures.

She stepped slightly closer to watch his large, square hands lift the first one. His wrists were sinewy, strong, his hands slightly callused but clean.

"I'd say your husband had a good eye for them. They're lovely."

"Lovely?" she countered. "Those are the most malevolent, ugly things I've ever seen."

He looked surprised at her vehemence. "My wife never liked anything in my shop, including sometimes me."

"I didn't mean to pry or to denigrate this art. These kachinas kind of haunt me, that's all."

"So," he went on, apparently all business again as he turned back to scrutinizing the figures, "no reason to have these just packed away somewhere."

"I didn't do that. They were still displayed, but I

think I'm ready to part with them at last. Someone who values and appreciates them ought to have them."

He nodded. "I'll give you a detailed appraisal with documentation for any or all of them. Quite frankly, I'd like to buy them, but I'd also show the ones that appear to be the oldest—like this one—to some Hopi or Zuni elders in case they want to make the first offer. You know these are sacred to them," he said, his voice deep but solemn now. "Magical powers for healing or destruction. Maybe I can stop by to examine the other ten you have next time I'm in town."

"Yes, that would be fine," she agreed hastily. He still seemed angry with her—or with himself—but the way he watched her gave her different vibes she couldn't quite read. "I'd appreciate that, Nick."

"I would expect you to get a second or third opinion too, and not just necessarily trust me," he added as their gazes locked again at this close range. She could see each separate eyelash and her own reflection mirrored in his coffee-black pupils. And she'd wondered earlier what he'd been chewing. She glimpsed a clove between his teeth, and its pungent scent assailed her.

Before she could tell him she had confidence in his judgment, he added in a rush, "I hope you didn't get the wrong idea about my designs on that clinic land the other day. I don't know your ties to the Stanhopes, but for some reason they abruptly changed their minds after I'd been led to expect they would take our fair offer for the acreage Silver sits on. And I take it, from talking to their clinic manager, Mr. VanHeyde, that it's the woman doctor who wants the land."

"Dr. Jasmine? She has more power there than she shows."

"You see, LH—Living Heritage—just wants to preserve the place and promote the study of it. More a living museum than some tourist magnet like Madrid nearby, if they're afraid of people making a lot of noise or gawking at clinic patients. That's what surprised me about seeing you there—the idea you might be doing a story on them if they're so obsessed with privacy."

"And then I said I wasn't, though it would be a fascinating one, so you were wondering about me even more."

"Alexis, I'm not in the investigation and reporting business like you are, but—are you remarried?"

His sudden shift in topics surprised her. She could tell he'd blurted out a question that had even surprised him. Even more she amazed herself by wanting to tell him that she was a patient there—and why—when she'd been guarding that from so many people who were much closer to her. At least here was an opening to avoid the line of questioning about being an IVF patient.

"No, I'm still single. And how's your wife?" she countered. "I can't recall her name, but she came in here that day we were doing the piece on the shop."

He moved around the counter to rewrap the kachinas, evidently so he could do it facing her. Or maybe he suddenly wanted a barrier between them.

"Yeah, I remember. She embarrassed me, horning in like that, but you handled it like—well, like a pro." He frowned. "We're divorced, Alexis. Last year. She's living in Phoenix."

She knew she should say she was sorry, but she didn't. She just waited, sure he was going to say more. She had always been skilled at reading people's mood or catching vibes. But nothing else was forthcoming, and she helped fill in the awkward silence by holding the canvas bag open for him while he replaced the wrapped kachinas.

This close, almost touching him, she could feel her heart beating. She really hadn't been so attracted to a man since Geoff, though this was terrible timing with the other complications in her life. But she felt so strangely in tune with this man, just as she had the other times they'd met. And she knew he was attracted to her despite how prickly he seemed.

"Will you go to lunch with me?" he asked in a rush. "We can just walk across the plaza to the La Casa Sena. I always tease people that there's something in the water there, so proceed with caution. The Casa's the restored home of a Civil War general and his wife who are best known around here for having twenty-three kids."

She felt pleased he'd asked her out but annoyed he'd added that last trivial detail and made a joke of it. But of course he knew nothing of the childless woman's world, where one avoided one's friends and sisters because they had cute kids hanging on their legs and you just couldn't bear it. He had no concept of despair so deep or fury so fierce that an ad for diapers could make you want to put your fist through the TV screen.

"I'd like that—lunch," she said. "And if you don't mind, I'll leave these kachinas here to be appraised. You know, I sometimes feel their black eyes are following me around the room," she added and forced a little laugh.

But he startled her again when he turned back to her with a somber look. "I've felt that way sometimes—with other things. We'll just put them under the counter here, and I'll write you a receipt for them later."

He locked the shop, and they walked toward the long, shaded portico of the Palace of Governors, teaming and buzzing with native artists on beach chairs or bright blankets selling their jewelry, bead work, and pottery to tourists. Yet Alex felt it was just the two of them here in sunny Santa Fe.

"I'm just wondering to what I owe this special occasion of a visit from my daughter," Marian Abernathy Spencer greeted Alex at the doorway to her spacious third-floor apartment overlooking the rugged Sangre de Cristo mountain range. Out the sweep of open patio doors, Alex glimpsed afternoon thunderclouds snagged on the peaks. The two women hugged each other stiffly, briefly, then stepped apart. As usual, her mother's floral-scented powder made her want to sneeze.

"I half wondered if it was an imposter on the phone saying she wanted to drop by," Marian added as if Alex hadn't taken her previous point.

Her sharp-edged voice took its first slice into Alex's self-confidence. "I have something I wanted to share with you, Mother. And you at least get to turn on the TV to see how I'm doing."

"I'm pretty busy with my new life and don't watch much TV."

Alex tried another tack. "Is Charles here?"

"Golfing. He's thrilled you're stopping by, of course, and hopes to see you before you go. I've made a little something special for a snack, Lexi."

Alexis was the youngest of six children born to Patrick and Marian Abernathy. The four eldest were boys, all of whom now served in the air force—two were fighter pilots—all over the world. Then came Sarah and last, Alexis. Sarah had lived in Honolulu with her country club chef husband and family for five years. Alex's siblings had a total of twelve kids among them.

"It's thoughtful of you to have something for me," Alex said, though she wanted nothing after her large lunch.

"Actually, now that I've seen you, I think I'd better fix you something more," her mother said, shaking her head. "They say those television cameras put pounds on, and I can see it's true. I don't want you wasting away."

"I just had lunch, a big one, really." Alex followed her mother into the kitchen, where she watched her take a prepared tray with nacho chips ringing guacamole from the refrigerator. The plastic wrap crinkled as she uncovered it.

To Alex—as always—her mother seemed to glow. Her plumpness kept her face and arms almost wrinkle-free, so she looked ten years younger, especially with the new shade of ash blond hair. She wore a patterned caftan that was quite slimming. But then her mother's exterior could cloak a lot of things.

"Are you still friends with that woman—Sandra?"

Marian asked. "Never married, did she? Has she ever really recovered from—the shock with her family?"

"I don't think anyone ever really recovers from something like that," Alex said as her mother delved into the fridge again and took out a cut-glass pitcher of what appeared to be sangria with orange and lemon slices bobbing among the ice cubes. "Mother, if there's booze in that, I can't have any."

"Well, by the time you drive back, it will be worn off. Or—" She straightened, staring across the small, immaculate kitchen at her. "Is there something wrong with you? You're not sick, on antibiotics or something?"

"No. Only sick of us dancing around things that should really matter. I came to tell you that—well, you know Geoff wanted a child every bit as much as I did— still do. And he froze some sperm before he went to the Gulf...." She made the mistake of stepping closer to look into her mother's face instead of just plunging on. The older woman pursed her lips as if she'd just eaten one of the lemons in the sangria. "Many guys going to the Gulf did that, Mother. Anyway," she blurted, deciding just to get this over with, "through artificial insemination, I'm trying to get pregnant again."

Marian looked stricken. She set the pitcher down with a bang, slopping out red liquid. She pressed both clasped hands to her ample breasts.

"You cannot mean that. Without a husband? If it wasn't bad enough before. Lexi, the whole thing could have been solved if you'd just not been so consumed by career, career, career. If you weren't so intense and— and driven. But now, without a man to care for you—"

"Mother! I'm driven, all right," Alex said, trying not to shout. She hit her fist on the refrigerator door. "Driven enough to tell you this is not the world you grew up in. Get with it. Women have careers, frequently with families. And there are single mothers. Geoff and I agreed to do this—he wanted me to promise to try— and I've been putting it off too long. Now, what I need— please—to know from you is something I asked you once before. Are you sure there was no possibility you ever took some form of that DES drug? Before when I asked you it was just routine, but the doctor's found out my cervix is kind of convoluted and—"

"Would you just stop? I don't want to hear all this," Marian cried and covered her ears with her hands. "I know some DES daughters have problems. But you think I needed to take that miscarriage drug when I had five children already? I read all about it when you asked me last time, and now you dare to bring it up again? You know what you're trying to accuse me of?"

"I'm not suggesting you lied or are to blame for anything."

"I read that some DES daughters get cancer young," she went on, taking her hands away from her head and leaning on a chair back with both hands while Alex stood her ground by the kitchen counter. "You don't have that, do you?"

"Of course not. I just want to know—"

"And I have answered you. Now, if you can just control yourself and sit here with your mother and have some of this—oh, dear, look at the mess," she went on and started to wipe up sangria.

Alex took another step closer, her arms now crossed and her fists jammed in her armpits. "I am looking at the mess. The one we've made between us because you can't accept how much I need this child. You can't want that for me."

"Lexi," she said, not looking at her, wringing out a dishrag, "I wanted it long ago, and it didn't happen because you wanted a career, and now it's too late. That happens. People have to grow up and pay the piper sometimes. Lexi, where are you going?"

"Why should I stay when we can't even talk to each other?" Alex cried as she headed for the kitchen door. "Excuse me while I go grow up. And do my damnedest to find a way to get your grandchild in my arms, whether you ever choose to see that child or not."

Her mother's voice, like the choking smell of her powder, pursued her through the living room to the tiny foyer. "You should be an actress, not an anchorwoman, Lexi. You were always too dramatic, too emotional for your own good, pushing yourself so hard you'd forget things around the house, though I must admit, that's why you're good at reading all that bad news on TV—"

The door slamming between them at least turned her off.

Alex gasped when she saw the knife on her kitchen counter. She could not recall for the life of her what she'd used it for.

Just back from Santa Fe, with her purse and car keys still in her hands, she stood staring, wracking her brain.

She decided to make a quick tour of the house to see if anything else was amiss. She started upstairs first, whispering to herself.

"Just too much going on," she told herself.

Her mother's accusations that she was overly emotional and driven ate at her. She was just too preoccupied to remember basic things, and here she was going back to work on Monday.

She peeked in room after room, snapping on lights and leaving them on, since it was after dark. "You've been like this before—college exams, those all-nighters." She talked aloud just to hear a voice. But she could not bear to put into words how distraught she'd been after she lost Geoff and walked through daily life for months like a zombie.

That's what her mother had referred to today. She'd find a stack of mail she'd put in the refrigerator or a meal she couldn't recall taking out of the freezer melting to softness in with the table napkins or Fig Newtons. Back then Alex would just shake her head and go on. Now she only whispered, "Damn that Cordova for giving me the heebie-jeebies. Man, I hope they get that bad ass back in jail soon."

But it was more than that scaring her, something else she couldn't describe or put a name to. As she went down the hall toward her bedroom, the hair on the back of her neck prickled.

She hesitated at the door. The hall light cast a gray glow into the room, falling across the corner of the big bed. She edged her hand in and fumbled down the wall for the light switch. Nothing looked disturbed, but sudden fear stabbed her, sharp as that butcher knife she'd just put away.

Hefting a heavy marble book end from the headboard of the bed, she made a quick circuit of the room, even looking under the bed with the little flashlight. Trembling, she checked the closet and the attached master bath. Her arms shook as she approached the partially closed jade green shower curtain, hesitated, holding her breath, then swept it back and jumped away.

Nothing. Nothing maybe but her own exhaustion and stress.

Still, after looking in the other upstairs rooms, even the linen closet where she'd replaced the cradle, she went downstairs to the first floor again. For once she was glad the house had no basement. Other than the kitchen counter, everything on the first floor looked perfectly untouched until, now carrying the butcher knife she'd retrieved, she went into the study.

When she flicked on the desk lamp by the master switch just inside the door, lights also blinked on for all three shelves of the corner cupboard, blazing the kachinas to life.

She gasped, jerking up the knife before her with both hands. The kachina collection glared at her in bright lights for the first time in years. Their blacks and orange, reds and yellows, hurt her eyes. Their feathers and weapons, masked faces and frowns, froze her in the doorway. The dolls were no longer turned to the wall as she had left them, but stared straight at her.

Shaking, she managed to get hold of herself. Maybe when she had packed the three dolls she had taken to show Nick, she had accidentally hit the hidden shelf light switch. But she couldn't recall turning them face out. And surely she would have left the spaces for the three she'd taken out not spaced them so evenly as they stood now.

She shoved the door farther open until it bumped into the wall, to be sure no one hid behind it. She didn't go closer to look at the dolls. She edged around the room to the desk phone. Though she'd seen absolutely no evidence of someone breaking in, she'd call Camelot Security. Or she could phone Bernice. But what would she tell her? I need police protection because I must have done some crazy little things around the house I don't remember because I'm so obsessed with bigger things? Damn, but she'd let her mother get to her again.

Still holding the knife in one hand, she yanked open the big middle desk drawer and rummaged frantically through pens and paper clips for a key. Not to the desk, but to the room. This time she not only closed but locked the door behind her.

5

"Gill O'Fallon, Ms. McCall. You called Camelot Security. Oh, it's you," he said, his long, freckled face breaking into a smile as he stood at her front door the next morning. He suddenly looked even more nervous. "You're on the TV."

"Yes, that's me."

Despite his boyish good looks, she guessed Gill was at least thirty. That fact made the crossed swords sewn on the pocket of his brown work shirt look even more silly. At least Camelot was willing to send their people out on a Sunday morning. She'd sleep much better once she had this taken care of.

"Not had any trouble, I hope," he said, as if she'd accused him of something. "I mean, the alarm for your number never sounded."

"No, no trouble like that," she assured him, wishing she could assure herself.

Redheaded men with Irish last names were few and far between in New Mexico. Especially since her last name was Irish and her father had sported a full head of red hair, this man's presence was already easing her worries.

She glanced behind him at his van in the driveway. The company logo emblazoned in bright green was a castle with a moat and high towers and parapets with two medieval-looking guards, holding the ubiquitous crossed swords as if they were ready to ward off some dragon or conqueror.

"Thanks for being prompt. I'd like you to take a look at the security control box just inside the door to the garage, then do a check of the interior and exterior entry points—all the door and window wiring. It's just that I've had the system a long time and want to be certain everything's working well."

"We check the system from our end all the time," he told her as he picked up his sword-crossed embossed toolbox and followed her in.

She kept a discreet eye on him while he worked. He seemed quick and efficient. He obviously knew the layout of the house, as there were quite a few of these floor plans in this subdivision Camelot serviced. He even checked her electrical breaker box and master switch in the garage. He was done in less than a half hour, which left her plenty of time to get to the clinic. The other decision she had made during her sleepless night was that, despite the fact she'd refused Beth and Dr. Jasmine's suggestion earlier, she was going to sit in on one of the Sunday session counseling circles.

"Thank you for joining us, Alexis." Dr. Joyce Prettyman gave her arm a little squeeze. "Especially," she added, leaning forward conspiratorially with a little lift of her precisely penciled eyebrows, "since I couldn't meet with you alone the other day."

"This is fine, really, Dr. Prettyman," Alex assured the attractive, fiftyish psychiatrist.

"Well, we just never know, do we?" the doctor said, suddenly annoying Alex so much she almost walked off. She had not attended these voluntary sessions before, and thought if anyone was the weak link in the clinic staff, it was Joyce Prettyman. She seemed to be a good listener, but too patronizing, even condescending. She was the sort of woman, Alex thought, who would have made a bouncy, bubbly first-grade teacher.

Dr. Prettyman had already turned back to the seated group as Alex took the last chair on the breeze-blessed, shaded front portico. "Ladies, this is Alexis." The doctor raised her voice to quiet their murmurs. "Alexis is sitting in with us today, and we want her to feel right at home, don't we?"

Several hellos and nods followed. "I think some of you may recognize Alexis from her job," the doctor went on. "But we all agree that our privacy is important here, so—as always—anything we share here will be for our ears only. Now, who would like to start today? Yes, Linda."

A petite, overweight brunette related how she was already dreading Mother's Day when it was nearly a month away. "I know our minister means well, but he always has all the mothers and grandmothers stand in the service as if motherhood is a special honor bestowed by God himself. Doesn't he realize how much that can hurt? I wish the church had a group of women like this who don't need nursery care for all their kids."

Women nodded and murmured. Some added similar stories of emotional longing and agony set off by the most minute but emotionally momentous of incidents.

Alex certainly empathized, but she could not bring herself to contribute. She was afraid that if she did, she'd soon be scraping raw her wounds about fighting with her mother. She could not bear to think about that, let alone share it. And yet it—and her growing attraction to Nick Destin—possessed her every second she was not thinking about a baby. How could she ever go back to work tomorrow? If only there was some way her career could help her solve her problems and those of others like her.

A loud sniff drew her attention. As bad as she felt, her heart immediately went out to the woman across from her, who seemed to be crying tearlessly, head erect, not moving but for a quivering lower lip and shaking shoulders. Among the predominantly Anglo women and one Hispanic here, she was a strikingly regal Native American, probably from one of the local Pueblo tribes.

Her bronze face was high and broad with a strong nose and cheekbones any model would kill for, but emotion thinned her full lips. A leather strap dangling turquoise and silver beads bound her hair in a knot at the nape of her neck. A wide silver belt cinched in her denim vest and long skirt to emphasize her full figure. She sniffed again. Alex fumbled in her purse and leaned across to hand her a tissue. The woman nodded, took it, and blew her nose loudly. Others spoke, but when the Indian woman began to talk, Alex finally snapped to full attention.

"My name is Rita. I know you don't see Indians— no Santa Cruz Pueblos—like me here. Our people, they just have children and lots, no problem. But the only ones I have, they are ones I make with my two hands with clay and paint."

When Rita paused to wipe her nose, Dr. Prettyman put in, "Rita is an artist who makes those lovely story-teller statues you may have seen. There is quite a display of them in the lobby."

Rita Twohorses, Alex thought. She was one of the artists whose work was displayed at Nick's shop, though she'd known about her for years. It had never worked out yet for her to do an interview with the artist, but she'd wanted to. She owned two of her statues, magical ones.

"For my people," Rita went on, her hair beads bouncing when she moved her head, "to trust the medicine— science—of the Anglos is not good. My husband, he says if the Creator does not give us children, we must accept. Only I cannot. And so I break our ways and give pain to my husband by coming here."

"But," the woman next to Rita began when she paused, "if your husband doesn't agree with this, then he won't cooperate, and how can you undergo IVF without at least donor sperm? I know my husband is having a fit about being tested. He says it questions his manhood."

"My husband said he will try that part once. But I

tricked him, worse than Coyote," Rita admitted. She looked annoyed by the murmur in the circle. "The *trick-ster* Coyote," she explained, frowning. "My husband, he gave one time a sample of himself I brought here. He does not know from one sample Dr. Jasmine can get many tries for a child. Only I am thinking Dr. Stanhope does not want to help me now."

That produced new whispers; no one, including Alex, believed such a thing. But Rita's voice had lost its wistful, confessional quality. It became hard, almost fierce.

"If he gets me a child or not, Dr. Stanhope maybe thinks my husband will cause this place trouble, but why—"

"I really don't think that's a proper perception, Rita," Dr. Prettyman interrupted, leaning forward as she always did when she spoke. "Dr. Stanhope wants to help everyone here. Perhaps you and I can discuss this later."

"The doctor too?" Rita demanded, her brown eyes shining like wet stones.

"Later," she promised and went on to someone else. But when the session ended, Alex saw her walk away with others in the group while Rita glared after her.

Alex approached Rita. "I'm sorry about your situation," she began awkwardly. They were just the same height, though Rita was built like Alex's mother, soft and pillowy. "I just wanted to tell you I love your art," she went on, "and own two pieces of it displayed on the mantel in my living room." She explained how she considered the statues a talisman for her career. She even found herself telling Rita how she was trying IVF without her husband, though for a different reason.

As she spoke, Rita's stiff stance relaxed and her defiant expression softened. Listening intently, she nodded from time to time. "Then we are the same blood, on our own for what is most important to us," she declared. "Come on, let's take a walk and tell some more true stories." She indicated the path that led back toward the long-abandoned town.

They went as far as the double barbed-wire fence with its no-trespassing sign that ran along the edge of the hillside. Alex had been down here once to peer over at the town before the fence went up, but had gone no closer. To her amazement, Rita gave a tug of the wires, and lifted them apart to reveal a gateway already cut. "I like it here," she said when Alex hesitated. Curious now, she followed Rita through and down the dusty, narrow, twisting path into the cliff-cradled valley.

"You know," Alex said, "the Stanhopes were going to sell this to a group that preserves and studies Western sites, but they changed their minds. A friend of mine, Nick Destin, told me, but the Stanhopes haven't said a word."

"That's them," she said, frowning, "but I know and trust Nick Destin. Nick Destiny, I call him to make him smile. Not a happy man these last few years. But he always honors our people with fair prices because he honors our work. I saw you with him, leaving the clinic several days ago. Watch your steps here," she called over her sturdy shoulder as she led their way down the snaking path.

Alex was hardly prepared to share what she thought
of Nick right now, but she did tell Rita she'd been to the
shop and seen her work prominently displayed there. As
they reached the valley floor, they both became silent.
Around them lay the ruined remains of once booming
Silver, now mere adobe and stone foundations lining a
tumbleweed and sage-clogged street.

Only one mine entrance of what must have once
been many was visible, with its fallen, interlocking
beams choking its mouth before its throat plunged into
darkness. A rutted road gone to grass ran to what was
once a creek, but in this dry season it was merely a barren arroyo. One clearly discernible feature of the ghost
town was a burying ground on the other side of the
shallow valley, with tombstones like crooked, broken
teeth.

"Even on this flat ground, be careful," Rita warned.
Her voice startled Alex as the Indian woman pointed.
"Pits and shafts hidden here."

They sat in the shade of a scrubby piñon pine on what
must once have been the foundation of a big building—
a church or saloon maybe. They gazed back up at the
clinic, with only its roofline visible from here. The
soughing of the breeze through the pine needles overhead was sad, but somehow it soothed Alex. They sat
in companionable silence for a while before Alex spoke.

"How did you happen to come to the clinic if your
husband and your people are against it?" she asked,
turning slightly to face Rita, who was watching a hawk
soar high overhead.

"Dr. Stanhope," she said, her voice almost a chant-like monotone. "He came to the Corn Dance Feast Day at the pueblo last fall. Paul and me, we live in Albuquerque above my studio near Old Town, but I go home to work some weekends. It's one way to advertise."

Looking at her, Alex could almost imagine they had walked through a time warp to the past, but a woman concerned with IVF and advertising was very real and modern.

"So," Rita went on, twisting one of several turquoise bracelets around her sturdy wrist, "I asked Hale Stanhope what he did, just like you would on TV maybe. He said he'd love to have some of my storytellers in the clinic. And I told him how I wanted a child. Later, we made a trade for two IVF cycles for twenty figures—statues, not money."

"Those figures of the woman with the children—a perfect trade for your own."

Rita frowned, glancing down at her bracelets. "But my husband, Paul, one night he was drinking, he came here and talked to Dr. Stanhope in the parking lot. So I think the doctor, he is now afraid of him or something."

"You mean he thinks your husband might harm him—if he proceeds with IVF or if he fails?" Alex pursued, leaning closer.

"Paul, he has a temper if I trust an Anglo too much," she admitted, not really answering the questions. "But I am desperate for a child, Alexis McCall." She sighed and looked down again. "That is how I heard them say it on *One Life to Live*."

"The soap opera?" she asked, trying not to smile.

"Right. When I work, I always turn on TV. I have

seen you, but I never saw dark colors from you until now—maybe the TV stops it."

"I don't know what you mean. Your TV has something wrong with the color?"

She shook her head in a rattle of hair beads. Briefly, she squinted as if studying Alex, then looked up at the hawk riding the thermals again. "I can't see them on TV. It has to be real people—in person. My gift from the Creator comes with a price, like everything. I can't have a baby, but I can make my hands give me what my heart sees in the statues. And I see colors around people that tell me things about them—maybe a curse and not a blessing."

Alex wasn't sure if she meant the colors showed a curse or if she herself felt cursed by this gift. "Is it an aura?" she asked as Rita regarded her solemnly. "You have ESP or whatever your people would call it?"

"No, not power like the tribal medicine men have. I just see colors. When I saw you leave the clinic recovery area this week, you were gold. But today when you came to the circle, you are deep green mixed with blue."

"Like those old mood rings," Alex marveled, realizing that she had felt relieved and hopeful the first time Rita must have seen her, but today… "Can you see your own colors?" she asked.

"Never, not even in a mirror. But Dr. Stanhope, he is dark brown when he sees me now, when he used to be just gray like his eyes. I have to talk to him, be sure our bargain is still good."

"Of course it's good," Alex tried to assure her. "I almost lost faith in him when he couldn't transfer my embryos, but he's discovered another problem I have and is just planning to do it another way. What a creative mother you will make for your child, after already birthing those beautiful terra-cotta ones."

For the first time Rita Twohorses smiled. Her teeth looked startling white in her copper face. "It is good to have a friend here," she said. "Can you tell me now about this new problem the doctor found for you?"

As Alex began to explain, Rita took a narrow silver band from her cluster of bracelets and bent it around Alex's narrower wrist as if they'd made some unspoken pact between them.

As Alexis drove back into town, it hit her. Though she had resisted getting support from Dr. Prettyman and the counseling circle today, she felt much better after talking to Rita. As different as their backgrounds and situations were, they had helped each other, one on one. It was just the way she'd always thought of herself talking to that individual TV viewer who had invited her into her home. Rita reached out through her art, but Alexis's gift was to reach out to individuals through the media.

She glanced around while her car idled at a red light. That woman in the blue Toyota in the next lane or that one carrying the sack of groceries on the sidewalk—that brunette driving the white van behind her—they might be just like Rita. Many women despaired over their infertility, even ones who got some sort of professional counseling. They thought no one understood; they didn't know where to go, or even what questions to ask.

"But that's what I do," she said aloud, thumping the steering wheel with her fist. Her art was asking questions, finding answers, and sharing information in a way people would understand and take to heart. Stripped down to its bare bones, her beloved job was informing people so they could make the right decisions for their lives. She realized she'd been wanting to do this story for years, but had been afraid. It had taken her own pain and determination—and now that of Rita's—to crystallize this for her.

When the light changed, she surged ahead, as if she could outrace her fear and the risks.

"You certainly didn't think you could keep something like this a secret—a baby, let alone a test-tube one?" Mike demanded the next morning.

"They don't call it that anymore," Alex said, sitting forward in her chair, struggling to keep calm in her excitement and frustration. "It's all under the umbrella of assisted-reproductive technologies—ART—or just IVF for in-vitro fertilization and a host of other names that sound like alphabet soup. But that's just the point about a series like this. I could explain and humanize—"

"*My* point is, you'd be an unwed mother," he interrupted, jumping up and going to the window to glare out between the vertical blinds. "The entire viewing audience knows you're widowed and still single. You did that charity-date auction piece just last month," he added, yanking the blinds open so hard they swung and smacked against each other as bright afternoon light leaped into the room. "Alexis, our viewing market is not the Bible belt, but there could be a P.R. downside here with this stuff, some real kickback."

"I realize that. And of course I would have eventually had to go public with an explanation if I got pregnant even without doing a series. But I've got to face the chances of failure, the way any infertile woman does. Even with new advances, the odds are stacked big time against conceiving and then a full-term pregnancy." She fought to keep her voice and composure from breaking. "Mike, I *have* to do this even if I don't have a child. It can really help other women and couples out there."

He threw himself back in the chair next to her. Evidently when he'd first seen her face today, he'd known not to take his usual high-backed leather throne across the vast desk. He took his glasses off and rubbed his eyes with one thumb and index finger.

"I admit," he said, his voice quiet, "there are risks in any important pieces of dynamite journalism."

"Exactly, and it's not like we're breaking new ground. We've both seen pieces and series on IVF. But to have the correspondent be the one going through it—with complications, with a past of failure, but hope for the future…"

When she hesitated, Mike thrust his glasses back on. She saw he was really listening now. "That's the angle, the slant," he muttered, as if to himself. "Not broken but brave."

"It's a crazed kind of courage, I guess, driven by desperation," she added, realizing they were automatically talking in sound bites now. She gripped her hands tightly in her lap, picturing Rita staring up at the hawk in the heavens, maybe seeing her child hovering there. She met Mike's gaze unflinchingly as he jumped to his feet and sat against the edge of his desk.

"All right," he said. "It could be great. What's that title you tossed out before?"

"'The Fertility Frontier.'"

"Okay, it's a go. But it's got to stay dramatic and personal—feel intimate even when you'll have to bring in the high-tech stuff. Though it will obviously be ongoing as you—your case proceeds—we'll launch it in a hurry for May sweeps, if you can get the foundation segments shot. Sandra's been our medical reporter, so she can give you a hand. And Alex, not only will you have to tell your own story, but get your doctors, their staff, some fellow patients—"

"That's what I can't deliver yet for sure," she said, rising and pulling her purse strap over her shoulder. "I'll need to consult with them, see what they think, then get back to you. I'll see if I can talk to them tomorrow sometime."

"You just tell them it will put their little clinic on the local and maybe the national map," he said and nodded smugly.

"National? Mike, the hinterlands out here are hardly New York or L.A. And this is a private clinic with all kinds of protection for patients, so I just don't know. I may have to promise anonymity, interviews with voices scrambled, faces blocked—even use other specialists— but I needed to clear it with you first."

"You get the staff to see this *our* way," he said, pointing at himself with both thumbs bobbing. She had to smile as she headed out. The idea was definitely going to fly now.

At the door, she remembered to explain her quick detective work to find threatening letters from Hank Cordova in her mail. "I'll be running an archive tape of his interview downtown to Detective Alvarez. I left her a message so if they've run the description of his vehicle, he may even be back in jail already after making bail the first time," she concluded breathlessly, expecting him to be pleased.

To her dismay, he kicked the side of his desk. "Alexis, why are you the biggest damn news maker in the city lately when you're supposed to be behind a desk merely reporting news? And why didn't you tell me this Cordova tie-in the minute you figured it out?"

She took a few steps closer. "I didn't think you wanted anything on the air about a car trying to hit me," she protested.

"Only because we didn't need you during a disciplinary suspension splashed all over the screen for a stupid fender bender in our own lot so we look like a bunch of morons. And you think Jack Fanshaw wanted that kind of publicity when he's in negotiations with us for a big lay-down for basketball games?" His voice got louder, his face ruddier. "But you ever so much as scent a possible story again, you bring it here first, that's your commitment, right?"

"That's what I just did," she said and closed the office door behind her.

6

"I know this request comes as a surprise," Alexis said, concluding her explanation of her ideas for the fertility series. She looked nervously from Hale to Jasmine to Peter VanHeyde, the clinic manager. "I'd certainly understand if you'd want to talk all this over privately."

"I don't think that will be necessary," Hale said. Alex's hopes fell when Jasmine cleared her throat as if in warning to her husband. If this conference table wasn't made of glass, Alex thought, Jasmine would have kicked him under it. She feared this request would go the way of Nick's desire to buy the ghost town land.

Alex tried to keep her hands lightly clasped on the table so she didn't appear to be begging them. Being in Dr. Stanhope's imposing office, where she'd had earlier medical consultations, didn't help either. She shifted slightly sideways in her seat.

"I can speak for the Evergreen staff," Hale said, hunching forward, propping his elbows on the table and steepling his fingers before his face. "It's our mission to help as many infertile women as is humanly possible, and we can only handle so many here. The reach of the media to enhance and expand our cause is very appealing. In a way, our helping you to do this series would be like *pro bono* work. Peter?"

Peter VanHeyde was pale, bone-thin, and spoke with a slight Dutch accent. He was European-born and educated, where much of the groundbreaking infertility work had been done. "I trust your vision on this, Hale," he said with a decisive nod, though Alex still wasn't sure of their position. "My only concern," he added, "is the privacy of our patients. But if any participation by them is voluntary and approved by one of the doctors or me, then yes."

"Approved?" Alex echoed, "You're asking for creative control of the series?"

"Of course not," Hale answered for him. "It's just that we would need to know your plans ahead, because there are some—ah, let's say, extremely delicate situations—where we would advise a particular patient not even be approached."

"Oh, I certainly understand that." Total acquiescence on this point went against her journalistic grain, but she agreed they had to protect their patients. "We're all set, then?" she asked, looking to Hale for further affirmation.

"My concern," Jasmine put in, "is that it would really be a problem to have outsiders in my lab." Her eyes pierced Alex like lasers. "I need a constantly secure area with controlled lighting, temperature, and air purity for my eggs and pre-embryos."

"Absolutely," Alex assured her, "although you must

admit what you do is at the heart of everything here, so we'd need at least a glimpse into your workplace." Alex knew very well that other IVF labs had permitted media visits, but it was essential to keep Jasmine on her side.

She breathed easier when Hale said, "We'll work that out, Jazz," and tapped his wife's arm before he turned back to Alex. "So you'd use yourself as the *entre* to this story? Would you want to cover the laparoscopic transfer of your pre-embryos, for example? I think you still show signs of being affected by DES, however much your mother protests. Bringing up something like that on the air could be very difficult if you're using yourself as a case study—"

"More like a guinea pig or laboratory rat, the way things are in this industry," Jasmine put in before Hale glared at her.

"I do understand your warnings, believe me," Alex admitted, sitting forward. "It's been a great sacrifice even to tell my closest friends."

She tried not to look shaken, but she was. With those incisive, personal questions, the enormity of what she was proposing finally hit her with full force. To have cameramen she knew recording her hopes and fears, to have everyone who had seen her grow up, her current neighbors, her mother, new acquaintances like Nick, know everything she had fought to keep private…

"Alexis?" Hale prompted, as if he had taken over the discussion now.

She nodded her head. "The intimate physical aspects of procedures we'd do with diagrams and graphics," she said. "But yes, I'd want to cover something of my surgery. I don't know about the DES yet. Still," she went on, once again looking at each of them in turn, "I would not ask you or other patients to help unless I intended to use myself as well. Frankly, that's what will make this powerful—pull people in."

She saw Hale and Jasmine exchange a lightning-quick glance she could not read. "You do understand," Hale went on, his voice taking on a soothing bedside tone, "that your ZIFT procedure will be invasive, if minor, surgery? You'll be unconscious, then quite groggy, when you come out from under the anesthesia. But," he added with a decisive tap of his knuckles on the table, "we'll have Beth give an interview that covers what happens. Before her divorce, she longed for a child for years, you know, but ART never succeeded for her."

"No wonder she's so supportive and concerned," Alex said, realizing another reason she'd been so instinctively drawn to Beth.

"And we're having a baby reunion next Sunday," Hale added, as if it were an afterthought, "so that will show results can be very real and rewarding."

Alex was surprised and impressed. Hale Stanhope sounded like Mike Montgomery at his best. She might have to buck both of them from time to time to bring this series to life from a woman's point of view, but she was grateful for the outpouring of ideas and support.

"That sounds great," she said, smiling, "I didn't know about the reunion—but then, I don't have a clinic baby—yet."

"I imagine," Jasmine said, rising and tugging her

jacket briskly down at each wrist, "now that you've got carte blanche here, Alexis, you'll learn a lot you never knew. Please just make sure you clear any lab visits with me way ahead. Speaking of which, I'm a bit backed up in there, so I hope you'll excuse me."

"Thank you for your support, Dr. Jasmine," Alex called out, twisting in her chair as the woman started away. At the door she spun around to face them, one hand on the knob, one splayed on her hip. Again, as the first and only other time Alex had met with her in person, she marveled at how poised she was, almost like an expensive mannequin, each external, separate part perfection. Yet Alex sensed that she seethed with some secret, deep-seated fury inside.

"I'm happy to help such a good cause, for you and for us," Jasmine said, but her crimson smile did not reach her eyes.

"I know this isn't what I said before," Alex told Nick as they sat in her living room with the ten kachinas he hadn't seen last Saturday spread out on the couch, "but I think I'd rather have you take them with you this evening. Except I have decided to put two away for the future, maybe to give to—to Geoff's relatives someday."

So that Geoff's son or daughter will have an opportunity to have something he valued, she almost said. She wanted to find a way to tell Nick about her *Fertility Frontier* series—and her own fertility frontier—but she just couldn't find a way to start.

"Sure, whatever you say. I'll probably buy several myself after I see what the tribal elders want. This one is an antique for certain. His name is Soyoko," he said and moved the carved and painted figure up and down so he seemed to dance.

She frowned at the hideous masklike face, with demonic horns sprouting from the wild hair and feathers standing straight up. Then just to appear to be interested in what he, like Geoff, found so fascinating, she asked, "How can you tell which ones are Zuni and which Hopi?"

"Without recognizing the specific different ones, the general rule is that the Zuni kachinas are taller and thinner and can't stand without support," he said, holding another one up as an example. "Why don't you pick out which two you want to keep, and I'll box up the others?"

She was relieved to get them out of her sight. Her mood improved considerably when they sat having cognac and after-dinner chocolates in front of the fire before he went to his other appointment, then headed back to Santa Fe. She wished she'd asked him to come to dinner, but she would soon.

In a little lull in the conversation, he angled his big body slightly more toward her. He seemed to fill the room, suck in all the empty space, tilt everything toward him. His left arm lay on the back of the leather couch so his fingers almost touched her. She wanted very badly to tangle her own in his hair, but she stared into the fire and said, "I have a very important new series I've been working on. I suppose you'll see teaser announcements for it soon."

"I like teaser announcements, as long as the series

itself will be all the teasers promise," he said. His mood seemed less austere tonight. The warm, intimate tone of his voice almost curled her toes. It often seemed that he said things which had a suggestive, sexy undercurrent, but it might just be the way she felt about him. Then at other times he seemed wary or even angry.

"I especially wanted you to know before it—it hit," she explained. The words were coming hard for her, which was unusual. "I told you I was not doing a story on the clinic. That was true then, but now I am doing one. With myself at the center of it."

She looked away from the flames to study his expression. His hand slid down to touch her shoulder, then clasp it. "The center of it how?"

"I tried to have an IVF baby years ago, when Geoff was alive. Before he left for the Gulf War, I promised him I wouldn't give up even if he never came back. I just hope you can understand that."

"I understand wanting a child," he said, his voice harder. "But you mean you're trying to get pregnant now? You'll be rearing a child alone?"

"If I'm fortunate enough to conceive with the problems I've had, yes," she declared defiantly, sitting up straighter.

He turned her to him on the couch, sliding her easily closer to him on the smooth leather. "So you want me to stay away?" he asked as the space between them shrank.

She put both hands on his chest, not to stop him but steady herself. "Stay away? I didn't say or mean that. It's just that I have so much on my plate right now that—"

"That you want me to take the kachinas, pay up, and run?"

"No, I didn't mean—"

"That you want to tell me you're on the Stanhopes' side if the discussion over Silver gets rough?"

"Will it get rough? And would you stop putting words in my mouth, please? I'm not asking you about any of that. I simply—"

"Before we argue, I simply this," he murmured and pulled her the rest of the way into his arms.

It wasn't a full embrace, for he touched only her upper arms and shoulders and her hands were caught gently between them. But his warm, firm mouth descended. The kiss started out soft, deepened, then lightened again until he was somehow feathering kisses along her jawline, tilted back for him, and then down her throat while her heart thudded and her breasts pressed against his hard chest. Somehow, she had looped her arms around his neck.

"I'd better stop," he said, setting her slightly back. "I don't usually make a practice of mixing business with pleasure or with kissing women, however appealing, who are trying to get pregnant—with someone else, dead or alive. Actually, you don't have to tell me any of this."

She felt breathless. More than anything she wanted him to hold and kiss her again. "But you do understand?" she asked.

When he just folded his arms over his chest, she had her answer. She felt totally abandoned at even the temporary loss of his touch and goodwill, but it was best to know now.

"Hell, no, I don't understand, if you're really asking and not just telling," he said. "I don't see why your husband would want or expect you to try to rear a child alone. My mother managed with me after my dad died young, but it was hard, and I don't just mean financially. Especially if it's a boy, it's going to be really rough."

He got up and paced to the mantel, where he glared at her storyteller dolls before he looked back at her.

"I see," she said.

"I doubt if you really do, not any more than I can really grasp what's brought you to this. Besides, you realize, I'm sure, that there are segments of your viewing audience who will think this is terrible, selfish, even immoral."

She stood too. She couldn't fathom why he'd kissed her after she'd told him if he really felt like this. "Including you?" she challenged, hands on her hips.

"I didn't say that, and you're the one who just accused me of putting words in your mouth."

"Since you feel that way, I think you'd better go."

"But that's my dilemma," he said, coming closer. "I'd really like to see you again, so—despite what I've said—I do value truth in our relationship from the beginning—if you want to try a relationship."

When she said nothing, only studied him, he went on, "I've already been burned by finding out things about someone else I thought I knew and could trust. And I've still got the scars."

"Your ex-wife?"

"Yeah. These last few years were difficult when we

were together and much worse when we were apart. I'd better get going, as I'm late already."

She escorted him to the door. He had told her he had to meet with a state representative on Living Heritage business. Since he hadn't shared whether it was about fighting the Stanhopes over Silver, she had reined in her natural curiosity to ask. No way she wanted to get caught up in that.

He hefted the two boxes of kachinas, but pushed one against the front door so she couldn't open it.

"I see this desire for a child is number one in your life. I can accept that. So do we have at least a truce? And if I call and ask to take you out this weekend, you'll at least negotiate with me about it?"

"Of course, though I'm on assignment all day Sunday at the clinic. They're having a baby reunion."

"Your face lights up even when you say that. You hinted that you've had a lot of trouble trying to have one—ah, the normal way?"

"Yes, though I must admit that hasn't turned me off on the normal way."

"Thank God," he said and chuckled. He leaned forward to brush her lips with his again. Since he held both boxes, this time she reached up to take his head in her hands to prolong the kiss. He moved again to tilt her body against his. She laughed low in her throat as she finally let him go.

"*I'll say* we've got a truce," he said. "But I'd look forward either to war or peace with you. I'll call you tomorrow."

She opened the front door and then his car doors for

him while he loaded the boxes. He squeezed her shoulder, looked as if he'd like to kiss her again, then evidently decided against it. He got in the driver's seat of his black Jeep and started the engine. As he pulled away and she waved, she noticed a light-colored van drive away from the curb in the dusk a few doors down. At least it wasn't an orange VW. Then she realized that it was probably the Camelot Securities van. She had asked Gill O'Fallon to drive by now and then if he had a chance, and he'd said he would.

Feeling both happier and safer than she had for quite a while, she hurried back into the house.

"I can't thank all of you enough for your support and understanding," Alex told her colleagues at the staff conference table the next morning. Mike, Sandra, events coordinator Anne Wheelwright, producer Maria Filmore, co-anchor Stan Jackson, even the station's on-call image consultant, Frank Townsend, had listened while she'd explained her proposal and Mike laid out the task and timetable. She'd talked so much the last two hours that her voice sounded hoarse.

"That's it for now, people," Mike said, "and thanks in advance for pulling out all the stops on this. Along with *From Cheap but Chic Great Weekend Escapes* and *Eating Lean and Loving It*, the *Fertility Frontier* has got to blast us way ahead of the other two network affiliates here in town for the spring sweeps."

"No wonder," Alex said to Sandra as they watched everyone rush off like rafters in white water, "they called the Nielsen rating months the sweeps."

"And speaking of being swept off one's feet," Sandra whispered as she dug a candy bar out of her suit jacket pocket, "I'm really glad Nick Destin doesn't think your mission to have this child puts you on the list of the dating disabled or romantically challenged. More power to him and both of you. Just don't get in over your head with him too."

"What do you mean *too?*" Alex demanded.

"The Stanhopes. I just don't trust doctors, and you're suddenly up to your neck in them, that's all," she said as Alex grabbed her desk phone on its first ring. "Hello?"

Sandra went back to her desk in the busy newsroom while Alex listened to Bernice Alvarez, then sank into her chair when she heard why she'd called. "You mean Cordova's jumped bond and left town?" Alex exploded.

"I mean he's at large, we've got an APB out. He may or may not have skipped town, so watch yourself, that's all. But I still have a gut feeling this loser's not worthy of stalker status. A perp stupid enough to sign threatening letters and sit around waiting in a TV parking lot reminds me of a rabid squirrel on the loose."

"Yeah, but I don't even need a rabid squirrel right now, believe me."

"Be in touch if you see anything even a little off, right? Any time, have them beep me or whatever."

"I assure you, I will. Thanks, Bernice."

The moment Alex hung up, she scolded herself for not telling her friend about the butcher knife and kachinas. But she was afraid she'd just been distracted and distraught—that she was back to being forgetful again.

She jumped straight up when her phone rang again. Wondering if Cordova would dare to call her here, she picked it up carefully and said slowly, "Alexis McCall speaking."

"Alexis, Lita at the front desk. There's a real upset woman to see you out here. I thought she had the same name as mine at first, but I guess she said Rita. I swear, she's full-blooded Pueblo." She dropped her voice even more. "But she's not on the guest list for noon news about the Powow Fiesta, so—"

"I'll be right out."

Alex walked Rita outside behind the station to the single employee picnic table, dwarfed by the station's tower. They sat on the bench with their backs to the table. Rita was in the same denim outfit as yesterday, down to the wrinkles. Alex wondered if she'd even been home to change. Didn't her husband care about the state she was in?

"What's upset you so?" Alex asked. "Did you talk to Dr. Stanhope?"

Rita nodded, arching her back against the edge of the wooden table to scan the tower, then looked back at Alex. As in the counseling group, she was not quite crying, but her expression made it seem she should be. "He wants Paul to go in to see Dr. Prettyman before he can proceed with a cycle for me, but I know he won't do it. And Dr. Stanhope said all six eggs made pre-embryos which would freeze just fine until things got more stable for me."

"They will, Rita—the eggs freeze, I mean." Maybe the clinic was right if they were intentionally going slowly with Rita. Alex reached for her hand and squeezed it. "That's exactly what they're doing for me right now," she assured her. "I've researched the procedure, and I heard Dr. Jasmine's supposed to be the best. She's fiercely protective of the lab. I'm sure—listen, if you're thinking that's not many eggs, I had only four."

"But six eggs? That lab assistant who did the count when Dr. Jasmine was sick the morning they harvested told me in the hall I had seven," she insisted, leaning so close to Alex their shoulders touched. "Now *she* insists it was always six, so he's changed his story. But I know what I heard!"

Rita looked so shook that Alex wondered if she could keep anything straight. She certainly understood. Or perhaps, like Paul, she did need a counselor—or psychiatrist—and not Joyce Prettyman.

"I see why you're upset, but maybe you misunderstood, especially if it was right after harvesting," Alex suggested. "I couldn't recall a thing until my friend who was with me that day in O.R. played a tape recording for me."

"So you're watching them too," she whispered, wide-eyed.

"No, not like that. We've got to trust these people or we wouldn't be there in the first place. Besides, I know you understand that some eggs and embryos can be lost after harvesting if they're abnormal or won't fertilize. I read that happens naturally and often in the human body, and we never even know it."

"Too much we don't know," Rita declared so darkly that Alex realized sharing her plans could help Rita now.

"As a matter of fact," Alex told her, "I'm going to do a news series to look at the whole fertility industry with a special focus on the clinic. Talking to you on Sunday helped me decide it would be a help to others. But it's going to be a positive, hope-filled series," she said, emphasizing those last words. Rita nodded at first, then pulled her hand back and frowned when Alex mentioned that no one could be interviewed without staff permission.

"You can't use me, then, that's for sure," she said as she stood and crossed her arms to hug her elbows. "So how am I ever going to make them—and Paul—listen?" Her shoulders and head slumped; she looked utterly defeated. "If it wasn't for my babies stored there just waiting to grow in me and be born, I don't know what I'd do."

Alex stood and put a hand on Rita's shoulder. Except for being her friend and letting her talk, she had no idea how to help her. But she did know if she could read people's colors the way Rita claimed she could, right now Rita Twohorses would be drowning in deep, dark blue.

7

Heavy blackness enveloped her, holding her down. She could not move. What day was it? Where was she? Distant voices wrapped around her, coiling tighter.

A man's voice. "Don't worry about me, my dear. It's for such a good cause—our cause—that I can handle it."

"But you could be deluged with desperate calls from women who see the TV coverage. A man of your looks and brilliance, Hale..."

"It won't come to that. This is a small, elite clinic. Its location and size will keep the things we value controlled. Besides, with the extra income from new patients this draws, we can expand on that land down the cliff."

Jasmine, Alex thought. Hale is talking her into it just as he said he would.

"But if we get too big, I'm afraid you'll be forced to become some pencil-pushing CEO overseeing a team of maverick doctors with rampaging egos and projects that drain funds and time."

Alex tried to hold on to what they said, but it all

drifted away from her. She wished her mother cared about the clinic, that she could hear her voice close by the bed. But maybe she would say it all again: *It's your fault, Lexi. Career, career, career. Your husband makes enough money to support you. If you'd just stay home and relax and try to get pregnant the right way before it's to late...*

Too late Alex swam up through the swirling depths, fighting for air. "Are you all right?" a woman asked, her voice very close.

When Alex dragged her eyelids open, praying it was not her mother, she thought she saw Rita bending over her.

"Rita? Why—you here?"

"I sneaked in just for a minute to be sure they don't hurt you."

"Hurt me? But..."

"And to tell you I'm going to have a pueblo curing ceremony and I want you to come. I'll talk to you later..."

She slipped out through the clouds of curtains. Alex drifted away again. When she woke Beth was there, as close as Rita had been—if she'd really seen her.

"Guess what?" Beth said as she squeezed a black bulb to release the blood-pressure sleeve around her arm. It hissed like a snake. "I'm going after your job."

"What?" Alex asked. Her mouth felt stuffed with cotton.

Alex saw Beth was smiling, teasing. "While you were under, I did the explanation of the procedure while your cameraman filmed Dr. Stanhope scrubbing up in the O.R. When do I get to do those voice -overs when they film a tour of the clinic? And when do I get a piece of your salary?"

Alex tried to smile in return, but her face felt like stone. She closed her eyes again and whispered, "If you want my job, get with it. It's not film anymore, but tape. And you've got a job where you're an angel…"

Now she remembered why she felt so drugged. She'd had the surgery. She needed to know if they'd put the embryos in her, the two embryos. Her try for her babies. Again, she struggled to lift one eyelid, then the other as the drapes around her bed whooshed open. Dr. Stanhope came in and leaned over her next to Beth. He listened to her heartbeat with his stethoscope.

"Did it—work?" Alex whispered, her voice so breathy she wasn't sure they heard her.

"It did," Hale said. "Now we watch and wait about two weeks to test if either of them implanted. And then to see if they're hanging on until the first ultrasound at four or so weeks. Even then we have to—"

"Just pray," Alex added with a sigh. But she was already so exultant she somehow found the strength to lift one hand to the back of his neck and half hug him before he straightened. Hale gave her a little hug back and kissed her cheek.

"Sure. And pray," he repeated, slowly releasing her. "One way or the other, I'm going to make you my first possible DES daughter to get pregnant here at the Evergreen."

He smiled down at her. Alex fought to lift the corners of her mouth in return, but Beth stepped in to settle the blanket and thump the pillow. "There!" she said. "I don't need you getting one bit excited right now, Alexis, because I won't have anything going wrong."

Alex wanted to scream. She saw no white cake mix anywhere on the stupid grocery store shelf where it was supposed to be, where they even had a sign for it at a special price. Darned if she was going to buy some of those sickening-sweet, ready-made yellow sponge cakes or just use Bisquick to make a shortcake when she and Nick were coming back to the house for dessert and coffee after they went out to dinner. She wished she had time to make something from scratch. She wanted him at least to think she knew what the inside of a kitchen looked like. She wanted everything—everything!—to go just right.

She tried to steady herself, leaning on her grocery cart, telling herself she was overreacting, working too hard, worrying too much about the clinic series. Teasers for it ran hourly, and they were launching it Monday, May ninth, in just two days. Meanwhile, this interminable wait to see if she was technically, as Dr. Jasmine put it, pregnant was preying on her mind. She had made it through eight days of the fourteen—the first two flat on her back in bed—but so much lay ahead. Though she was on no drugs now, she almost felt as if Pergonal had taken over her life again.

Or maybe she'd caught Rita's overwrought agitation like some disease. But, she thought, pushing her cart again, she was already running late and hardly had time to drive to another store where more senior citizens—and mothers toting entirely too many kids—clogged the aisles with their carts.

Ahead of her, two older women had made a real roadblock. "Excuse me, please," she said, trying to keep her voice in check.

"Oh, Susie, look, it's Alexis McCall," the plumper one told the other with a shy grin. "We watch you all the time," she assured Alex. "And we like your new hair color—lighter. It makes you look years younger."

"Not to say your hair isn't always darling," the other put in, not budging. "And I love that red suit with the black collar you wear sometimes. We saw your new ads today about your coming fertility series, but we thought you meant in flower gardens at first." The woman raised both eyebrows and shook her head.

Forcing a smile and managing what Mike called happy talk, Alex finally breached their barricade and pushed her cart into the next aisle. Ordinarily she liked meeting viewers and getting their opinions on things, but not today. No matter what those women had said, she could have bitten their heads off. She'd like to think it was new natural pregnancy hormones surging through her that made her like this, but—despite her trust of the clinic staff—she was afraid to hope.

"Hi, Alexis. I see you're going to do a series on having babies—with outside help, of course," a raven-haired woman told her.

Her cart too blocked the aisle. She smiled tightly; her blue eyes sparkled. She was dressed in baggy gray sweats. She wore no makeup, and her short hair looked like she'd combed it by clawing her fingers through it.

The strange thing was that Alex felt she should know her, but couldn't place her, a common problem when she'd done thousands of brief interviews over the years. Still, the way things were right now, it bothered her more than usual. All this forgetfulness made her fear she might be starting to lose her mind. Maybe that Santa Cruz healing ceremony Rita so much wanted her to attend would help her too.

"Thanks so much. Glad to be back," Alex replied curtly and tried to get her cart past. The woman's tone or choice of words made her uncomfortable. Her eyes didn't really sparkle but glittered.

When she just stood and stared, Alex did an abrupt U-turn. The woman pursued her with a cart that had a loose wheel and knocked and rattled. "I was just wondering," she called after her, "if I could have your autograph?"

Gritting her teeth, Alex stopped. What was the matter with her, panicking like that? "Of course," she said, stopping at the end of the aisle. "Do you have something I can sign it on?" she asked, producing the pen she'd been checking items off with.

The woman fumbled so long in her purse that Alex got nervous again. "I feel I should know you from somewhere," Alex prompted. When the woman didn't respond, the hairs on the nape of Alex's neck prickled and she began to perspire. "Here, that's okay," she told her. "I'll just use this." She ripped off one of the coupons in the dispensers and scribbled her name on the back of it and thrust it at the woman.

She took it but didn't even look at it. She stared

straight at Alex and whispered, "I hope you signed it *seducer—husband stealer—adulterer.*"

"You must have me confused—" Alex began, then decided she'd do best just to get out of here. She grabbed the few things from her cart, left it as a barrier, and hurried toward the front of the store. Thank God no one was in the quick check-out line. She kept glancing over her shoulder as the cashier rang up her items.

"Something wrong, Ms. McCall?" the clerk asked.

"There's a woman back there—black hair in gray sweats—who is acting really strange," Alex told her, but she didn't wait around while the clerk went back to look.

In her car, she clicked down all the locks, then glanced in her rearview and side mirrors as she backed out. Maybe she'd think of who that was and where she'd seen her later, probably in the middle of another sleepless night or out at dinner tonight with Nick.

Then, as impossible as it was, a memory jolted her like a sonic boom. Her hands trembling, she pulled over to the curb and just sat there with the engine idling. She craned her neck, looking back, even up ahead to be sure she wasn't being followed. She grabbed her car phone to call Nick's shop, but his machine picked up and she realized she'd never gotten the number of his home. She had no choice but to face him down tonight.

Sandra felt like a stalker as she hid in a clump of pines and watched the staff leave and Jasmine Stanhope repeatedly jog the circumference of the clinic grounds.

That hot pink spandex sure looked good on her, even sweating and running with extra weights in her hands.

Sandra shook her head. This sort of masochistic exercise was beyond her understanding. Her own people came from generations of hard physical work, picking other people's pinto beans for $1.50 an hour. She always managed to get enough exercise just doing her job, she told herself as she savored her last *empanada* and brushed the remnants of fried dough off her hands.

She noted that Jasmine did stop, however, on the ridge above the ghost town at each pass and stare down as if she saw something there—or maybe envisioned something for the future. Nick Destin had said the Stanhopes, especially Jasmine, wanted the place for expansion. *Madre de Dios,* she'd seen Anglos like them before, the West Coast or Eastern-educated elite. They thought they could have everything their way out here where other people had lived and worshiped three hundred years before Anglos ever came over the mountains or the Rio Grande to buy up or take everything.

Sandra walked down from the edge of the forest and put herself in the woman's path on her next circuit. "Oh, hi, Dr. Jasmine, how are you today?" she asked, trying to sound surprised to see her. Frowning, Jasmine slowed.

"Are you a patient?" She didn't even seem out of breath, now jogging in place a few yards away.

"No, I'm Sandra Sanchez, KALB-TV advance team for the big event Sunday—the reunion party."

"Advance *team?*" Jasmine repeated, pointedly glancing around to see no one.

Sandra didn't break eye contact. "Just to get the lay of the land for the live coverage."

"I recognize you now. Alexis's friend in the O.R. I don't have time to watch much TV. The lay of the land, how?"

"I'm deciding on places for camera angles, looking for spots to keep our staff unobtrusive, things like that," Sandra assured her with broad hand gestures she hoped looked more convincing than she sounded.

It was all white lies, but she didn't want anyone— not even Alexis, if this got back to her—to think she'd been digging as deep as she had already, not only into procedures but personnel. Jasmine might clam up if she knew Sandra had a complete academic résumé on her, down to her lofty premed point average at Cornell.

Not only did Sandra not trust doctors, but Rita Two-horses had tipped her off to the possibility of something awry in the embryo lab, which she'd heard Beth call "the womb kitchen," as if they were cooking up something in there. In talking to Rita after she left Alex at the station yesterday, Sandra had learned that she'd gotten two different stories on her egg count. Had someone "in the kitchen" just made a careless mistake or misspoken? Looking at the precision with which Jasmine dressed, even out here, she doubted it.

Trying to fill the awkward silence, Sandra plunged on, "It's great you're giving Alex a tour of the embryo lab Sunday, even without a camera allowed. I'd love to see it. What a fascinating career you have—such power to affect the future."

That admiring tone seemed to snag Jasmine's attention. Her stunning face glowed with more than perspiration. "You're right about that," she said, slowing her mechanical movements to an in-place walk but still swinging her hand weights. "Women deserve that—an opportunity to have children now or even far into the future. More than one mother has said my work and research meant salvation for her."

"All that seems so fabulously high-tech to someone like me," Sandra said, excited she'd somehow pushed the right button. "What kind of research?"

A curtain of mistrust came over Jasmine's features, just when she thought she'd gotten a glimpse backstage. "I've got to get going," Jasmine said, moving faster again. "Maybe we can talk more on Sunday. My husband believes your coverage of the Miracle Baby party will help us share our mission with those in need," she called back over her shapely shoulder.

Sandra glared as those flat abs and tight buns left her in their wake. Why, she wondered, did so many of these clinic people speak with an almost evangelical zeal? *Mission. Outreach. Salvation. Miracle baby.* They were starting to sound as if they believed they were delivering angels—or gods.

Clenching her fists and swinging her own arms stiffly, Sandra plodded toward her car in the parking lot. She wished she was the one getting a tour of Jasmine's inner sanctum because she didn't trust Alex's objectivity anymore. She'd been so on edge lately that Sandra was scared to death that one more setback for her miracle baby would crack her up.

* * *

Nick felt Alexis had kicked him in the stomach when she told him.

"That can't be," he insisted, grabbing her shoulders. They stood inside her front door in the tiled foyer. "Carolyn's living in Phoenix, and she's under a psychiatrist's care. And I just talked to her last week—"

"Oh, great, just great, Nick," she said, smacking her hands outward against his wrists to make him release her. "And told me nothing about it. You're still in touch with her, and she evidently wants you enough to come back here and follow you. I assume she saw us together, then decided to insult me. This is all I need right now."

"I swear I didn't know. And I still can't believe this. She's not a brunette like you described, so maybe you're mistak—"

"I'm not! At least—I don't think so."

"See," he said. "You're under a lot of strain, aren't you? You sounded so upset this week that I wish I'd seen you. Let's sit down in here, and I'll phone her doctor. No, I probably can't call her office until Monday. But maybe she'd answer if I left an emergency message."

He suddenly felt as harried as she looked. He could not stand it if Carolyn had come back to haunt him again. He'd figured he could keep from any real commitment to Alexis because of her passion to have a child, but if Carolyn was going to threaten that, he'd have to get involved.

"So you'd call the psychiatrist and not Carolyn directly?" she asked.

"Yes—I—if I call her we always end up arguing, and it doesn't do either of us any good."

She nodded and walked with him into the living room. "I understand dreading that," she told him. "And I *am* under some pressure, but I have a good memory for faces." Her voice quavered at that; she looked doubtful. Damn, but he hoped she was wrong about this, for her sake, for his, even Carolyn's.

"I don't suppose you carry her picture with you so I can be absolutely sure," she said, turning to face him. Her face and voice were challenging again; her hands rode on her hips.

"No, I don't have her picture. I thought she was out of my life. You carry Geoff's with you?"

"That's different."

"Do you?"

"Not anymore. I have some around the house. Look, let's not argue," she said, crossing her arms over her breasts as if she were cold. He wanted to hold her, but they finally sat facing each other on the couch before the empty hearth. As bad as this was, he figured he'd try the truth. Carolyn never had, and that had cost them, even in the beginning.

"Even after Carolyn and I decided on the divorce," he explained, "it seemed she couldn't do anything on her own. She drove me absolutely wild. She kept showing up at the shop—yes, and following me."

"There, see? It's got to be her, Nick."

"But she called a couple of months ago to say she got a new job—sales rep with a Phoenix pharmaceutical company. She does travel some but not in this area. She can't be just taking off from a new job to follow anyone," he insisted, trying to convince himself as well as Alexis.

"I recall she hung around that day we did the interview. You were married then. Didn't you know she was so unstable?"

"I tried to get her help for years, but nothing worked—until this new doctor in Phoenix, I thought. She used to stalk me, but…I'll check into this. I've got the number of that psychiatrist in the car."

He jumped up and went out, closing the door behind him, then realized too late he'd probably locked himself out. He wouldn't blame her if she was so upset she didn't let him back in. Damn, he'd thought his long nightmare with Carolyn was over. He fumed as he rummaged in his glove compartment. He'd planned never to risk love or trust again, and it made him furious he might be even indirectly responsible for Alexis's endangerment.

He scanned the street, relocked his car, and went back, lifting his hand to knock. To his relief, Alexis met him at the door and opened it again. She was a strong woman, he thought, no matter what she'd been through.

Like an idiot, he dropped his keys in the doorway and stooped to pick them up.

The backfire of a car cracked close. The explosion of the small window in her door followed instantaneously.

He shoved Alex back inside, forcing her to the floor, covering her body with his while shards of glass shattered onto the mosaic tiles around them.

"Nick, my babies!"

"What? Stay down!" he ordered as he managed to slam the door with his foot. He moved beside her, still holding her. Glass crunched under them.

He rolled out of it and, keeping low, got to his feet and darted for the cell phone he'd seen on her desk in her study. The damn door was locked. He cursed and tore to the phone in the kitchen.

By the time he'd punched 911 she had joined him. "Ask for Bernice Alvarez," she said. "I know her." She dabbed at his cut arm with a kitchen towel.

"I'm going out through the back door to look around in front," he told her, pulling away.

"No!" She grabbed his hands as he fumbled with the back door lock. "What if she's out there? There's a bullet hole in the wall behind the door."

"She? Did you see that woman again? Alexis, it can't be Carolyn. She was always scared of guns, wouldn't touch one."

"Times and people change. They get desperate, they crack up, so—"

"I know," he admitted, feeling scared to death. "Just stay here and keep down. I'll be right back. And—I didn't mean to hurt you. I didn't know you'd had that done—the embryos put in."

"I was going to tell you tonight. Now I won't have a chance—we won't go out, I mean…"

She looked as angry as afraid. If he had one brain in his head, now that her husband's embryos were in, he'd be on his way out for good.

"I'll be right back," he repeated and went out the door to circle around in front.

Bernice Alvarez interviewed both of them a second time while a forensic expert dug the bullet out of the wall—"Hey, Bernie," he'd called. "Looks like a nine-millimeter to me"—and took photos of the pattern in which the glass had sprayed. Officers searched across the street for signs of whoever had shot at them—or at whichever one of them was the target. Alex felt really bad that officers were also going door to door to upset her neighbors with questions.

"Okay, so your ex-wife's shrink just told me the same thing on the phone," Bernice told Nick, flipping open a little notebook from her macramé purse as she rejoined them in the living room. Bernice had inherited a rich mixture of ethnic bloodlines and tastes. She dressed eclectically, today in an outfit that looked Afro-Mexican, as if there was any such style. Her dark hair had been severely layer-cut short and was blond above her ears and its natural sable below. She and Alex had been friends since a series of on-air interviews to teach kids about "stranger danger" years ago.

"So," Bernice went on, "this Dr. Gwen Arlington also told me she thinks Carolyn is much better. Under her brilliant counseling, of course," she added, lifting one eyebrow. "Beyond that, she cites doctor-patient privilege, but admits Carolyn still might be somewhat possessive about Nick—but doesn't blame him for the breakup of the marriage."

"If she doesn't blame Nick," Alex put in, "she might be blaming a woman he sees socially. The woman in the grocery store called me a 'seducer and husband stealer.'"

"Yeah," Nick agreed, "but why would she call you an adulterer?"

"But," Bernice said, frowning at her notes, "none of that's enough for any arrests. And the doctor says she's never seen Carolyn with her blond hair dyed black. Alex, it could be some friend of Cordova's."

"I doubt it. Rich TV bitch is his name for me." She sighed and put her head in her hands.

"You sure no one else hates your TV self right now?" Bernice plunged on, perching on Alex's other side on the couch.

"I'm not sure of anything anymore," she admitted.

"Okay, I know this was a shock," Bernice said, "but I've seen the promo spots of your new fertility exposé. We can't overlook it might be someone ticked off about that too. Any chance you can postpone that first segment Monday, maybe the whole piece for a week or so?"

"No," Alex said, shaking her head adamantly. "And I'm not going to let myself be blackmailed by some lunatic viewer, even if that's what this is. It's an important series, Bernice."

"As soon as I get that photo of Carolyn from Mr. Destin, I'll check with the people at the grocery. So, my advice right now to you two is to be careful—and keep apart, at least for a while. The only way to find out who this perp's after is to see what happens next when you're separated." As she rose, she added, "Listen, you two, be damn careful."

As soon as the police and Nick left, Alex called Hale. When he didn't answer his emergency number at home, she tried the one at the clinic, though she couldn't fathom why he'd still be there this late on a Saturday night. She offered up a silent prayer when she heard his strong, steady voice.

"Dr. Stanhope, I'm so glad I caught you. It's Alexis."

"I decided to stay a little late tonight. You sound upset."

"I—had a real shock and fell—kind of, well, someone fell partly on top of me on a tile floor, and I'm worried about the implantations—my babies," she blurted out in one breath before slowing down to fill him in a bit more.

"Thank God you weren't shot," he kept interjecting as he listened to her explanation, but he quickly returned to what was worrying her.

"Are you bleeding or cramping?" he asked, then rattled off more questions. She began to breathe easier when she was able to answer in the negative to each. "Listen to me, Alexis. I'm glad you called, because you and that pregnancy are very important to me. And I don't mean because you're a high-profile patient or helping the clinic or because I'm still worried you're a DES daughter, because as soon as we make sure you're pregnant, we'll face your mother on that together."

"I really appreciate that. I know all the clinic babies are important to you."

"And that's why if you have any of the symptoms I just listed, you call me back immediately, day or night, and I'll come to you. I can take care of you or at least consult if there's any hint of a problem. Should you ever end up at an E.R. or your own ob-gyn's, call me too, promise?"

"I promise, Hale—Dr. Stanhope."

"All we're going through together, Hale will do just fine. Now go get in bed for some more of that flat-on-your-back rest and call me if there's a problem. Just do what the doctor orders, all right?"

"You've made me feel so much better. I won't be half so scared going through this with you."

When they said good-bye, Alex cradled the phone for a moment before hanging up. But in the instant after Hale cut off, she was certain she heard someone breathing and then another clear click before the dial tone began.

8

The illuminated digital clock on the dashboard of her car read 3:34 when she slowed on the block behind Alexis's house. She'd done a brief dry run of this before; she knew the neighborhood. She killed the headlights and the engine before she got out.

It was pitch dark, but her eyes were already adjusted, so she darted between houses and into the McCall backyard, trying to avoid even the dim light thrown from the distant telephone pole.

Quick and quiet, she told herself. Everything tonight had to be quick and quiet. So she was annoyed that the syringe and the keys in her fanny pack she'd strapped across the front of her black jeans bounced as she jogged along. She pressed them to silence. At Alexis's back door, she sucked in several deep breaths as she unzipped the pack and brought out the two keys she hoped worked. She'd taken careful impressions of the ones in Alexis's purse in her patient locker when she'd been under the anesthesia.

Her heart pounded hard as she inserted the keys, one

in the doorknob of the back door and one in the dead-bolt lock. To save herself time inside, she turned them both at once and went swiftly in. She held the screen door so it wouldn't bang but didn't take time to close the storm door yet. Gill said she had exactly one minute after entry either to punch in the disarming code by the front door or turn off all the electricity. And there was no way to get the code—yet.

Turning on no lights, she darted to the kitchen door to the attached garage and fumbled with that dead bolt from the inside. She opened it, but a chain lock above held fast and yanked once. The sound, she thought, was deafening.

Damn that stupid ass Gill! He'd forgotten Alexis had a chain lock here, unless she'd just put it in.

But she wasn't going back. She fumbled for her flashlight in her fanny pack and slid the chain bolt open. No time to listen to see if that single thud had awakened Alexis. She whipped the door open and ran for the master switch near the breaker box on the garage wall. And pulled it down, just as Gill had taught her.

But the surgical gloves she wore made the touch strange. She should have practiced in them. She stood tensely against the wall, sweating hard, staring at the shadowed silhouette of the single car in the double ga-rage, hoping the alarm didn't sound in the Camelot of-fice. If it did, Gill would be the one to respond, but she didn't need Alexis or the neighbors being wakened and looking out their windows if she had to run for it.

Surely a minute was up; no alarm sounded. She breathed again. As Gill had promised, this system did not reactivate when there was a power outage; nor did it automatically trigger the alarm until the owner reset it. She had time now.

But not time for another thorough tour like before. As she went back in and closed the kitchen door, she wondered if the knife she'd left on the counter and the way she'd rearranged those Indian dolls had the desired effect. But that was nothing compared to what came next. Alexis kept stepping over the line.

She tiptoed upstairs, annoyed that the surgical booties she wore made her feet slip on the carpeted steps. Enough light sifted into the upstairs hallway, so she turned off her flashlight. Perched on the top step, she pushed the needle up into the plastic vial and drew back on the plunger. After it was full, she snapped it sharply with a finger to release the potentially deadly air bubbles inside, though that was pure habit. What would it matter in a situation like this?

She saw Alexis slept with her bedroom door to the hallway open, unless she'd changed rooms since she'd been here. Leaning outside against the wall, she could hear her breathing. This had to be quick, quiet—and sure, she lectured herself again. No way they could prove that this hadn't been done by the others harassing Alexis, like Nick Destin's poor ex-wife, who Alexis told Hale had taken a shot at them. The bottom line was, there would be no reason for anyone associated with the clinic to harm their star patient. And even though Hale would be furious, even if they did an autopsy and found a puncture mark on her or traces of the boric acid in her, he'd have to protect the clinic.

She shuffled sideways into the bedroom. Alexis slept on her side with her face turned away, cuddling the second bed pillow in her arms like a person—a baby.

The intruder stopped, stared, and nodded. Now she knew what she could do if she must. If further warnings did not work, she could and would do exactly this—and next time plunge this needle in.

She turned and replaced the needle in her pack as she started downstairs. She opened the back door for a quick getaway, then hurried into the garage and hit the master electric switch on.

But as she closed the back door behind her, she glimpsed the digital clock on the microwave and realized she'd made a mistake. After the electricity had been off and on, clocks blinked, so Alexis would know. But know what?

She smiled smugly, then grimly all the way back to her car.

The huge eye stared unblinkingly at her. The red light over the camera clicked on. So much was at stake that for a moment Alexis feared she'd go blank. Besides, she'd overslept this morning because the power had been off and screwed up her alarm, and it seemed she'd had to rush all day to catch up. But her long-honed skills took over, and she bonded with that person, that face out there, just beyond the lens. And, for the first time, fought hard to block out the image of someone malevolent watching, someone with a face as ugly as one of those demon-like kachina dolls.

"Because infertility affects more than five million

Americans"—Alexis read her own copy smoothly from the teleprompter—"I know I'm talking to a lot of you who share the same problem I do. Actually, that's one of ten in the reproductive population. Or if you're one of the fortunate who has no problem having a baby, I still hope you'll learn a great deal from our new series, *The Fertility Frontier.*

"I could give you a lot of statistics about infertility, but I'm not going to do that today. Because it's the people behind the numbers—their desperation, pain, courage, and triumph—that you need to know to really understand the scope of this problem and this booming high-tech industry."

"We're going to take a journey into the Fertility Frontier, and I'll be your guide. Not only because I'm the correspondent here, but because for years I've been struggling with the daunting challenges of infertility. But let me introduce you first to someone who will be our interpreter in this strange new land, Dr. Hale Stanhope, fertility doctor at a very special reproductive health clinic here in the Albuquerque area."

"Roll tape," she heard in her earpiece as the monitor began to run the previously recorded conversation between her and Hale they had shot in his office yesterday.

"Let's get to the main question everyone wants to know about reproductive technology, Dr. Stanhope," Alex said on the tape, leaning slightly toward him. They sat close together in matched, high-backed burgundy leather chairs in his office. "Does it really work? Is it worth the pain and cost?"

"Of course, everyone must make his or her own decision on that, Alexis," Hale answered, managing an expression between serious and friendly. He angled his body slightly toward the camera, though he kept his eyes on her. "Let me just say that here at Evergreen Reproductive Health Clinic, we're taking problem couples—and some individuals—and giving them a pregnancy rate comparable to the normal, fertile population. Recently well-publicized adoption fiascos have scared a lot of people away from that option, which of course, I also champion. But, yes, in many cases our clinic and others like ours across the country can help those who want a biological child. Frankly, I'm hoping you will soon be one of our many success stories."

"Man, that guy's telegenic," her co-anchor Stan said from beside her at the anchor desk. "His popularity rating's got to beat ours combined."

She nodded, intent on the rest of the brief tape. Yes, Hale looked and sounded good. But none of that was the reason she believed in him. She was just so certain she was sitting here pregnant right now that she was tempted to make the prediction on the air. After all, Hale almost had.

"Granted," Alexis went on when she was live again, "the financial and emotional costs can be staggering. Very few states currently cover in-vitro fertilizations through insurance claims, and New Mexico is not one of them. Actually, it can cost six to eight thousand dollars per IVF cycle, and we'll cover more of that tomorrow, when we really begin to explore this fascinating high-tech and high-stakes frontier. But to get a glimpse of the rewards—live, cuddly, and noisy—also tune in *Live at Five* next Sunday for a visit to a Miracle Baby reunion at the clinic."

Sunday morning a few hours before the baby reunion, Alex stood with Jasmine Stanhope in the middle of her lab, grateful she was trusting her to be here.

"These are embryo tracking sheets," Jasmine said as she pulled open a file drawer and showed her the meticulously recorded information.

"That's not the consent forms everyone signs?" Alex asked.

"No, those are kept on file in the outer office under Alice Prettyman's aegis. These are under my control, and I'm an absolute fanatic on keeping all specimens labeled. As a matter of fact, I suppose I'm a perfectionist in general and protective as hell of my work. I hope I didn't come off as negative, because I'm for anything that helps women like you, Alexis. Look, here's yours."

Standing closer to her, looking over Jasmine's shoulder, Alex skimmed the tracking sheet, noting especially that her two pre-embryos, which were still frozen, were marked by letter and number. "What does this mean?" she asked, pointing at the labeling.

"Those indicate which cryopreservation bank they are in. Come over here. Rather than just lecture you, I'm going to show you one of our basic procedures—defrosting a pre-embryo. Maybe—if we get permission from a patient later—we can do one of these for the camera."

"That would be great. I think Rita Twohorses would give permission."

"Step closer," Jasmine said, not responding, but maybe she was just concentrating on what she would say next. Alex was disappointed she'd gotten no reaction from her one way or the other to try to read because Rita was so convinced the Stanhopes were refusing to help her.

Alex watched as Jasmine rolled out a squat, round, gray, thigh-high tank from under one of the lab tables. Alex glimpsed others hidden away in the shadows too. When Jasmine snapped the lid open, a fog of super-chilled liquid nitrogen whirled into the room.

"The pre-embryos are cooled gradually, but this is at minus 385 degrees Fahrenheit, and if the level of nitrogen or temperature drops too much, an alarm goes off to warn us," she explained. "If no one's here—which is rare—the security system calls my or Tom Anders's beeper."

With a padded glove over her surgical ones, she lifted out a tiny, tear-shaped glass ampule covered with frost and wiped away the ice crystals to read the name and date etched on the side. She checked that information against a tracking sheet. "You see," she said, "I am very careful with these, for obvious reasons. I want to deserve the faith of my patients."

Alex began to relax. Just because the woman looked and acted like an ice goddess—she still thought her bedside manner was as chilly as this storage bank—didn't mean she wasn't to be trusted.

"By the calendar," Jasmine explained as she closed and rolled the freezer tank back under the counter, "this pre-embryo, which Hale is going to transfer early tomorrow morning, is eighteen months old, but it believes it's only three days old."

To Alex's amazement, she crooned, "Time to wake up, little one." Alex had read and heard that most fertility doctors were careful even to avoid calling these cells an embryo until they implanted in a womb. But Jasmine saw the potential.

"Come over here but close your eyes," Jasmine ordered as she stepped to a counter and held the ampule over a metal pitcher. At that strange command, the dimly lighted room suddenly seemed an eerie place with shadows and strange sounds—the wheezing storage banks and other muted moanings.

"Why?" Alex asked, shuffling slowly closer.

"Unfortunately, the ampule might explode in this lukewarm water when you least expect it." Alex closed her eyes when Jasmine covered her own. "Like life, you know, right, little baby?"

Alex heard her plunge the ampule in. "It's fine now," she said almost immediately. "You can look."

Alex was thrilled to see the milky ice inside the glass slowly clear. Two of her own had been resurrected like this, thanks to Jasmine's skill. Adjusting her mask to make sure it was secure, she hovered over Jasmine's shoulder as she opened the ampule with a diamond-tipped glass cutter, then suctioned out the liquid and the tiny pre-embryo, no bigger than a pinpoint.

"This is the first of six glucose solutions to get it back to normal size and shape," she explained, indicating a peach-hued petri dish set in a circle with five others. "We actually use a sort of antifreeze before they're frozen so the water in their cells doesn't explode. Will you remember all of this?" she inquired, her voice so gentle that Alex wondered for a moment if she addressed her or the so-called "baby."

"This is a brave new world you control here, Dr. Jasmine," she told her on their way out. A young male lab tech had come in to oversee things during the party on the patio and lawn.

"In the best sense, yes," Jasmine agreed with a proud nod. "This room has seen success and failure, a kind of pre-birth and death." She pulled down her mask and stared directly into Alex's eyes at last. "Frozen, they are not alive, nor are they dead, but just hanging in the balance."

"The balance of what you do," Alex whispered as the door to the vaulted lab quietly closed behind them.

Jasmine smiled, and this time her eyes lighted up too.

"You doing okay, Alexis?" Jerry, her cameraman, asked her at the clinic party as he hefted the camera to his other shoulder.

"Seeing all these kids is kind of like riding an emotional roller coaster," she admitted as a couple carrying triplets crossed their path. Although she had thought it would be hard that the KALB staff knew what she was going through, they had been very supportive. So had Bernice, though she was still urging she and Nick to stay apart for a while. That and the supposedly anonymous attack on her had really depressed her. If one's own front door wasn't safe, what was?

Even the pastel decorations and festive atmosphere

here failed to lift her sinking spirits. Pale blue table-cloths with pink swags covered a long buffet table, which had been set up on the back portico. Balloons bobbed in the breeze above teddy bears on individual tables the catering service had set up. A yellow canvas dropcloth filled with huge stuffed animals was a popular place for pictures.

Laughter permeated the crisp, sunny mountain air. Occasionally, Joyce Prettyman made an announcement through a loudspeaker in her best nursery school voice. All staff members except the receptionist, Alice Pretty-man, who welcomed people in the front lobby, circulated through the crowd of about a hundred. One- or two-year-olds—the clinic itself was only three years old—toddled or crawled everywhere.

Alex had interviewed many parents and had held many of the children. She even recognized some of the names—everyone had jack-in-the-box name tags on—as the same ones in the tiles of the front walk. But one thing she had never noticed before kept tugging at her objective, journalist instincts. Except for four of the couples, the parents were all Anglo.

Granted, maybe the Hispanics, Afro- and Native Americans in the area couldn't afford or would not trust the clinic, but Albuquerque had a number of ethnic professionals. Sandia National Laboratories and similar big research and development firms abounded. Some of their brightest, most affluent employees were Asian or Indian. Yet there was only one Chinese couple here, one Indian—the mother even wore a sari—two Afro-American, and of course she knew of one American Indian couple in Rita and Paul Twohorses. But the ethnic babies she saw here were darling, so maybe word of mouth—or her series—would bring in others of their races and countries to trust the Evergreen.

"So where do you want that live shot with the Stanhopes holding the babies for the five o'clock remote?" Jerry interrupted her thoughts.

"How about over there by the clinic back door? You know, a little symbolism, like the door's open for new people." She frowned, thinking of the door to her own house again.

"Sure, that's good."

"Jerry, have you seen Sandra?" she asked, scanning the crowd again.

"Nope. Poking around somewhere, that's Sandra. Or," he added as an afterthought, "hitting the food table."

"I don't see her there. Excuse me just a minute. I'll be right back."

Alex had spotted Rita on the fringe of the crowd, windmilling her arm when she shouldn't be here at all. This party was for parents who had clinic babies. If Alex was having trouble holding it together here, Rita could be disaster. At least today she didn't look as if she'd slept in her clothes. She'd changed to jeans and a blue T-shirt with one of her storyteller figures on it.

"What's the matter? Why are you here, Rita?" she asked as she hurried to her.

"I need to tell you something right away," she said, sounding slightly out of breath. "You know Pamela Wentworth, that new patient from Taos?"

"I've met her briefly," Alex said, turning back to skim the crowd again. When she saw they weren't being watched, she steered Rita a bit deeper into the trees. "She isn't here, is she?"

"No, but I overheard her talking to Dr. Prettyman after our counseling group yesterday. Her and her husband just got their phone number changed. So she had to change the forms she'd filled out. Alice at the reception desk, she was really busy. So she said just go ahead and fix it. But Pamela, when she looked it over again, she saw something really wrong."

"What do you mean, wrong?" Those background and consent forms were agonizingly detailed. Alex had spent hours digesting and filling out the various permissions and rights of the three single-spaced pages.

"Where it asked if her extra eggs could be donated, yes or no, Pamela and her husband checked no. But now it was checked yes. She was real upset, but they just showed her another form that said no and told her the other was in error. So I got to thinking maybe my forms got switched too, and that's where my extra egg went. The doctors, they don't want to admit it."

Alex frowned, staring into the shade cast by thick pines and piñons. There must be a perfectly logical explanation. She wished there was some way to check out what Rita had claimed without letting the Stanhopes think she didn't trust them—because she did. And what would she say to them anyway? Can't you count correctly? Are you losing our precious eggs? Selling them?

"Why did you want me to know this right now?" she

asked warily, afraid Rita would make some wild demand about putting this on the air.

"I'm gonna demand to check my form, even if it ticks them off. Maybe you should too."

"You have every right to see that form," Alex assured her, putting her hand on her arm to calm her.

"Only then I got to thinking if I do that—especially if it's screwed up—the Stanhopes, they might retaliate somehow, even more."

"Retaliate? More? Rita, I know you think they're putting you off and maybe they are, but—"

"You are on my side, aren't you?"

"Do we have to take sides here? Fertility work can fail if everyone doesn't work together."

"Yeah, tell me about it." She pulled back, then propped her hands on her hips.

"I don't mean to be on their side if there's really a problem here, but—"

"Oh, no? You're as good as doing free advertising for them right now," she said with scorn in her voice and a sneer on her face that infuriated Alex.

"Rita, I thought you agreed this series could help others like us. I'm really busy right now, because we're going on the air live at five, but it you'll just give me until tomorrow, I'll see if I can find a way to check into this that won't get you in hot water. And I will look at my own egg donor form too. Will you do that, just go on home today and I'll call you tomorrow?" she asked, leaning close to the distraught woman.

Rita stared hard at her. She sighed as her broad shoulders slumped. "I guess I'd do about anything if I thought it would get me my embryos, like little lives just waiting to get in my body and my hands."

Alex looked at the artist's large, skilled hands, but she thought of how Jasmine's hands had plunged that tiny glass cradle, shaped like a teardrop, into the warm water to thaw the pre-embryo. She had said they were neither dead nor alive, but that sounded now like some old horror movie of tales from the crypt, not the nurturing heart of the lab.

"But," Rita said, "if they keep giving me a bad time, I'm going to demand my embryos back. Even if *she* made them, they're my property. I'll go somewhere else for help. And talk to the newspaper or something if they won't let me talk on TV!"

"Rita…" she began but just flopped her hands helplessly down at her sides as the woman turned and trudged away, deeper into the forest. She could only hope she would circle around toward her car and leave. She did, however, have an idea of how to settle this dilemma right now.

Alex skirted the busy scene at the back of the clinic and headed for the front door. Beth suddenly crossed her path.

"Isn't it great to see all these happy parents?" she asked Alex, her arms full of a lively blond boy. "This will be you next year, Alex, I just know it."

"Thanks for helping keep my spirits up. Oh, Beth," she called, motioning her back. "I was just wondering about what percentage of the clinic babies are from minority families. There should be some way to encourage them to try the clinic too."

"Good idea," Beth said, bouncing the squirming child once to get a better hold on him. "After all, we are an equal-opportunity inseminator." She grinned and Alex shook her head as Beth hurried off.

Alex went in the front door, hoping it was late enough that everyone had arrived. Perhaps, she thought, it was time for Alice Prettyman to abandon her post here.

"Hi, Alice," she greeted the older lady, who sat drooped over the sign-in desk in the center of the now deserted lobby.

"Oh, hello, Alexis. How's that filming going?"

"We go on the air in"—Alex dramatically checked her watch—"about eleven minutes, so I hope you'll at least be able to pop outside for that. Can't you just lock up and join us?"

"Oh, I'd love to—and stop by the rest room on the way out. The tech's here to watch over things this afternoon anyway. But why are you in here if you're going on the air?"

"Just taking a moment of quiet from all the confusion outside. You know I'm trying to take it easy more now—hoping I'm really pregnant this time and it's going to last. Listen, as long as I'm here, why don't you just go ahead to the rest room?" Alex said, gesturing in that direction. "I'll be here for a few minutes in case anyone else comes in late."

"Thank you, dear. I'll be right back, but I'm going to comb my hair and put on some lipstick too, in case I get on camera," she said, already patting her white hair in place as she took her purse and headed toward the lobby's rest room. "I just got a new permanent and can't do a thing with it," she called back.

For a moment Alex regretted taking advantage of the kindly woman, but one glimpse at the lighted *nichos* with Rita's storytellers energized her again. This was a risk, but she had to do it. She had to make certain that Rita's worries about the donation forms were nothing— were downright wrong.

Thank God she'd been right about the reception room not being locked. She opened the door, hit the light switch, propped the door open so she could hear Alice returning, and bounded in. Behind the desk, she scanned the labels on the files for the first letters of last names. She needed the T's and M's in a hurry.

Her hands shook as she located Rita's folder. When she fanned the material to find her consent forms, a single page caught her eye. "Oh, no!" she whispered. Rita had been under psychiatric care two years ago for depression and severe swings of mood. *Has a tendency toward delusional visions and misperceives reality,* was written in someone's bold script. She flipped more pages, looking for the egg-donor section. When she found it, she breathed a sigh of relief.

Rita was wrong. Nothing was amiss here. Pamela Wentworth's form must have been a single mistake. This was clearly marked no. But as she flipped one page further, she saw an identical page underneath, and this one was marked yes. Rita's signature looked as authentic on this page as on the other.

She stuck everything back in its folder and shoved it in the drawer. How long would it take Alice to relieve her bladder, comb hair she couldn't do a thing with, and put on lipstick? Straining to listen for footsteps outside, she bent to scan for the M's one cabinet away. She pulled open the rolling drawer. The Ms's weren't in alphabetical order here but must be at the beginning of the M's. She'd never have time, never make it now.

But she grabbed her folder. Knowing what page to look for, she flipped to it. "Damn!" Hers was marked no, but also had a page behind it marked yes. And she had never had a moment's indecision about that. What in hell was going on here?

She heard the rest room door close. Alice's footsteps got louder.

She rolled the drawer shut with both knees and darted out into the hall, clicking off the light behind her. "I hope you're feeling better, dear," the older woman said as she came around the corner. "I know I do. Let's go so we don't miss your show," she urged, carefully locking both doors behind them.

Although Alex never had nerves about going on the air, she felt shaky hurrying around the building. Jerry was already shooting the lead-in of the Stanhopes sitting on the tarp amid stuffed animals. Hale had a cute blond baby in his lap, and Beth was handing one to Jasmine, a black-haired one. At least someone had already wired both doctors. She rushed up and took her own tiny mike, clamping it on her lapel and wriggling to hide the wire down the back of her jacket and clip the power box on the back of her skirt belt.

She settled between Hale and Jasmine, smiling, chatting away. A worried-looking Beth frowned at her—

probably for almost being late—and plopped a baby in her lap, a darling Afro-American boy. As always the sweet scent and squirming softness of a child almost swamped her senses. And then she saw Beth had given Jasmine an Asian child. Of the three clinic babies on camera, two were not Caucasian.

Her eyes sought Beth, who nodded, smiled smugly, and folded her arms across her chest. It wasn't, Alex thought, truth in advertising, but she nodded back, surprised by Beth's quick, clever move. She probably shouldn't have let her do this, but then, she shouldn't have been in the clinic files without permission either.

She managed to keep calm on the air until she saw, to her dismay, that Rita had come back into the crowd and was standing quite close. She was muttering something. Evidently Beth and Dr. Prettyman saw her too, for they were trying to coax her back, out of earshot of the mikes.

Hale was saying, "As you can see, we do our utmost to help couples who come to us to achieve their dreams, and—"

"No, you don't!" Rita screamed. Blessedly, though everyone in the crowd turned to her, Jerry kept the camera steady. "No, you won't give me my babies! I think you—"

Suddenly the baby Jasmine was holding wailed into her mike and drowned out Rita's tirade. Both Hale and Jasmine began comforting the child. The baby screamed louder; his parents ran forward, arms outstretched.

The interview in shambles, the camera off, Alex got

up and started for Rita. She realized too late she was still wired; she yanked the mike and connections loose and threw them back on the tarp. Behind her, she heard Hale trying to recapture the attention of the crowd through the loudspeaker. Peter, Sandra, Dr. Prettyman, and Beth had surrounded Rita and were moving her away.

"Wait, wait!" Alex called to them. "I'm going to drive her home. Please, just let her go," she insisted. With a frowning glance at each other, Peter and Beth loosened their hold on the distraught woman.

"Beth, you go with them," Peter ordered.

"I'll be fine just with Alex," Rita insisted, rubbing her arms where they'd grabbed her.

"After that outburst, Rita," Dr. Prettyman scolded, "I can't be certain Alexis will be just fine with you. Go ahead with them, Beth, and I'll follow in a car to bring you back. Rita can retrieve her own later."

On the way into town, Beth's presence and Rita's volatile state made it impossible for Alex to tell Rita what she'd learned about the consent forms. She was determined not to overreact until she dug deeper. She wasn't even sure about telling Sandra, because she had a habit of jumping in with both feet at the merest hint of impropriety, but she needed her help.

Paul Twohorses was not at their apartment. Rita insisted he was on his way back from the Santa Cruz pueblo and would be here soon. After Beth and Dr. Prettyman left in the extra car, Alex talked Rita into calling her psychiatrist and making an appointment for early tomorrow. Alex said she'd drive her in case Paul—who didn't approve of that either, Rita said—didn't want to.

If Rita wondered how Alex knew she had a psychiatrist to call, she didn't ask. But she did ask something to make Alex recall that Rita had sneaked into the recovery area to see her after she'd come out of the anesthesia from the embryo implantation.

"Will you come to a healing ceremony for me?" she asked, gripping Alex's wrist over the bracelet she'd given her the first day they'd met. "And be my supporter?"

"You asked me that at the clinic, didn't you? At your pueblo, you mean? Would I be welcome?"

Rita shrugged and sat up straighter against her pillow on the couch. "You're sure good at asking questions, but that's what we need at the clinic. Anglos, they are not usually at healing ceremonies, but I'd appreciate it. Paul will be there, my two sisters, and the tribal doctor—the medicine man. I will have Ada and Vengie tell you what it all means that day. But you are the only one who will understand my need. Please, my friend."

Alex stared into the deep pools of the eyes. "Then you've given up on the clinic?" she asked.

"No, but I have to do everything I can. I have to be sure—what is it they say?—I cover all the bases."

"If it's that important, I will go with you. But there won't be any of those kachinas in the ceremony or dancers dressed like them I've seen before, will there? You won't believe it, but I've actually had a couple of nightmares about them chasing me—shooting at me."

Rita frowned and shook her head. "Kachinas don't shoot. But no kachinas," she promised, apparently just accepting the crazy dream. "Besides, maybe if you drink some of the medicine water, it will help you too."

9

When the telephone shrieked, Alex jumped, knocking Shredded Wheat and milk onto the place mat and table. She bounced up and reached for the kitchen wall phone. Bernice with news? Rita? Nick? She missed him already, and hated that their growing relationship had been—at least temporarily—aborted.

But it was Hale Stanhope.

"Oh, good morning," she said, leaning her shoulder on the kitchen door frame and closing her eyes to concentrate on his words. "I really regret the upheaval yesterday in front of your guests and the immediate world."

"It was hardly your fault. That poor woman is disturbed and needs help."

"You'll be happy to hear I'm leaving in a few minutes to drive her to a psychiatric appointment. And she's also reaching out to her tribal elders for help." She didn't tell him it was a healing ceremony with a tribal medicine man. How could a doctor like Hale understand or accept that?

"Good," he said. "She's really confiding and trusting in you, isn't she? But listen for a minute. I know you've been worried about the shock of getting shot at and jostled. You looked really distressed yesterday— and I understand perfectly, I assure you."

The words, his tone, soothed her, yet she tried to remind herself that one reason she was upset would upset him too. She really needed to find out about those egg-donor forms, but she didn't want to alienate the Stanhopes. She should probably just ask Beth.

"Aren't you going to be out here mid-afternoon," he went on, "to interview Beth and shoot some of the nurses' activities anyway?"

"Yes."

"Then let's do the first pregnancy test and get some of this waiting over."

"Today? Find out if I'm pregnant today?" Her legs gave out and she slid right down the door frame to sit on the floor. She huddled there, excited and scared.

"You said you'd want to record it. The cameraman will be here, won't he? We'll plan on it later today. And if the result isn't positive, we'll try again with those other two frozen pre-embryos, so don't lose heart."

Don't lose heart. Her heart was still singing with hope a half hour later when she parked in front of Rita's shop and went around to the back door to access their apartment above.

At the clinic that afternoon, Alex was so nervous she couldn't give a urine specimen for the standard hCG, so they took a blood sample to do the test instead. While it was analyzed, she went to interview Beth. As Jerry set up his equipment in the lobby, Alex took Beth off to the side.

"Mind if I ask you an off-the-air question about general clinic procedure before we get started?"

"Sure, go ahead," Beth said, her face serious. "But how are you doing after some jerk took a potshot at you? Hale says you called him. I wish you'd told me too. You don't know who did it?"

"The police—and I—have several theories," Alex said, not wanting to share all Nick's past problems.

"People just don't know the downside of the so-called TV rich and famous, do they?" Beth said, shaking her head. "Maybe I don't want your job after all," she added, punching Alex lightly on the arm with her fist.

Beth turned away and fussed with her bangs, using the glass in the display *nichos* as a mirror. She was obviously nervous about the interview, and Alex longed to set her at ease the way she always did her.

"I really admire you," Beth continued, "for going on with this when some viewer does something insane like that. Probably some nut in the religious right who doesn't want any tampering with God's plan for 'be fruitful and multiply,' even though some people just can't.'"

Her expression darkened. Alex sensed she was recalling her own failure to have a child, and her heart went out to her.

"We don't know it is *any* sort of viewer, Beth," she said, realizing how much she sounded like Bernice now, "but I really appreciate your concern. Now, about my question—I just don't want to bother the Stanhopes with it."

"Hale especially, not a man with all the demands on his time. Ask away, and if I can ever run interference for him, that's one reason I'm here, though I don't know all the technical stuff he deals with," she added, turning to face Alex.

"I was looking over my original permission forms the other day and noticed that the one which asks about egg donation was duplicated," Alex explained. "I saw the original form where I checked no, but another one with a yes was right under it. And apparently my signature on both."

"Standard procedure, though I can see why you're asking," Beth said and stepped away to the glass covering a display of Rita's figurines. She used it as a mirror again, this time to adjust her collar. "The one on top is the operative form. But at a later date, some women who checked no become very willing to donate—when they have a child or two of their own." She turned back with a smile that Alex read as personal encouragement.

"But then," she went on, "often they're busy then or have moved away, and they wouldn't authorize it if it caused them time or trouble. But they're willing via phone, and then we've already got the duplicate form to mail them and get countersigned at their leisure. Sometimes it's even a need-that-egg-quickly kind of thing, when it would take too long to exchange forms by mail or whatever to allow the recipient to have a chance at a child."

"I see. But what about just sending the forms by fax? That would be quick."

A little frown perched between Beth's brows. "Not everyone has a fax, and we don't want a faxed signature for something like this. Besides, who can argue with such success?" she said and swept her arm out as if to encompass the clinic. "You'll soon be a believer too."

As Alex waited for Hale later in the same spot where she'd done what she considered to be a very touching interview with Beth, she saw him come in and head straight for her. Was this it—word on whether she was pregnant or not? *Even if you are,* she told herself, sinking back in the chair where she'd done the interview, *that doesn't mean you're home free.* Mountains higher than the Sandias stood between the start of an assisted pregnancy and a safe delivery. *And if you're not, like Hale said, don't lose heart.*

But her heart began to thud. It was instantly obvious to Alex that Beth had been crying when she'd just talked to her and she'd looked fine. Was it over the bad news Hale had to give her?

"Are you ready?" he asked, craning his neck to look at Jerry. "Alexis, do you still want this on tape?"

She nodded but was frozen with doubt. Though she prided herself on psyching people out, she could not read the man's expression. Surely he would not push for this if he had to give her bad news, no matter what they had decided earlier. She became an instant coward. Hale sat in the chair next to her. Beth hovered. Jerry's auxiliary lights kicked on again. She blinked into their brightness. Her mind went blank.

Time seemed to topple into eternity, like that awful moment those two air force officers had stood at her front door to tell her Geoff was gone. She gripped both arms of the chair.

"You're pregnant, Alexis," she heard. She turned to look into Hale's shining gray eyes, tilted up with his smile. "I don't know yet if it's one or both pre-embryos hanging on, but you're definitely pregnant."

She sucked in a big breath and leaned back in the chair and covered her face with both hands, then bent over so her forehead touched her knees. A torrent of emotion drowned her, joy and fear and hope.

"I'm pregnant!" she cried when she sat up. She hugged Hale. Beth cried, and Alex realized it was from relief for her, even when she could not have a child of her own. "Everybody—so far, so good," Alex said, smiling into the camera and crying at the same time. "I'm pregnant, and it's really going to work this time. The first thing I'm going to do when I get home is get my family's heirloom cradle out of the linen closet for good luck."

Hale tugged her back in her seat and did a little slice-across-the-throat motion to Jerry. "Huh? Oh, yeah," Jerry said and turned away to cut the taping.

"Listen to me, Alexis," Hale said, getting right in her face. "This is fabulous news, but you've been through a lot the last weeks—years. And this terrible shock about someone harassing you—shooting at you—not to mention the fact I still think you're a DES pregnancy can't help. I'd like to suggest we go to talk to your mother together about it."

"I'd appreciate some help with her," Alex admitted, "*if* she's willing to see me again. You had mentioned you'd hardly had time to see Santa Fe, and I could show you around to make it worth your while."

He took both of her hands in his. "Knowing about the DES will make a difference in how I proceed—and how I advise your ob-gyn to treat you. Yes, it would be worth my while." His gray eyes shone so intensely in such an intimate stare that she almost wondered if he was attracted to her. Embarrassed, she slowly tugged her hands back.

"Now you've got to start thinking of this future clinic baby above all else. In a few weeks I'll do an ultrasound to verify one fetus or two. We can count the oval sacs then, but still not be sure they're viable. Then we'll do our damnedest from there. But meanwhile, you're to kick back mentally and emotionally, as well as physically. Do you understand me?"

"Oh, yes. I can try, but…yes, of course."

"Good. I'll let Beth give you some parameters then. Meanwhile, you or Sandra let me know if you need any help for the series."

"Thank you, Doctor. I think we both know you—and Dr. Jasmine too—have already done the very best thing for the series."

He grinned like a boy and gave her cheek a quick peck. Not talking at first, Beth walked Alex outside to her car while Jerry went ahead to put his gear in the van. He said he'd wait for her in the lot, and they'd hightail it to the station.

"Hightail? To the station?" Beth repeated, suddenly

sounding angry. "I think the doctor just gave you orders to take it easy."

"I will, I will," she promised. "I'm sorry to see you so distressed today, when one of the most wonderful things about you is how much you care about your patients."

"Alexis, can I tell you something and have it be like lawyer-client privilege or doctor-patient?" Beth blurted, frowning out toward the cliff above Silver. "I know some journalists have even gone to jail protecting their sources."

They stopped walking. Long blue-green shadows threw themselves across their path. Alex turned to face Beth, who finally met her gaze. Her eyes were bloodshot, and she sounded as if she had a cold.

"Of course you can tell me," Alex whispered, touching her arm. "I give you my word, as a journalist and a friend."

"A friend—I'd like that."

"What is it, then? Something really serious?"

"I didn't mean to sound so dramatic. It's only that Dr. Jasmine was furious with Rita for shouting at the party, and I overheard her say she'd like to get rid of her—as a clinic patient, I mean. But I'm afraid if Rita had no hope for a child, she might actually harm herself—or someone else. I can sympathize with her desperation."

"I can too. And Hale mentioned something about your own situation. I didn't know if you wanted to keep it a secret from me, but you don't have to, you know."

Beth looked surprised, then angry again. "He told you?"

"I didn't mean to give away a confidence. He really cares about you, as he does all of us."

Alex hoped she hadn't opened up some kind of emotional wound or caused trouble for Hale. "Was that all about Dr. Jasmine?" she prompted, hoping to change the subject.

"She also said," Beth went on, "that the clinic ought to get a restraining order preventing Rita from being on the grounds. Since they can both be volatile—I mean, I just wanted you to work on Rita if you can. I wouldn't like to have to break up their next confrontation."

"If I work on Rita, can you try to calm Dr. Jasmine?" Alex asked.

"Ha! *That* would be good. No one, but no one—including poor Hale—does that. I've got to go back in. I'm glad to know I can confide in you, that's all. And I don't mean to interfere in patients' lives but—"

"I don't think any of them see it that way. I know I don't. And I don't mean to interfere in yours, but sometime I hope you'll share what makes you relate so well to me and all of us."

With a stiff nod, Beth hurried up the walk. At the lobby window, Alex was certain she saw someone staring out, but when she blinked there was nothing but the mirror of graying sky.

"Alexis, it's Nick. I need to talk to you."

She had her answering machine on, but she snatched the phone.

"Nick, how are you?"

"Happy for you. I saw your announcement on TV

about the pregnancy taking. Your station keeps showing you screaming and hugging Dr. Stanhope."

"Thank you. I can't tell you how much your goodwill means—after everything."

"And how else am I? I'm lonely for you too. I can't believe we had some police officer telling us we shouldn't see each other, like a couple of teenagers caught out after curfew. And we were both so shook we went for it. But this is not a police state, thank God."

"You're also angry."

"I sure as hell am. And not just at Detective Alvarez."

"At Carolyn?"

"And myself."

She twisted the phone cord around her finger so tightly the color blanched out of it. The rich mix of passions in his voice swamped her senses. She closed her eyes, wishing he was here to see, to touch…

"I was thinking," he said, his tone tense, "since we can't prove one way or the other that Carolyn was the shooter—even though you ID'd her photo as the woman in the grocery store—we ought to do something instead of just waiting for whoever's after one of us to make the next move. We can't go on like this. It's not fair to you or me."

"I'm willing. I'd do anything to end this waiting, except I have to take it easy in this lovely state I'm in. But you have an idea to flush the shooter out?"

"What if there was a safe way—safe for you—to lure the person out, set a trap—with the police there for protection? You think they'd go for that? You're the one with connections."

"I can find out. But, Nick, what if it really is *her* they catch? Carolyn."

"If she's that sick, she needs to be caught and helped. I've been agonizing over this, but I can't accept or condone that she'd do something like that to herself, or to me, let alone a strange woman she's only met once. And God forgive me if this sounds callous, but I want to protect you more than I do her."

She heard his voice break. He cleared his throat. Unshed tears burned her eyelids. "All right," was all she could manage Once a family member's hurt or betrayed you, she thought, picturing her mother, it was so much harder to trust outsiders, even friends. At least she had Sandra, and now Beth and Rita. Maybe Nick too, but she wanted him to be more than a friend.

"The only touchy thing," he said, "is that the place I think would work for the trap belongs to the clinic, and we'd have to ask the Stanhopes for help—permission. And I'm not on their good list."

"I hear you," she said. "Exactly what do you have in mind?"

"Here's the tape, and I had audio engineering do a sound enhancement on Rita's voice like you wanted, *amiga.*" Sandra produced the tape from under her raincoat and tossed it on a chair. As always lately when a guest came in the door, Alex re-armed her security system right away.

"Whew, is it ever wet out there," Sandra said. "Know anybody who builds arks?"

Alex took her wet coat into the kitchen and let it drip

over a chair onto the tiled floor. The weather forecasters had warned that a rare but heavy rainstorm would swell the concrete and natural arroyos, not to mention the Rio Grande, and produce flash floods.

Sandra picked up the tape again. "The VCR's in your study, right?" she said, making for the door. Alex hurried to get the key off the end table to unlock it.

"So why's that closed——and *locked?*" Sandra asked, her eyes riveted on Alex in her best journalistic, you'd-better-tell-me expression.

"If it wasn't you, Sandra, I'd make something up. But the truth is, I've been having bad dreams about selling Geoff's precious kachinas—and to Nick Destin."

"You and Nick still tight? After his ex maybe shot at you?" she asked with a nod toward the front door.

"You didn't see anyone out there, did you? The police and security service go by and check, but—did you?"

"You kidding? They'd be drowned by now."

"But Nick and I—we're tight only on the phone these last two days, but yes, I care and I think he does too. And about the locked door—that's the room where the kachinas used to be displayed, that's all," she said as the key grated in the lock. Thunder thudded against the house like mammoth fists.

"Vell—as ve Freudian doctors know, dreams is *mucho* Freudian, *mi carida.*" Sandra's Hispanic accent made her attempt at a German one ridiculous. Relieved to see the shelf lights didn't come on, Alex followed her into the study.

"Just lie down on ze couch," Sandra went on, "and tell

Dr. Sandra all. I diagnose guilt cloaking forbidden desire for a new man in your life. And it's about time—"

"Would you stop? At least the electricity hasn't gone out," Alex interrupted her as she turned on the VCR.

"Where's your control box if it does?" Sandra asked.

"Just inside the garage by the kitchen door. I had to rearm it after my electricity went off once before. Why?"

"Just wondered. I didn't even know where mine was in my new place until last week."

"As for the kachinas," Alex said, anxious to confide in her, "some are going back to their tribes, so that's good. Actually, I didn't sell all of them but kept two back for the baby—or babies. They're wrapped up in the bottom drawer under the shelf where they all used to stand. Sandra, would you please quit looking at me that way?"

"I'm just trying to cheer you up," she said, speaking like herself again. "You all right here? Want me to move in for a little while, or you want to come live with me?"

"I'm fine, really, especially now with the worries about getting pregnant are past. All I've got to do is make it through eight and a half more months, which may not be easy, especially if I turn out to be DES-affected."

"You believe Hale on that over what your mother still claims?"

"My mother might be like me lately—forgetful, distracted—and occasionally demented."

Sandra stepped forward to give her a swift, silent hug. Though they'd always talked a lot, when things had been toughest—especially during Sandra's traumatic times—they had learned to comfort quietly.

"I've been worried sick about you," Hale told Jasmine when she came into the kitchen through the garage door. She was dripping wet. She fully expected him to lecture her, so she was prepared for the tirade.

"I hate your driving on that twisting road at night," he went on, "let alone in a deluge like this. Research paper or not, I don't see why you have to work so much after hours. If you can't keep up with the daily load, we can certainly hire an extra lab assistant."

"No! Thank you, but no," she said more quietly. "It's quite enough for me to make sure Tom does things my way. I don't need anyone else hanging around."

She pecked a quick kiss on his cheek, then just kept going toward the master bedroom of their sprawling one-floor home, stripping off damp garments as she went, leaving him to lock up behind her. But she knew she had to break her shocking request to him and turned back to loop her arms around his neck. She kissed him full and hard on the lips this time, pressing against him in slip and panty hose, rubbing her hips against him.

"I know, I know," he said, his angry tone softening, as she knew it would. "You always did want things your own way."

"And I want that tonight—want my wicked way with you, that is."

She saw she had him hooked now. She whirled away, tugging him after her down the hall. "I've got to get undressed, to keep up with you," she said, indicating his plaid shorts and open robe. "And then we'll do some research together." Even Hale had no idea when the real import and impact of her work could be. She laughed throatily, hoping she could carry this off.

"So your work is going well?" he asked as he sat on their king-size bed.

To make him forget his question, she slowly stripped off her hose, slip, and bra. Hale loved it that she wore sexy lingerie under her stiff, pristine lab coats. The first time they'd made love had been on the floor of the Cornell embryology lab. You'd think with a beginning like that, they could have managed at least one natural pregnancy between them.

"You haven't hit a snag in the research, have you?" he asked doggedly.

"It could be further along, but I've got to get to a certain point before I deliver my manifesto at the Miami conference next week."

"Maybe I should come too, so I can get the latest on your new freezing techniques," he said with a sly smile. "But not with all that's happening with the media. And this mess with Rita Twohorses. It worries me that Alexis seems to be getting close to her. I don't want Rita's negativism, to put it mildly, to affect Alexis's pregnancy."

"Or her TV coverage. But Rita's the last person I want to talk about tonight," she said. "Or Alex. You know, I could get very jealous watching her hug you on TV over and over."

Completely nude, she sauntered over to the bed and lifted one long leg over him to sit facing him in his lap. As many years as they'd had sex, his admiration of her body had never wavered. Above all, she loved to see his need and hunger for her in his eyes—and elsewhere.

"Hale, I have something to ask you, more than a favor," she whispered, rocking slightly in his lap. "A fervent, a passionate need."

"Anything, my darling, if it's within my power. Ask for anything." He looked heavy-lidded, the skin over his fine features stretched taut with desire. His hands on her waist, his thumbs stroked her flat belly.

"Actually, the two things you do best, my love," she said in his ear. "Start me on another IVF cycle tomorrow and make love to me tonight."

He tipped her slightly back and stared at her. "Another cycle? But—Pergonal? You hated the drugs, and they really affected your moods. But I'm—I'm deeply moved you want another try for a child, and we'll celebrate that with your other request right now...."

He rolled her over and straddled her. She murmured love words to him as he showered her throat and breasts with kisses, but her mind was miles away. In the lab. Rolling out the secret storage bank. Lifting its lid to stare into eternity. Though Hale could think what he must, she didn't want a child from him, not even his sperm, whatever brilliance his DNA would carry. From him she wanted only the harvest of her eggs.

"There!" Sandra cried and pointed with her bread stick. "Back it up again. You're right—the illustrious Dr. Jasmine pinched that poor little kid."

"Which only proves she can be sneaky and deceptive," Alex said as they watched her lightning-quick move again. "And very nasty."

"And is wily enough to shut Rita up at any cost," Sandra added.

"Beth says Jasmine wants Rita out of the clinic. I can't tell you my source, but I know Rita has an unstable past. I want her to have a child, but maybe it's for the best if she would wait until she can get hold of herself."

"Sounds like you're on Dr. Jasmine's side," Sandra stated as Alex finally clicked the VCR off. They kept turning their rotating barrel chairs toward each other, then away as they talked.

"No, I'm not on her side. It's just I want desperately to have this story—and my own—work out, and I need the Stanhopes."

"At least you're honest," Sandra said, raising her voice above the rattle of rain on the windows. She took a swallow of the wine Alex had poured for her while she stuck to cranberry juice. "But then, you always were."

The guilt Sandra had teased her about earlier assaulted Alex again. She wished she hadn't promised both Bernice and Nick she would not inform the station about "the sting operation," as Nick called it, that was in the works. The Stanhopes, however, had to be let in on the plan so Sandra and Mike would probably be doubly furious later. But Nick had it figured out so she couldn't possibly get hurt, and when it was over, she'd explain everything to Sandra and Mike.

She did, however, tell Sandra now about the double

egg-donor forms and Beth's explanation for them. "And since I've looked at them without permission, I hope you don't ask somebody something to give me away. I feel really bad when I have to keep things from you."

"Then don't anymore. We've been joined at the hip these last few years—until Mr. Destin."

"I'll tell you what else is worrying me, though," Alex admitted, afraid that another discussion of Nick would have her blurting out their plans to entrap their assailant. "*The Fertility Frontier* is starting to take on a life of its own. Already, with Hale on the air just once and the coverage of the Miracle Baby party, the station's getting a lot of feedback. And the clinic's inundated with women wanting initial consultations. They're getting a waiting list a mile long." The memory of Rita's accusing voice poured through her like a torrent outside: *You're as good as doing free advertising for them right now!*

"But's that's all good, isn't it? Mike's happy, and the Stanhopes are getting their payoff for helping us with the series."

"By the way, I'm meeting with the Mei-Luns tomorrow, the parents of that Asian baby Jasmine was holding, but not for the series. No camera, no interview per se, but I'm going to try to see if they think Jasmine pinched their son. But what really worries me," she said, sitting forward, "is—what if something *is* wrong? If I've misled anyone—including myself—I'd just die."

"Something wrong? Such as?" Sandra demanded, narrowing her eyes.

"What if the Stanhopes have ripped Rita off just to

get her valuable figurines, or what if they are tampering for some reason with those egg-donor forms I sneaked a look at?"

"And that's where you found out Rita's been mentally unstable. *Madre de Dios,* if this is the sacrament of holy confession," she said, crossing herself with another bread stick, "I gotta tell you I been looking for something too, just on the principle that you can't trust doctors, and the most powerful are the worst. So I'm starting to collect résumés and bios of the clinic staff." When Alex only nodded, she went on, "I mean, I can understand Jasmine getting all starry-eyed when she talks about her research, but she clams up when asked to explain *what* research, and there's no record of it in her background. As a matter of fact, there's a lot of holes."

"Talks about her research. You've been interviewing her too? And didn't tell me?" Alex raised her voice over the rain.

"We still friends, *chica?* We can work on this together. But you're not gonna do something wild like demanding she explain her work, are you?"

"Yes, but not quite yet," Alex said solemnly. "I am, however, going to search until I find some experts to explain the cutting edge of egg and embryological research and, if I have to, trek to Timbuktu to interview them."

10

The first thing the next morning Alex waited the required three interminable minutes, then checked the indicator strip of the test. She stared so hard, so long at it she almost felt her eyes cross.

"Yes. Yes, yes! Oh, thank you, Lord God—and the Stanhopes too!"

Two blue lines—she was pregnant, all right.

She hugged herself, then whirled in a circle before she got hold of herself and perched on the edge of the tub. She should not have mistrusted the Stanhopes for one moment. Why should she resort to this cheap drugstore test when she had a high-tech—and high-cost—clinic helping her? The doctors had not lied about anything. They wanted only the best for her and her pregnancy, as well as all their clinic babies. The whole secret investigation she and Sandra were planning would probably lead to a dead end.

Then she did what she'd promised on the air. She got out the maternal family cradle and shined and waxed it. It looked so empty and vast that she tucked an embroidered and ruffled towel inside until she could get some small bedclothes and a pillow. She carried the cradle downstairs to put it on the hearth, then decided she didn't want others to see it, not yet at least.

She took it up to her bedroom and put it on the far side of her bed under the front windows. From the other end of the room on the pecan dresser, Geoff's picture looked down at the cradle. If only, she thought, the nine months could be gone now, safely over. If only the sting at Silver planned for next week was safely resolved and Carolyn or whoever had shot at her and Nick could be stopped and—and helped. Then she and Nick would have time together…

She walked to the photo of Geoff. She studied it, that brash face and cocky stance in the picture of a pilot's private joke. Suited up for his F-15 with his dark-visored pilot's helmet in one hand, he only had his foot on the step of his own little Piper Cub.

She bit her lip and stared at herself in the mirror, pregnant with his child but going on without him. She lifted the picture and held it to her cheek, then lowered it and laid it in the drawer on top of the folded American flag from his funeral.

"Jonathan's a darling baby," Alex told George and Jing Mei-Lun later that morning. The window in the living room of their ranch-style home in the Volcano Cliffs neighborhood had a stunning view of the Rio Grande and rain-washed city skyline. But what thrilled Alex was that they let her hold their sleepy one-year-old. She had to remind herself she was here for a specific, serious reason.

"I hope," she said, slightly rocking the child, "that Jonathan recovered quickly from his crying bout at the clinic party. And that it wasn't our camera that scared him."

"It was not your fault," his father said, sitting up even straighter in his chair across from the gray futon sofa where Alex sat next to the baby's beautiful mother. "But we appreciate your and the doctors' concern."

"So the doctors were concerned too?" Alex asked. "I believe Dr. Jasmine was holding him."

"That is so," Jing put in with a tight smile and purposeful nod at her husband, as if to warn him of something. His eyes darted around the room. Little in this home bespoke an Asian heritage, except perhaps the taste in spare, sleek furnishings. Yet Alex's careful questioning today had revealed this couple was native-born Chinese, who as children had fled their homeland with their families. Though Jing had taken a leave of absence when her pregnancy began, the Mei-Luns were designing engineers at a small nearby research and development firm, which did a lot of contract work for NASA

"Well, maybe it was the camera," the father said.

"But we do not criticize you or your television people," Jing added. "It is good that your series lets others know they do not have to give up on having a child of their own."

"Right. That is good," George said.

Alex felt very uncomfortable with this. He was defensive, and both parents were extremely nervous. She had no right to press them further and didn't want to accuse Dr. Jasmine directly. "If you'll excuse me," she told them, "I really must go. It's been a great encouragement to me to be able to hold your beautiful son." But as she handed the child back, with her hands grasping his waist, he flinched and wailed.

Suddenly Jing, who had sat nearly motionless, took her son and stood. "I will walk Ms. McCall to her car, and I'll be right back, George," she told her husband. She started out the door before he could respond or Alex could rise. George Mei-Lun looked very worried as Alex said a hasty good-bye and followed Jing outside.

"Thank you for your time," Alex told Jing as she dug in her purse for her keys. Once she was in the car, the woman leaned down to look in the open window with the baby balanced on one hip.

"Sorry, but I don't suppose we were much help for what you really wanted to know," Jing said, her voice so low Alex could barely hear her. Now Alex was certain Jing wanted to tell her something out of her husband's earshot. But the woman only silently lifted the little shirt the baby wore to expose two purplish marks along his fluted rib cage, one on each side. Each was a fingerprint-sized bruise.

Jing's jet eyes met and held Alex's stunned gaze, even as she gently tucked in the baby's shirt.

"She pinched Jonathan hard to make him cry," Alex stated. "I saw it on the tape. That's why I came."

"Yes, I guess she did it to stop that woman's accusations. But they always say they love and protect the clinic babies."

"Perhaps she just panicked," Alex said, ashamed she was offering any excuse for such behavior. Neither of them had used Jasmine's name as if by tacit agreement.

"If so, then she knows how it feels—panic," Jing whispered. She rolled her eyes and held Jonathan even tighter. "I thought I would never have this child, our son. It was so hard to carry him—hospitalization, time in bed at home, fear of miscarriage. I got extra help from Dr. Stanhope as well as my own doctor—I am eternally grateful to the Stanhopes and the clinic."

"You're torn. I understand. But..." Alex prompted.

"I would never go through it again anyway, so it doesn't matter," she insisted and stepped away from the car.

"It certainly does matter if anyone deliberately hurt a child that way," Alex called to her. "I'll talk to her—"

"No! We want only our son, no trouble. Even the other eggs, I don't mind."

Alex realized she was gripping the steering wheel so hard her fingers had gone numb. She flexed them slowly, but her mind raced. "You donated your eggs—after Jonathan was born?"

"No, I told George I would and we argued, so we still said no. But they—her assistant called later to say—they were lost anyway."

"Lost?"

"A little lab accident. Lost. Sometimes it just happens. But I must tell you, Ms. McCall, if you ever put this on the television, we will sue you," she declared. "From the first moment we saw an ad on TV telling about your series, George was very angry with you for digging up clinic business. Where will it end?"

The tightly controlled tirade stunned Alex. "Then why do you even tell me—hint at this suspicion about your eggs being carelessly or deliberately lost? That is what you believe, isn't it?"

"No suspicion, but the truth," she said with a decisive nod. She looked directly into her eyes again. "I asked that woman about it at the baby party. I could tell she lied about their just being lost. And now I tell you because, of all people, you must understand. I tell you so that without pulling us in, you can do something about it, stop it from happening ever again."

"I will go find my sisters and get ready," Rita told Paul and Alex when they reached the Santa Cruz pueblo.

Alex dreaded being left alone with this aloof man who obviously didn't approve of her friendship with his wife, let alone her coming today. He had smoked in his Ford pickup, and Alex felt assaulted by the smell, even though she'd rolled down her passenger window. Rita, who sat between them, hadn't seemed to notice. She was intent on what she called "this trial."

"Okay," Paul told his wife and gave her a hard hug. "We'll see you inside."

Although Alex had visited several of the local pueblos over the years for feast days or TV coverage, she had never been to Santa Cruz pueblo. Not a tourist site, the small town of Rita Twohorses' people protected its privacy and sacred traditions.

Lying along the Rio Grande about thirty miles north of Albuquerque, Santa Cruz was one of the southern pueblos which had once united with the northern ones in a bloody revolt against their Spanish masters. At that time this land had already been in Indian hands for hundreds of years. Later Anglos both enslaved the Indians and "saved" them with their Catholicism. Now, Alex knew, most pueblos blended that faith with their ancestors' religious beliefs. But Rita had given her no hint of what she would be getting into today.

On a small bluff overlooking the Rio Grande floodplain, clustered around a central dirt plaza, the pueblo buildings were a monotonous blur of tan adobe and brown tuff, a stone made from volcanic ash. Few people seemed to be stirring. Alex appreciated the color accents of the place: blue corn and red chile *ristras,* bright blankets, curtains, painted doors, and pots.

When she walked a bit away to look down at the river, Paul followed. Swollen with the recent spring rain, it rushed over rocks and boulders. He propped one foot on a low tuff fence while she glanced at his bronze, hawklike profile. The breeze ruffled their clothes and hair. Alex had learned that Paul's family owned what they called an adobe farm, where bricks were mixed, cut, and dried, but she couldn't think of any *entre* to conversation about that.

"I hear you will have your Feast Day here next week," she said, trying to sound pleasant and interested. "I'm sure that takes a lot of preparation."

"I'm in the deer dance. The chant in our language asks for the deer mothers to have many children. Rita cried during it last year."

"I'm sorry things aren't better for her now. I wish I could help," she said, turning slightly toward him.

"Then stay with your own kind and tell Rita to." His voice was quiet but cutting. "When she heard you are going to have a child, she talked of nothing else, but she was sadder too."

"She told me it gives her hope."

"No." His wide brow clenched. "I am telling you to stay away or else—"

A woman's voice cut him off. "Paul! Paul, over here!" Dressed in high, turned down moccasins, a long skirt, and a striped red blanket worn like a shawl, the attractive young woman hurried to meet him. Alex introduced herself when Paul didn't. This was Vengie, one of Rita's two sisters who would be the other supporters today. She was a thinner, younger version of Rita with her hair loose instead of pulled straight back.

"Rita, she told me explain it all to you," Vengie said, gesturing for them to follow her. Alex smiled to see she had a neon yellow Nike T-shirt under her blanket and aviator sunglasses stuck in her pocket. She looked about twenty. "And she says you're pregnant," she went on with a nod and a smile. "Then you'll have to close your eyes when the tribal doctor dances later, because you can't see anything ugly or your child won't be good-looking."

"Vengie, just cool it," Paul put in, throwing away another cigarette outside the blue-door pueblo on the very edge of the little town. "Anglos think that's all crap and superstition."

"And never," Vengie said to Alex, rolling her eyes

and ignoring his warning, "start out a door and turn back or start eating and then stop, or the baby will hesitate to come."

"I'll remember that," Alex told her.

Inside the dimly lit house—a main room with others partitioned off by hanging rugs with zigzag designs—Vengie showed Alex where to sit on the floor on another rug. Vengie whirled a red shawl like her own around Alex's shoulders. When her eyes became adjusted to the light, she saw a delicate sand painting on the floor near the far wall, one with bear prints, feathers, and ears of corn in a sunburst pattern.

Paul ambled in and sat, cross-legged, next to Vengie. Soon the second sister, Ada, entered and sat on Alex's other side. She looked young, but was heavier, like Rita. No, Alex saw, feeling a stab of sadness for Rita again, the young woman was pregnant. They began to speak in whispers.

Soon Rita entered behind a stern-looking man. Alex's breath caught at the sight of her. She resembled some painted powwow poster. Like her sisters, she wore a long skirt and fawn-hued moccasins turned down. Her hair flowed full and wild in all its abundance. She looked excited, almost feverish. Two large red spots of paint bloomed on her cheeks. Just then Ada leaned toward Vengie and Alex to dab similar circles of red on them.

"Crushed amaranth blossoms," Ada said. "A blessing. The flower that never fades."

Alex began to relax. Surely, however strange these customs were to her, this ceremony was going to help

Rita. If it just calmed her, it would be, as Ada said, a blessing. She watched, wide-eyed, as the doctor began to chant and Rita lay down on her back along the far wall, next to the sand painting. How she wished she could bring this unique, amazing experience to her television viewers, but she knew better than to even breathe the thought here.

"What are those items next to Rita?" Alex whispered to Vengie.

"Corn for fertility. We're from the Corn Clan. Eagle feather, a bear's paw, and water bowl. Powerful magic, that's all."

The sudden screech jolted Alex. A masked man—no, his face was only painted black—exploded into the room with a long dagger in his hand. He postured, glaring each way around Rita as if protecting her from unseen terror. Then he bent to dip his hand into the bowl and flicked water in six different directions. Some sprinkled Alex's arm. She imagined it burned her, but she dared not rub it off.

She calmed down again as the chanting slowed. Thank God, this man—he must be the so-called doctor or medicine man and the other just his assistant—didn't look anything like the kachinas of the Hopi or Zuni she'd been dreading in coming here.

A memory flew at her, sharp and clear. She'd forgotten it years ago. With her family she'd attended a ceremony somewhere where male dancers had dressed like kachinas, towering ten-foot ones with huge eyes and horns. They had postured, threatened, and she had screamed so loud even over the beat of drums that her family had been forced to leave the reservation. She must have been only four or five then, but she recalled too how her brothers, annoyed and angry, for months after had jumped out from doors and bushes with horrible expressions and shrieks.

She shoved the painful memory away, watching what happened next. But she was startled when Vengie tugged her shawl. "All supporters step outside now. You can't see this part."

The sun blinded them. Alex fumbled for her sunglasses in her purse. The four of them walked out where Alex and Paul had stood earlier. The ceremony hadn't been bad, Alex thought. Not at all.

But a screech shattered the calm, drawing a few others from their pueblos to watch. The painted doctor exploded from the house, dagger in hand, shrieking, dancing not to drums but his own imagined beat. Slashing the air, twisting and writhing, he threw himself on the ground, rolled, kicked, then scrambled up, dust-caked and wild.

He ran right at Alex. She screamed and ducked before he veered away down the twisting path toward the riverbank.

"I told you not to look at him!" Vengie cried. "He's got to fight the witches that made Rita a victim. He's got to kill them and bring her heart back healthy that they stole."

"Witches?" Alex stammered. "I didn't know…"

"It's not for you," Paul muttered darkly, narrowing his eyes. "None of it."

But while the doctor shrieked and cavorted below

them, Vengie and Ada coaxed her back inside. "It's quiet from here on," Vengie promised. "It will take all the strength he has to fight them and keep moving so he doesn't have to breathe their breath."

Alex nearly collapsed on the blanket in the dim, now quiet house. She shouldn't have come. Hale had told her to take it easy.

Following the sisters' lead, she also ignored Rita. Her friend lay as if in a trance, on the floor, staring unblinkingly up at the ceiling. At some point she had flopped one arm in the sand painting, smearing some of its fine lines. Alex wondered if she'd been drugged with something. She thought how savage and primitive this was until she remembered lying drugged, staring at the ceiling, with Sandra as her supporter, waiting for Dr Stanhope to help her get a child.

Finally, the tribal doctor dragged himself back into the hut, gasping for breath, his once proud stance now sagging. But in his hand was still his dagger and in his other a crude rag doll.

"That's what the witches have been tormenting to hurt Rita," Vengie said.

Like voodoo? Alex thought, but held her tongue.

The doctor tore a piece of the doll away and produced a silver-hot coal to burn the piece on a flat dish. The smoke, which he wafted toward Rita with an eagle feather, was sickeningly sweet. He gathered the ashes and stirred them in the medicine bowl with the feather quill. And in the ashes was something else which he held proudly, exhaustedly up for them to see between his thumb and finger.

"What's that?" Alex mouthed to Vengie.

"Rita's heart."

"What?"

"Corn."

Transfixed, Alex could not even nod as he dropped the single kernel of corn in the medicine bowl. Her cheeks glazed with tears that smeared her red spots, Rita sat up and drank the water from the bowl, first solemnly, then greedily while both curers chanted.

"The words are," Vengie said, chanting slowly too, "'It is good. The Corn Mother holds us in her heart. Our mother holds us in her heart.'"

For many reasons she could not name or explain, like Rita, Alex cried.

11

That Saturday evening after the curing ceremony, Alex amazed herself by feeling physically stronger, as if she too had received a new heart from it. Her fear of the kachina nightmares eased now that she'd recalled her childhood trauma. She became more convinced things would go well for her tenuous pregnancy. She'd had no other incidents of misplacing things in the house, being forgetful, or harassment. Even such sobering future events as the sting at Silver tomorrow and her and Hale's visit to her mother in the near future didn't seem so daunting.

For one thing, she had great success tracing who the most prominent fertility and egg-preservation specialists were—not just in the country but the *world*. Through a combination of on-line searches and phoning contacts at other affiliate stations, she had learned that the WFO, the World Fertility Organization, was having its annual conference soon in Orlando.

"Listen to this, Ms. Sanchez," she'd told Sandra, hurrying excitedly over to her desk in the newsroom yesterday. "Not only is British specialist *Sir* Nigel Givens-Jones lecturing at the symposium on the future of fertility next week, but Jasmine too."

"What?" Sandra asked, grabbing the fax sheet from Alex. "Her royal highness, Queen Jasmine? And there's a trade show too, with all the latest gizmos on display?" she added, reading the printout.

"You don't call cutting-edge medical and scientific breakthroughs gizmos. You know, I think I can pull some strings at our Miami affiliate to get us press passes. Want a two-day escape to Florida?"

"*Perfecto, mi amiga,*" she declared, smacking both palms on her messy desk and leaping up. "Who knows, but if we can use interviews and footage from the trade show, the station might spring for the tickets."

"Except Mike's going to flip when he hears the name of the official conference hotel, not that we'd be staying there. It's the Gone with the Wind. Can you believe the gall of those doctors to hold this conference at the Reel World Amusement Park, built around old movie sets?"

"I can believe anything weird about doctors," Sandra muttered, sitting back down when her phone rang.

Alex had decided to go upstairs right then to ask Mike about attending the conference. She'd tell him Dr. Jasmine was speaking there, though she didn't intend to tell Jasmine they were going. They needed to keep an eye on her, perhaps surprise her *after* her talk.

Alex began pacing at eight-thirty that evening, though Nick wasn't due until nine. She walked the entire perimeter of the house, upstairs and down, peering out every direction through narrow cracks in the closed blinds or drapes. She watched the front street for a long time. She saw the Camelot security truck drive slowly by, so she felt good about that. Then, from the living room, she saw the Jeep swing in. The headlights blinked twice before they went off.

Alex disarmed her security system. So he could drive into the garage and park beside her car, she hurried to the kitchen and hit the automatic opener for him. She waited until she heard it rumble open, then closed. Two knocks sounded on the kitchen door. She opened it and surprised both of them by hugging him.

He held her, instantly responding in one long, searing kiss while he leaned and balanced her against him in the open doorway between the kitchen and garage. When they came up for air, still holding tight, he whispered, "There's a parked police car just down the street, so I stopped to tell them who I was. Nothing like a little cloak-and-dagger stuff to spice up a romance. Now, I've heard of some women who only respond in dangerous situations, so—"

"Don't say that, not with what we're facing. And for me, the cloak-and-dagger stuff does *not* enhance romance. That isn't it at all. I've just been worried about you, thinking about you."

"Then we have a lot in common."

Holding his hand, she led him through the kitchen to the couch in front of the fireplace. A log settled to scatter sparks. He took his denim jacket off and tossed it on a chair. He was dressed casually, like her, in jeans and a shirt. He threw an arm around her shoulders, and she pulled her legs up sideways to settle against him, as if they were old married folks looking forward to tomorrow. But tomorrow was the sting at Silver.

She could tell he wanted to kiss her again. He shifted slightly closer so her thigh pressed against his. He cleared his throat. "Business first, I guess. Everything's cleared with Bernice and the SWAT team. I talked to her on the phone this afternoon. She says even though you'll be in that protected area, she's bringing a bulletproof vest for you too. I just wish you'd agree to having someone impersonate you."

"If it isn't both of us, Carolyn might get spooked. Or we might not know who she's after. If it's her. I know you still don't want to accept that."

"I don't want to accept a lot of things I should." He squeezed her shoulder and looked away, frowning, repeatedly rubbing his free hand on the thigh of his jeans.

"Did you talk to Carolyn to set it up?" she asked quietly.

He nodded. "I worked into the conversation that I was finally starting to date someone. And then mentioned I'm excavating Silver before it becomes off limits—described where it was—and that I was going there tomorrow on a kind of picnic. I feel terrible setting her up—unless it is her. However bad I want anyone who could harm you locked up, I'm just hoping it's not her and no one comes…." His voice got rough and trailed off as he frowned at his boot tips.

"I understand, Nick, really. And I'm sorry we got—tangled up like this when we're just—well, starting out."

"But not," he said, turning to look at her with eyes that reflected the hearth flames, "that we got tangled up. Are you?" He transferred his big hand from his thigh to her knee. They tilted even more together, their foreheads touching.

"No," she admitted softly. "The timing's crazy, but no—no!"

When he touched her with his hands and mouth, she got dizzy at the scent and feel of him. Lime aftershave, that clove scent of his breath. It had been so long. Had it ever felt so powerfully out of control like this? She matched his kisses and caresses until they were both breathless. His big hands cupped her breasts and bottom, his knee rode insistently higher between her thighs. They ended up sprawled on the couch, but he was careful not to press too tightly against her.

"Time out," she whispered, her voice as ragged as her breathing. He cradled her, then pulled them both up, settling her in his lap. She felt the room was spinning. She gripped his shoulders to steady herself, but staring this close into his dark eyes hardly helped. Firelight etched each crag and crevice of his face.

"Tomorrow," he said, and she watched his mouth as he talked, "we're going to do what we have to so we can start over without any worries. Now—if I can think and talk straight, let's go over the plans once more, however much Bernice has already talked to both of us. And then we'll enjoy this fire a little more."

He nodded at the fireplace but grinned at her, looking boyish before his narrowed gaze dropped slowly to her mouth, her breasts, waist, thighs, legs, then up to her face again. She shifted on his lap and knew he was completely aroused. The impact of his intensity staggered her. For now, the way things were for her, an intimate relationship with him seemed impossible and forbidden, yet so—utterly desirable. She felt the impact of his gaze deep in her belly, and that slapped her sober.

"There's not just us to worry about," she told him, her voice suddenly so strong and clear it even surprised her. She put one hand almost defensively on her stomach. "I'm committed to having these babies."

"I know that, Alexis, and I'm still here. Now let's talk about tomorrow."

"I'll be really glad to get this over with," Hale told Alex in his office, where they were meeting with Bernice and the department heads of the clinic staff around the conference table the next morning. SWAT officers had already been deployed in Silver to await Alex's and Nick's staged arrivals. "And I'm relieved that your being shot at is probably not related to the clinic story. Since we've gotten some negative feedback too, I though surely that was it at first."

"What sort of feedback have you had, Dr. Stanhope?" Bernice asked before Alex could. Alex looked at Beth. If she'd known about this, she wished she'd have told her.

"Enough that we're going to beef up the security around here, even though we're somewhat out in the boondocks," he admitted.

"A remote location can actually be a liability," Bernice observed. "You haven't had any incidents, have you?"

"Nothing more than a few phone calls from so-called colleagues," he said, shaking his head. "I knew we'd stir up a hornets' nest at other Southwest hospitals that do IVF. One thing I guess I've never mentioned—even to Alexis—is that there's a lot of resentment toward private clinics in the industry, especially ones doing research and doing well."

"And getting major publicity," Beth said, her voice tense.

Alex wanted to ask Hale what kind of research they were doing, but she forced herself to wait until later for that. "You think some rival doctor could be upset enough to do something to you or the clinic?" she asked him.

"Let's hope not. So far it's been a few bitter or snide phone calls or comments in chat rooms on-line, but I just thought I'd mention it. They resent private clinics being relatively unmonitored—which means more progress and state-of-the-art techniques for patients and—"

"In short, sour grapes," Jasmine interrupted. "Never mind all that, Hale. It's getting this burden off Alex's back that we want to focus on today."

"We appreciate your help, Dr. Stanhope, Dr. Jasmine," Nick said, looking bulky with his navy blue bulletproof vest under his denim jacket. "I know you were against my even being on the land down there."

"Perhaps, Mr. Destin," Jasmine went on, "we can work out some sort of arrangement for your organization collecting artifacts before we build on it. Frankly, the idea of a ghost town with that horrid old cemetery down there—with some babies' graves, my lab assistant tells me—where we hope to put labs and O.R.s dedicated to the future good of babies and their parents someday…"

Her voice trailed off and she shuddered dramatically. Alex just glared at her. This from the woman who pinched that innocent baby so hard he was black and blue. She was of the same stripe as that child abuser, Hank Cordova. If Alex hadn't promised Jing she wouldn't say anything, she'd really like to tell her off, however much she wanted her help for the series. She regretted how much she'd come to dislike, and maybe distrust, Jasmine, however grateful she should feel toward her.

"All right," Bernice cut in, "the SWAT guys have been hidden in the crevices and the mine entrance for over an hour, so it's time for the key players. You'll be completely covered. Nick, you go on down to the valley floor to draw attention to yourself. Alexis will make her entrance through the forest in"—she glanced at her watch—"exactly twelve minutes. I've got 10:37, so everybody reset your watches. Alexis I'll help you with the vest."

After Nick left, those twelve minutes dragged. Her stomachache got worse, but she knew it was just nerves. If this didn't work, they'd look silly, but the SWAT team leader had said it would be "a useful operation whether the suspect showed or not." If only life had such practice sessions where dangers didn't really count.

The velcro ties Bernice ripped open on the vest seemed to scream at Alex. The padded kevlar was heavy and hot. Bernice had agreed to get one too big for her so it covered her stomach instead of stopping between the navel and pelvic bones. Beth came over to the corner to see if she could help. Just staff, no patients in today, not even for counseling circles, to keep the area clear from possible mishaps. If Carolyn showed up with a gun, Nick had been promised, they would just contain and then arrest her.

"He's really good-looking," Beth said, "your Nick. I feel terrible I told him off that time, even if he was trespassing. He's a lot sexier than the guy I've started dating," she added with a sigh.

"You have? Who?" Alex asked, desperate for any kind of pleasant talk to fill the void of worrying and waiting. "Someone I know?"

"No, and no way I'm talking about him," she said, leaning against the wall with her arms crossed. "I have a little superstition it's bad luck to tell a friend about a new guy until she actually meets him. You know, like if you tell a dream, you'll never have it again."

"Then I hope I get to meet him soon. I never heard that about dreams, but it could be true," she said, explaining she'd told Sandra and Rita about her kachina nightmares and they seemed better now. "Did you ever hear that about nightmares, Bernice?"

"Nope," she said, evidently too busy for normal conversation. It made Alex even more nervous to watch her purposeful preparations. Bernice put on her own vest, strapped her holster back on, then turned away to give orders over a hand-held two-way radio.

"But you and Nick—you're pretty serious?" Beth

asked, surprising Alex with the change of subject. "I mean, there's no one else in your life—that way?"

"Where do I have time to stash someone else— someone secret? After all, with everything—"

"It's time," Bernice interrupted. "Thanks for all your help, Beth. Keep everyone inside, like I said. And lock the doors once we get out."

Alex's legs felt stiff. This seemed suddenly so unreal. She became aware of every breath, every motion and step. Covered by one SWAT officer, she and Bernice darted out the back door of the clinic, then walked a ways into the forest to approach the edge of Silver unseen. With the Stanhopes' permission, three entrances had been cut through the barbed-wire fence in hopes that if Carolyn took the bait, she would come through one of them.

"Any sign of the suspect's car or anyone else suspicious?" Bernice asked the sullen-looking officer. As if he were going into war, he had blackened his face.

"No one. But we're still a go for the next three hours."

Three hours, Alex thought. Until almost one-thirty today. That seemed as much of an eternity as did nine months—minus almost three weeks now—of a danger-fraught pregnancy.

"I've been saving some good news for you," Bernice told her, glancing at her watch again. "Just confirmed before I got here today. I didn't want to tell you in front of everyone."

"What? Anything good I can use."

"Your old nemesis Hank Cordova has been arrested

for shoplifting, of all things, in North Dakota, of all places. Over a week ago, but I didn't think to try searching for him with the NCIC computer link until last night. I still thought he was the top candidate for the nine-millimeter bullet that came calling through your front door."

"Which still doesn't prove it was Carolyn Destin. See, I'm starting to think like you—or Nick."

"I should have known that Destin's insistence his wife knew zilch about guns means nothing. Like always, desperate women do whatever they believe they have to," she added grimly.

"I know," Alex admitted. "I know."

Now that it was actually happening, Nick admitted to himself he'd never been so scared in his life. He'd been putting on a good show for Alexis, for the police, even for himself, but he was sick to his soul about this. And now, like a sitting duck—flak jacket or not—he just knew, too late, that Carolyn had done it.

Because the creepy feeling he'd had before here at Silver and dismissed was back full force. It was the sensation he was being watched, not just by someone from the clinic staff back then and not just by Bernice and the SWAT sharpshooters now. Carolyn must have been here that day, so she probably knew the area. And if she'd watched—stalked—him that long, that recently, when he believed she was living somewhere else and was better, it must have been him and not Alexis whom Carolyn wanted to control. Damn it, right now she was succeeding. But things were set in motion like a big boulder rolling downhill, and he could not stop it.

He glanced up at the ledge where Alexis would be protected from above and from every angle below by the officers' rifles. As scripted, she appeared in her big hat and bright jacket. She waved down to him, and he waved up, wishing he could scream at her to go back to the clinic. He should have insisted she use a double or set this trap some other way. She took her place, sitting against the cliff face.

He readjusted his backpack and pretended to be poking around. He stopped occasionally to make notes so that if Carolyn were watching, she'd think everything was normal. She'd gone with him on several trips and digs like this, years ago, when he had been happy to have her with him.

His hand shook as he wrote, "Alexis, I'm sorry. I really hope we have a shot"—shaking his head ruefully, he crossed that out—"a chance to be together." He tried to concentrate, not to keep scanning the cliffs. He tried to watch where he walked because these thorny mesquite bushes often hid old wells, dug randomly to get water when the mining polluted the streams. Funny how the information part of his brain worked when red fear screamed at him.

"There's a carcass of a broken upright piano down this hole!" His voice echoed off the walls as he yelled up the planned comment so they'd know he hadn't spotted anyone yet. He could glimpse only the one marksman lying prone in a crevice just above Alexis, but no one else. They had done a great job of hiding.

He felt sweat roll down the middle of his back. If Carolyn was still as sharp as she used to be, the fact he was down here in a bulky jacket in this heat could tip her off. He moved closer to the mouth of the old mine.

"That could be deep. Be careful!" Alexis's shout jolted him as it echoed, *careful, careful...ful.*

She wasn't supposed to say that. Then he knew that she was scared too, and that she cared. Guilt sapped his strength because he actually expected her to lose her dead husband's baby—or babies. He'd read up on it, the tremendous odds against her, especially since she'd told him about her earlier miscarriages and her mother's possible use of DES. If tragedy struck again, he'd want to help her through it, but even that would take the commitment that turned desire into love, and he still wasn't sure he could face that, not even for Alexis.

He glanced at his watch—only fifteen minutes gone. *Come on, Carolyn,* he thought. *Let's get this over with for both of us. I hope they trap you before you even hike clear in here, but you'd better have the gun on you that will match the bullet in Alex's door. You'll be all right if you just don't turn a gun on one of the men. You were afraid of guns, but I'm so afraid it was you.*

The sun rose higher over Alexis's position, right in his eyes. He knew he'd see better if he could just step back into the shade of the mine's mouth, the adit, old-timers called it. One of the SWAT guys was hunkered down in here, had been for over an hour, so that—if necessary—he could cover the cliff directly above Alexis from this vantage point.

Feeling safe in knowing that, Nick stepped in, shuffling carefully because—after the sunlight—the darkness dumbfounded him like going into a black movie theater. He could barely see beyond the old boards and beams that choked out light from outside.

"I hoped you'd come in here," the feminine voice whispered.

He whirled toward it. Bernice hadn't told him any of the SWAT team were women.

His eyes adjusted and he realized his mistake. That voice— "Carolyn?" he croaked out as a figure all in black, wearing a baseball cap, stepped out from the depths, holding something in each hand.

A wooden club and a semi-automatic. She shook her head hard and her cap flew off. Her once long blond hair was black and short, just the way Alex had said. And he saw the SWAT officer slumped almost at her feet.

His stomach went into free fall.

"Surely you were expecting me," she whispered. "I'm glad I didn't just have to shoot you from in here."

"You—could have shot me many times."

"No, I needed to do it with her watching. And if I hit her too, she deserved it."

"Carolyn, this is—" He kept himself from saying crazy. "This is going to get you in prison or worse. Now let's just—"

"You know what, Nick? There's a ledge just down the dropoff there, not far at all, where somebody can hide. Especially someone who comes hours early to spend the night here."

"You—didn't—shoot that man?"

"I hit him with this old pickax I found in here. I didn't want anyone to hear a gunshot. I thought he was you."

His pulse thudded through him. She pointed the gun toward him, but worse, she could step to the mouth of this mine and shoot straight up at Alexis without this SWAT officer to stop her. He couldn't risk that.

"Dr. Arlington said you're better, Carolyn, that she helped you," he said, stalling for time so someone could get down here.

"Oh, she has. To assert myself more, to take my life into my own hands and not hang onto the past—to you. To just let you go. Not to blame myself for failures. That's exactly what I'm doing."

"Put the gun down and let me call the doctor so—"

"No! How long have you been seeing her, Nick, that TV star? Since that time she did the interview years ago—when we were still married?"

"No, I didn't see her after that until just recently. I didn't see anyone else when we were married."

"How noble, you liar. She's always so pretty, so upbeat. You wanted that instead of someone who was suffering, didn't you?"

"That's not true. She's suffered. Carolyn, God knows, I have too."

"Not like me!" she cried, and her voice echoed. That would bring them, wouldn't it?

"Now come over here," she went on, "and just slide down over this ledge where I spent the night. I want to have you there, in the dark, under me. I know that men can be really weak, and I forgive you that, now that I realize my own strength."

"That won't work. There are others like that man out there, and I wouldn't want them to shoot you."

"Then what in hell are they for?" She lifted the gun, straight-armed at him.

"To capture you and get you help."

"Get down there, Nick, before I shoot you here. And I won't miss this time."

"I thought you wanted her to see me shot," he said. He moved closer, peering down into the abyss. Was there a ledge or nothing if he jumped? He kicked a baseball-sized rock down and heard it bounce and bounce into oblivion.

He threw himself low at her in the same moment he heard the bang, and the dim light went out to nothing.

Consciousness came back with a crash—and the sharp sniff of ammonia up his nose.

"Mmm," Nick muttered. "N-no."

His eyes flew open and fixed on Alex, leaning close, holding his hand. The pain in his leg—foot—somewhere shocked him. He squeezed her hand so hard, she winced. "What—happened?"

"You're going to be all right. Dr. Stanhope has stopped the bleeding and brought you to."

The words hardly sank in. Above her head the sky was a shattering blue. He blinked as the brightness bored into his brain. He was outside. In Silver.

Reality slowly sifted back. Bernice hovered too. He could see SWAT team officers; Beth and Dr. Jasmine stood a ways back.

"These men will carry you up to the clinic, and the

emergency squad will be here soon from the city," Hale Stanhope told him. "When the woman shot, the bullet must have ricocheted off the wall and hit your ankle. The men rushed in and got her."

"Got her?" Nick cried. Carolyn. Shot? Dead?

"They collared her," Bernice put in. "Arrested her, that's all."

"How's the officer—in the mine?"

"A concussion," Bernice said, leaning over him to touch his shoulder. "He'll recover. I'm sorry you took a bullet, Nick, but you sure helped us with this, and I won't forget it. Don't talk now. It's all over."

"Over for you too," Nick gritted out to Alexis as they lifted him on a stretcher and carried him past the old graveyard.

Maybe, he thought, trying to hold on to consciousness, he wouldn't be so afraid now. Afraid to really love Alexis. But she was so intent on that baby, the way Carolyn had been on him. Wouldn't she snap if she lost the child…lost that hope and chance, lost…

He stopped fighting the tall rock walls of pain and let them crash down on him again.

12

After Jasmine spoke on the phone to Alexis, she checked her watch. Damn, she was late. "I'll be back in a few minutes, Tom," she told her lab assistant and hurried toward the door.

"You're like clockwork every afternoon," he said, looking up from studying the monitor of what they jokingly called the sperm-speed computer. "I think it's really nice that you and Hale make time for yourselves." He dared to grin smugly. That ticked her off, but then, lately, lots of things did.

"I'll be back in a few minutes," she said and let the door bang shut. He no doubt pictured her and Hale going at it hot and heavy on his desk late every afternoon or even on that hard conference table in his office.

She knocked on Hale's door. As usual, Beth was just leaving, her arms full of charts they must have been going over. Then she realized they were probably working ahead to prepare for Beth's few days away to see her mother in Schenectady. This place would really be in slow-mo without her and Beth for a few days this week. Suddenly the charts in Beth's arms reminded her of something else.

"Just on my way out, Dr. Jasmine," the nurse said with a nod as she stepped past her.

"I've been meaning to talk to you about something," Jasmine told her. Beth turned back, and Jasmine caught her grim look before she hid it. "I pulled a patient's records this morning and saw the double permission forms for egg donation are not both filed. And Alice says you changed the policy? On your own?"

"I didn't change the policy, just the procedure. After Alex asked me about them—and Rita Twohorses asked too—I realized it looked funny."

"Funny?" Jasmine's voice rose.

"I think we should keep the alternate forms in a separate place not to rile the troops, especially since the alternates are usually the yes forms."

"Alex asked—and Rita?"

"Rita asked because that new Pamela Wentworth asked, so that's three. Your policy's one thing, but—"

"The policy to keep both forms in the folder is exactly in case someone does ask. I don't want to appear to be hiding them, because, of course, I'm not."

"Perhaps," Hale cut in, though he was still behind his desk, "we need to review the entire policy."

"If so, perhaps we need to review a lot of things," Jasmine clipped out, frowning at Beth as she closed the office door in her face.

"I know you've been on edge," Hale said, "but let's try to consider the feelings of others and not argue."

"I wasn't arguing, she was, and you sided with her."

"Ah, my Jazz," he said and sighed. "I love you no matter what. And I love how you're always right on time for this Pergonal that drives us both crazy even if you're late for everything else. But how in God's name are you going to keep control of yourself at the conference when you're on this personality poison?" He screwed the top back on his fountain pen and rose from behind his desk.

"I'll handle it. By the way, Alex just called, and they put her through to me since you were supposedly in conference. She says Destin's left tibia was splintered by that bullet, and the E.R. doctor praised you for stopping the bleeding. They're operating right now to put a pin in it. He'll be in a cast and on crutches for weeks, she thinks. I just hope when Sandra Sanchez interviews him, he doesn't bad-mouth us about Silver, after we helped him by letting him 'borrow' it for that fiasco."

"Actually, I was just trying to help Alex. But he won't fight us now that he and Alex are close. You see, she's doing a lot of good for us."

"That's assuming Alex stays close to us too. But I think we can see to that."

"What's that supposed to mean?"

"Beth says you and Alexis have a mutual admiration society, and I think that's good. Frankly, compared to Rita, Alex is a real trouper, just like you, my darling."

She remembered to go back to lock the door. Taking out the syringe and tiny bottle of clear liquid from her jacket pocket, she went to the desk. Frowning in her concentration, she filled the syringe from the bottle of Pergonal, tapping out the air bubbles before she handed the needle to him.

"Here, take this," she prodded when he just stared so hard at the tip of the needle she wasn't sure he was even listening. He took it from her.

She turned her back to him, thinking Tom would really have a fit if he knew she was down here mooning the illustrious Dr. Hale Stanhope every afternoon. She lifted her skirt, slid her panties down almost to her knees and leaned over the edge of his desk, exposing both bare cheeks to him so he could, hopefully, pick an unpricked place. At least he didn't try to get cute with her as he had at first, sliding his hand all over her. For a doctor whose female patients—and some of the staff—were mad about him, he was amazingly obtuse about feminine feelings sometimes.

"Hale!" she said when he didn't approach her right away. "Could we please just get this over with?"

"I'm getting a cotton ball with alcohol," he said as if snapping back to reality.

She wondered what mental mountains he'd been climbing and wished fleetingly that she dared confide in him about her project. But no, it was all hers, just the way these eggs would be.

"Besides, I really do like the view," he told her.

She felt the touch of icy liquid against her buttock. Even that hurt. Her beautiful butt she'd been working on toning was starting to look and feel like a pincushion.

"I just hope," Hale said, putting one hand on her flank to stretch the skin and steady her, "if we can get you a viable zygote and through a pregnancy, you'll be home a bit more often. I have no intention of bringing my child up with a nanny."

"Ouch! Damn!" Jasmine said inadequately as Hale administered the painful, deep-muscle gonadotropin. Twin tears tracked down her cheeks.

"Sorry. I told you to get Beth to do it. She takes care of all injections for me."

"I don't want Beth to do it," she muttered for the tenth time. "I don't want her or anybody else to know about any of our private business."

"You're just the opposite of Alexis," he said as he dabbed the cold ball of cotton to her again and stepped away. "She shares everything to try to help and encourage others."

"That's untrue and unfair. I do my work in private, that's all. She's just more visible and vocal." She tugged up her panties, flopped down her skirt, turned around and glared at him. Suddenly, she really wanted to hurt him. No matter how much hard work she'd done, he'd always gotten the glory, but not anymore. Not after the conference in Miami this week.

"Hale," she said, fighting for control, trying to make her voice silky, not shrill, "I have a confession to make." She sauntered toward him and gently squeezed his upper arms.

"Which is?" he prompted, frowning.

"All this—the shots and my asking you to harvest my eggs—as badly as I've always wanted your child, it's not that I really think we should—or I could—have a baby. I—the truth is, I just couldn't face that kind of defeat again."

"What, then?" he asked, surprised. He didn't look angry at her first admission, but then he didn't want a child either—only clinic ones. His next expression encouraged her: mingled concern and fear.

She bit her lower lip for a moment, hoping she looked and sounded vulnerable and not violent as she felt. "I want my eggs for an experiment I'm doing," she said in her best rendition of a fragile female voice. "To freeze long-term. I don't want to be left out of that part of it—the future."

"Then your secret work—it's that close. I think you'd better explain everything to me."

"I will. I'll need your help. But after I give my paper in Miami. Trust me, darling, just trust me the way I always have you."

That night, her lab work complete until after her trip to Florida, Jasmine shook with excitement. She got on her knees and rolled out the front cryopreservation tanks from under the lab's counter so she could get to her real treasures.

She could not resist staring into her special tank, like some witch over a boiling pot of pure, powerful magic. The cold air danced like steam she stirred with her hand. She almost thought she should have some chant or mantra to say over them—the many eggs she had taken for her experiments no one knew about.

But she snapped back to reality. This would not take long and would provide the money for her to purchase another state-of-the-art cryopreservation tank at the trade show in Miami. Ethnic eggs were a specialty item which could command more money. She wondered how much she'd get for Rita Twohorses', but

Amerind ones were so rare she wanted to keep those for herself.

She retrieved the eggs she'd decided on and packaged them in a tiny plastic six-pack of vials. She printed labels for each, including race, hair, eye color, and profession of the parents. In this case three vials were marked Asian (Chin.), black, brown, and resrch. scientists and the other three Afr.-Am., black, brown, dr. and coll. prof. She filled in the dates of harvest and freezing.

She placed the six-pack in dry ice in a plastic picnic cooler. This trip would be a picnic indeed. She'd be the toast of Miami—and soon the world.

She hurried out into the night.

Alex came back home bone-tired from briefly seeing Nick in recovery after his surgery. Thank God the doctor had said he had every expectation of walking normally again after a recuperation period and physical therapy. Carolyn was under arrest for aggravated assault. When Alex had told Nick, he'd muttered that he'd like to assault her Phoenix psychiatrist.

As exhausted as she was, Alex felt free and safe with Cordova also under arrest. No more watching over her shoulder or peering in the rearview mirror. The police cars didn't have to go by at night, and she'd told Camelot Security to relax, because she could too. She'd just concentrate on this baby, Nick, her job—and trying to help Rita, no matter what her husband said.

She kicked her shoes off and tossed her jacket on the couch. She got some cranberry juice from the fridge.

Above all else, she wanted to see and rock the heirloom cradle.

When the phone rang, she turned back, strode confidently into the study, and hit off the answering machine. No more being afraid of anything, no more worries she was going a little crazy herself.

She picked up the phone on the third ring, expecting it to be Sandra, who would do interviews with Nick and with Alex tomorrow on the SWAT team's stake-out of old Silver. Mike hadn't been half as angry as she'd expected because they had scooped the other two stations with news of it tonight. Since one of his mottos was "If it bleeds, it leads" on the newscast, they were emphasizing that Nick had been stalked and wounded by his ex-wife—and that their own Alexis McCall had been an eyewitness to an earlier attempted shooting. Besides, the tremendous outpouring of interest in the fertility series—including requests from network affiliates to run segments—had greatly improved Mike's outlook lately. Once again she was his fair-haired girl.

"Hello. Alexis McCall."

There was silence, but she could hear the line was open. A click and then noise. At first she could not even tell what the dreadful sound was.

"Waaaa. Waa-aaa!" built to a shrieking pitch.

A baby. Crying, screaming, until it was almost out of breath, gasping for life. It seemed somehow familiar, so close. She pictured the Mei-Lun baby, Jonathan—and then her own faceless, unborn children.

Her pulse pounding, she slammed the phone down.

It rang again, the cries repeated, piercing her heart.

Sapping her strength. Her confidence. But she was angry too: she stabbed her finger at the caller ID button. Her hands shaking, she scribbled the local number down, one she didn't recognize.

"I've got you now," she said when she hung up, but from the frustration and fury of being harassed again, she could have wailed herself.

The third time she did not pick up but heard it slightly muted on the answering machine she had turned back on. She sat in the desk chair, bent over with her arms around her knees, listening. Then she bounced up to copy this caller ID down—a new number—as she strained to listen for other background noise while the screams went on.

She stared at the wall, shaking with anger and frustration. This was worse than the bullet through the front door. This threat—unspoken but not voiceless—invaded even deeper into her house. Her ears, her head. Even her womb.

She pressed her hands to her belly and sat like a statue as the rings and shrieks kept coming.

"That's really sick," Sandra said as she listened to the answering machine tape. "And I think you're right. It could be a recording off the TV of that Mei-Lun baby crying at the Miracle Baby party, played repeatedly. We can get that checked. And none of the ID numbers match. I'll call Bernice for you."

"I wouldn't blame her if *she's* sick and tired of me," Alex said.

"Come on, don't get down, *chica*. I'll go make us

something good to eat. Of course," she said when Alex just shook her head, "I can just check these numbers myself. I've got my sources."

"I know you do, but I can't believe it. I can't face this again. The thing is, I know who it isn't now, so who the hell is it?" she demanded, hugging herself and rocking slightly back and forth.

"At least you're getting out of the house for a couple of days. A change of scenery will look good to you—lots of green grass, real lakes, sand beaches, the blue Atlantic."

Alex just punched Sandra's shoulder. "I told Nick I wouldn't go, but he insisted. He said he'll be medicated anyway, but I hate to leave him now."

"He's going to make a good man for you. He understands how important your work is."

"Don't count your chickens. He's been so badly burned by his first marriage that he's not big on commitment. And I won't accept less."

"If we can't count chickens yet, let's count eggs. That's what I'd like to tell the illustrious Dr. Jasmine in Miami after we scope out the place and hear her talk," Sandra said, fists perched on her ample hips.

Alex slumped at the desk with her head in her hands. "I'm so glad you're going with me. You know, a lot of other careers are starting to look really good lately. Landscaper, dishwasher, baker, candlestick maker…"

"Don't beat yourself up," Sandra said, squeezing her shoulder with one hand. "I'll stay the night, and then we'll go to my house early while I pack. Things will look a lot better in the morning, and Bernice will have these calls traced when we get back."

"Traced to half the viewing population? It could be anybody who hates the infertility exposure. I just thought it was over, Sandra, and now I'm scared to death its only begun."

The woman slumped in the seat of her car after she made the last call from the pay phone near the drugstore. She had originally planned to make them at different exits on the way to the airport, but they might figure that out and she didn't need Gill knowing more than he already did.

It didn't do to underestimate danger of failure, she told herself as she stuffed the minicassette recorder in her purse. That's why she had rehearsed the ultimate the other night. Besides, now that she'd seen what had happened to Carolyn Destin, she'd have to lay more plans. She felt sorry for the poor woman. Someone should help her get out of jail on bond. After this Miami trip she might do just that, if she could find a way to do it anonymously.

She turned into the next side street and pulled up at the now familiar Hacienda Heights apartment complex. She shook her head, amazed at her power: he was waiting for her with suitcase in hand. She unlocked the car doors. He put it in the backseat, then bounded in, bouncing the whole car.

"This is great, just great. So romantic," he said, his face and voice sincere as he leaned over the console to kiss her.

"Save that for later," she said, grateful for an excuse to hold him off for once. "You know we've got to check in early these days, and the Orlando plane leaves before the Miami one I'd rather have us on."

"You think of all the angles, baby. I never met a woman smart as you. It's really exciting to help a security agent protect the clinic's work when competitors are trying to find out your secrets. We're kind of like that old TV show, *Mission Impossible,* where the team just gets in and gets out of places, and no one knows what hits them—and for a real good cause."

"Yeah, it is kind of like that, Gill."

"And, like you promised," he said, putting a heavy hand on her thigh and squeezing it through her slacks, "I got *you.*"

13

"Look at this," Sandra said with a low whistle. "Making babies is big business."

They stopped just inside the entrance of the vast Miami convention center and gaped. "At the clinic," Alex said, shaking her head in amazement, "everything seems so personal and intimate. But this…"

With their press passes she'd managed to finagle pinned on their lapels, they walked the crowded aisles lined with commercial displays of the trade show of the World Fertility Organization. Shiny helium balloons in the shape of sperm and eggs floated over one pharmaceutical booth which promised, WE CAN CONTROL THE FUTURE! Salesmen and women—some of the latter bulbously pregnant—passed out sample ovulation kits, infant-shaped wall magnets, posters and baby calendars, and milk chocolates shaped like thermometers, which Sandra kept eating.

"You can raise your clinic fertility rates sky high," a voice boomed from a TV monitor they passed, which showed a space shuttle blasting off to the sonorous music track from *2001: A Space Odyssey*. It then segued to a scene with an unborn child in its embryonic sac floating out into the universe.

"You sure the initials for this organization aren't UFO instead of WFO?" Sandra joked, but neither of them laughed.

Sales reps handed them prescription pads with corporate logos, a birth-date calculator, and reams of information about how to expand a client list. They kept stuffing everything in sacks from a pharmaceutical firm which promised, SEX-SELECTOR KITS, NOW VALUE PRICED.

They had about an hour to decide what they wanted the cameraman from their station affiliate here to shoot when he arrived. They felt so overwhelmed, they weren't sure. They argued about hooks and slants. Alex thought it would be good to give the international scope of the industry; Sandra wanted to keep the focus only on how this could affect the Evergreen. But Alex won since so many companies based in Europe, Australia, and Hong Kong had booths. And a huge banner draped across the exit doors declared: KEEP IVF AN INTERNATIONAL FREE MARKET BRANCH OF MEDICINE! They walked and stared until their legs felt dead from the concrete floor.

They soon realized that freezing and immunology studies were the two cutting edges of the industry. They talked to several salesmen who had cryopreservation units on display. PRESERVATION TO LAST FOR YEARS—DECADES—ETERNITY! one sign boasted.

"I imagine," Alex said to one tall, energetic sales rep while Sandra questioned another, "the ramifications for long-term freezing is mind-blowing. In other words, if we'd had this sort of thing in the past, we could have offspring of Queen Elizabeth I, Marie Curie, or Susan B. Anthony alive today, whether any of them bore children back then or not."

"You got it," he said, squinting to try to read her name tag in the glare of overhead lights. "But so far it's only sperm freezing that's good real long-term. After a few years embryos don't unfreeze safely. But if we get egg freezing knocked, the talented, bright, and famous women of today could leave their heritage to the future."

"In other words, famous, powerful, and rich women."

"Hey," he said with a grin and a grandiose shrug, "money talks. What's the prize tag on biological immortality? With hardy frozen sperm *and* eggs, the embryos would never risk being frozen but just be freshly implanted."

"But where do scientists and doctors get the eggs to experiment on—to test-freeze and later see if they fertilize, for example?" She raised her voice to ask in the buzz and din around them.

He looked taken aback at what must have been a stupid question. "Obviously, donor eggs." He began to lean around her to pass out literature to others going by. "Eggs aren't embryos yet, and even fertilized ones are just pre-embryos until they implant, if you're worrying about ethics or morality, ah, Ms.—McCall."

"You know," she shot back, flinging out an arm to encompass his display, then the huge room, "with all this, who'd want to worry about a little thing like ethics or morality?"

Sandra hurried over to grab her arm. "Come on, *amiga*," she said and tugged her away. "Let's get out of this *loco* place un *momentito* and talk things over. I think it's getting to you."

"And it isn't to you?"

"Sure, sure, but you know how I feel about doctors in general. You're just realizing what I already know."

"That's not it," Alex protested as they went into a curtained alcove with small tables for snacks and drinks off the main floor. "I'm just awed—and scared—by how much can be done. With all this, it must be easy enough to get two little babies to come safely—namely mine. And your godchildren, if you'll agree."

"What? Really?" Sandra said, beaming.

"I didn't mean to spring it on you here. But I guess I needed to have something real and personal right now. So what do you think? Do you accept?"

"With love and gratitude," she said, giving her a quick hug. Then she sobered and looked down at the floor. Her voice faded. "You know, my mother and sister—they'd want me to have kids, but since I'm not married—"

"Yet..."

"Sure, yet, so I will be happy to spoil your kids rotten," she said, looking back up at Alex. "And they're gonna be bilingual right from the first."

Alex squeezed her hand. Sandra, who their TV competition claimed was hard and cold enough to skate on, wiped a tear from each eye. Alex wondered if it was from joy of being asked to share her children—or her own mention of her mother and sister for the first time since the tragedy.

* * *

"Absolutely unbelievable," Jasmine muttered.

She ducked behind the big display divider for the egg-bank booth. Without saying one word—as tight-mouthed as she had been—Alexis McCall and Sandra Sanchez had turned up at this conference. Were they stalking her as Nick Destin's wife had him? But she shook her head and got control of herself. They could be here for the TV series, but too much was at risk for her to trust that.

Jasmine's stomach sank to her feet when she realized they were reading the bulletin board about the seminars. What if they were here for something more serious— sinister? What if those permission forms or that pain-in-the-ass Indian had gotten them on to her? She'd have to bluff it through—after all, how much could they really know or understand about all this?

"Damn you both," she mouthed. She turned away, heading back into the press of people so they wouldn't see her. She had to do something. She glanced back once to be sure they hadn't seen her. And saw they were greeting some bastard with a TV camera.

After they got the coverage they wanted and inter-views with a few more vendors, Alex and Sandra re-turned to the bulletin board listing symposium doctors and topics. They'd been interrupted before, but now they copied down the time and place for the two talks they wanted to hear. Dr. Nigel Givens-Jones had the keynote speech tonight, entitled, "And Where from Here: Options and Prognostications, Promises and

Problems." They had already phoned and convinced him to give them an interview in the lobby of his hotel after his speech, though he didn't want it taped. Jasmine's so-called paper tomorrow morning was called, "Freezing the Future: The New Women's Liberation."

"I think we're about to learn what Jasmine's been doing with extra eggs," Alex whispered. "Maybe embezzled eggs."

"And then all we have to do is prove it *before* we blast her with a big exposé," Sandra gritted out as they made their way out through the booths and still crowded aisles. "And hope Mike doesn't can or kill us both for the fertility series that promoted her." Their sacks of samples kept bumping together as they walked. They slowed and stepped off to the side.

"I know," Alex admitted, raising her voice over the noise. "It's not just that she maybe took eggs from Rita, me, and others, but that I've put a kind of *Good Housekeeping* seal of approval on the clinic. I've brought people to her, I made it sound so good, especially since I got pregnant, that—"

"Look," Sandra insisted, punching the air between them with her index finger, "we only reported what we knew to be true, and that's exactly what we're going to keep doing. Whatever rich and famous doctors we bring down."

"The other question is," Alex said, staring at a tape of an IVF procedure that was running on a TV screen beside them, "how far would Jasmine go to protect herself if someone started snooping around?"

Sandra glanced at the screen, then stood between it

and Alex. "You mean phone calls to scare you off?" she whispered. "She never knew Cordova got collared, did she? And you said she and Hale kind of laid the groundwork the other day that rival clinics or some disgruntled idiot in the audience could be angry with you. So she'd never figure we'd suspect her for a few anonymous calls."

"Since it was a baby's cries, the message is I might be hurt—or, indirectly, my babies—if I don't cool it," Alex said with a shudder.

"It would make sense that she'd use a baby screaming. Actually, one *she* made scream, if that turns out to be a recording of the Mei-Lun kid. On the other hand, she's helped us with the series and let you tour her precious lab," Sandra admitted, shaking her head.

"But she didn't want to at first. Then she probably realized the financial boon the TV coverage would mean to them—so she could build those new buildings and forge ahead with—with whatever she's doing."

"And Hale?" Sandra challenged. "They *are* partners."

"I still trust him. That lab's her realm, that's clear. Even if he knows what she's doing, he might not know she's stealing eggs to do it—if she is. I—I just don't know. But I've got to find out."

"We will. I've got some ideas for when we get back."

"I think this place is getting to me. Let's get out of here until we have to come back tonight."

That evening they stood in the very back of the crowded room, waiting for Dr. Nigel Givens-Jones to give his speech. They were also keeping an eye on the crowd, watching for Jasmine.

"There she is, second row, just sitting down, yakking to a couple of others," Sandra said. "At least she won't see us way back here."

"From now on we don't take anything for granted or trust anyone except each other," Alex insisted, grabbing her pad and pen from her purse to take notes.

"And that includes Hale?" Sandra asked. "You're not going to go with him to talk to your mother about DES when you get back?"

"I didn't say that," she whispered as the lights dimmed.

When the speaker was introduced with his lengthy string of credentials, they learned that he had been on the staff of the elite English doctors who had helped bring Louise Brown, the world's first "test-tube" baby, into the world in 1978. And last year he had been on Queen Elizabeth's honors list and was now properly addressed as Sir Givens-Jones, or even "my lord." That brought muted, nervous laughter followed by thunderous applause before he even spoke.

Much of his speech, however, went right over their heads with its medical jargon and enough acronyms to make alphabet soup. But they got the bottom line about the financial future of IVF: "Our industry has always been, of necessity, run on the desperation of wealthy individuals, rather than fairly funded by government grants like other branches of mainstream medicine," he declared. "But billions—of pounds, not patients—would be brought in by the discovery of a way to freeze eggs long-term."

Alex scribbled down the rest nearly word for word: "And I predict, my colleagues, that the first victorious battle in this noble—or should I say Nobel prize—struggle will go to some privately funded, almost cloistered individual."

"That's our girl—or she thinks so," Sandra whispered.

"Sh."

"Unfortunately," Givens-Jones went on, "you doctors from the big hospitals with the big reputations are being watched. Watched by patients, colleagues, the media, even moralists—and occasionally—big government, though they haven't yet caught on to the import and impact of all this. You will have a much harder time finding eggs with which to legitimately experiment. But we shall see, indeed, at long last, with success, that government grants—unfortunately with attached, small-minded restrictions—will pour in too."

"Typical doctor's ego," Sandra muttered. "Anyone against them is small-minded."

"And so in closing, I thank you very much indeed for this sunny Florida escape from foggy London town and the opportunity to address you."

They stayed put as applause swelled and ebbed. Alex's exultation came and went too. If Jasmine was guilty of stealing eggs for experiments, why did it have to be in the place that had given her the chance for her child? She could hardly just ask her—or Hale—outright.

Sandra elbowed her. "There she goes with the two others. How about I follow her, maybe try to eavesdrop while you follow up with Givens-Jones?"

"And if she spots you?"

"I'll dart from potted palm to potted palm," she said with a tight grin. "And she's going to see us and that cameraman who's coming back tomorrow to get some of her speech anyway."

"Right. But be careful. It's not just a headline in a local paper or a few new clients Jasmine's angling for if she's into all this. Like Bernice says, desperate people can do desperate things."

"Tell me about it," she said and hurried off into the crowd.

In the heart of the large complex of hotels and golf courses, Alex met with Dr. Givens-Jones in the vast resort hotel a half hour later. Up close the man seemed much healthier and younger than he'd looked on the podium, wiry rather than gaunt with a complexion which glowed ruddy rather than florid. His wire-rimmed glasses magnified his hazel eyes up this close rather than catching the stage lights to make his gaze seem white, blank circles. His nasal voice, however, still leapfrogged in jerks and jumps, as though he'd never gone through puberty.

As she introduced herself and began to question him, she saw he was edgy and distracted. Perhaps, she thought, he was just tired. As darkness fell outside, they sat facing each other in rattan chairs under tropical foliage. She wondered if the foot-weary tourists trooping in and out or the orchestral music floating in from the pillared porch was drawing his attention—or if he was nervous about the path she was taking with her questions.

"Yes, lately research on the possibilities of egg cryo-preservation has been my specialty," he admitted, taking out his billfold and checking inside it for something before he looked back at her.

"I really admired your talk, but I'm afraid some of it was a bit over my head," she said. "Could you tell me in layman's terms what a lab would look like which was engaged in such long-term, experimental egg-preservation research? Would there be, for example, certain instruments or machines which might be visible?"

In the awkward pause, she watched him open his billfold again to take out two slips of paper. "Ms. McCall, if it wouldn't be utterly rude of me, what say we do this interview en route into the park? I've been so bloody busy since I got here, and they gave me these passes, but I've got to catch a jet home tomorrow—if you wouldn't mind. Come along and be my guest, eh?"

She could see she had no choice if she wanted to talk to him. She wished Sandra had come along, but what could happen in an amusement park filled with families and children? And what right did she have to keep this busy, brilliant man from enjoying himself here? Maybe he'd even quit fidgeting like a kid if he wasn't worrying about missing Reelworld.

As he explained about the early days of freezing eggs and embryos, they walked through the thickening dusk to the train station and took the old replica around the large lake to the gates of the theme park. The old man brightened considerably and talked more readily as they strolled toward the center of the park.

"Now, your original question about what an egg-freezing lab would look like," he said, "how does that tie in to your series you described?"

She realized she'd have to lie. She could hardly tell him she was planning on examining and maybe exposing one of his colleagues.

"I'm hoping the final piece of the series can touch on some possible breakthroughs for the future—looking beyond the present fertility frontier, so to speak."

"You do know the woman who runs the lab at the Evergreen clinic you're profiling is at this convention, I assume? I don't know her well, but there's good buzz on her paper to be presented tomorrow, and I'm going to have to miss it," he said, shaking his head regretfully.

"I know Jasmine Stanhope quite well, and she's given me a tour of her lab," she admitted, desperately searching for a way to get him to trust her. "However, I wanted to expand the scope of that narrow focus on one clinic and one American expert—to cite one of the real pioneers, Sir Nigel. Since the fertility industry is international, I know how much weight your name and ideas would carry."

She could tell that calmed and pleased him. As darkness descended, his ruddy face turned even redder in the glow of streetlights and strings of bulbs strung along the storefronts.

"Ah, I see," he said, nodding sagely. "Can't blame you journalists for cross-checking sources or wanting to quote an expert, can I? But I've so little time, as I said..." He walked rather quickly now.

"Please, just a few questions." Alex looked back over her shoulder, trying to keep her bearings straight as they walked farther into the park. Right now they were heading for the noisy, brightly lit High Noon Saloon. That was a good landmark.

"So," she said, looking back at him, "if I talked our viewers through a virtual-reality fertility lab of the future which was working with freezing eggs long-term, what would I see?"

"There are three ways the futuristic research is going today," he explained. He took another turn through the gates of Casablanca, despite the fact everyone else seemed to be streaming out. She took notes but tried to keep her eyes on his face. She stubbed her toe and almost stumbled.

"First," he said, catching her elbow and steering her out of the flow of human traffic, "some are trying to place the unfrozen eggs in a culture with tissue from fallopian tubes to abet strength in freezing. That means the researcher must have access to tissue from Caesarian sections—noncancerous, of course—or young cadavers."

"Oh," she said, so surprised and horrified her pen jumped off the page and she almost stabbed herself with it. Thank God, she thought, rubbing the ink mark off her wrist, Jasmine couldn't be into that, however legal it must be.

Gratefully, she sank onto the bench next to the doctor when he evidently saw she couldn't walk and write at the same time. But he perched on the edge, watching people pass, obviously anxious to be on his way.

"Secondly," he went on as if lecturing by rote, "some researchers are banking on the simple oxygen-induce-ment theory. Low oxygen levels can mean chromosomes tend to scatter, so ways are being sought to simply induce more oxygen to eggs. The arguments are whether to induce the oxygen before or after freezing and how."

"So, there would be oxygen tanks around that kind of lab?" she asked.

"Most likely. And of course, any of these labs would need a good supply of eggs to work with, so that means extra preservation banks—squat little tanks."

"Yes, I've seen those."

He hunched over to prop one bony elbow on his knee. "And thirdly, perhaps the newest hope for long-term freezing, is championed by the dimethyl-sulfoxide believers. I think if you'd ask Dr. Stanhope—if what I heard is correct—that's where she's put all her eggs in one basket." His shoulders shook with silent laughter.

"Could you spell that please, Sir Nigel?" she said, pen poised and entirely serious.

"I won't insult you by spelling basket, my dear. Just write down DMSO and look it up that way. Bottles of it would be stored at room temperature, so it could be sitting out. Or not. Labeled or not. And I really think, so that I don't get my illustrious colleague in trouble on your telly series, you'd best attend her talk—or question her personally about the risks—because they are serious indeed and most controversial for using DMSO."

He sat up straight and slapped his hands on his knees. "If you'll excuse me now, I really must be off. Best of luck with your series—and your IVF babies."

When he stood and nodded a curt, definitive farewell, light reflected in his glasses so it looked as if he glowed from within. Lines of vibrant colors jerked and darted as fireworks exploded in the sky behind them.

"Oh, dear, that means the park's closing soon, so here's your monorail pass back," he said, handing her a ticket. He looked terribly nervous again. "I really just need some time to walk and think after today—so many things. Will you be all right now?"

"Of course, thank you, but I'd like to…" she began, but he gave a limp wave over his shoulder and disappeared, almost at a trot around the corner of a big building toward the gate to Frontier Land.

Alex just stood for a moment, deflated, upset, and annoyed. She scolded herself for doing an uncharacteristically terrible job on an interview, but at least he'd given her a lot of fodder. *Serious, risky, and controversial,* he'd said about experiments with DMSO. But risky how? To whom? And DMSO was another of sonorous-sounding acronyms, one that reminded her of the dreaded DES, though there was obviously no connection.

She shook her head and looked around, trying to get her bearings. Suddenly she felt so alone. She wished Sandra or Nick, even Beth or Hale, were here. As the rides closed down, most of the visitors had drifted out toward the fireworks across the water. Shafts of lights and the illumined spires of Robin Hood's castle stabbed the sable sky over the tops of the other buildings. She jammed her notes in her purse and started out.

But she was terrible at directions—navigationally

impaired, Geoff had always said. She turned right until she saw she'd come up against the now chained and gated entrance to the African Queen with the vast black backdrop of trees and twisting canals. She turned back again, out of the dead end. No one was in sight in this corner of the park.

She walked faster. "Just keep calm, at least for the babies," she whispered to herself. Gripping the strap of her purse tightly, she turned the other way, back toward the distant tinkle of saloon music—she remembered the High Noon Saloon, at least.

But a man—or was it a woman?—stood dead ahead of her.

The tall, thin silhouette that blocked her path wore a blousy shirt, baggy pants, and a huge hat. And a funny mask with a big nose Alex glimpsed when he turned slightly to the side.

She almost relaxed when she saw the figure carried a thick, curved scimitar at his side. *You're in Reelworld, you idiot,* she scolded herself. *And you passed the Reelworld Treasure Island ride a while ago, so what do you expect? Next you'll be terrified of other tourists.*

But then, in the figure's other hand, she saw the smaller silhouette the figure lifted toward her. It glinted. A knife? A gun?

Raw fear energized her. She tore toward the looming building just ahead, careening around the cluster of palms at the corner of the jungle ride. She could hear the person running after her, hear her own gasps for breath, her footsteps. The nightmare of kachinas chasing her leaped at her, grabbed at her, making her feet feel like lead. Yet she vaulted sideways, ran zigzag, waiting for the pain of a bullet tearing into her. But none came, not even a voice. She didn't want to run, to jostle her babies. But she had to get help.

She saw ahead that ride attendants—pirates too, but with scarves tied around their heads, no big hats or masks—were chaining off the stalls for waiting in line under the entry. Yet the boats still moved by on their tracks, swishing through water into the depths of the now black building. She screamed once for help, but she'd never get all the way over to them. The side door looked closer and stood ajar, even if the sign over it said EMERGENCY EXIT ONLY.

Emergency, emergency, she thought as she ran. She could duck in there, come out the front for help.

When she got inside, she wasn't even sure if her pursuer was after her. Had that been a knife or gun? Could it have been something harmless? But he'd chased her. Dear God in heaven, help me. Don't let my babies be hurt.

The wan red reflection of the exit sign inside was the only dim light at first. After the relative brightness outside, it seemed pitch black here. She edged inside as the smell of the place assaulted her: a musky dampness, dust. This was how Nick must have been afraid when he stepped in the mouth of the mine and heard Carolyn's voice. She felt closer to him than ever, wanting, needing him.

When the urge to sneeze hit her, she pressed her index finger under her nose. And then, even over her panicked breathing, she heard someone else shuffle inside.

14

Alex tiptoed farther into the cavernous blackness, then turned back and saw, dimly outlined against the door, the darker form of her pursuer. The fact it was a pirate—maybe just someone who worked here—did nothing to calm her.

She held her breath, though her lungs were bursting. He filled the door and, shuffling slowly, came closer. Arms outstretched, she felt her way along over uneven ground, hearing rushing water nearby, feeling and smelling stale air from the occasional whoosh of an empty pirate's boat as it went mechanically past on the ride.

She bumped into someone who barely budged. She gasped. Her hand touched a standing person—a body. It was cold, dead—oh, damn, one of those alive-looking robots.

She heard and sensed her pursuer coming closer, thought she heard the click of the hammer of the gun as he cocked it. Another boat whooshed by. If she could only get to the next one, in it, wouldn't it take her out to the operators of the ride?

She could see better now, but it was all figures standing, leaning, half lunging, grotesque or lunatic expressions, some with guns, swords, as if she'd wandered into a nightmare waxworks. She'd been on this ride once years ago, but she could not remember one thing about it but the noise of guns and shouts in pirates' attacks. She was going to get in the next boat on the curve here where it slowed down....

Just as she bent over and inched forward, the lights came on, nearly blinding her. Everything began to move. Shouts and bangs. Terrible laughter shrieked around her, coming from speakers, some in the figures. She crouched behind a barrel as a pirate war exploded around her. Puffs of smoke, crackling guns, bigger bangs. Darting a glimpse, she saw, amid the moving, shouting figures the one with the real gun who had maybe thrown the light switch and could shoot her now—

She half rolled into, half sat in, the next boat and huddled facedown in the bottom of it with her arms wrapped protectively around her belly. The booms and blasts of pyrotechnics, recorded screams—she wasn't sure if one was hers.

Praying she hadn't hurt herself, she stay curled up in the bottom of the boat while it rounded the next corner into another scene, this one dark and silent as a tomb.

Then all sound and movement stopped. Lights dimmed as if some giant had snuffed them out. The water hissed, slowed, so the boat barely rocked. She got to her knees to peer over the gunwales into the return of darkness, blinking to make her eyes adjust. But what if her pursuer followed her here? She had to get out now.

She was not near enough to the walkway to just step over, but she could not call for help. Somewhere in the distance she thought she heard normal voices. Even as she edged up slowly to sit on the side of the boat, to balance and reach for dry land, she concentrated on how she felt, terrified for the embryos she carried. Scrapes and bruises on elbows and knees with a stitch in her side from running, but no cramps—hopefully no blood but maybe on her shins. Crablike, panting, she wriggled onto the dry floor, then scrambled up to find her way out.

She went toward the hint of gray ahead, but she still felt that this place clung to her. The two attendants looked as if they'd seen a ghost when she ran out of the ride toward the light, crying, "Call your security guards! A man—a real man—with a gun's chasing me."

"So what did you find out?" Sandra greeted the park security guard who knocked on the door of their hotel room early the next morning.

Alex recognized Jon Pulling, the same man who had taken her story last night. He had also located Sandra and driven them back to the hotel. His plastic pocket liner still sprouted a brace of ballpoint pens, and he tapped one on his knuckles as he talked. Last night it had driven her crazy.

Sandra escorted him in to the small table where Alex sat, forcing herself to eat fruit and toast from room service. She had no appetite for food any more than she did for facing Jasmine this morning. At least, once again after being bounced around, her babies seemed intact and that—that alone—was a good omen.

"Since you claimed there was a gun involved," the stocky, crew-cut man told her when he was seated stiffly across the table, pen tapping away on it, "we called in the Miami police too. Obviously, this is still early in our investigation. But no man with a gun—especially not some masked pirate figure," he added, barely stifling a grin—"has been found or was seen by any staff we interviewed so far. Still, one of our workers closing the Treasure Island ride last night saw and heard you running."

"Just saw *me?*" Alex demanded, standing. She began to pace. "But the pirate I described was not any part of that ride?"

"No, except"—he paused dramatically again—"we do sell tricorn hats, shiny cardboard cutlasses, and big-nosed masks in a park gift shop."

"There, you see?" Alex insisted as much to herself as the hovering Sandra and this damned amused man. "I'm not making this up, after all, am I, Mr. Pulling?"

"No, ma'am. But those outfits are tied to the Hook movie ride—Captain Hook kiddie-type stuff. And there's no bigger-than-life Captain Hook who walks the grounds, only a lifelike one in the Hook ride." He shook his head and smothered another grin while his pen bounced. "So unless he's come to life, we'll have to just keep looking into it."

"I certainly hope you will and that I will get your reports promptly, even back in Albuquerque, since we're leaving later today," Alex said, putting a fist on the table and leaning over him. His pen stopped its nervous patter at last. "Although I agreed for now not to give our affiliate TV station here the story, I'd hate to think that coverage would air later suggesting that somebody's getting their kicks out of terrorizing park visitors and the sharp guards can't do a thing about it. Surely, that would not be good for the family world of this park— or your job."

That wiped the smirk off his face. He left huffy and frowning.

"Here we go again," Alexis said, lying back down on her bed, though they were both already dressed to attend Jasmine's talk. "Why me and why all the time lately? Cordova and Carolyn Destin are locked up, I'm thousands of miles away from Albuquerque, and someone's still threatening me—or intending worse."

"But the pieces of the puzzle don't fit," Sandra protested, going over to finish her doughnut. "I was watching Jasmine yakking to other doctors in the bar at the time you were being chased, so she didn't do it. She doesn't even know we're here."

Alex sat up slowly. "But, taking away the Cordova and Carolyn incidents, there has to be a pattern emerging lately. I found a butcher knife on my counter and knew I hadn't put it there—no more than I turned those kachina dolls around to face the room." She shuddered at the possibility someone could have been in her home. At first she'd accepted that she could have done that, but not now. She'd have to change her keys and the code she used on the alarm. "Someone," she said, "either wants me to think I'm cracking up so what I know is not reliable or to keep me out of commission or away from something."

"And right now it's working, because we're going to be late for our prime suspect's talk if we don't hustle." Sandra put her cup in her saucer with a clink that made Alex jump. "You sure you're up to facing the Queen of the Evergreen this morning? I can go alone."

"No way," she said, getting up. "We're sticking together. Besides, I want to hear what she says because we may have to use it against her. You know, she could have discovered we were here, could have hired someone to scare me, especially if she found out—maybe Dr. Givens-Jones even told her—that I was interviewing him and she knows we'll find out what she's doing. And that reminds me," she murmured, mostly to herself, "when we get back home, I'm going to find out what could be so dangerous about the DMSO she might be using if she doesn't mention it in her talk."

"Come on, let's go *pronto, chica*," Sandra said, clapping her hands. "We gotta meet the camera guy from the station in fifteen minutes."

Alex ran a brush through her hair and pinched color into her cheeks in front of the bedroom mirror. "Just wait until I tell Bernice and Nick that I identified the man pursuing me as Captain Hook from Treasure Island," she told Sandra as they made for the door. "They'll put me in the psychiatric ward like a judge may do to Carolyn."

"You mean Nick Destin drives women crazy? Hey, bad joke, I know. Just don't tell Mike anything until we figure this out." Sandra pushed Alex ahead of her out the door, then had to dart back for the room key.

"Jasmine's missed her calling," Sandra whispered to Alex as they took their seats off to the right side in the front row in the long, narrow conference room where people were gathering for her talk. Jasmine had spotted Alex and Sandra already and, all charm and charisma, had come over to talk to them, "so pleased they were here to cover the breadth of the field—and to hear her call to action for all women." Round one for her, they'd admitted after she returned to the podium. Still, they'd told the cameraman on loan what they wanted— Dr. Jasmine Stanhope's entire speech on audio, even if he took only a short segment on video tape.

"What do you mean, she's missed her calling?" Alex asked, squinting at where Sandra pointed on her program. "Because she looks so fabulous, she could bump Sharon Stone or Madonna out of their jobs?"

"She may be one hell of an actress, but I'm talking evangelist. Or maybe she should have been head of the ERA movement that fizzled. She'd have gotten that amendment through Congress," she said, pointing to the name of Jasmine's topic, 'Freezing the Future: The New Women's Liberation.' I bet when she's done with us this morning, we'll be ready to burn our bras."

"Hey, don't knock it," Alex protested, ever aware how Sandra thought all doctors were arrogant egomaniacs. "Not until we've heard her."

But Sandra was right. As the talk progressed, Jasmine made Alex want to jump up on her chair and wave a banner. Sperm cryopreservation was way ahead of that for eggs, Jasmine claimed, because the interest and income, as in American medicine in general, had been skewed toward male diseases. Her speech briefly included observations on the three major experimental techniques to freeze eggs, including, briefly DMSO.

Alex scribbled down every word, since Dr. Givens-Jones had mentioned using it could be risky: "Before they are frozen, if eggs are treated with dimethyl sulfoxide, it will help protect the cellular membrane." That sounded nothing but good to Alexis. Jasmine didn't mention any dangers with DMSO, or how close she was to a breakthrough if she was using it. She was obviously more focused on arousing interest in funding—and breaking through sexist barricades.

Alex even thought her navy blue and red fitted suit looked like a battlefield banner. Surely, such petty things as harassment of a TV anchorwoman would be far beneath this brave, brilliant woman's concern. But then, maybe that's just why she could act with impunity, looking down on all lesser beings.

"But now, standing on the brink of fertility equality for women, I make a plea to our long male-dominated industry to prepare to fund anyone who can bring equity to cryopreservation of eggs.

"And," she went on in ringing tones, "I would challenge my many illustrious male colleagues, who are thinking sperm—perhaps even *their* sperm—will be immortalized by fertilizing future female eggs, to think of it this way. Unless you are the Jonas Salk or the President Clinton or the Prince Charles of this generation, will women of the future want their fresh ova to be mated to yours?"

Smothered laughter greeted her examples of this particular president and prince, but Alex saw Jasmine's eyes gleam as she plunged on. "You need to reward royally and support wholeheartedly anyone who can preserve the ova of the women of your era, the women you know and love—and admire. And that means our entire industry must herald the breakthrough Dr. Nigel Givens-Jones mentioned yesterday. It must come at any cost, any sacrifice—and soon," she concluded to surprised silence, then sporadic applause.

Despite her dislike of the woman, Alex was awed at the fervor of the messenger and the message. She grabbed Sandra's arm and pulled her back in her seat when she tried to rise to ask the question they'd discussed about the legality and morality of finding egg donors.

"What?" Sandra squawked. "*Madre de Dios*, she hasn't converted you?"

"No, but why challenge her on this? It will totally tip her off. Besides, she answered that question already— she'd do *anything* to succeed. It's her cause, her mission. Fanatics are always doubly dangerous and deceptive. So we're going to have to get as sneaky as she is," she whispered, "maybe get inside that lab without her knowledge."

"Oh, thank God," Sandra said, flopping her hands in her lap. "I thought for a minute I'd lost you."

"No way. She didn't exactly say ends justify the means, but that's what she believes. She's setting herself up for fame and fortune, and if she's stealing clinic eggs no matter how grand the cause, we've got to stop her."

The minute Alex got to work the next morning, she went to Sandra's desk in the newsroom to borrow her thick book *The Physician's Desk Reference,* commonly called the PDR. Ironic, Alex thought as she opened it to the D's that Sandra, as KALB's medical editor, distrusted and detested doctors. Yet her reporter instincts had kept her fairly objective in this witch-hunt so far. Alex only prayed that, with all she had personally at stake at the clinic, she could keep unbiased too. She sat in Sandra's chair and shoved her morning sack of her favorite *empanadas* out of the way.

"Find anything there?" Sandra asked as she came back with a cup of coffee to lean over her. "We can go back online again. Or maybe somebody will answer one of our SOS e-mails we sent out."

They had been up half the night searching web sites about government regulations of fertility clinics and reproductive rights laws. And they had left queries about DMSO with several local doctors and scientists Sandra had interviewed on her medical segments.

Alex shook her head. "Some of that online medical information is so arcane. I just thought this might help—that we'd better go to the keep-it-simple-stupid tactic."

"That's the way this medical gobbledygook usually makes me feel," Sandra muttered, leaning now on the edge of her desk and reaching for an *empanada.* A piece of the flaky, fried dough and a few raisins fell on the open book, and she hurried to brush them away. Alex was so focused, she ignored it.

"'DMSO is a clear, odorless chemical,'" she began to read, running her fingernail along the lines of tight, small print. To speed things up, she began to paraphrase. "Some claim it can treat arthritis, sprains, bruises, skin infections, burns, and general wounds."

"In short, a magic cure-all," Sandra muttered.

"No, whether or not it works for all that is highly controversial," she explained, frowning and skimming. "The only thing that has been proved and approved by the FDA is it helps cure cystitis in the bladder."

"You're kidding. So the more they've worked with it, the worse the side effects or something."

"Maybe. Get this. It's evidently so powerful it can be simply absorbed through skin and muscle. And its use can give off a garlic-like odor from the breath and skin. Warning—here it is! Do not use if pregnant, as it may cause birth defects. Oh, no. Oh, no. She's soaking egg membranes she's going to freeze in it, but those will be fertilized and become babies. What if not only a pregnant woman using DMSO—but also her eggs soaked in it—will cause freaks years later when they're unfrozen and used?"

"Madre de Di—" Sandra said with her mouth half full, then began to choke so Alex had to jump up to pound her back. Others in the newsroom looked up, then returned to work. "Don't you remember," Sandra whispered, her eyes still watering, "she smelled like garlic when she spoke to us before her talk?"

"But surely she's not pregnant or doesn't plan to use her own eggs. Let's not get totally paranoid. Maybe she had an Italian meal the night before and the garlic smell lingered. Or if DMSO is absorbed through the skin, despite those latex lab gloves she wears, maybe she got some of it on her wrist or something."

"If you're not still admiring that talk of hers, you're at least scared to believe the worst, aren't you? I can understand that but—look!" Sandra interrupted herself so loudly that Alex jumped and scanned the room for something wrong. But Sandra's gaze was riveted to her computer screen. "More messages on my e-mail than the ones we've checked—let me scan them," she said, switching places with Alex so she could use her keyboard while Alex hovered. "Here's one about DMSO," Sandra cried triumphantly. "But—from a vet?"

The message was posted by a woman veterinarian at Ohio State University in Columbus, Ohio, whom they didn't know and had never heard of. She had evidently been queried by one of the doctors they'd e-mailed last night. They stared at the bright blue screen silently until Alex began to read aloud again.

"There is much disagreement in the veterinary research community—some studies show DMSO causes birth defects in mammals, others claim it inconclusive. However, no studies of pregnant women have been done, and until then it must be assumed there would be a potential risk to the fetus. If DMSO was used to help freeze human eggs—before each egg becomes a fetus— we cannot possibly predict future results without experimenting on many eggs."

"That's exactly what she's doing, even if she ends up with hundreds of freak births years after," Alex declared, smacking her hand on the desk. "And we had to have a vet tell us because she's pushing the limits for humans, skirting what's legal and moral and planning to get away with it, damn her."

"And with eggs she's stolen," Sandra muttered, "including maybe Rita's, Jing's, and yours."

A shudder shook Alex. "If the illustrious Dr. Jasmine is taking big risks, I've got to too. I'm getting in her lab if I have to march—or sneak—through hell to do it."

"Did you find out Jasmine's and Tom Anders's lab schedules?" Sandra asked Alex the moment they walked away from the clinic that afternoon. They'd finished their last interviews of staff members, and Jerry had already left with his camera equipment. Now Alex was anxious to pick up Nick at the hospital and drive him home to Santa Fe.

"Not a schedule we can trust," Alex told her. "The chart in the nurses' office I checked when I knew Beth wasn't there is probably only reliable for nurses. It's obvious Jasmine practically lives here lately, and after being away for a couple of days, it will probably get worse. And you know how it is when you come back from conventions with colleagues. The competition, got-to-get-to-work bug bites worse than ever."

"I might try to get in through the cleaning agency people," Sandra muttered as if she weren't listening. "But then, if I ask for time off, we'd have to tell Mike what we're up to before we even know if—"

"Alexis!" a voice called. Squinting back into the sun, she turned around to see Dr. Prettyman gesturing wildly to her. "Rita's inside very upset, and I thought you could help us reason with her."

"Did you see Rita anywhere in the clinic today?" Alex asked Sandra as they turned around and hurried back.

"No. But since you said she was suddenly standing over you when you came out of the anesthesia that time, maybe we'd better consult her about how to sneak in there. She's starting to remind me of those Indian skin walkers."

"That's Navajo, not Pueblo," Alex corrected, so concerned about Rita it took her a second to realize Sandra was kidding.

Rita was in the foyer, determinedly removing her storyteller figurines from the first of four lighted *nichos* where they were displayed. From the looks of everyone—Beth, Peter, Jasmine and the Prettyman sisters—poised like vultures around her, Alex surmised they would have jumped her again if they weren't fearful of breaking the pottery.

"No eggs fertilized, no IVF transfer, our deal is over," Rita's voice rang out. "The clinic owes me some of these back."

"If you will just wait a moment, Rita," Dr. Prettyman said in her best soothing voice, "when Dr. Stanhope's free, you can talk to him."

"I'm done talking," Rita declared with a shake of her head that rattled her hair beads. "Except maybe to the authorities or the media—someone sympathetic, someone I can trust," she added sarcastically when she saw Alex approach.

"Could I talk with you privately, Rita?" she asked.

"Why? So you can convince me to let them off again? I thought I could trust you, I really did. Even shared my curing ceremony with you, and all I have left now is this."

From the cardboard box where she'd been placing her statues, she pulled out a crude, foot-and-a-half kachina doll. Alex jumped back when she saw it, bumping into Sandra, who grunted. Rita thrust it on the now cleared *nicho* and closed the glass door with a bang. Alex was surprised it didn't shatter.

"Want a little background information about that kachina for the next TV segment, Alex?" Rita asked, her voice goading. "Pueblo women, if they desire children, sometimes carry around a kachina baby for good luck. Like real people, kachina can be bad or good, bring blessings or curses. And," she said, whirling to face them all, hands on her hips, "I'd just like to curse every last one of you. You've all turned to dark colors, every one—"

Before Peter could lunge, Alex elbowed him out of the way. She took Rita's arm while Sandra blocked Jasmine and took hold of the distraught woman too. Nodding the others out of the way, they took her down the hall and out the back door into the bright sunlight. Fortunately, the area was deserted. Of her own accord, Rita collapsed into the closest rocking chair.

"My period started," she blurted out, slumped over. Sandra looked shocked at Alex and mouthed,

"PMS?" But Alex understood the catastrophic impact of starting menstruation when desperate hopes ran high.

"I'm so sorry, Rita. I do understand," she said quietly, leaning over her to place a hand gently on her shoulder.

"I don't believe in all that kachina and tribal curing stuff anyway," she said with a sniff. "But I did it for Paul. And now I'm worse off than ever." She propped her elbows on her knees and leaned her head in her hands. "I'd just like to die."

Alex's wide eyes met Sandra's. Without speaking they decided what they had to do.

"Rita, listen to me," Alex said and knelt beside her chair. "Sandra and I are working hard not only to publicize IVF but to check into it too—and the people here who participate in it. I told you that once before, and I meant it," she insisted when the woman looked up and slowly, hopelessly shook her head. Tears trembled on the ends of her sable lashes, but didn't fall.

"We're hoping we can trust you to keep this a secret, Rita," Sandra put in. "You have to, or you'll blow everything to kingdom come."

"I'm listening," she said wearily, leaning back in the chair.

"Please realize you are not alone," Alex pleaded. "That you're not the only one frustrated and angry. You mentioned Pamela Wentworth, and I've interviewed another former patient who is very upset and believes something is wrong about egg donation here. Sandra and I spent last evening at the university law library and talking to legal experts on-line to see what we can do about—this situation."

"Can you get Dr. Jasmine arrested?" she said, looking from one of them to the other.

"We don't know," Alex admitted. "Now, just a minute—listen to the rest before you glare at us that way. The ultimate insult is that fertility clinics are not government regulated. A 1992 federal law supposedly went into effect just this year to mandate publishing and policing clinic data, but it hasn't been carried out yet for lack of funds."

"It figures," Rita muttered, but she sat up straighter. "What else?"

"Criminal law," Sandra explained with an approving nod from Alex, "hasn't quite caught up with medical progress either."

"In other words," Alex went on, "stealing eggs is not even medical malpractice, let alone theft. American laws are on the books against stealing eggs and embryos from cows and horses, but not from humans."

"What?" she cried, bounding up, just as Alex and Sandra had done when they discovered this. Rita reeled off a string of words neither of them could translate, though they got her meaning well enough. They only hoped her knowing they were pursuing this helped to stem her desperation so it didn't eat her alive.

"The only good thing in this whole mess," Nick told Alex as she helped him into his apartment across the courtyard from his shop, "is getting you into my bedroom."

But he was exhausted from their drive back to Santa Fe. Paler, thinner, he'd had to sit in the backseat to keep his leg up. She saw him grimace as she helped him ease himself to a sitting position on his double bed. Alex took his crutches and leaned them against the wall next to the big, carved headboard. This room as well as the kitchen, dining, and living area were done in old mission-style furniture with bright splashes of art and color. She was relieved to see no kachinas here, but instead the popular carved and primitive wooden saints called *santos*.

Trying not to look around so curiously, she concentrated on carefully lifting his leg in the knee-to-foot cast on the terra-cotta-colored bedspread.

"Right, you really look ready for romance," she responded to his teasing, scolding herself for blushing at his lame comment when he looked so whipped.

He seized her wrist, his big hand like a thick, warm bracelet. His strength surprised her. "Try me," he said. "It could be just what the doctored ordered."

"Ni-i-ick," she protested feebly, then gave in to the tension he created in her by leaning closer. She intended to give him a quick peck, then get him his pain pill and some water and be on her way. But he quickly deepened the kiss and she responded fervently. She wanted to cling to him, to be crushed to him, to feel safe. But she felt more, much more. The avalanche of sensation scared her. Her life was already careening out of control in every other way.

"Nick, Nick," she said breathlessly when his kiss and one-handed caress of her hair and shoulder lightened for a moment. "Do you think we'll ever be able to really build something together when this is over?"

His dark eyes widened. She could see her face reflected in his coffee-dark pupils. He was scared too. And she couldn't help him when she was struggling to save herself. She wished she could tell him what Jasmine might be doing and what she had to do in return. "From now on," she said, tossing her hand and pulling slightly back, "I'm demanding a happy ending, or else."

"Sometimes," he whispered, looking out a window drenched with late afternoon sun, "that doesn't work. But you know that." He shook his head slowly, sadly.

It was then Alex wished she didn't have that sixth sense about people when she interviewed them, questioned them—that feeling she could read their motives or agendas. He didn't believe she would have a happy ending—have these babies. And if that was the way he felt, even if she maybe owed him for taking a bullet for her, she would not let this or him go any further.

"I'll go get your medicine," she said, starting away. "And then I've got to head back. Dr. Stanhope and I are driving here tomorrow to face my mother. She's never really believed I could have a child, so we've been estranged...."

Her voice broke as she went into the other living room and headed for the kitchen. "Alexis, come back here for a minute," he called to her. "Alexis!"

As she found cold water in his fridge, she blessed the knock on the kitchen door. The old neighbor woman who was going to keep house and fix meals for him must be here. She'd just send her in with his medicine.

"Alexis!" she heard him yell again when evidently he saw Rosa.

"I've got to run, Nick," she called. "I'll be—in touch." Quickly, determinedly, she let herself out the door.

15

"If you are a DES daughter, you're a rare specimen these days," Hale told her as they drove into Santa Fe late the next afternoon. He drove a jade Jaguar sports model, slung low to the ground. Sandra would have a fit about doctors' egos again when Alex told her that. Ahead of them the Sangre de Cristo mountains turned crimson in the sinking sun. Alex wondered how Nick was today. Last night she had let his phone calls go onto her machine and hadn't called back yet.

She had been so sleepy on this ride she had almost dozed off, much to her embarrassment with Hale driving and talking. Though, as far as she was concerned, he was not in any way a suspect in any underhanded doings at the Evergreen, she knew she should have been listening to every word he said. She and Sandra had been pulling out all stops to find out everything they could about the entire clinic staff.

"I don't blame you a bit for being sleepy," he said and reached over to pat her arm. "First of all, you're pregnant, so I'd expect you to be tired."

She couldn't help herself; she beamed at him.

"And secondly, you said you made the same trip yesterday to bring Nick back here. How's he doing?"

"He keeps saying he's going to look more like lame Chester on the old reruns of *Gunsmoke* instead of Marshal Dillon. He's been a real western fan for years."

"But how's he doing? I guess a tough guy like him will walk well enough again if it takes him hard months of p.t."

"I'll tell him you said that. I love the way you're always so upbeat. I hope my mother thinks so too and realizes we are not accusing her of anything." She looked at the road ahead. "She never believes that of me."

"If I hear her say your fertility problems are your fault, I'll set her straight."

Alex managed a rueful smile. "Turn at the next light," she said and put her hands across her belly, as if she could protect the baby—or herself—from the mere presence of her mother.

Inside Marian Spencer's apartment, at first things went about as badly as last time, from her stilted greeting of Alex to her fussing over drinks and snacks. Alex watched Hale put the older woman at ease, even charm her, and wondered if she had let him do the same thing to her when he should be a suspect too. After all, he was Jasmine's boss and husband.

"I must explain to you, Mrs. Spencer," Hale said, sitting slightly forward in his padded wicker chair on the patio, "that although I don't want to criticize any of my colleagues, some doctors have misled their patients. And I came along today because I knew Alex probably just asked you previously about DES when that's also very misleading."

"How so, Doctor?" she asked, passing him a plate of crackers and cheese. Alex breathed a sigh of relief that at least her mother was still listening.

"I realize there's so much mumbo-jumbo in medicine about terms, names of medicines and the like," he said, his voice so assuring, his smile so warm. "Here," he said, reaching in the interior pocket of his hunter green sports coat, "sometimes I can't even remember all of the names. Do you mind if I just read you the list of other names for DES—a final check, and then I won't bring it up again and neither will Alexis. The thing is, though, if we could just know if she's DES, it could actually help me save the baby's life."

"Well, all right," she said, repeatedly smoothing a purple paper napkin over her knee. "But it's all so hypothetical—the idea of her getting pregnant again at this age after she lost—well, the other two long before they were born."

Tears Alex thought she was far past stung her eyes again. Her mother should have been the first person she told about this pregnancy, and she hadn't even called her. Suddenly, whatever rebuff or cruelty she met here, she had to say it, to share it. Hale was looking at her expectantly.

"It's not hypothetical, Mother, thanks to Hale and— the clinic staff. I'm pregnant and determined to do anything I can to carry my one or two babies to term—and love them as you have tried to love me."

Her mother clasped her hands together between her breasts. "You are? Pregnant? And Geoff so long gone?"

Alex stood. So it was going to be that now. She couldn't bear it. Let Hale talk to her. But as she turned away, her mother got up too and touched her arm and raised her hands toward her shoulders.

They hugged tightly, both crying, and Alex never noticed until later that Hale had tiptoed inside to give them time alone.

Later, as Alex and Marian sat side by side, holding hands on the couch, Hale slowly read through the brand and generic names of DES, the drug formally known as Diethylstilbestrol.

Alex felt her mother's hand stiffen and begin to tremble. By the time he finished the list, her body shook the patterned silk of her pastel caftan.

"I'm so sorry we haven't been together, Lexi, so sorry we argued," she said, suddenly ignoring Hale. "So sorry, but—it was hard for me. If you thought I blamed you, I had to because I couldn't blame him."

"Who? Your doctor back then?" Alex asked and felt a shiver slide over her skin.

Marian pulled back and wiped under her eyes with both hands. What was left of her mascara blurred and ran. "It was because I was afraid…"

"Afraid of what, mother? Please tell me."

"It was really his fault," she said vehemently, her words muffled behind a handkerchief she produced from one voluminous sleeve.

Alex leaned closer. Hale sat up straighter. But they both let the older woman cry. Then words poured from her, brokenly, but finally making sense while Alex sat frozen in the warmth of the late afternoon sun and Hale sat watching in shadow.

"Your father didn't want another mouth to feed. That's exactly how he said it—mouth to feed—as if you were just mouths, devourers, not giving anything back like smiles and love. I know airplane mechanics didn't make much, and he worked hard. But he blamed me when I told him to be careful so soon after Sarah came along, when we were in bed, you know what I mean. At least there was never any question that I would—I would carry you to term. But, Lexi, I could never, never tell you that your own father turned against me and didn't want you!"

Alex sat stunned. She'd adored her father and blamed her mother. But she did not allow herself to react to that blow, because she wanted her to go on. Out of the corner of her eye she could see Hale was nodding to encourage her.

"It's not your fault," Alex whispered, and that was enough to unleash the final torrent.

"I got very ill," Marian said, her words coming quick and quiet as she twisted her handkerchief. "Even with the other kids to care for, I kept to my bed. He had to care for his children then, oh yes. Maybe he even learned to love them some. And the doctor was so very kind, so understanding. He said he had a wonder drug, a miracle pill to make me feel better, and I believed him. And it helped me—helped me then. It's that first one you read, Dr. Stanhope," she said, finally looking at him. "The one called Meprane."

"Oh, Mother," Alex cried, scooting closer to hug her

again. "Knowing this will help, really it will!" She felt betrayed by both parents—but somehow deeply relieved. Hale would know what to do now. He could consult with her ob-gyn and help protect her pregnancy. And she could work not only on being a mother but on having one again.

Alex could tell Hale felt triumphant on the way back, but she didn't.

"I'm really scared now, Hale. Everything's stacked against this pregnancy turning out successfully, worse than the others, so don't tell me it isn't."

"Not everything. You have me. And I have a very good trick up my medical sleeve, if you'll just trust me."

"Which is?" she asked, turning slightly toward him in the confines of her seat belt.

"You see, as the fetus develops—though if you end up carrying two, it will be harder—the womb and uterus are, of course, stretched, even in a normal patient," he explained, gesturing with one hand as he drove. "But most DES daughters have weakened wombs which need special strengthening—a rather clever but very rare suturing procedure I can do—to keep the growing fetus from miscarrying. Just some light anesthesia for you. It's that simple."

"You can do that for me?"

"Of course, but the timing's important too. I don't want to do it before two months or so—unless, and here's the caveat, you do something to bounce them loose early, so to speak, start to cramp or spot. But to replay one of my earlier lectures, if you get enough rest and don't work too hard, I'll bet we'll make it. You'll be my first DES daughter here, so don't let some run-of-the-mill E.R. room doctor or even your ob-gyn man—"

"My doctor's a woman—"

"—woman do it without me at least there to consult. I helped with several cases of this when DES was more common in the East. I swear," he said with a little snorted laugh, "your mother must have had some quack of a doctor out there in the boondocks." He shook his head, his voice derisive. "Some old coot way past his prime and the times handing out dated, dangerous drugs."

The sudden shift in his earlier caring tone slapped her. A scratch just beneath Hale's smooth veneer revealed the arrogance that tainted Jasmine. Again, she agonized over whether he could be hiding something else. But she needed him more than ever now. And if she and Sandra exposed or ruined Jasmine, what would happen to his miracle suturing for her then?

Sandra felt like a criminal, sneaking around the clinic after dark. Not that she hadn't done a few questionably marginal things to get a story before, but this was really getting to be cloak-and-dagger. Dressed all in black, she shuffled through the dry carpet of pine needles, waiting for her contact to show in the back door of the clinic. She paced slowly, popping chocolate mocha drops in her mouth from time to time.

She squinted up at the sickle of pale moon, then down at the greenish cast the clinic windows emanated at night—her perfect childhood picture of a haunted house. "Might as well be Halloween," she grumbled. "Let's get those ghosts up from the ghost town and the skeletons out of the closet."

She just had to get the chance to look around inside. She only hoped the woman she'd talked to at the cleaning company needed two hundred bucks badly enough. But however she or Alex got in, it had to be soon since Beth had let it slip that a motion-sensor security system was being installed around the circumference of the building next week.

As exhausted as Alex without the excuse for it, Sandra finally sat down on the ground with her back to a tree. She just hoped things had worked out for Alex and Hale in Santa Fe facing down that witch of a mother of hers.

But Sandra smiled just thinking about Alexis's pregnancy and the chance she'd have a godchild or two to spoil. However attracted Sandra felt to Mike Montgomery—a secret she would take to her grave before she'd tell anyone, especially him—she was afraid she'd never marry, never have kids of her own this late in life.

Suddenly, though it was a warm night, she felt chilled. She walked faster, recalling that time Mike had held her tight when she'd come back to work after her mama and Carla had died. He was enough shorter that he could almost rest his head under her chin, but she'd tipped her head, bent her knees, and curled into him so it wasn't so noticeable.

She'd even taken to studying how Princess Diana was skilled at looking shorter than she was, back when she still tried to kowtow to Prince Charles. Not that

Sandra Maria Theresa Sanchez was one to bow her head to a man, any man, like Mama had. And she remembered that Jill Eikenberry on *L.A. LAW* was taller than her husband, Michael Tucker, and they seemed happy enough, both on-screen and off. She wondered if Napoleon had been a lot shorter than Josephine, or was that another reason—besides the lack of an heir— he'd divorced her.

And she worried too that Mike would think she was too plump, but some men liked a little meat on a girl's bones. Her mama and Carla had both been shapely. But now she could only cherish Mike's single, sweet embrace. She supposed their difference in height, maybe in size, would be enough to keep a proud man like her little Napoleon from so much as thinking of her as a possibility for him. It would never work anyway, since he'd been her boss, one she'd argued with and criticized. Still, sometimes when he glared at her and she talked back to him, she sensed that electrical jolt of feeling from his eyes so intense—

The back door of the clinic opened to throw a pale rectangle of light onto the portico. Sandra got up and hid behind the tree. The cleaning woman trudged out toward the parking lot without the high sign she'd arranged so that Sandra could dart inside. Then, before the door completely closed, she heard a voice—Jasmine's. The woman was practically living here. And that meant it was Alex who would have a better chance to somehow sneak into the clinic.

Nick leaned away from the dinner table and slumped on one elbow into the thick window alcove of his apartment to watch four young boys play a noisy, ragtag game of soccer in the small, empty parking lot behind the row of shops. Their young brown bodies looked so strong, their voices sounded so exuberant and carefree.

"You not eating Rosa's *comida, Señor Nick,*"—she always pronounced it "Neek"—the old woman said, interrupting his thoughts, bustling back into the room. "I make for you *carne adovada and sopapillos,* some of your favorites, *sí.* That broken bone not keeping you from eating. It that TV woman, I think, and she not even here, not even on the air right now."

Rosa stood over him like a mother, arms crossed over her full breasts, glaring at the food still on his plate. Though he had hired her to keep the shop and apartment clean, sometimes she made him feel like a kid.

"It's delicious, Rosa, *es verdad.* And I'm going to eat it all. I've just been watching the boys outside and thinking, that's all."

"Humph! You better eat. I not planning to spoon-feed you when I take this job."

"And I'll clean up after myself. You go on home now, and I'll be fine," he urged her with a forced smile.

Shaking her head, Rosa banged around in his small kitchen some more, then sang out, *"Hasta la vista y vaya con Dios, Señor Nick,"* before she let herself out the door.

He sighed and shoved his plate away. "Hell, Destin," he muttered to himself, "broken bone, broken marriage—but no more damn broken heart. You're not going through all that again, no way, so cut your losses and get out now."

He jammed his fists under his chin. He wanted Alex but so what? Too complicated, too risky. He'd been trying to phone her, but no more. Let her hasty exit be the end for them. It had to stop now before either of them got hurt—more than she was already going to.

He sat as sunset dimmed his world, seeing her face, thinking of the child she might never have, maybe a son, loud and alive like those kids, bouncing that ball after dark like the beating of his heart.

Alex was surprised to glimpse the Camelot Securities van coming out of her street when she and Hale turned down it, but then why should she be? Though she had told them earlier they did not need to drive by anymore, she was hardly the only customer they had to service in this area. But it did remind her she needed to change her keys and the alarm code.

She thanked Hale again, and he waited until she got safely in and punched in the code to disarm her alarm. She waved to him before she closed the door and punched in the code to rearm it once again. And then she went back and changed the code—from the date of her and Geoff's anniversary she'd used so long to the numbers of the date she had found out she was pregnant. She felt better now. And she'd call a locksmith tomorrow.

She drank some milk, mentally sending it to her babies Soon she'd have an ultrasound to see, as Hale said, if both were hanging on or just one. She wanted both, but she could read between the lines of what he'd said today. As high as the odds were against a normal pregnancy, she'd be better off trying to carry one than two, especially with the suturing procedure acting like a safety net for the fetus.

Turning off the lights in the kitchen, she went upstairs. She smiled at herself in the bathroom mirror more than once as she removed her makeup. She and her mother had a chance to build a better relationship now. And she'd had the beginnings of one with Nick, before she'd run from her fears and his. But she'd call him soon. She'd let Sandra sleep for once, because she'd see her first thing tomorrow.

As she took a shower, she struggled to clean everything bad from her mind. She too needed a good night's sleep. She had to take care of herself and this pregnancy above all else.

She got into bed in her shortie silk nightgown and stretched luxuriously between the cool sheets. Then she decided to set her alarm on her bedside clock a bit earlier. It was when she reached over to turn off her table lamp that her eyes went to the heirloom cradle on the floor. The ruffled towel she'd tucked in was bright red with scarlet blotches which also splattered the beige carpet. And a long butcher knife protruded from the chest of the ugly kachina doll staring up at her from the cradle.

16

"I can't believe you insist on doing this tonight after that scare you had last night," Sandra said. Her empty candy bar wrapper crinkled loudly as she wadded it up and jammed it in her purse.

On the access road near the clinic, Alex pulled the car off into a thicket of trees, then maneuvered to turn around so they'd be heading out in case they needed to make a fast getaway. That's why she hadn't let slowpoke Sandra drive. She turned off the engine; she'd been driving without lights since they pulled off the Turquoise Trail.

"It's partly *because* of that scare," Alex explained, giving the ignition keys to her for safekeeping. "I can't live under a hanging sword like that, and we've got to stop someone that horrible. And I won't have my baby threatened further by threats to me."

"I still say since it was a kachina and real blood in that cradle, you have to consider Rita now. She could be jealous of your pregnancy, and she was furious at you last time we saw her."

"Not once we talked to her. Whoever came and went at my house is the same coward who fooled with the kachinas and left that knife out on the counter before. As soon as Bernice checks for fingerprints—and the blood type—we'll know more," she said determinedly, but she could tell Sandra knew her bravado was an act.

"Right. Anyhow, my money's still on Jasmine."

"She obviously has more access to blood than Rita. And I've mentioned the kachinas at the clinic, so that's not something just Rita knows. Actually, if she went home last night and told Paul we'd given her hope again, I wouldn't be surprised if he was angry enough to do something. He told me to steer clear of her, and Rita once told me he has a temper if she trusts Anglos too much."

"I just had another awful thought," Sandra said, leaning forward to stuff her purse under her seat as Alex had done. "Bernice is back there busting her buns to help find out who's breaking in your house, and we're here doing this. Mike and Nick are not the only ones who would string us up if we get caught."

"Do you see another way?" Alex demanded, turning in her seat to face Sandra. "Do you want to go back?"

"No way. We're in this together, and it has to be done."

"I'm grateful you're moving in with me for a while," Alex said, "even though I got the keys changed and the security system checked again today." They spoke more quietly now as they got out into the breezy darkness.

"One more thing happens and we're going to my

place," Sandra whispered, "however cramped it is compared to yours."

"That's a deal. And speaking of deals," she said as they made their way through the whispering, shifting pines toward the lighted clinic, "you did promise me several times that you'd wait for me outside and not try something overly brave if it takes me a while inside?"

"Sure, *bueno*. The plan is good because it's simple. And if Hale told you he finally got Her Highness to go out to dinner with him for once, the timing's good too. And this had to be done before their installation of that motion-detector alarm system next week."

Alex hoped they'd reasoned out every contingency. If she was caught, she was going to tell them she had fallen and bumped her head and had no idea how she got back inside. She'd insist on another pregnancy test, and that would distract and worry them. Jasmine and Hale were always worried about legal liability for someone falling on the grounds—if that wasn't a laugh now with all Jasmine might be doing.

She and Sandra synchronized watches again and separated, Alex to the front and Sandra to her post in the edge of the forest above the back patio where Alex would make her exit later. Looking like a cat burglar in her black pantsuit, Alex began to feel very alone.

As she had arranged by calling ahead, she rang the bell at the front door and waited until the lab tech on duty opened it. Expecting her, he had in his hands the briefcase she'd intentionally left in Hale's office earlier, out of the way where even he wouldn't see it.

"Oh, thanks so much," she told the serious-looking

young man in thick wire-rimmed glasses. "I need some things in it tonight or I wouldn't have come out so late or bothered you."

"No problem," he said, handing her the briefcase. "I understand working all hours, believe me. 'Night now."

She started away and the spring door behind her began to close. Quickly, she darted back and thrust a folded piece of cardboard in it at the lock level. Sandra had found out from a cleaning woman that this would keep the door from relocking. Standing there with her heart thudding and the door barely ajar, Alex counted slowly to ten and pushed it.

At first she thought it must have caught, but it moved inward. With an excuse on her lips in case the tech was still in the foyer, she shoved the door wider and tiptoed in, closing it carefully. She heard the lock catch.

The foyer was lit only be the exit sign leading into the back hall and the *nichos* where Rita's storytellers—all of them—stared at her. It made Alex angry that the staff had just put them back after Rita's protest two days ago. She tiptoed down the central hall toward the lab.

She heard someone else in the intersecting hall, walking toward the corner. The tech or someone else? She ducked into a nearby supply closet and spent an endless fifteen minutes huddled behind piles of towels, feeling doubly trapped. Unfortunately, she admitted to herself, she had sunk to a level she detested, lying, hiding out.

Finally, when she heard no other footsteps, she tiptoed down the back hall toward the lab. But as she peered through the small, high window in the door, she saw the tech inside. Not panicking, she went to wait in Hale's kingdom of the O.R. transfer room. She and Sandra had strategized that in case Jasmine and Tom Anders locked the lab door when they left, she'd access the lab through the O.R. hatch. It was definitely large enough to get through, and she'd never noticed a lock on it. Now, if that damned tech would leave for a while.

Just in case whoever was walking the hall entered, Alex hid in the corner behind a draped, wheeled cart. Indirect ceiling light shone here so she didn't need her little flashlight yet. She sat on the cold tile floor, hugging her bent knees, wishing she didn't have to tote this dummy briefcase around. Unless she could make photocopies of incriminating evidence, she'd not carry anything out in it. She shuddered. Like most doctors' offices and exam rooms, they had the A.C. up way too high.

She was startled the first time she heard the tech clear his throat through the closed hatch. No, the sound was coming through the A.C. duct just above her head.

It seemed an eternity, but she heard footsteps coming closer in the hall, doors opening. A woman's voice. Thank God, not Jasmine's. One she didn't know.

"'Scuse me in there, sir," came the voice, even louder. She was evidently shouting through a closed door. "Can't find where's I left my mop."

"I don't see it, Ruby."

Alex rolled her eyes in annoyance, until she saw a mop leaning against the wall two feet from where she hid.

"And I know I'm not 'sposed to open the lab door

more than once a night or that lady doctor like to skin me alive."

Alex grabbed the mop and slid it across the floor toward the door. "I'm about done in here," the tech called out, "so I'll look around again before I leave the lab."

Alex heard the door to the O.R. open. "Oh, there you be," the cleaning woman said, luckily, speaking to the mop.

When the door closed and footsteps trudged away, Alex felt immensely better, as if she'd received some heavenly sign things would go well. And the tech soon left the lab, though she clearly heard him jingle keys when he locked it, then again when he locked the O.R. room door to the hall. But she was ready for that.

When all was quiet, the only thing she could find to get up to the height of the hatch was the rolling cart. Leaving her briefcase behind, she jammed blankets from a cabinet under the wheels so it wouldn't roll away while she sat, then knelt on it. The hatch doors slid easily, quietly open. No wonder once the lab was closed for the night, they locked this room too.

Hunched over, moving slowly and carefully, Alex got one leg, then the other over the narrow countertop and through the hatch. Suddenly it struck her that these babies she carried had been through here once before—no, more than once, starting that dreadful day Hale could not implant them with a catheter. Beth and Hale had passed it back and forth several times.

Holding on to the formica ledge, she let herself down into the wan aura of the embryo lab.

Tonight it seemed an alien world. Indicators blinked.

Greenish, gold, or red lights blurred before her eyes. Angular lines, like some extraterrestrial language, crawled or darted across several small screens. The two main computer screens at rest seemed to shot stars of galaxies at her, like windows from the bridge of a space-craft as she was swept out into the universe. The freezing banks and other machines wheezed, hummed, and moaned; the A.C. made the entire atmosphere cold and forbidding.

Fishing in her pocket for her little flashlight, she forced herself to action. The beam was feeble, but her eyes were well accustomed to the dim light, so it was enough. She gasped when she opened the door to the first low cupboard and saw tanks clearly marked O2. So Jasmine might be using enhanced oxygen to freeze eggs, but what about DMSO? If other canisters or bottles contained it, they weren't marked, but maybe she would keep that hidden or even carry it around with her.

Tiptoeing to the counter which covered the freezer tanks, she bent to peer into their lair. Four bright, single red eyes stared unblinking at her from the blackness.

As she had seen Jasmine do here and as she had seen demonstrated at the fertility trade show, she grasped the first tank by its handle and rolled it out. It came at her like a squat robot with its single eye glowing, dragging its own electrical umbilical cord.

She shined her light on the label on its belly. Yes, this was one of the embryo tanks, probably the one from which Jasmine had taken the glass vial to defrost. She stooped and rolled out the second tank. It too was clearly marked as an embryo tank with earlier dates than the first one.

The third tank held sperm, the fourth one eggs—if Jasmine's markings were true. And then, far back in the corner, with a cord around its neck in addition to its electrical life line, was a fifth tank. It had been wedged in the corner as if guarded by the others. On her knees, Alex crawled back in and, when she couldn't easily reach the handle, tugged at its noose.

As if it had a life of its own, the last, squat tank came rolling at her. She put up her hands to stop it. It looked shinier than the others. She moved it out and read the label. It read simply, EE.

"Embryo or egg—what?" she whispered to herself. "Egg Experiments? Eternal eggs? Excellent embryos? No, they always call these pre-embryos, so she'd use a p for that. It must be eggs."

She didn't want to, she feared to, but she knew then she would have to look inside. She stood and scanned the counters for Jasmine's padded glove. There it was, looking like a thinner version of an oven mitt. She pulled it on, then opened the clamps on the neck of the tank.

Icy air whirled out into the room like unearthly atmosphere, stinging her face, stealing her breath. She stepped back and bumped into another tank, which rolled into another and thudded a third. She fanned at the frost, steadied her little beam of light, and lifted the first rack of iced vials from the depths just high enough to get at one. Wishing she had a second glove, she carefully lifted one vial and held it up before her eyes.

Fortunately, she could read its label. On three tightly hand-printed lines, this one said, 9/4/93/cau./bl.hr/br.e/+/lawyer/#78.

Alex whispered the statistics aloud before she replaced the vial, rattling the others in their cold cradles. The date of collection or freezing, she estimated, came first. Then the physical characteristics, although she wasn't certain what the plus meant. Maybe that the egg donor was above average height? Or did that indicate intelligence? Was the donor a lawyer or did Jasmine somehow decide that's what a child coming from this egg should be in a future Brave New World of her own making? And if she was using DMSO in her experiments of freezing these eggs long-term, couldn't an egg meant to produce a brilliant lawyer turn out to be some sort of freak?

Alex reached for another vial, hoping she could find one she could match to its owner—by the date, hair and eye color, or occupation. Maybe Rita's extra egg or her embryos were here and it would say Ind. Instead of Cau. Were there any of her own eggs here?

She gasped as she heard keys jangle and the handle of the lab door rattle. Realizing she'd never make it back through the hatch, she dropped to her knees and had the rack of vials lowered and the lid clamped back on when she heard a string of angry words from a man just outside the door.

While the keys rattled again, she shoved the storage banks under the counter, hoping she had them in the correct order. When the door opened, she stayed under the counter and crawled along over the bumpy computer cables and electrical cords into the corner opposite the huddled storage banks.

The room burst into light—or so it seemed, though the overhead ones he clicked on were muted and indirect. Her pulse pounded in rhythm with his fast footsteps across the floor, around the center counter, and into the very corner where she'd been. She could see it was the lab tech when he squatted and reached for the first cryopreservation bank.

He cursed when it rolled out jerkily, bumping against its own cord she hadn't had time to rearrange. He finally got all five banks out into the aisle where she'd had them. Alex took the opportunity of the noise to crawl even farther away, wedging herself behind a rolling chair and an orange medical waste bag. Trembling, she held her breath.

She heard him shuffle his feet and the unmistakable sound of him punching phone buttons, with their electronic sounds making a dissonant, muted melody.

"Yes, Doctor, it's me. No…you can calm down. The safety light's glowing red on all of them. I don't know why your beeper went off. I've only been gone from here a few minutes."

Alex could not hear what she assumed was Jasmine's reply. She remembered to breathe. Or what if that was Hale on the phone? What if he knew?

"Yes, something malfunctioned. Well, if you would feel better about looking yourself. Mr. VanHeyde's coming back too in about a half hour. He just called. Okay." Jasmine evidently said something else. He hung up.

Alex pressed her balled-up hands to her nose and mouth. Damn, but she'd made a real mistake. Jasmine had mentioned that if the level of nitrogen or the temperature dropped too much in those tanks, she would be beeped. She had obviously phoned to check before she rushed back. And Alex hadn't expected Peter Van-Heyde would be here tonight either. But it sounded like she might have as much as a half hour. She could think of no place close Jasmine and Hale could have been having a nice dinner.

But this tech stood between her and finishing her search here—and between her and freedom outside. She heard him rolling the tanks back in place, still muttering. Would he look around now?

It was then she realized she'd made another blunder. She hadn't closed the hatch. If he saw that, he'd surely suspect something and search the lab to trap her here.

But he shut off the overhead lights and went out, relocking the door again. She let out another shaky breath it seemed she'd held forever. Hoping she had even a few minutes before Jasmine arrived—or perhaps before the tech realized the hatch had been open—she scrambled out. She darted over to the files beside Jasmine's desk from which she'd pulled the embryo tracking sheets she'd made such a big deal of. *I'm a fanatic on keeping all specimens labeled,* she'd said that day of the Miracle Baby party. *I suppose I'm a perfectionist in general...*

At least if she hadn't lied about that, there might be some sort of records in here to explain if she was using DMSO and the amounts, reasons, anything.

But unlike Alice Prettyman's files, these were locked. Suddenly, Alex felt so angry and desperate she could have ripped the drawer out with her bare hands. But she steadied herself again.

She checked Jasmine's top desk drawer, then Tom's. Just before giving up, she saw two lab coats hanging on a Plexiglas clothes rack in the corner by the big glass water cooler. On a hunch inspired by where she'd misplaced her car keys more than once, she shook both coats and one jingled.

Three keys on a brass ring! Just like one a winner grabs on a merry-go-round, she exulted silently.

The second key fit Jasmine's file drawer. Frantically, Alex flipped, then fanned through what seemed reams of tracking forms. Next, lab notes, either computer printouts or in Jasmine's neat, printed handwriting, which she recognized as identical to the labeling on the freezer tanks.

And then—yes!—DMSO records—amounts, times, some sort of percentages. She'd give anything for a photocopy machine in here. Dare she take just one of these pages for proof? Quickly, she pulled one out at random and folded it in quarters. Unzipping her jacket, she shoved it into her bra and zipped the jacket back up.

Then she noticed that the metal file holder stopped before the back of the drawer, leaving behind the last files a dark space she couldn't see into, even though the drawer was pulled way out. Maybe a bottle of DMSO was here. She didn't have time to search everywhere else, but Jasmine wouldn't want it out where her lab assistant could see it, would she?

Gingerly, despite her haste, she put her hand behind the divider. She touched a four-inch-wide, hard cylinder rolled in paper. It could be a glass bottle of the drug. She pulled it out and put it on Jasmine's desk, holding her small flashlight in her mouth to free both hands.

She unwrapped the paper. When the cylinder rolled out, it was really two of them, stacked. She gasped.

In one, a tiny, well-formed fetus floated in clear liquid. MY OWN—TO THE FUTURE, was labeled in Jasmine's precise printing on the glass tomb.

In the other, the thing was grotesque, like an alien being. Where an arm should be above one froglike leg, the head sprouted. Its single, lidless Cyclops eye stared straight into her screaming soul.

17

Alex had to lock her knees and grab the edge of the desk to stand. She stared down at the thing, mesmerized, horrified. She thought she would be sick. Especially when she saw the printing on the tiny label said, IF AT FIRST YOU DON'T SUCCEED…

She dry-heaved once, but voices in the hall, including Peter's, jolted her to silence. But it had not been a half hour.

Shaking so hard she could barely control her hands, she rolled both cylinders inside their wrap and placed them back behind the file divider. She shoved the file drawer closed but didn't have time to relock it. Darting across the room toward the door, she dropped the keys in the pocket of the hanging coat as she heard Peter, just on the other side of the door, ask someone if anything else unusual had happened tonight.

The tech's answer was muted, but she knew he must be mentioning her late visit. She had to get out of here.

She climbed on the counter to get to the open hatch, knocking a tray of test tubes so they rattled and clinked.

She got one leg up into the hatch, over, and down, then sat there, straddling it like a horse.

She was in such a hurry that the cart on the other side shifted a bit away from her. She gasped as she went slightly spread-eagled, holding on to the frame of the hatch with both hands. She felt something pull. But it had only been a thigh muscle, hadn't it? With her foot she snagged the cart and got it back in place. Biting her lip in pain and panic, she wriggled the rest of the way through the hatch and slid off the cart to crouch on the floor.

"—great responsibility, because this isn't some regular doctor's office or drugstore you're watching at night," Peter was saying. It sounded as if they stood in the open door of the lab now.

Fearful to draw attention to herself by closing the hatch doors, keeping low, Alex scuttled to the door of the transfer room. If only Peter would go into the lab with the tech, she could get out into the hall and out of the clinic. She kept seeing that fetus—MY OWN—staring out at her, deaf but watchful, as if guarding all those other pieces of human lives. Jasmine—dear God, please not Hale too—were playing with eggs and embryos here like Dr. Frankenstein. But the monster in that other big test tube had been worse, more horrendous than that kachina in the cradle.

Feeling sick again, lightly, carefully, she put both hands flat on her stomach to get hold of herself. Then she remembered her briefcase and went back for it. She could hear the men in the lab; she'd make it outside to Sandra. She fumbled with the latch and opened the door into the hall. Its normal lights almost blinded her.

Though the lab door still stood open, it was blocking the men's view of her unless they moved. She limped toward the back door, wondering which way Jasmine would rush in when she arrived. As she turned the corner, she heard Peter's sharp voice echo down the hall behind her.

"Look, the O.R. door's ajar! It was just closed. Someone's been in there and the cleaning woman's gone. Come on and help me check the halls. That way. I'll go this."

Her blood pounding, Alex fumbled with the back door lock and ran haltingly into the dark night. She tore toward the trees.

"What happened?" Sandra demanded, emerging from the gloom.

"The worst. Let's go!"

Sandra grabbed her briefcase. They tried to make a wide circle of the clinic, but Alex's leg was giving out in her loping, jerky scramble. "Slow—I better go slow, for my leg, the babies." Panting, drenched with sweat, they stopped several times behind trees to get their bearings and breath.

Though almost staggering from nerves and exhaustion, they made it back to the car. "You look like you're in shock. I'll drive," Sandra insisted, producing the keys. "Don't worry, I'll get us out of here fast."

Alex collapsed in the passenger seat, massaging her thigh. At least she felt no cramps, no telltale bleeding, only horror. But she was proud of those babies. They were in there for the long haul. "But what are we going to do now?" she asked.

"They saw you?"

"I don't think so, but they know someone was inside and I saw plenty. I've got one thing that may help."

"What did you see?" Sandra asked as, without the headlights still, they bounced back up onto the access road and took off. Still, Alex thought, Sandra wasn't setting any speed records.

"DMSO records and a freezer bank full of what are either extra or experimental eggs—and two fetuses—one evidently with DMSO and one without. I'll explain later. At least one of them is Jasmine's."

"What? *Madre de Dios!*"

"Just drive."

The highway seemed silent and deserted as they turned onto it and finally hit the headlights. The digital watch on the dashboard said 11:04. They began to breathe easier.

Sandra did a better job than usual, pushing the car on these curves. Then, from around a turn, coming fast, another vehicle suddenly appeared behind them, its lights leaping into the rearview and side mirrors. Alex craned around to look back. Could Peter or the tech have gone for a car, playing a hunch he'd find the clinic's intruder making a run for the city? Or could Jasmine—even Hale—have arrived and...

"I—I see him too," Sandra said, her voice taut. "I'll never outrun him. I wish you'd driven. I'm sorry I'm still such a coward."

"It's all right. Just keep going. Watch the turns."

The car behind them came so close it seemed he must either pass or hit them. Since Sandra's hands gripped the wheel, Alex tilted her rearview mirror to let his headlights—his brights, damn him—out of their eyes. It seemed like a big car, which Peter drove, but she couldn't tell the make or color. They would never outrun him on this stretch of twisting road or on the freeway with Sandra driving.

But one look at her made Alex decide to take the wheel, even from the passenger seat. Her friend's eyes were wide, fixed straight ahead. Alex knew she was seeing it all again, playing it over in her mind, the tragedy that haunted her.

"Listen to me, Sandra. If we take the next turn, he'll overshoot us, and we'll ditch him. Then I can drive."

"But that road—it's a dead end."

"We can hide. We have to try. All right, *amiga?*"

As if she were in shock, she didn't nod or blink. "Yes. Y-yes," she finally said.

Alex sucked in a ragged breath when their headlights slashed across a sign that read

NM 536
Next Right
Sandia Crest
Tinkertown Museum

By now their pursuer only thought they would try to outrun him. To her amazement, on the two-lane road, the car roared alongside, as if he would push them off.

"Are you crazy?" Alex screamed at the driver, but her voice only echoed in her closed car and Sandra sobbed.

Leaning to look past Sandra, Alex took one lightning

glance at the neck-in-neck vehicle, but it was dark inside. Maybe the windows were tinted, not uncommon here. She saw her car reflected in its closed windows. It seemed to have no driver. It could even be some jackass who did this for thrills. But no, she'd never believe that this assault was any more random than the one in Florida. But who?

Grateful the car was not momentarily behind them, praying Sandra would at least respond, Alex cried, "Hit the brakes to slow down!" Fighting her seat belt, she helped Sandra turn the wheel. They slowed with a squeal of brakes and fishtailed neatly onto the 536 turnoff while the dark car roared on by.

"Oh, *Sacre Cristo,* help us," Sandra cried. "I keep thinking of them wrecked in the car, Alex—on the highway, Mama and Carla."

"Just pull in here so I can drive."

Alex knew they had a few minutes even if he turned around to pursue them. She didn't want to take any of these early scenic-site turnoffs where they could get trapped. They changed drivers, and Alex drove uphill through the thick Cibola National Forest until she saw the Tinkertown Museum driveway on the left. No one had come up behind them, and only one car at them on this even narrower two-lane road with treed ravines on one side and the mountain on the other.

She pulled into the tiny parking lot behind this museum oddity she'd done a segment on once. The place had a vast collection of miniature wood carvings of a western town and circus. She parked her car beside the bizarre cement wall studded with glass bottles which surrounded the place like a medieval fortress. She wished they were hidden safely away inside, but secreting the car behind it would have to do. The glass glittered like a thousand eyes before she turned off the headlights.

They sat silent, wilted, just breathing for a few minutes.

"I've relived it a million times," Sandra whispered, "but never like that—so real."

"You did great," Alex said, reaching over to squeeze her shoulder, "I was scared at first you were going to— I'd lose you, but you're better now."

Sandra turned to her. "I'll never get over it," she insisted, her voice angry. "To be sent out to do that story on a two-car wreck and get there—and then see it was Mama and Carla in that old rusty pickup coming all the way from Chimayo to stay with me, their supposedly rich, famous, crusading daughter, because Papa was drinking again. That other guy was speeding and hit them. And to have the rescue squad take them in to the E.R. and have those damn doctors take so long when they maybe could have saved them."

Alex squeezed Sandra's shoulder again. After being in shock and then mute for two months after the accident, Sandra had never spoken of it, not even to the psychiatrist who had tried to help her. Now, at last, she had at least gotten it outside of her with words.

They waited fifteen minutes, sometimes talking, sometimes not, staring at Sandia Crest, which rose like a much vaster, blacker wall ahead of them as if to balance the museum wall beside them. Alex thought the shadowed face of the nearly full moon looked like an ultrasound of a baby curled in a womb when it rolled into view above the mountain. Soon she could have an ultrasound of her own, but she didn't know if she could bear to have it—or anything—in the clinic ever again. It was no haven now but a place of horror.

"Those cliffs," Sandra said slowly, finally breaking their silence, "are really deceptive. They look so stunning, but they've taken lots of lives. I was thinking of that last story we covered, where those two fell who were tethered together—"

"Don't," Alex commanded. "No more talk of death right now." She shuddered as gooseflesh gilded her skin again. She hugged herself for warmth and comfort. But even that didn't help because she had to go to the bathroom so bad.

"Before we drive back to town, I've got to get out and use the bushes."

Sandra still seemed dazed. "Huh?"

"Nature calls. It's just nerves. Be right back."

She went over into the first stand of pines before the dropoff began. She wished she had a skirt on, not a pantsuit. She'd just hold onto this sapling and lean a bit.

She managed to get her slacks and panties down to clear her bottom so she could squat. She was concentrating so hard on her balance that the sound of an engine didn't register at first. Was Sandra starting the car for her? Surely she wasn't planning to drive back into town.

Through the scrim of pine needles, headlights leapt

at her, then swung right. That wasn't her car. Instinctively, she huddled behind the nearest tree, off balance, trying to see. Caught in her own clothes, she sat down hard on twigs, maybe even briars which scraped her bare skin. And then she realized the lights and engine for sure were from another car. Had their pursuer searched and found them?

The intruding car killed its headlights. The next sound terrified her. A hit! "Sandra!" she screamed when realization of what was happening came to her.

That other car was bumping—shoving her car off—off into the black ravine....

An engine revved and roared. Metal on metal, a grinding, then the sound of snapping trees. Only one car's silhouette in cold moonlight while the crash went on endlessly.

"Sandra—aa" she screamed again and fell flat over a vine or root when she tried to scramble out to help. Her slacks still wrapped around her knees, she heard the engine near her roar away. But the crash came from below: metal scraped, smashed, then silence.

"Oh, dear God, oh, dear God," she heard someone keep saying as she yanked her clothes up and scrambled out to stand where her car had been. If only Sandra had gotten out before it went over...

"Sandra!"

Leaning carefully over, she could see the car had stopped on a ledge, maybe just ten or twelve yards down, pointing toward the deep abyss. Had trees stopped its tumble? The ledge?

"Sandra!"

It was only then, when all the sounds subsided, that she realized a stuck horn was blowing, but no one up here at night could hear it. And she'd seen those movies where a car burst into flame with the injured inside.

Sandra. She was not going to let her die down there—if she hadn't already. Not the way her mother and sister had in a wreck.

A phone. She needed a phone. Help. A squad.

She dragged a heavy metal trash can around to a window of the museum and somehow broke it through a window. She got through the jagged glass, fumbled to a phone and dialed 911 even though an alarm went off, shrieking at her.

She ran around to the back again. How much time before the car blew up? Before Sandra burned or died? She'd never be able to help even if she went down there because the ledge didn't look big and she'd never get them both back up. The path was cleared where trees had snapped off in the car's careening fall. If she had been in the car—her babies. If she went over now…

But she had to help Sandra.

She heard the car shudder and shift below her. More limbs or tree trunks snapped. She couldn't let the car go on down, into the valley far below. Maybe she could at least get Sandra out of the car. If a fire hadn't started by now, maybe it wasn't going to.

She sat down, then went slowly over the side to the first tree, grabbing it, sliding over the edge, clinging to the trunk. It wasn't too steep here at first, she tried to tell herself. She could go from broken trunk to trunk, for the forest had been thick here. But if she slid or fell…

She could hear Hale's warnings to her about taking it easy. But she could hear Sandra's words that they were in this together, that she'd be there for her no matter what.

How long would it take for someone to respond to her 911 call? She'd only shouted for help, then run back out. She hoped Ross and Carla Ward, who owned this place, had a security system that sent police too. That's what she needed—security. She wasn't just dealing with someone trying to scare her but kill her now, and she wasn't going to let them win.

Thank God, the moon was full. She dug her heels in and, on the edge of the jagged scar the car had made when it plunged down, went just small distances from pine to pine. She panted from exhaustion; her muscles strained. She had never had a fear of heights until now. She kept seeing that awful scene from *Jurassic Park* where the dinosaur had shoved the amusement vehicle to the edge of the cliff and the hero had to get the kids out. She had to rescue Sandra, but save her kids too.

Eternity passed, until she made it to the ledge with the car tilted partway off it. "Sandra?" she screamed. "Sandra!"

The car horn stopped as if to answer her. Carefully, staying close to the hillside and away from the edge, she shuffled toward the car. It looked poised to leap into black oblivion. She peered in the driver's window, then the front. No Sandra. Surely, she had not made it out before it went over. And the doors were all shut—crumpled shut—so she couldn't have been thrown. She tried to recall if Sandra had her seat belt on when she'd gotten out of the car.

And then she saw something, a huddled form on the floor of the backseat. An arm sprawled. She'd been thrown there.

The car shuddered again, but Alex did not jump back. "Sandra! Sandra!" she screamed, trying to get the back door to open. She rattled the handle and shrieked so loud that she didn't hear the sirens or shouts above her until she was on her knees beside the door, sobbing.

The rescue team that came later took Alex up top first, two men in harnesses helping her. By the time others were lowered with a grappling hook and chain from a tow truck to stabilize the car and cut Sandra out with the jaws of life, two TV teams had showed up and the KALB night reporter on site had phoned Mike Montgomery.

He showed up in slacks but with his pajama top for a shirt. His hair stood straight up in back from being pushed against a pillow.

"What the hell happened?" he demanded, leaning in the back open doors of one of four blinking emergency vehicles where Alex sat, wrapped in a blanket. For a moment she looked at him blankly, as if he couldn't be here. The place was drenched with bright rescue and TV lights. Though she had no idea what she'd said, she'd already given a statement to two reporters.

Then she heard herself say something like she must have told them. "Sandra came with me out to the clinic to get a briefcase I forgot." Her voice didn't sound like her own. "Heading back to town, someone tried to push us off the road. We turned off the trail and drove back in here to hide. He—they found us and pushed the car off when I was in the bushes going to the bathroom— you know—and then Sandra went over…. Oh, Mike, when that car chased us she finally talked about her family's accident tonight, and then this—"

"But how is she?" he cried, gripping Alex's wrist so hard her hand went numb.

"They got her out, but they won't say yet, so—"

He swore and turned to the closest medic. "How is she—the victim?" he asked, grabbing his arm. "I'm general manager of KALB-TV. That's Sandra Sanchez, my top reporter, my very best…" His voice cracked, and Alex saw him swipe at tears made shiny by the bank of lights. Though she still felt dazed, she read there something deeper than just the boss's concern—

But shouts drew their attention. Mike turned away, and Alex followed to the circle of men working above the car. Shoulder to shoulder, Alex and Mike edged forward, but the police pushed everyone back while firemen and paramedics half carried, half winched a covered stretcher up from the ravine. The figure was unmoving, strapped down.

"She can't be—not dead!" Mike cried, his voice a jagged sob. Alex took his arm, but he seemed not to even know she was there.

"Alive…barely," whispers buzzed through the crowd. "TV reporter…real bad…murder attempt… won't make it."

The medics slid her into the back of an emergency vehicle. Mike cried out as if he'd been punched. Alex bit her lower lip so hard she tasted blood. But for the bounty of black hair—even shiny with blood—it did not look like Sandra with the purple, swollen face.

"But she's alive. Alive, alive," Mike chanted. He still wiped tears from his eyes with his pajama sleeves. "She had no family but you and me, Alexis. She's not going to die, no way. I'm going with her."

"Me too. I'll ride with you," she said until a medic took her arm.

"After all you've been through, we're gonna have to transport and admit you, Ms. McCall," he said. "Especially, like you said, if you're pregnant. There's nothing you can do for her right now but pray. She's comatose and the E.R. will have a lot to do. Come on now and stretch out in the back of this other vehicle so the doctors can look you over too."

She nodded as she saw the third TV station's team get out of their satellite van. But it was KALB's crew that approached again. Harsh TV lights glared in her face. Mike stepped in to shield her.

"Get those the hell out of here!" he shouted, gesturing wildly as if he'd swing at someone. "Show some decency here, or I'll can your ass!"

That didn't even snag Alex's attention. She'd taken too many blows tonight and for too long. But she was going to hold on for Sandra and these babies.

18

Alex felt herself falling off a cliff, into a grave. Alex in Underland—that timeless rabbit hole where everyone was tumbling down, down.

Sandra went by. Extending both arms, she tried to scream, but no sound came out. Alex ducked as a car rushed at her and fell past too.

Rita went by, shouting, "Help me. Help me!" Her storyteller dolls went falling, falling with kachinas chasing them. And then all the faces turned to that grotesque thing in Jasmine's glass tomb.

Alex tried to swim upward, kicking hard, flailing her arms through the choking water. She wanted to save her baby. If only Nick would come to help—if someone would hear her—

"Ms. McCall, Detective Alvarez is here to see you again," a woman's quiet voice broke in.

Alex's eyes flew open. A nurse. The hospital. Thank God, she'd just been dreaming. Then she remembered everything and wished reality away too. Bernice had been here earlier to interview her about what had happened. She had told her everything—except about breaking into the clinic lab. She wasn't sure what to do with that yet, and now she'd have to decide without Sandra.

"Hey, mama-to-be, I hear they gave you an ultrasound after I left." Bernice's serious face replaced the nurse's. She leaned down to take her hand. The nurse went out, and the door of the private room closed quietly.

And then that other reality—that sorrow—crashed into Alex again. "Yes," she told Bernice. "The ultrasound showed bad news and good. I'm still pregnant, but there's only one sac. Only one chance now, but for the two embryos I still have frozen—at the clinic. Still, Dr. Stanhope"—her voice snagged on his name too—"said I'd probably be able to better carry one to term than two."

"See there, a cloud with a silver lining," Bernice said and let go of her hand to slide a chair up close and perch on the edge of it.

"Anything new on Sandra?" Alex asked.

"Still comatose and they have no idea for how long. Nothing actually broken but ribs, if you can believe that. The front window on her side was so smashed it's probably a blessing in disguise—another silver lining, see?—that she had her seat belt off while you two were talking there and she got thrown onto the back floor. Mr. Montgomery's still with her, driving the ICU nurses crazy."

"I think he really cares for her, Bernice. I've often thought 'my lady doth protest too much' when she carried on about him, that she really liked him too. You know what I mean," she added and crossed her hands lightly on her belly.

"Sure do."

"I'll never forgive myself for parking that car where I did if she—she doesn't pull through. But I never realized whoever chased us would come searching every nook and cranny up there. Still, you're here to tell me something else, aren't you?"

"You always were good at reading people. Yep, I am." She leaned closer to the bed again. "I told you before that I put a guard on Sandra's door in ICU. If you weren't going to be released this afternoon, now I'd have to put one on yours too and not for why you think."

"What is it?"

"Alexis, Carolyn Destin got out on bail yesterday, and now she's missing."

"I thought she couldn't make that high bail!" Alex cried. She struggled to sit up before Bernice pushed her back, and hit the lever that tilted the top part of her bed. "But someone had to sign for the money, and state where she'd be," Alex protested. "It—it wasn't Nick was it?"

Bernice frowned and shook her head. "It was supposedly her brother from the East Coast—Ithaca, New York— but Nick says there's no such person, despite the fact the so-called Boyd Gilbert who put up the money had an apparently valid driver's license. Alex, after the same thing happened with Cordova—I mean, no one got him out, but he skipped—heads are going to roll. I don't get what's going on here with any of this, but I'm gonna, I swear it."

"So Carolyn was out of jail when my car went over the cliff," Alex said, speaking slowly, though her mind raced. "But she was in jail when the knife in one of my kachinas showed up in my house. Either way, it's not her, Bernice, any more than it's Cordova, I just know it."

"Tell me why you're so sure." Alex could see Bernice was really upset now, and maybe with her. She kept punching the edge of the mattress with an index finger. "I'm not just accepting it's your reporter's sixth sense about people again. You tell me who you think it is and why."

"I'm trying to reason it out, my friend, really I am."

"Okay, okay—for now," she said, though she sounded angry. She heaved a huge sigh. "Revelation number two."

"There's more?"

"I hope you'll like this one. When I drove to Santa Fe to tell Nick he was in danger again, he asked me to bring him back here to see you—to protect you, no less, though how a guy on crutches is gonna—"

"He's here? Now?" Alex cried as her hands flew to smooth her hair.

"In the hall outside," she said with a nod. "He had some crazy idea you might not want to see him, but your reaction tells me he's wrong."

"I'll see him. I need all the friends I can get, and I've made a mistake with him." She sat up straighter, intently straightening the sheets.

"You mean your sixth sense doesn't work with guys?" Bernice asked as she rose. "Better keep an eye on the clinic icon Hale Stanhope, then." Alex looked up at her. "Just food for thought," Bernice threw back over her shoulder as she went to the door. "But if you have any hints about who shoved your car off the road, I'm the first to know. Got that?"

Alex nodded, feeling guilty not only about defying Bernice but Mike's ultimatum that she tell him first about any breaking story. She couldn't believe she'd dug a hole for herself where she was keeping things from them—and, of necessity, Nick.

He filled the doorway the minute Bernice opened it. He seemed quite dressed up in a red golf shirt, navy blazer and slacks, though even without his usual western garb he looked as roughly handsome as ever. And amazingly more dexterous on his crutches than a few days ago.

"I wanted to see you," he said as Bernice closed the door to leave them alone, "but sure as hell not here."

"I won't say we should stop meeting this way. I'm glad to see you too, you don't know how much."

She sat up, tugging the sheet closer over her breasts and this awful split-back hospital gown they had her in. Suddenly, she felt warm all over to have him standing so close when she was so—undressed. She pressed her knees tighter together. His eyes swept her as always, and that didn't help her composure. It scared her to realize that she wanted and needed this man in many ways.

"Sandra's gonna make it—I just know it," he promised, coming closer.

"She has to. But will I, Nick? And my baby—there's only one now, and I didn't even know the other was lost."

"Sweetheart, I'm sorry."

"The thing it, I didn't feel the loss but do now—like with you. I ran from you because you didn't believe I could carry a child. You were still struggling with your past, and I couldn't help you when I'm trying so hard…."

Her voice broke, but she didn't lose control. "It's true—don't deny that," she went on when he shook his head. "And maybe that you thought we'd have a better—cleaner—start without another man's child."

"All right, I don't deny all that, but now I know I was wrong. I don't know quite where I'm going, but I know where I've been was wrong. I don't expect you to try to help me—but right now, please let me try to help you."

She searched his face. His intense gaze didn't waver, even as he sat stiffly in the chair Bernice had vacated, then evidently changed his mind. Putting his crutches aside, he stood and leaned his thighs against the high bed, taking her hand in his. From that single contact point she could feel the strength and heat of his body. His craggy face looked almost fragile for once, as if his rigid expression could shatter.

"Whatever I've thought about your baby, us, or me— I believe in *you*, Alexis," he whispered. "Yes, I was trying to protect myself and—I just can't bear to see you hurt. And, lately, you keep getting hurt."

"But I want *you* to believe in this baby too. Not that you have to have a thing to do with it when it's born— I knew I'd have to do that alone, so—"

"The point is, I don't want you going back to that

house alone. Bernice told me what's been going on, with some idiot getting in to pull bizarre stunts—and that Sandra was going to stay with you. I know I can never take her place as a friend, but I'd like to ask you to let me move in with you—don't look at me that way. I'll bunk downstairs on the couch and act like a boy scout if I have to. I don't know what I can promise you—and your child—after that, but let me help for now."

"But if Carolyn's free again..."

"I might draw her to you?" he asked, shaking his head. "Bernice says the police have traced her to Phoenix and maybe beyond, so I think she's running *from* me this time. But the way I've been piecing this together, your worry is whoever bailed her out. Bernice has already shown the corrections officer who dealt with the so-called Mr. Boyd Gilbert KALB video of all the men on the clinic staff and the TV station."

"The TV station?"

"Just covering all the bases. And the officer can't ID anyone."

"She didn't tell me all that." Tears stung Alex's eyes.

Nick reached for her chin and tipped her face up as he leaned closer. She smelled the sharp, seductive scent of cloves on his breath. "You need a bodyguard—you got one, crippled or not."

"If not exactly a bodyguard," she said, blushing. "I'd love a house guest."

"Love a house guest—sounds good to me," he said and, balancing carefully, bent to kiss her, a brief, warm caress on her hot cheek. She smiled as he shifted closer.

This time he slanted his open mouth across hers, harder and longer, a kiss full of promise and possession. It made her want to get out of here, no matter what she had to face right now.

By the time the hospital released Alex at four p.m., she'd given Nick the keys to her house and Bernice had taken him there hours ago. Because she felt unsteady on her feet and didn't want another nurse walking in on her, she went into the bathroom to get dressed sitting on the toilet.

But when she came back into her room, a nurse in pale green scrubs stood looking out the window by her bed. She was one Alex hadn't seen, tall, big-boned... who wore her raven hair in a bun on the nape of her neck decorated with turquoise beads.

"Rita?"

She turned around. "I had to see if you were all right, then figured you were in the bathroom, so I just waited."

"But why are you dressed that way?"

"The doctors and nurses here, I didn't know if they'd let me in."

Alex nodded, but she recalled that time Rita had just suddenly appeared at the clinic, apparently to see if she was all right. An instinctive chill made her shiver. "I'm fine, but Sandra's not," Alex said.

"I saw the TV. And you're not really fine. Your color, it is swirling dark blue."

"I'd forgotten about your hidden talent. Maybe it's something like the way I can sense people's moods."

When Rita only nodded, Alex went on, "I had an ultrasound, Rita. I'm only carrying one of the two babies now."

Rita balled her hands to big fists and took a step forward. "But you won't just let them scare you into going home to stay in bed? You'll keep working to be sure you get your others back from that woman too, won't you? Because if someone doesn't help me soon, I'll have to do it for myself."

"How? What do you mean?"

"You're not the only one can get on TV, you know." She crossed her arms defiantly and took a step toward the door.

"Rita," Alex said, stepping into her path, "what are you planning? Please, just give me some more time and don't blow this. You promised Sandra and me."

"You better go see her," she said, not meeting Alex's eyes now, but easily moving Alex out of the way with one arm. "Even if the worst has happened, a friend needs a friend."

"Yes, I'm going now. Can I call you later?"

"Sure," she said, turning back in the open door. "But if Paul answers, better hang up."

Alex signed out at the nurses' station, refused their offer of being taken out in a wheelchair, and went down the hall toward the elevators to go to the ICU. But coming straight toward her was Jasmine. Alex wondered if she'd been lurking out here waiting for her and steeled herself for the worst.

"I'm glad to see you're all right," Jasmine said without a greeting. Her tight smile did not begin to light her ice blue eyes.

"I've just been released."

"So I see. I also see you're limping. From going so heroically down that hill after Sandra? What thrilling television coverage that would have made."

Alex leveled a narrow look at Jasmine's to match her own. She would not let this woman cow her. Could she have pushed her car off that cliff, thinking she was in it? The clinic staff had to know her car. The only doubt she had was if Jasmine herself could have driven the car or if she had some sort of help— maybe someone named Boyd Gilbert who sprang Carolyn loose, whoever he was. Surely, not Hale, even if she had been with him. They often drove separate cars.

"A pulled muscle is nothing," Alex told her and stood her ground. She could not take her eyes from Jasmine's mouth. A smear of crimson lipstick marred the perfect teeth.

"Hale will be so relieved. He was determined to march in here and try to take over your care," she said, propping one hand on her hip and shaking her head. "It took both me and Beth to calm him down when he thought his DES patient—and her clinic babies—might have been harmed."

"As a matter of fact," Alex said, clearing her throat, "they did an ultrasound here, and I have lost one of the embryos, maybe from the very beginning. But this one's going to make it," she said, more vehemently than she intended.

"I should hope so. I'm sorry about your loss, as I have a stake in all the eggs I fertilize, of course. But Hale doesn't know I'm here, so you can tell him yourself later. I need to talk to you privately."

"I'm exhausted and need to see Sandra," she countered, edging around her in the hallway. "I'll call you later."

"No, now," she insisted and stepped forward as if to pin her against the wall. "You've got to help me figure out who could have broken into the clinic lab last night. It's a life-and-death situation."

"The clinic lab..." Alex began, but Jasmine snagged her arm and steered her into a nearby door marked PATIENT LOUNGE. Unfortunately, the spartan room was deserted. Alex pulled free of Jasmine's hold and spun to face her. She smelled strong garlic on Jasmine's breath. Sandra had mentioned she'd smelled it on her that morning of her speech in Miami. Was this woman crazy enough to use DMSO on herself? And wouldn't that mean she was trying to produce eggs or even get pregnant?

"That's terrible about the lab, but why do you think I can help you with that?" Alex asked, hoping she sounded sincere. She hated herself for lying again; she was stooping to this woman's level.

"You don't seem surprised. Aren't you shocked to hear someone's been in the clinic that cradles your embryos—that I gave you a tour of for the TV series, so you know it well?" Jasmine demanded, thrusting her face close to Alex's.

"Of course I'm shocked," she said, trying to keep

eye contact and brazen it out. "But stop trying to implicate me."

"But you were at the clinic just before it must have happened. Did you see anything or anyone weird outside when you got your briefcase from Steve Matthews?"

"No."

"Really? My theory is that you and Sandra were in the clinic and the lab—got in right through the front door Steve somehow didn't close, no matter what he claims. God knows what you were looking for since I've been so open and trusting with both of you, but when the tech or Peter almost caught you, you took off. Were you and Sandra in that lab?" she shouted.

"No, we were not. But let me tell you my theory, Dr. Jasmine," she said, pointing a finger right in that perfect nose. "You thought we were and came looking for us. We were only out for a drive, but you spotted my car and chased us, found us when we tried to ditch you, then hit the car over—"

"That's outrageous, absolutely asinine!" she cried, turning away and smacking her hands to her sides. "Peter and the tech can vouch for Hale and me rushing back in separate cars—"

"I have no doubt your own people would vouch for you to cover what you're doing in the lab or on some dark cliff. But what did you mean before that what happened in the lab is a life-and-death situation?"

"Futuristic mass murder," Jasmine declared, turning back, "not that anyone would prosecute it. But I'm not taking the blame for it—for any of your imaginary TV story scenarios." Her voice became more strident as she came closer again, as if stalking Alex.

"Whoever it was who came through the hatch door from the O.R. and got flushed out by Peter or the tech tampered with one of my freezer banks, Alexis. And either accidentally or deliberately unplugged one and left it open so the top racks of eggs and embryos defrosted—though I don't want a word of this printed or blabbed anywhere until I can contact the patients who lost property."

Alex collapsed in a chair, her face in her hands.

"Well?" Jasmine demanded.

"That's horrible." Her voice came muffled. "Eggs and embryos," she repeated, realizing what the EE designation on the inner freezer unit could have meant. That was the one she had pulled out by the noose around its neck and opened. She'd been startled and rushed putting it back in place when the tech returned, but she'd closed it, hadn't she? *Hadn't she?*

"Ordinarily, I wouldn't have had eggs and embryos frozen together," Jasmine was explaining, "but until I get my badly needed new cryopreservation bank I ordered in Miami, I had to make do—and now this catastrophe. Our unfounded accusations aside, can you help me?" Jasmine repeated, hovering over her, her voice so close. That garlic odor enveloped her again. "Anything you remember…"

Alex felt physically sick. Jasmine called it property, but it was people's eggs, their future babies, their dreams and hopes. And her tampering, as Jasmine put it, had—had destroyed them when she so desperately wanted life for all of them.

"I—can't tell you anything else," Alex said, leaning back, stunned, the last of her strength sapped. "Hale said maybe a local fertility competitor."

"Possible but not probable. Someone like that would know the equipment, Alexis."

"Who—who do I know who lost eggs or embryos?"

"I am glad you're sitting down." Jasmine's voice was as strong now, as if she were giving another call-to-arms speech at a conference. She stepped away at last and put a hand to the doorknob. She had a stranglehold on the straps of her suede purse. "Because I regret to inform you, Alexis, that your two extra pre-embryos were in the top rack, along with Rita Twohorses' six eggs. I take every precaution, but this was sabotage. I had no choice but to destroy the ruined remains. I'll be informing the others of the unfortunate accident and just pray that our new security system keeps thieves and worse away from now on."

She spun, strode out, and slammed the door shut behind her. That clap quaked clear through Alex. She sat, staring at the blank beige wall that seemed to shift and swim before her.

Rita's…her own…others'. In agony she bent over her knees again as she gasped for breath, for control. And trying to get so close to her one baby she had left.

But then she thought of something. With a hiccup she sat up. On the phone from the lab last night, the tech had told Jasmine that the safety light was glowing red on all the tanks. And that was after she had closed it, shoved it back. She'd seen Jasmine and several vendors in Miami clamp the lid in place, and she had done the same.

She hit her fists on both arms of the chair. Damn Jasmine! Either she was lying about the loss of the eggs and embryos, or—or she had done it herself. Had she disposed of the remains to get revenge, or just taken advantage of the situation to relabel or hide them, totally unharmed, for her own uses, as she had Rita's or Jing's or maybe countless others with other excuses? Even her own. By putting Alex on the defensive, by subtly threatening her, she hoped to make her keep out of this.

She looked in the mirror on the other wall on her way out. Her total lack of makeup made her eyes look washed out and puffy. It was so unlike her appearance in normal or heavier TV makeup she didn't even look like herself. This Alexis—the inner, stripped down one—still was staggered by the loss of her embryos, and she shuddered to think what Rita would do when she heard.

Now, Alex told herself, she knew how a mother felt who had her child kidnapped. The torture of not knowing what had happened was as bad as the loss. Was Jasmine going to use them for her dreadful experiments? Get them transplanted into someone else and see if they turned out to be monsters, gargoyles like that one hidden in her desk drawer?

"No!" Her single cry echoed in the empty room. She went out and down the hall toward the ICU.

Alex sat in the single chair by the bed, as stone still as Sandra. The nurse on duty had said it sometimes took weeks or months for brain swelling to go down. Mike had finally gone home for a while, but she couldn't face him right now anyway. If she and Sandra hadn't been so determined to get into the clinic in an underhanded way, this wouldn't have happened, at least not like this. She began to blame herself.

"Sandra, I'm not cut out for this dirty-tricks stuff," she said aloud. "It's just not me. I think I'm going to have to go at this a lot more head-on, use my strengths. You know, *amiga,* talk to suspects or character witnesses, psych them out as I would on the air. And then hope I can challenge them or appeal to someone's sense of right and wrong—maybe Hale or Beth—who will help me stop Jasmine."

Alex scooted closer and gently grasped Sandra's elbow, the only visible place she didn't look bruised or have tubes or needles in her.

"Sorry for just yakking. Can you hear me? They say comatose people can hear. It's Alexis, Sandra." She said each word deliberately. "All those times after you lost your mom and sister, when we were together and you didn't talk but I did—it can be like that again. But you have to get better, promise me."

Nothing. No movement, only the respirator and those maddeningly scary, repetitive green lines on the black screens and the whispered *thip-thip* of her heart monitor registering life in there somewhere.

When the guards on Sandra's door changed, the one going off duty drove Alex home. He pointed out the unmarked police car four doors down and waved to the plainclothes man inside as they went by.

"See, that duty ain't so bad," he told Alexis. "I saw

him eating with chopsticks in there, so he's not starving. Alvarez got this stakeout set at least for a coupla days." When he pulled in the driveway, Nick had obviously been watching for them, because he came right out and stood in the open door. She waved to him before she got out.

How secure, though strange, Nick's presence made her feel. She thanked the officer and hurried up the walk, trying to forget the last time she and Nick had stood here together and Carolyn's bullet had come calling.

"Oh," she said when he put his arms around her the moment he closed the door, "it smells so good in here." Her voice came muffled against his chest. The embrace included his crutches, but she didn't care. She was desperate to tell him everything, but she couldn't. About the loss of her other embryos, yes, but not about breaking in the lab—or that she was going to nail that dangerous, deadly bitch Jasmine at any cost.

She saw he had the dining room table set, including cut lavender iris. "You're smelling delivered flowers and carry-in Chinese," he told her, letting her go at last. "I even got some for the cop down the street—food, not flowers. It will take me a while to get to know your kitchen. Right now two mixed cranberry juice and ginger ales waiting, milady, but I fix some mean chile dishes."

"And you were waiting, Nick, that was the best. Let me just pop upstairs for a moment, and I'll be right back down."

* * *

He didn't like how she picked at her food. She'd been through one hell of a lot, but she should be eating for two. She kept fussing with the Japanese iris he'd had delivered too, deep in thought. It amazed him that she seemed so calm and controlled all of a sudden. Something had changed—coiled even tighter—in her. That winsome vulnerability that had moved him from the first had hardened to something else. If she'd shut out her fears, he wished he could change so easily.

"I'd like to keep you here with me all night," he told her, "but I think you'd better get some sleep. I'll clean this up. I'm getting good at carting things around on crutches."

"I'm sorry I'm such terrible company."

"I'm not expecting company—just you and me."

She looked at him and nodded. "Just you and me sounds good in the middle of this terrible storm I've been walking through for so long."

"You and me—and that baby."

She looked surprised he'd said that, but didn't comment. He knew she was keeping something back—or she still didn't believe him. He didn't believe himself. When they kissed good night, he forced himself not to encourage more than that. Timing was going to be everything with her.

When he heard the bathroom door close upstairs, then the shower start, he carefully carried the last load of dishes to the kitchen and punched the number he'd memorized into the phone.

"She's here with me now," he said into it without preamble. "Don't call me, and I'll call you like we said. What? Yeah, I'm downstairs guarding the doors, and I know the alarm code. And the cops are still down the street. Be careful."

He hung up quietly and leaned against the sink a moment, staring out the kitchen window at his dark reflection.

amble. Then I said that she should calm down, that you said what I said. For downstairs reporting the moon, and I know the alarm code. And she says she will pass the same to camera.

He came up calmly and looked around the pink a madman, walking, and on I rather welcome at his fury to the rest.

19

"What are you doing with those?" Mike demanded.

Alex jumped and shuffled the papers together, then stuffed her red pen in her purse. She had been so intent, sitting at a hospital cafeteria table, she hadn't heard him come up behind her. She hoped he thought she was clearing things so hastily just to give him room.

He sat down across from her with his tray. They were both evidently here to check up on Sandra between newscasts. If Mike's tray held lunch, it showed the state of his mind: two pieces of apple pie and two cups of black coffee. Mike was a health fanatic, seldom ate desserts, and got his caffeine only from soft drinks. If she hadn't known better, she would have thought this Mike was an imposter lately.

"Did you bring the carbon copies for me?" she asked him, gesturing at his tray. She held her papers in her lap, hoping he was distracted enough not to ask about them again.

"You're welcome to half of it," he told her. "I'm not hungry anyway. Not since she…" He cleared his throat and took a big swallow of coffee. "Hate this stuff, but it keeps me going, that and sugar. Want some of this?"

"Thanks, no. I'm trying to be careful what I eat and drink, just like you used to."

"Yeah," he said, "and I'm not even pregnant."

"Mike, I know this is lousy timing, but if everything works out all right for me, I was hoping you'd agree to be the baby's godfather—Sandra's the godmother, you know."

He froze with his fork and a hunk of apple pie halfway to his mouth. He nodded; his eyes actually teared behind his thick glasses. He put his fork down, looked down. "Sure," he whispered. "A great honor. Hey," he went on, obviously trying to look happy about it, "you think our girl would get through the christening without sticking her hand in her suit coat to mock me for being a little Napoleon?"

Alex's mouth dropped open. She had no idea he'd known. "She never meant it to be mocking, Mike—"

"Like hell she didn't, the little witch. Now, I know I'm shorter but…I always liked to think it was her way of teasing me, that it showed she cared too."

"She did, Mike—she does."

He went on as though he hardly heard her. "I should have laid her out for it—you know what I mean—but it amused me. But when she comes to, she's going to hear about a lot of things I never said…."

His voice broke again. "I think I'll go on back up to see if they're done bathing and turning her yet," he said quietly. "You been up there?"

"Yes, yesterday. But I'll give you some time today before I come up."

"Thanks, Alexis. For everything—said and unsaid. You and I, we're in this waiting together because she means a lot." He meant to say more but couldn't go on.

Alex reached across his almost untouched food and squeezed his hand. Mike had already insisted the station run continual pleas for tips about who could have shoved Sandra—in Alexis's car—off the cliff, and they were offering a reward for information. He'd jump in with both feet and ruin her plans worse than she was afraid Rita would if she so much as breathed it could be someone at the clinic they'd been promoting. And no one had told him about the lab break-in.

Mike started to get up, then sat back down again. "I forgot. I'm hoping you won't mind working a few hours this Saturday at the Fiesta—if you're up for it and not overtired. Without Sandra…"

"I'd be glad to help, especially with you being shorthanded."

"Yeah, without her, really short. She loved covering Fiesta," he said, his voice becoming almost wistful. "The only soft news she'd deign to touch. She's really proud of her Hispanic heritage. I'd like to have you take a camera crew and just get some on-site personality pieces—participants and tourists—soak in the color for it. You're great at drawing people out, getting them to trust you."

Her eyes met his. She was banking on exactly that in her next moves to find out how culpable Jasmine was and prove that she was the one who had harassed her and hurt Sandra. "It will be hard without Sandra, Mike, but I'll gladly do it for her—and you."

"Thanks, Alexis. Oh, yeah—why did you have all those bios and résumés of clinic people spread out here?" He asked the question she'd been dreading as he stood. "What's the problem?"

"I thought maybe you'd let me fill in for Sandra in the medical reports too," she said. That much was the truth, at least, she told herself, before she plunged on. "I thought a good angle would be how much training, cost, etc., doctors and nurses go through to get where they are."

"Yeah, but the fertility folks are hardly typical," he argued, his voice strong and combative again. "And why the arrows and circles in red?"

"I'll explain it later," she said, looking him straight in the eye. "You'd better get on upstairs, and I'll be up soon."

He looked as if he'd challenge that or argue, but he only rapped his knuckles once on the table and left, forgetting his tray. Alex picked at his untouched apple pie as she put the papers back out and tried to trace connections, a pattern.

Of the entire clinic staff, Hale, Jasmine, and Beth were linked from way back. Hale's medical career was an open book, but there seemed to be gaps in what she and Sandra had gathered on Jasmine and Beth. She'd have to make some more phone calls this afternoon. She might have to eventually ask Bernice to run background checks, but she'd try her own contacts first. KALB had an affiliate station in New York, where Cornell Medical College was, and that was the first common link for the three main "fertility folks," as Mike had dubbed them. Meanwhile, she was going to find a way to speak privately with both Hale and Beth again. Someone had to give something up on Jasmine she could use.

The Albuquerque Fiesta of San Felipe was always the first weekend in June. It filled the old plaza with religious parades, dancing, mariachi bands, little food booths called *cochinitas,* and Indian art and jewelry sales. With her heart thudding in her breast, Alex stopped in Rita's shop, just off the main plaza, when she and the camera crew broke for lunch.

Attired in jeans and a pink T-shirt, another Indian woman was in the store filled with storyteller statues and other art from Rita's Santa Cruz pueblo. Brightly striped blankets decorated the walls. When the woman turned around from repinning one of them that had come loose, Alex saw it was Rita's youngest sister, Vengie.

"Hello, Vengie." Alex greeted her as the slender woman nodded and smiled a silent greeting. "Is Rita here or upstairs?"

"Not today, Mrs. McCall. She been real upset lately, not been working much, gone somewhere right now."

"Here at the Fiesta?"

"Naw, drove out with Paul, angry words like before."

"I'm sorry. I've tried to call her several times this week, but I couldn't get her, and my messages on the shop phone didn't get returned."

Vengie nodded and shrugged. She looked very sad. "Your pregnancy going good?" she asked.

"Yes, I—I believe so. Did Rita learn about the accident at the clinic? I wanted to talk to her about that."

"Oh, yeah, she heard. But she says she's not talking to nobody but everybody about that."

"She said what? Nobody but everybody? I don't understand."

"Me neither," she said with another shrug. "Hey, you know sometimes I think Rita's little people are the only happy ones around right now," Vengie said and lifted a large figurine close to Alex's face, then bounced it slightly so the tiny children clustered at the skirts of the Pueblo storyteller seemed to dance and move. The finely painted dots and stripes on the clothes of some of the figures zigzagged and blurred before her eyes.

"Thanks, Vengie," she said. She put her hand on the doorknob to steady herself. "Tell Rita to call me, please."

As Alex went back out toward the bustling, noisy plaza, she kept seeing those children and the Indian woman dancing, though all around her Hispanic *señoritas* spun by with their ruffled, rainbow-hued skirts flared out to the lilting beat of mariachi bands. Men in *serapes* and *sombreros* walked by in the parade, carrying the wooden carved and painted figures of San Felipe and Madonna and Holy Child shoulder high. Little clusters of singing children, rosary societies, Sunday school classes, streamed by singing songs. It was suddenly too much and she felt dizzy with everything flying, whirling by.

She leaned against a shop wall, then went inside the sprawling La Placita restaurant next door. Though a few noisy groups were here, by comparison with outside it seemed dim, quiet, and cool.

"What you have, *señora?*" the waiter asked as he plunked a basket of corn chips down in front of her along with small dishes of green and red chile salsa.

"Just lemonade, please," she told him.

She leaned her head back against the huge supporting beam behind her chair. The music was muted here. Her dizziness receded. Maybe she'd worked too hard. Having Nick sleeping downstairs had the opposite effect on her getting the rest she'd hoped for. But today she'd only done four of what Mike called personality pieces for the station and some live coverage with voice-overs.

"Limonada, señora." Her waiter jolted her alert and placed the frosted glass on the table. "You want to order now? Oh, it's you, right? TV?" he said and simulated a little screen around his fat face with both hands. He grinned at his own cleverness.

"Yes, that's right. But don't tell anybody else, because I just need a little rest now, all right?"

"Bueno, bueno. But the reason this such a good place to rest is 'cause La Placita is the best, the oldest in Old town, *sí?"*

"Sí," she said, then pointedly gave her attention to her lemonade. When he bustled off, she realized that the lilt of his voice, even his sprinkled use of Spanish, made her miss Sandra terribly again.

And then she looked across the big restaurant at the door she'd just come in and saw Beth Bradley.

She was standing in the doorway, talking to someone Alexis couldn't see, looking up as if the person were tall, but then Beth was quite petite. And she was laughing, almost flirting. With great effort Alex got up from the table and hurried toward the door. Both Beth and Hale had been so busy with the deluge of new patients—ones Alexis's *Fertility Frontier* had brought them—that they'd begged off what she'd called follow-up interviews until later. But if she could just snag Beth now—

"Beth, hi! I saw you from inside. Oh, aren't you with someone?"

"Alexis. No—I'm alone. I was just talking to some people I didn't know. Who are you here with?"

"I just taped some TV segments, but I don't have to be back to the station van until three. Come on in and have something with me. Come on, I'm buying, as I owe you more than I can say," she said, taking her arm when she obviously hesitated.

"I don't know, Alexis…"

"If nothing else, we're going to celebrate you actually having some free time away from your calling. The Stanhopes remind me of my boss some time—do this, do that," she said, forcing gaiety when she didn't feel that good at all.

"All right. But you should be here with Nick."

"When he heard I'd have half the TV news team here to keep an eye on me, a friend of his took him to Santa Fe to hire someone to keep his shop open while he's living here. He's seen plenty of fiestas there, believe me."

"He's living here? Where?" she asked as they sat at Alexis's table.

"Actually, at my place, but it's not quite what you think."

"Sure, Alexis. You're just nursing him, right?" Her voice seemed taunting, not teasing. "Want some pointers about bedside manner? But," she went on, "you're trying to tell me he doesn't mean anything to you? That he's just some kind of a protector—or cover? Is that it?"

"Come on, Beth, lighten up. I hate to admit it, but neither of us is willing to commit to much yet. We've both been through a lot, you know that. Now he's kind of nursing me after this terrible thing with Sandra—and the loss of the embryos at the clinic."

"Unbelievable," Beth muttered. Alex suddenly wasn't sure if she was referring to what she'd said about the lost embryos or Nick.

"What is?"

"Hale thinks it was some fanatic who broke in," Beth explained, though Alex didn't miss the fact she'd shifted subjects. "Or maybe someone who believes we're something like an abortion clinic or whatever, when we're actually just the opposite, of course."

"And Jasmine?" Alex asked as Beth started eating the chips and salsa. She suddenly looked very nervous. "What does she think?"

"Oh, wow, this stuff is hot! Can I—" she asked and took a swig of Alex's lemonade, then opened and fanned her mouth.

"The green is hotter than the red," Alex told her. "I forget you're a mere babe in the woods around here."

"Oh, that helped, thanks," Beth claimed.

Alex only nodded. Anyone who was a native here knew no liquid but milk soothed chile burn. Beth had been stalling, faking. Alex's senses sprang even more alert, because she had no idea why—unless Beth too suspected Alex and Sandra had broken into the clinic.

Beth's watery gaze snagged with Alex's before she looked away but she could not read the woman's expression. Now, Alex told herself: interview time for Beth. So much for the feel-good warm-up.

"Beth, I've been through hell mourning those lost embryos. That's why I really wanted to talk to you this week. I just knew," she repeated forcefully, looking down at her folded hands, "you'd understand."

"Of course I do," she said, her voice normal again. "And I know how afraid you've been you can't have a baby. Believe me, I know about all that." The intensity in Beth that so often came out as humor or concern for others sharpened her voice. Her face, shoulders, and backbone seemed to stiffen. She bit her lower lip and looked across the room, her dark eyes suddenly angry.

"At least, I hear, you've got one good chance to hold to," Beth went on. "And for us to help you—especially Hale. You know, in a way, maybe the only way that really matters to him, I'm one of his few failures. I mean, no pregnancy after he tried everything. But he's still helped me so much. This job, moral support, a purpose in life."

"I gather you know him and Jasmine well and have for quite a while."

She shrugged and pursed her lips. "Hale, yes, but

she's something else. I don't know if Jasmine even knows herself well."

"I remember," Alex prompted, trying to keep her voice calm, "you told me outside the clinic one day that she had threatened Rita. She's very protective of Hale and the clinic. They really seem a team."

"Unfortunately, they are," she said, her voice bitter, "because she doesn't deserve him. Well, maybe deserves him professionally, but not personally. I knew him before I knew her back East, even before they got married," she said, her eyes getting distant again. "I desperately wanted a baby and went to the Cornell Medical Center, where he worked. I drove sixty miles each way for my fertility appointments because I knew from the first time I met him he was the best."

When her voice trailed off, Alex said, "I've felt that way about him too."

"I know. My husband," Beth went on with a sharp sniff, "was totally threatened. I suppose he feared our infertility might be his fault. So damned selfish and insecure. But it turned out to be *my* fault."

"You know it's not like that—someone's fault," Alex said, reaching over to squeeze her hand. Her instinctive rapport with Beth rushed back. "Not unless you abused your body."

"No. Never. But his emotional and verbal abuse broke up our marriage. He wanted children, blamed me, and found someone younger to make him feel like a man. The bastard even got her pregnant before he told me and left me. About that time Hale admitted that we were out of options for a baby. He was as shattered as I was," she whispered, still looking at the far wall.

"I'm so sorry. You know, I felt we had so much in common from the first."

"I got really suicidal," Beth went on as if she hadn't heard her, "but Hale encouraged me to find a purpose in life, to go back to school in nursing. I'd already started med school once but left because my husband kept getting transferred, the bast—"

She shook her head again. "I guess I said that was his name before, didn't I? Mr. Bastard Spaulding."

"Bradley's not your married name?"

"I wanted nothing of him clinging to me. I tell myself it's a good thing he left, because there was a time when I could have killed him." Her eyes darted back to Alex's and focused from the depths of memory. "My story's so different from the way you lost your husband, Alexis. Maybe I envied you a little bit and couldn't bear to share it, but now—I'm glad I did."

"Me too. Different, yes, but I admire your tough spirit through it all. It takes a lot of love to face women daily who are succeeding where it hadn't gone right for you. Thanks, Beth, from me and all of us."

Beth sniffed, nodded, and leaned over to give Alex's hand a quick squeeze in return. She was tough all right, Alex thought. Though tears had blinded her throughout that wrenching story, she had not cried. And she didn't blame her for not wanting to talk about her tragedy.

"As much as I like the company," Beth said, her voice and expression brightening, "I'd better go back out. As you said, I don't get many days off, and I wanted to see everything. With the way you've increased our client list, I may not get another day off for years. Just get me a ball and chain attached to Hale that's in that nice plum color Jasmine ordered for all us prisoners, that's all," she added before she said her good-byes and walked out.

Alex declined to order but offered to pay for the few chips Beth had. "No, no," the waiter told her, writing up only her lemonade. On her way out, she glanced at her watch. She had a half hour yet, but she headed back across the crowded plaza toward the van and ran into Mike.

"What are you doing here, boss? Did you think we'd need help without Sandra?"

"Nothing like that," he told her, shouting to be heard over the Spanish song four guitar-strumming *hombres* were singing. "It's just—you know, she wanted me to come down here for this last year and taste something called *posole,* but I was too busy."

"She makes a great *posole,*" Alex said. "Pig's feet, onions, cabbage, spices…"

"Whoa," Mike said, hitting his fist into his midriff. "But I'd eat it for her," he added. "Maybe next year, huh, but you'll be home baby-sitting…"

She could tell he was trying hard to pull them both out of the dumps. She linked her arm through his, and they wove their way back toward the thick fortress walls of the Church of San Felipe as the hot sun drenched the plaza.

"I wouldn't mind baby-sitting the rest of my life," she told him. "Changing diapers—anything."

"I understand wanting something that bad now," he told her, his head down, his short strides stretched to match hers. "Oh," he added, "I meant to tell you I saw that head nurse from the clinic you like so much with her boyfriend."

"Beth? She told me she was alone today. Maybe someone was just trying to pick her up, though…"

"Though what? I didn't see him close up, but they had some real tight body language going."

A revelation hit Alex so hard she stopped walking. She'd been occasionally thinking it, but not admitting it. She knew Beth adored Hale, but then so did most of the women at the clinic, and Beth worked with him so closely and he'd saved her, as Beth put it.

"Mike—she wasn't with Hale Stanhope, was she?"

"What?" he squawked, yanking off his sunglasses, then putting them right back on. "There some hanky-panky going on at the clinic behind the scenes?"

She almost told him, just the way she'd almost told Nick and Bernice, but she just couldn't until she had talked once more to Hale. Then she'd know now to accuse them and whether Jasmine was working completely alone as she suspected. She'd have more proof than breaking in a lab, one DMSO sheet she'd stolen, and two bizarre embryos she'd seen. And she had to talk to Hale off by himself, out of his royal realm of the lab.

"His wife's such a looker," Mike was saying, shaking his head, "but Beth Bradley's cute and perky—kind of a Katie Couric type. No accounting for taste, though, I learned that years ago, so—"

"Mike," she said, frustrated now, "the man with her…"

"No, it wasn't Dr. Stanhope running around with his nurse. He was tall like him, but thinner and red-haired, not that silver fox look the ladies evidently like."

"I shouldn't have asked," Alex said as they began to walk again. "Then good for Beth—with the guy. She works too hard and internalizes everyone's problems. And she's so busy guarding everyone else's privacy, I don't blame her for wanting some of her own."

She was also relieved that Beth had not accused her of being in the clinic illegally. But her mind was still racing. Beth had once before refused to say whom she was dating. Why had she lied today about not being with a man when she'd supposedly just bared her soul about everything else?

20

Alex sat straight up in bed, then flopped back down.

"This isn't working," she muttered, staring at her bedroom ceiling. "Nothing is."

She'd promised everyone from Hale to Mike to Nick to herself—even her mother—that she would get some extra rest today. And she had thought it would relax her to have Nick in the house. But his nearness—the scent of those cloves he sometimes chewed, his offkey humming of no tune in particular, even his breathing, his mere movement now downstairs…

Her brain and body were working overtime, as were her damned hormones, and not only ones caused by the first trimester of a pregnancy. Despite her worries and fears, with Nick nearby, her pheromones were roaring. He was downstairs fixing a special dinner for the two of them, and she still could not relax.

Giving in to the inevitable, she got up and pulled on workout shorts and a top over her bra and panties. She washed her face, appalled by how drawn and pale she looked. She pinched color into her cheeks, put concealer on the dark shadows under her eyes, brushed her hair, and headed downstairs barefoot.

She could hear the rhythmic thump, thump of a knife on a cutting board; he had the kitchen TV on, a Sunday afternoon football game with the volume low. She watched him working for a moment, his dark head bent, his broad shoulders slightly tensed. He too wore a workout T-shirt and shorts—black ones displaying his tan, muscular legs, where his right calf and ankle weren't covered with the cast. His crutches were not in sight, but she'd seen him get around well in the kitchen with its counters to hold on to.

"It's me," she told him from the doorway. "Didn't want to surprise you and make you cut yourself."

"Can't sleep?" he asked, craning around to eye her. "Am I bothering you?"

She bit back a grin. "No—just too much to think about. And I have to make a couple of phone calls to set up interviews early this week." She didn't tell him one would be with Hale.

He nodded and returned to his work as she walked closer and leaned one hip against the counter to watch him. He was cutting dark green *poblano chiles* to make a salsa for the *chile renellos* he'd promised her tonight. She could taste their hot, smoky flavor already. She saw he wore kitchen gloves as knowledgeable cooks always did when working with hot chiles. The mere touch of them could burn skin. She went to the refrigerator and took out the jug of ice water she kept there.

"Tell me what you're thinking right now and let me

help," he said as she went back to watching his big hands in her too tight kitchen gloves.

"Looking at those gloves, I was thinking that I might know why Bernice didn't turn up any fingerprints from the couple of times someone must have been in the house."

"Kitchen gloves?"

"Or surgical ones."

"There's a lot you haven't told me, Alexis." He turned around and leaned back against the counter, watching her, the knife in his hand. "You think someone at the clinic is behind your house break-ins? Or the attempt on your and Sandra's lives? If so, who and why?"

Bernice had said much the same thing. She ached to tell him. It was so dreadful going through this without Sandra. But if she shared what she knew, he would probably face down Jasmine himself or insist on going with her when she finally confronted Hale alone. Take charge, jump in—that was the Nick she knew from the ordeal with Carolyn.

His high brow furrowed when she didn't respond, and he chopped the chiles even harder. "I still don't have a lot of answers," she said and poured herself some water.

"And you're risking yourself and the baby to get them, is that it? I'm here, but I'm just kitchen help or a bodyguard." One thick black eyebrow tilted up; his lips pressed together in a taut slash.

She banged her glass down. "Nick, you're my friend."

"Friends confide and trust, Alexis," he said, gesturing with the knife until he saw her staring at it. "Sorry." He turned and smacked it down on the cutting board. "It's not a good knife, but if it's the best you have to give me right now, I guess I have to use it."

"I hear you. And I have a sharper knife, only that's the one Bernice took to check for prints, the one that was out on the counter and stuck in the kachina. Nick, I do trust you or you wouldn't be here."

She walked closer to him as he grated cheese with a vengeance, then stuffed it by hand in the chile peppers. He tore the first one and swore under his breath. He looked suddenly so angry he might as well have been jamming his clothes in a duffel bag to walk out the door—if he could have walked without his crutches. She put her hands on his shoulders and laid her cheek in the shifting valley between his shoulder blades.

"Be careful," he warned, stopping to lean stiff-armed on the counter. "I think you know this stuff is really hot."

"I do," she murmured, standing slightly on tiptoe to rub her smile against the nape of his neck. "But I'm touching you and you're not touching back, so who can get burned?" She stepped lightly against him, her lower belly to his taut buttocks. She felt breathless, as if she stood on the edge of some precipice, wanting to hurl herself over.

"Al-ex…" He gave a little groan when she began to rub her hips across his butt. She felt his muscles tighten, then relax as he heaved a huge sigh. "I've steeled myself not to crowd you," he said, his deep voice even huskier than usual. "I've tried not to push for too much right now for several reasons—and you're making me forget every damn one of them...."

She wrapped her arms around his flat waist, pressing her palms against his ribs. Her breasts flattened to his back; the jolt was electrifying. He moved his good leg back to separate her thighs. Then holding his gloved hands up in the air as if he'd just scrubbed for surgery, he pivoted slowly to face her. Her embrace still circled him. His leg without the cast still rode gently between hers. She could feel every taut inch of him.

"Good," she murmured. "We both need to forget some things."

They lost themselves in kisses and her caresses. She got bolder, crazier. She stripped his shirt off, and he ripped his gloves off and yanked the faucets on to thrust his hands under running water while she ran her hands over his chest, snagging her fingers in his crisp, curly hair. She laughed aloud for the first time in days as he turned her away to pull her shirt over her head with wet hands. They both glanced at the TV on the counter. Rita Twohorses stared out at them, furious and frenzied.

"Nick, Rita!"

"Oh, hell—forgot..." he muttered and steadied her as he reached across her for the remote control, hopping carefully on his good leg.

"You knew she'd be on?"

"Forgot to tell you her husband called here wondering if she was with you..."

"Oh, no. Sh."

They stood, leaning against each other and back

against the edge of the counter as he punched the volume up. Alex saw the channel was not KALB, but a rival—the one who had tried to pirate Sandra last year and Mike had had a fit and topped their offer.

"…malpractice for the terrible way I and many others have been treated at the Evergreen Clinic, no matter what you saw on another channel," Rita was saying. "Eggs and embryos hidden and kept from us, and I can name names too."

"Oh no, oh no," Alex cried, clapping her hands to her mouth. Only when Nick's arm tightened around her bare shoulders did she remember they were both shirtless.

"…going to bring a lawsuit and have my lawyer subpoena those who have been keeping an eye on Drs. Hale and Jasmine Stanhope and the clinic. They won't give me my artwork or my babies…."

She continued to talk about the fact she and her husband could not have a child, and she was the first Pueblo Indian to trust the Evergreen. With that voice-over, the station ran a close-up of several of Rita's storytellers. Alex could tell that had been shot at her shop; it was followed by dated file footage of the Santa Cruz pueblo. If anyone believed her claims, it was going to hit the fan before Alex could gather enough evidence to make anything stick, but helping Rita came first now.

"I've got to call Paul," she told Nick, scrambling for the phone. "It looks like this is a live interview, so she's at the station. We've got to get to her before everyone else—her husband, the Stanhopes."

"I meant to tell you her husband called," he began to

apologize again. "I know Paul from times he's dropped off her work. I told him she wasn't here; then when you came downstairs, I forgot about it."

Alex only nodded. She felt guilty she was also angry that Rita had ruined something else—where she and Nick had been headed just now.

Once Rita got the phone call she wanted at the station, she did not take the others, even the ones they said were from Alexis McCall from KALB or her husband, Paul. Instead, she withdrew five hundred dollars from the bank, then drove her car out toward the clinic. She turned off onto a dead-end dirt road just before the grounds began, as the phone call had instructed.

She drove in and hid the car behind a clump of pines. She knew this area above Silver well, so she could easily approach it from this side as well as from the clinic across the valley. If the call had been from the Stanhopes, she never would have come without her new lawyer, but she was not afraid. She was eager to get her chance at her babies back.

"I knew you were lying about losing them." She held an imagined conversation as she walked through thick brush to reach the edge of the cliff opposite the clinic. "Read your history books, Dr. Jasmine. My people, we fight back fierce and always will," she said, slashing a fanciful knife in a broad arc.

She already had her new fertility clinic doctor lined up, one at a downtown hospital, the same one where she'd visited Alexis. Soon she'd be just like her, pregnant and hopeful. Then maybe someday they could be friends again.

As she walked the uneven ground, she dug in her fringed leather pouch for the wad of bills. She had not asked for money, but this was worth it to her, worth everything. If she bore a daughter, perhaps she might even name the child for its savior.

Names were sacred to the Pueblo people. She said her future daughter's name aloud on her lips, picturing herself talking to a group of children clustered about her skirts: "Beth. Beth Twohorses."

"You made good time," a voice called to her.

Rita turned and shaded her eyes. Beth Bradley emerged from behind a twisted piñon tree and waved. She carried a small plastic cooler. Rita clasped her hands tightly together to stop shaking. She was so excited, but she saw the nurse was too. The aura of seething colors around her were yellow and orange.

"I had no idea," Beth told her, "that Dr. Jasmine was keeping your—or anyone else's—eggs or embryos from you. You should have talked to me about it, not gone on TV, where Hale got pulled into this. But if you ever tell where you got these, it will mean my job. I'm hoping she just thinks her lab assistant misplaced or accidentally relabeled them."

"This is all I want," Rita assured her. "I won't tell anyone. And here, I brought this for you, for your trouble and the truth—and your bravery." But even when she tried to reward the nurse by paying her, her colors only got sharper, redder.

"No, no, put that away. I do everything for love of

my work—and because I understand how it is for desperate people like you. Here, let me just show you how I've packed them."

"At least she didn't sell them. Was she going to give them to someone else?"

"She's doing secret experiments," Beth confided, taking her sunglasses off and laying them carefully on the rock face, though she squinted even more in the sun. "I'm trying to find out exactly what she's doing to either confront her or turn her in—to make her stop, maybe go away…." Her voice trailed off as if she were deep in thought.

"Then you should work with Alexis," Rita assured her. "She wants to stop her too."

"I know. Here," Beth said and squatted as she opened the cooler a crack and peeked in. "Take a look."

Rita squatted and leaned over too, hoping to shade the cooler from the sun. It was a hot day, and a nurse should know not to open it out here. Yet she was thrilled to get a glimpse of what was inside: a whole beautiful future in those tiny vials.

She reached for them, just for a brief touch. The inside of the cooler was not cold at all. "But why are…" she began and snatched one up before the nurse could snap the lid shut.

"Empty?" Rita cried, holding it up to the light. No colors came from the empty tube at all. Empty.

Catching her squatting, intent, the nurse leaped and shoved her. Rita rolled once and tumbled, empty, empty.

Shocked beyond belief, Rita did not scream, but thrust out her hands to grab the hard face of cliff. She tried to dig her nails in, but they only ripped, and she had to save her artist's hands. The rock slid by, upward, as she skidded, bumped, and spun into empty air.

Then she was twisting, flying free, all skirts and arms and mouth opened in a silent scream. And little children climbed on her knees and sheltered themselves in her skirts as she told them tales of her life and the truth about how much she loved them.

"It's your fault too—maybe it's mine, but it's yours too!" Paul Twohorses dared to yell at Alex on the phone at work the next morning. "You got to announce on the air she's missing, find out who's seen her."

Alex raked her fingers through her hair with her free hand. "Paul, I can't do that. Then we'd have to do it for every missing person. I want to help, but I can't—not that way. Nick and I tried to find her yesterday too."

"I know. I'm scared for her."

"I am too." She shook her head as if trying to convince herself that what she said was right. Still, she had an overwhelming urge just to blurt out a plea about Rita on the air, then take the consequences later. Next to other possible repercussions awaiting her, Mike's anger over such a breach of decorum seemed a small price to pay. "Paul, my hands are tied about making an announcement until the police agree—"

"I had to admit to them that she gets—you know, off balance—and that we'd argued for months over a baby. I couldn't lie about how crazy she can act—not after how she's carried on publically before..." he said, evidently referring to her outburst at the baby clinic party. "But I didn't harm her, never would…"

"All right. I'll talk to my detective friend about maybe looking for her sooner than they usually would. I'll—"

"They won't do nothing—just like you," he cried and slammed down the phone.

But she did want to do something, find out if, even indirectly, Jasmine could have anything to do with Rita's disappearance. So she called Hale to ask for a private meeting. To her amazement he was out of town, and she had to leave voice mail. In Boston on family business, he said when he'd phoned back, because his mother was in a nursing home there. Wednesday evening he'd meet her for dinner anyplace she wanted, he promised.

Still hearing Paul's and Hale's voices in her head, Alex forced herself to type her script for the Monday midday newscast. But she'd find herself sitting with her hand still, seeing Rita's face on the screen. Staring at the emerging sheets of paper as she printed out her script, she admitted she was a mess of jumbled, jagged emotions.

Suddenly, Anne Wheelwright, the events coordinator, screamed. The buzzing, busy newsroom came to a silent halt.

"I just got—" Anne cried, evidently talking to none or all of them, "the latest printout of police radio calls." She rose to her feet at her desk on the elevated platform where she did assignments and kept track of everybody's location during the day. Staff froze where they were, poised, expecting to leap to action at the word of a local tragedy. Alex stood as Anne waved the computer printout at them. Ordinarily, whatever the catastrophe, Anne kept her cool, but she was visibly shaken.

Over the other heads, Anne's eyes locked with Alexis's. "Out near where you—where Sandra had the wreck—" she began, then stopped to clear her throat. "On the clinic grounds, that Indian woman friend of yours, the artist... The lab assistant from the clinic, a Tom Anders, found her dead. She fell or threw herself off a cliff there...."

Chaos ensued. Someone very close to Alex screamed, someone inside her. Her. She screamed in fear and rage because Rita and Sandra couldn't anymore.

Fifteen minutes later, Alex heard Mike's voice outside the women's rest room again. "It's four till twelve. Get her out here if she's going on the air at noon."

Anne popped her head back in. "Mike wants to know if you can go on," she said. "With Stan on location at the university..."

"Yes, I'm going on," Alex said, wiping carefully under each eye to clear the mascara that had run. "I want to do her obit—I have to."

Cursing the fact she didn't have time to repair her makeup, she tore out and strode toward the studio at the back of the station, with Mike at her heels. "We can just do a voice-over," he rattled on. "We'll have to can our previous lead and scramble everything else. I've got footage of her—"

"Not from the time she interrupted that baby reunion at the clinic."

"No, hell, no. Of her working in her studio. Alexis, you're not going to lose it on the air, are you?" he asked as he shoved open the soundproof door for her. The icy temperature at which they always kept the place for the Doppler radar weather equipment smacked her, but it felt good. "I mean," he went on, "I'd understand, but last time—"

"If I cry it will be truth in journalism, Mike. But I'm getting through this for Rita." She took her place behind the anchor desk and automatically fixed her earpiece and tiny mike. She felt very alone with Stan away for a remote today, but she had felt alone all the time lately, and it was her fault for not telling anyone what she was going through.

"This accident site is so damn close to where Sandra got hurt," Mike muttered, voicing her worst fears. He stood on first one foot and then the other, just out of the range of the cameras and lights. "It can't be pure coincidence."

Alex nodded her head. She was on the air.

They made Rita's story—native American artist falls to her death—their lead, even though the reporter they'd sent to the scene had barely arrived and had not had time to talk to the police yet. He had, however, interviewed Tom Anders about having lunch across the valley near the clinic where he glanced down to see the body, "with her big, bright skirts all spread out like wings." A vivid picture flashed through Alex's brain: Rita sitting in that valley the first day they met, staring up at birds soaring in the thermals.

As they ran more live coverage, Alex stayed rivetted to the studio monitor. She glimpsed Hale, Jasmine, and other clinic staff standing behind the fluttering neon yellow police tape on the cliff beyond Silver. Beth had said how worried the Stanhopes had been about someone falling on the grounds and suing them. She wondered if they were relieved to have their fiercest critic silenced. But perhaps they knew the one who would inherit her fallen mantle was on the air right now.

Again the red eye of the camera blinked back to Alex. She read the copy her producer had hastily written for her. "The police have not given the cause of death, but a police source has told KALB there are no signs of foul play, and it is known that Rita Twohorses sometimes took walks in this area. Her husband, Paul, admitted she had been despondent lately. But I hope you will allow this reporter a personal observation as we show you some of this Santa Cruz pueblo artist's beautiful pieces called storytellers."

She cleared her throat. She had no script for this. Blinking back tears, she ignored her producer's voice in her earpiece telling her they could just run a soundtrack of Pueblo music. She ignored Mike's gestures to "just keep it down, under control."

"I knew Rita Twohorses personally," Alex adlibbed, "and found her to be not only tremendously artistically talented but brave and caring. Her art shows her love for children and the value she placed in telling them of the precious traditions of the tribe."

She blinked back tears and cleared her throat again. "In this age when the politically correct thing is to talk of family values, Rita Twohorses gave us a symbol of real family values. Former first lady Barbara Bush and her longtime literary campaign could not have had a more eloquent spokeswoman than Rita Twohorses' pottery of tribal elders and mothers telling traditional tales to their precious children. Rita will be sorely missed by those of us who knew and admired her, by her Santa Cruz people, and the world of art."

She might have talked forever. She wanted to throw out a challenge to those who had hurt Rita—at the clinic, maybe Paul, maybe even herself. She wanted to say it was a terrible accident or a tragic suicide, but she was suddenly convinced it was more than that. Though a car had not shoved Rita from the cliff, this time the murderer had won.

21

"I don't like it, Nick," Alex protested and pulled back against him as they approached Rita's shop that evening. "It's pitch-black in there and in the apartment upstairs."

"He said he'd be here," Nick insisted, resting a moment on his crutches. "I wouldn't have let you come if I didn't feel it was safe. I know the man and what he's been through."

"I feel sorry for him, but he didn't need to be so hostile toward Rita—or me." As far as she was concerned, Paul Twohorses had been as cruel to Rita as Beth's husband had to her—refusing to support his wife's desperate desire for a child, basically blaming her for all her problems. But now was no time to quarrel. For once Paul had asked her to come see him instead of telling her to stay away.

Alex jumped when Nick banged his fist on the door of the shop, rattling a loose glass pane. "Paul? You in there?"

A gray form emerged to unlock and open the door.

This close, without the streetlight in their eyes, they could see a low, single lamp in the store behind the counter threw strange shadows on the beamed ceiling. Paul hit a switch and an overhead, hanging wooden wagon-wheel lamp came on, casting cold light over the blankets on the walls and the clusters of figurines. Their once vibrant colors seemed dimmed, muted.

"Thanks for coming," Paul said and sniffled. He wiped his nose with his shirtsleeve. His face looked gray and gaunt, his eyes in shadow. Alex smelled liquor on him. He seemed worse than she'd expected, slumped, shuffling, not furious, as she always thought of him, but fearful. He didn't look at them, but kept glancing into corners as he led them into a small back room, shoving aside a heavy blanket over the door. In the makeshift office which also held Rita's potter's wheel, bags of clay, and a kiln, a desk lamp puddled pale light on a cluttered desk.

"Can't stand sitting out there," he said, his words slightly slurred. "All those eyes of her women and children."

Paul indicated they should sit on a bench along the wall, while he slumped in the desk chair. He clinked a beer bottle against another as if to make room for his elbow. He showed no embarrassment at the array of empties on the desk.

"Paul, we're so sorry for your loss," Alex said, wishing her words didn't sound so stilted. Nick had already given his condolences to him on the phone, but she hadn't talked to him since Rita had been found. "I'm sorry I can't find the words to—"

"You found good words on TV."

That helped her as nothing else had. "Thank you. What can we do to help?"

"Both of you, come to the funeral—please. She'd want that." He did not look at them; his eyes darted here and there. "It has to be soon—real soon."

"We'd be honored," Alex assured him. "I will miss Ri—"

"And never say her name—bad luck, real bad," he said, shaking his shaggy head, then hiding his face in his hands. He looked slowly, warily out through his spread fingers. "The people—we don't say she died— just gone away."

"All right," Alex agreed, nervously waiting for what else must be coming.

No one spoke for a moment until Nick reached for her hand on her knee and explained, "Paul's people believe the dead and the living must be kept separate in every way, or sickness and death might come." Alex shuddered; Nick gripped her hand tighter.

"Paul, besides the funeral," she prompted, glad she had talked Mike out of trying to interview this broken man, "what else?"

"Burial gotta be fast, the next day if it can, but soon, very soon or her ghost cannot rest." He glanced into a corner again. "I know you probably think that's crap, but I don't care. The police want to keep her body when they already cut her up—"

"What?" Alex cried, leaning forward. "You mean an autopsy? But that's standard when it's a question of suicide or an accident or—"

"Or?" he asked, leaning forward, his face intent at last. "Or? It has to be murder because she'd never fall there, and I sure as hell didn't touch her. You know she was surefooted. She said once she walked with you there."

"Yes, but…"

"I don't even care if they think it was me. It was murder. Never suicide." He spat that last word out with contempt. "Did you tell her never suicide for my people, Nick?"

"But you admitted she was depressed," Nick said, his voice so quiet compared to Paul's. "And Alex mentioned your wife said she'd like to kill herself over her lack of a child."

Paul leaped to his feet, ready to lunge. He stood, weaving, one hand on the desk. "She didn't mean it. Our people fear death. We would never kill ourselves—a people with no suicide, few murders within the tribe. I want you, Alexis McCall, to ask the police to give me her body back for burial. You have power. Help me, help her."

He gestured wildly, knocking one bottle over, but paid no attention to it. "I could not stop her from wandering," he went on, "broken in life, but I can't let her ghost do it now she's gone away."

"Yes, of course," Alex said, trying to soothe him, however hard her heart was thudding. "But did you ask the police?"

"My people did, the elders. The coroner's office called. They said soon, not sure when. But I see her everywhere," he said, wide-eyed.

Fear prickled up Alex's neck. As exhausted as she was, she'd imagined she'd seen Rita's face staring at her from her computer screen earlier today.

"She wants to leave and rest," he went on. "It has to be now." He banged his fist on the desk and the bottles clanked.

"I'll call my contact at the police department," Alex promised. "I'll do my best."

"It's for you too," he said. "If she comes back it will be to those who made her angry in the end. And the touch of a ghost is—is, you know…"

He made a sharp slicing movement across his own throat, then led them out into the shop. More deeply shaken than when she came in, Alex now peered into corners of shifting shadows. She didn't believe in any of this ghost talk, yet she could not stop trembling. She felt haunted, all right, not by Rita's spirit but by her own burden of proof against Jasmine.

"Here," Paul said just before he opened the front door for them. "Take this gift from her." Frowning, he lifted one of the largest storytellers from a table. His hands trembled; she thought he would drop it. But he thrust it at her, and their fingers touched. His were ice cold.

"I will work to deserve this gift, Paul. I'll do my best to get her body back and find out what happened to her on that cliff." Her words trailed off as she realized she'd said the same of Sandra.

His voice was so weak she had to lean toward him. "She heard your sacred vow," he said. "So now you have to do it."

* * *

"Are you going to tell me what's been going on at the clinic or not?" Nick demanded the minute they walked back in her house after seeing Paul.

Alex could tell he was trying to control his temper, but he was seething. She stalled giving him an answer by carefully placing the storyteller on the end table by the front window. She would not put it with the other two on the mantel right now, but keep it with her, perhaps up in her bedroom.

"Nick, I want to, but you have to prom—"

"Let me guess before I promise anything. You and Rita were getting ready to blow the whistle on the clinic for stealing eggs, and she exploded and went on the air. And Sandra was in on the investigation, and someone at the clinic knows this and is picking off their problems. So far you're too much of a kingpin to touch, so they've only been threatening you, but you figure you might be next."

She crumpled in a chair. "Yes," she admitted breathily, "but there's so much more. I think it's all Jasmine, but I'm not sure. I'm going to get the police in on this, but not until I know. There's too much at stake if the culprit just takes off—or runs amok more. And if Hale's not involved, I can't ruin his reputation."

"I also owe him, for stopping my bleeding when I got shot. But if you and your baby are at stake, you'd better hide out somewhere. I know a couple of spots where you'd be safe." He perched on the edge of her chair, his injured leg straight out. He took her hand.

"I can't do that, Nick, baby or not. My gung-ho series for the clinic has made a lot of people trust them. If they or Jasmine are betraying that trust, she has to be stopped."

She gripped his hand hard in hers and blurted out, "Sandra waited outside the clinic while I more or less broke into the lab and found some evidence that Jasmine's doing experiments, terrible things that can cause birth defects. When we were followed, then the car shoved off the cliff, they—she—probably thought I was in it too."

She refused to cry, shoving hovering hysteria back as best she could. Stopping the Stanhopes was the only way she and her child could live here with their heads up over the years, the only way she could protect Sandra and make Rita's loss count for something. She couldn't just sit here shaken and scared. Right now she had things to do, calls to make about getting Rita's body released to her people.

She stood, tugging her hand free of Nick's. But in one smooth move he slid into the big armchair she had just vacated and pulled her onto his lap.

"Nick, your leg."

"Shut up and stop worrying about everyone else for once when you're putting yourself in the line of fire."

"I don't believe you're saying this," she insisted, pushing her palms flat against his chest. "Not the man who took a bullet to stop his ex-wife from hurting me, the man who does what he can to get the Pueblo people their treasures back instead of just selling them. And the man who moved in with me when you know someone's after me…"

"All of that aside, *I'm* after you, sweetheart," he said. "I love you, Alexis, and I'm not going to do without you. So I don't want you going out on some quest unless I'm at your side—or unless you tell Bernice what's going on."

"I'm going to call her now," she said, determinedly and reluctantly getting off his lap. "And—just like with you—I'm going to make a deal with her. I need just a little more time to try to sort this out—and then if I can't—I'll get her in on things. Please, Nick, trust me that much—if you love me."

He nodded, but she couldn't quite read his expression. She sensed he wanted to say he didn't trust her in this *because* he loved her. She leaned back down to kiss him. "Nick, I value and treasure your feelings for me. If I could unscramble my own right now, I'd return them, but you don't deserve another woman who's confused....I'll let you know what Bernice says about getting Rita back to her people for a decent burial."

Wanting only to throw herself into his arms to hide, she squared her shoulders, went into her office to make the call. She looked up the number, punched it in, then heard Nick yell. She hung up and tore back out. He stood in the living room before the hearth, staring down.

As if they'd leaped off the mantel, her two original storyteller figures lay shattered on the tile. And in their place stood the two glaring kachinas she had saved to give her baby.

Silence swept the hill above the Rio Grande as the Twohorses and Ortiz families and other members of the

Corn Clan of Santa Cruz pueblo prepared to bury Rita the next afternoon. Alex was ashamed that the TV stations, even KALB, which had caught wind of the "hasty burial," hung about like vultures down the hill, but tribal members had set up a roadblock and they could come no closer. Though Rita's body hadn't been carried up yet, Alex wondered what their telephoto lenses were stealing from the scene.

She and Nick were the only Anglos at the funeral. Alex had done the one thing she could to get Rita's body released this fast.

"Sure, I could lean on the M.E.'s office to give up her body sooner, Alexis," Bernice had said on the phone, "but now that it might be murder, we've got to hold it even longer. It would be a nightmare to try to exhume her later from a Pueblo burial if some other forensic concerns came up."

"The initial police reports said no foul play suspected. Now you think it might be murder?" Alex had demanded, gripping the phone receiver tighter.

"She withdrew money from an ATM after she left the station. The bills of nearly five hundred dollars floated down with her body and blew around in the valley. And she had a shattered but apparently empty test tube clutched in her hand, so could she have met someone there to pay for that? It doesn't make sense. The clinic people say it doesn't either."

Alex had swayed back into her chair, feeling dizzy. "Do you have any suspects?"

"The husband's a possible perp, but after that on-air attack she did on the clinic you've been touting—"

"You don't mean me?" Alex had cried.

"No way. I'm talking clinic staff, Alexis, I'm talking the same brazen bastard who pushed your car off the cliff with Sandra in it. But because Rita's demise could have been suicide or an accident, I don't have the green light around here to dig any deeper. But you want Rita's body released, how about you trade what you know for it? Man, I sound like a reporter now, don't I?"

"I can tell you she was surefooted and that the Pueblo people hate death and detest suicide. What else do you want in return for helping her people get her body back so they can fulfill their traditions we've been trampling on for years, Bernice?"

"I hear you, but you can't have it both ways, my friend—protect the clinic, however much good they do, however much you owe them personally, and protect a possible murderer there."

"Can you give me a little time—just over twenty-four hours?" she had asked, fumbling to take out her desk calendar. This was Tuesday night. Hale would be back tomorrow afternoon. She'd question him at dinner; then if he couldn't or didn't clarify things, she'd maybe have time to get to Beth. If not, she'd let Bernice jump in, come what may.

"Bernice, I'd have more to give you then, maybe everything. And yes, I don't want to destroy the whole barrel of precious apples at the clinic if there's just one bad one in it. A fertility clinic that's worked the miracles they have…"

"All right, then. I'm going out on a limb with this. We've been friends awhile, though I won't cut you any slack if you don't appear in my office Thursday morning at nine a.m. sharp. This is kind of a plea bargain, Alexis, because I will have you arrested for withholding evidence if I don't see your face then…."

"Alex, you look faint," Nick whispered to bring her back to earth. The funeral went on, the chanting, the hot sun and wind in her face. "Do you want to sit down?" he asked.

"No, I'll make it," she told him and tightened both hands around his upper arm, though on the slick rock surrounding the stony, barren graveyard with its mixture of crosses and wooden tombstones, he was leaning on her too.

That touched her deeply: they needed each other, they could depend on each other. She was glad she had told him her suspicions about Jasmine, a sort of rehearsal for talking to the police. And for talking to Hale, because he could turn against her. In case she could not hold this child in the womb, she'd have to find someone else who could do the suturing procedure and soon.

The men's chanting got louder. She didn't understand a word of it, but its mournful tones and cadences spoke for itself. She began saying her own prayers, her own good-bye to one of the most unique people she had ever known.

The four men carrying the open wooden casket came slowly into the graveyard and laid it next to the newly dug, shallow hole. Alex stared at Rita's body, laid out in Pueblo regalia. Her profile was elegant, serene. Sacred meal dusted her face, whereas wild mustard pollen covered the faces of the mourners so they would not miss the dead too long. Rita's artist's hands, though torn and bruised from her fall, were clasped quietly now. Alex longed to say Rita's name in farewell, but she sang it in her heart, hoping that maybe the Lord in heaven could spare just one cherub for Rita to mother.

The tribal doctor—the same one who had done Rita's curing ceremony just over two weeks ago—chanted again as he covered Rita's face with a white cotton mask sewn with feathers to make the body "light" for travel to the other world. He tucked in the rabbit-skin rug that wrapped her. Paul himself stepped forward and hunched over to close and fasten the coffin lid. But for the chanting, no one made a sound and only the breeze rustled the dry grass.

Then Alex jerked back into Nick. His arm tightened around her. She shook her head to clear it. All of a sudden she had glimpsed Sandra lying there on her white bed, white pillow, so white, her face covered. And her own face still and calm.

Blessedly, Nick pulled her away. It was over. The mourners made their way back to Rita's sister Ada's house for the funeral feast. The mood changed instantly: life went on. Mutton stew, roasted piñon nuts, side dishes, and fragrant cornbread fresh-baked in the domed *horno* ovens abounded. People crowded in the small central room chatted, children squealed, even dogs wandered in and out. Paul's old grandmother, her face a web of wrinkles, sang a dissonant tune but occasionally broke into an old western song called "Happy Trails to You."

"I'm not telling Mike one word about any of this funeral for him to use on the air, even if he fires me," Alex told Nick. He sat next to the hearth with his leg propped up to keep it from swelling from all the standing.

"Bold words, especially since you've got more you're hiding from him than that," he warned, reaching to take her hand.

One of Rita and Paul's numerous, luminous-eyed nephews edged closer to Nick, staring at his cast through the long slice in the leg of his black jeans.

"Horsie?" he asked, putting one brown finger up his nostril. "White horsie?"

Alex didn't know what the little boy meant at first, but Nick did. "You can't ride the white horsie, but here's a black one," he told the child and reached slowly toward him. The round face broke into a huge smile as Nick pulled him closer and crossed his good leg over his broken on.

"Come on, take a ride, kiddo," Nick said. "What's your name?"

"Horsie?" the mite insisted.

"Then let's ride, Tonto."

Alex watched as Nick held the boy's upper arms and bounced him up and down on his booted foot, making neighing, whinnying sounds the child soon imitated. Alex stood against the wall, smiling, laughing when he did. Her arms ached to hold the little boy—and her own child. And then it hit her what a wonderful father Nick would make and how her child, boy or girl, would need him as much as she did now.

22

When Alex rushed home from stopping off to see Sandra that night, Nick hugged her at the door, but he was frowning.

"Bernice just called," he said. "She tried to get you on your car phone, but it didn't pick up. She expects to see you tomorrow morning at nine in her office, no matter what time Mike expects you in. I told her I'll be with you. Alexis, I hate to sound like a bully, but I'm not letting you out of my sight until then. You'll have to be content with the police interviewing Hale and Beth, not you."

She didn't argue, though she could not allow that. "I wonder why my phone didn't pick up," she said, stepping past him into the house. She tossed her purse in a chair she'd like to sink into. Neither Nick or Bernice knew she was meeting Hale in about an hour.

"I can check the batteries," he said, limping into the living room after her. Alex noticed his crutches were nowhere in sight. "By the way, I've turned this place over with a fine-tooth comb while you were at the hospital and still have no idea how someone got in to break those storytellers last night. I told Bernice—since you evidently forgot to—and had her send a forensic guy over to gather up the shards, because they still may find prints."

"Not if they didn't before," she said, pacing the room to glance out at the street through the front window. "I don't know how, but I'm starting to think it's some kind of inside job. But as you said, how?"

"One more thing. The forensics guy also brought back the butcher knife they took," he said, folding his arms over his chest. "It's in a brown envelope on the kitchen counter, in case you didn't just want it put away with the others."

"Thanks, Nick. For everything," she told him, and their eyes met across the room. He looked as tightly coiled as she felt.

"Anything I can do. I mean it. I wish I were the police. I'd haul in anyone and everyone for questioning, from the clinic and anyone from the station who could be professionally jealous and—"

"And the entire KALB viewing audience who might be against a single mother?" she said. "I just wish it was that easy."

She was too distracted and distraught to stand as he talked. She paced, feeling she was on a treadmill rushing toward something and she couldn't get off. Even if people like Bernice or Nick extended their helping hands, she had to trust only herself right now. She continued to make a circuit of the downstairs.

Her biggest immediate concern was telling Nick she

had to go back out—and alone. If she hadn't decided she wanted to tape-record what Hale said, she might have just kept going, but she didn't want Nick to think she was in danger or missing. She also needed to stop here to check on her messages. She had several important calls into various TV stations in New York state, asking about both Jasmine's and Beth's pasts, and she'd given them her home number as well as work.

"Why don't you settle somewhere?" Nick suggested as she walked into her office. "I'm going out to check on your car phone. Why didn't you put the Jeep in the garage instead of out front?"

"Sandra's showing some improvement, and I'm going back to the hospital to check on her," she called to him, then jammed her hand over her mouth. Sandra had shown improvement, but she had no intention of going back tonight. She'd lied to Nick, but nothing could happen to her in the public place she was meeting Hale.

"Then I'm going too, even if it forces us to leave the house unguarded," he yelled.

She didn't answer, but she'd find a way to get out alone. She had set up a safe situation to talk to Hale. She checked the calls on her answering machine. All business—some of it Nick's—and the fax tray was piled with junk. As soon as she heard him go out the front door, she opened the top desk drawer and took out her microcassette tape recorder. It was the one she'd used what seemed ages ago to play the recording Sandra had secretly made for her during the harvesting of her eggs. "Egg!" she could recall Jasmine calling out on that tape.

"Egg!" That was where this struggle for this baby—and this nightmare—had begun.

Alex clicked a fresh tape into it and put it down the front of her suit to be sure it wedged in her bra between her breasts. Yes, good, she thought as she taped it in. Hale would never know it was there. Now all she had to do was get out of here without upsetting Nick too much.

She heard him come back into the house and mutter something about batteries. He must be on his crutches now, because they made a particular sound on the tiles. When he went toward the back of the house, she hurried into the downstairs bathroom and checked to be sure the tape recorder didn't peek out or bulge. She used the toilet and flushed it. She'd just insist she was going to see Sandra alone, say that Mike would be there and could follow her back home.

Then it occurred to her that it was amazing if Nick knew where she kept the extra batteries in the house. He must have really scoped it out quickly and thoroughly, no matter what he said about being slow to learn her kitchen.

As she opened the bathroom door, she heard him on the phone. Had it rung when she flushed the toilet, or had he called someone? No matter, she'd tell him she was heading out alone—

"I want to get this over soon," she heard him say, almost in a whisper. She froze, pressed to the wall just outside the kitchen. "I'll keep her here tonight, and that should do it. Yeah, she changed the house alarm code again last night, but I know the new one. Just get over here and make sure you don't get stopped by the police...."

Alex darted quietly away. She grabbed her purse and hurried out the door, not even daring to make the noise by closing it. She had the Jeep—his Jeep, she regretted now—started and backed down the driveway before Nick even made it, limping without his crutches, onto the front patio to yell at her to come back.

Nick felt furious—betrayed. He should have known better than to trust another woman after Carolyn had so thoroughly screwed up his head and heart. Though he wasn't supposed to drive, he'd get out of here for good—if she hadn't dared to take off in his Jeep.

But after he slammed the door and made it into her office to see if something in here had set her off, he calmed down. He had come to understand Alexis, to see her desperate determination for a child, her drive to control her life and succeed in all she did. Unlike Paul, who had let Rita down—and maybe he'd let Carolyn down too—he could learn to accept and even appreciate that in Alexis. But never deceit.

The phone rang, jolting him just as he was ready to reach for it to call Bernice. He grabbed the receiver and said, "Alexis?"

He cursed silently when he heard a man's voice, then again when he realized he held Alexis's car phone in his hand. He missed the guy's name and asked him to repeat it—Jack Daniels, no less, at a TV station in New York.

Nick shook his head. He'd like a good slug of Jack

Daniel's bourbon right now. He was going to tell Mr. Daniels there was an emergency and please call back until he listened to what he way saying.

"So when I saw Ms. McCall had phoned the other day and gave me Beth Bradley's other name, it all fell together. The thing is, I've been on assignment and just got back to see this note. Spaulding—that rang a bell, all right, a story right out of that weekly show *Most Wanted*."

"Beth Bradley—the clinic nurse," Nick said, leaning over the desk to scribble notes. "But her name used to be Spaulding."

"You got it. A married name. Listen, just tell your wife that Elizabeth Spaulding pretty much matches the photo she faxed me. She was once questioned for drugging, then bludgeoning to death her ex-husband and his pregnant wife."

"What?" Nick cried. "That cute, upbeat little woman."

"Yeah, but she was never arrested, let alone tried, because, for one thing, there was nothing but circumstantial evidence and no one had any idea how she could have gotten into a burglar-proof house. Besides, character witnesses came out of the woodwork for her, including one other name Alexis sent me—Stanhope—the man and not the woman doctor. I don't think the woman Stanhope, ah, Jasmine, was even in the picture then."

"She is now," Nick whispered.

"What? Anyhow, whoever would believe—like you said—a petite, sweet woman who gives her life helping people have babies could murder people like that—one of them pregnant?"

"I—I've got to get this information to the police right now. Thanks. I'll have Alexis call you back when she can."

"You got it. Tell her we ran some of the fertility series here, and it really made an impact."

Nick shuddered. He could only hope that Alexis had gone out to meet with Hale and not Beth, but then if Hale had testified for her, maybe they were working together. Either way—wherever she was—he was getting Bernice and her boys to cover the clinic, their houses, anywhere Beth or Hale might be.

He heard the automatic garage door go up just as he punched in the first number. Thank God. Alexis was back, and they could decide how to handle this together.

He grabbed his crutches, hurried out into the kitchen, and undid the kitchen door to the garage. Already he could hear the garage door going back down, then hitting. A car door slammed. He yanked the door open. "Alex—"

The car that had driven in wasn't hers. It was a white van with Camelot Security on the side. A tall red-haired man got out. Nick thought a woman still sat in the passenger's seat, but he couldn't see who. "Alexis?" he said again, but he knew better when the man leveled a gun at him.

Alex clutched her purse strap tightly and leaned her head against the glass window of the gondola to stare out at the vast panorama below. The parking lot, then the treetops and the city dropped away beneath her view as the tramcar climbed the west face of Sandia Mountain on its triple-stranded safety cable, passing the gondola heading down.

This was the longest aerial tramway in the world, and she had grown to love it years ago. Geoff had once said it was almost like flying. Below, lights came on in the city, and above, stars struggled to peer through the deepening darkness.

The sky's-eye view of lush forests, soaring eagles, and an occasional glimpse of bighorn sheep climbing the cliffs usually put life's little problems in perspective for her, but not today. Like some of the wildlife below, she felt increasingly endangered.

Even Nick, whom she had come to trust, might have betrayed her. It could not have been the police on the phone with him. All she could think of was that perhaps Jasmine had offered Nick the land with Silver to keep an eye on her. But no, there had to be some other explanation. It made her feel more alone, but she had to face Hale. If this didn't work, she would just let Bernice do it all—in, she thought, glancing at her wristwatch, about eleven hours. And then she'd settle things with Nick one way or the other.

She had chosen the restaurant at the top of Sandia Peak because it was neutral ground, far away from Hale's supporting cast at the clinic. And he couldn't easily run off if he didn't like what she was saying or demanding. It was a long, slow way down. Suddenly she wished she'd chosen someplace not on a cliff.

As the remnants of daylight faded, the tramcar

bumped and swung its way into the roofed terminal. Usually the impact of bracing air at this altitude perked her up, but not tonight. She still felt drugged with despair and had a nervous stomach the moment she stepped out on firm land.

She had relied on Hale, been so grateful to him. In a strange way he was the spiritual father of her child. He had given her this last chance at a pregnancy, helped her get her mother back, then become the lifeline to her DES baby. And he did many good things for other Evergreen patients. Jasmine was about to ruin everything he'd hoped and worked for. She sympathized with him deeply if it meant the loss of his dreams.

She waited just inside the restaurant, where she could see gondolas arriving from below. The terminal was well lit, and few people were coming up this late on a weeknight before the tourist season got in full swing. When she finally spotted Hale in a tramcar—alone—she even waited until the next one came up to be sure Jasmine or even Peter or Beth didn't get off. Meanwhile, she'd watched Hale emerge from the terminal in blue sports jacket and slacks and walk up toward the restaurant. She had already cased, as Bernice would say, the people inside the sparsely populated restaurant to be sure she recognized no one.

She ducked into the rest room and turned on the tape recorder hidden between her breasts. She didn't even care if he tried to claim entrapment when Jasmine finally went to court. After all, her recording could actually help to keep him out of whatever Jasmine had done—if he wasn't guilty.

When she went to meet Hale by the hostess desk, his

whole face lit up and his eyes swept her. Warning alarms went off in her head. Surely, he didn't think this was some sort of tryst she'd set up. If so, he was going to be doubly disillusioned. But no, she realized, he was just possessive about someone carrying one of his clinic babies. She tried to steady her legs and her voice. She just felt sick about this.

"I really appreciate you're agreeing to talk, Hale," she told him as the hostess seated them in a table for two by the window overlooking the tramway as it plunged into the valley.

"Love the view. And the name of the restaurant— High Finance." He chuckled.

"At least you've always seemed to me to be in your career for other reasons than money, though I'm sure your work is lucrative as well as altruistic." In tough interviews she always tried to put her subject at ease with compliments or talk of personal concerns. "How's your mother doing?" she added when he merely nodded at her observation.

"Actually, she's dying of Alzheimer's," he admitted, putting down the menu the hostess handed him without looking at it.

"Oh, Hale, I'm sorry."

"Scares the hell out of me—the genetic ramifications, I mean, aside from losing her. It's like she's had one of those amnesiac drugs we use, Alexis, only she's getting stronger and stronger doses."

Alex shuddered at the memory. She sipped some water their server poured before telling them the specials and then disappearing again.

"Forgive me for playing doctor, Alexis," he said, leaning closer across the table on folded arms, "but you don't look well. I know Rita's death took a lot out of you after the tragedy with Sandra, but you've got to take better care of yourself. I've told you that all along. I can only do so much."

"I realize that. And I am."

"I don't think so. You risked your pregnancy going down the cliff after Sandra when the emergency squad was on the way."

"I'll never regret that, Hale, because—"

"And are you eating? I'm going to make sure you do tonight."

She could barely stand to think of food, but she ordered. Her stomach was tied in knots at facing him— facing him down like this. She felt so nervous, really shaky, but she relied on her long-honed on-air skills to seize control of herself.

"Hale, I have always respected you deeply, as have most of your patients. And been grateful for all you've done, but I have some real concerns I need to discuss with you before this goes any further."

Crumbs flew when he broke into his roll with his butter knife. "Before what does?" he replied, his voice tautly controlled. "I hope you're not implying that someone on my staff could wish any of our patients or your colleagues harm. Or do you mean those claims Rita made against the lab and Jasmine and me?"

That he would go on the offensive surprised her. She tried not to show it.

"Hale, Rita is not the only patient who has become

convinced that something is amiss, to put it mildly, with eggs and embryo counts in Dr. Jasmine's lab. She's experimenting—"

"Of course she is. Too damn many hours to please me."

"Then let me ask this. Is Jasmine pregnant?"

"What? Hell, no. That's not on her agenda," he insisted, but he looked either embarrassed or angry now. The tips of his ears turned red.

"But she has been before. And, like Beth, failed to come to term," Alex prompted.

He clunked his knife down, hitting his other utensils. His uneaten roll hit his plate. "So what? A lot of people are in the fertility field because of personal tragedies. At least half the psychiatrists in the world go into that specialty to solve their own problems, I swear they do. Have you been talking to Beth, or are you just playing twenty questions about Jasmine? The two of them don't get along personally—I'm sure you've figured that one out. Beyond that, it's none of your business, Alexis, but yes, Jasmine has been pregnant twice and miscarried twice. I believe you share that with her and probably more than you know."

Alex nodded jerkily. She was starting to feel even worse—her head, her stomach. She fought back the vision of those two embryos in jars in Jasmine's desk. But if she mentioned those to Hale, they would probably be gone by morning when Bernice might want to get a search warrant.

"Jasmine spoke in Miami on the call to arms for egg research and freezing." She shifted topics a bit, fighting to keep her concentration. "She mentioned DMSO, and I think she's been using it. But if she had been pregnant—Hale, it can cause birth defects. She's had garlic breath—you must know that—which can indicate she's been working with it. But if it can possibly cause birth defects in a pregnant woman, what can it do to eggs once they are fertilized and implanted to make a woman pregnant? Maybe that woman wouldn't even have to get near DMSO to have a child with birth defects."

"Alexis, your imagination's going crazy. Where in the hell is this going? I've no doubt Jasmine's used experimental tactics in the lab, but she wouldn't—just wouldn't risk that."

"Then answer this. Where is she getting all the eggs or embryos to use experimental tactics on, as you put it?"

"You know, *Dr.* McCall," he mocked, openly hostile now, "I think you'd better calm down and just stay in your own area of expertise. You're flushed and trembling. I think all of this has been too much for you, and if you don't want to be joining your friend Sandra in the hospital, I suggest—"

She noted he'd shifted topics but chose to ignore the veiled threat. "Hale, for starters, I think Jasmine's taking eggs from your patients, a few here and there, more when she can get them. Something's got to be done to stop her. It may not be illegal, but it's immoral—you know that, and I'm terrified you know what she's doing."

She took another swig of water. Her pulse was pounding. She really did feel sick. She'd gone too far.

"Listen to me," Hale said, reaching across the table to seize her wrist in a grip hard enough to make her hand go numb. "You're ill and imagining things—you're becoming paranoid like Rita—and it's going to cost you your child, a clinic DES baby I don't want you to lose. Do you hear me?" he added, giving her a little shake.

She could tell he was panicking. "Don't try to frighten me," she insisted, pulling free of him.

"It's exactly what you need. Alexis, do you have cramps?"

Her wide gaze slammed into his narrow one across the table. She had to admit it was a bit like that. Like menstrual cramps, only worse, building, radiating out to make her feel prickly hot, then cold, clamped by pain. Dear God, not—not that. Not now. She couldn't need Hale now, now when she was taking him on, not when he'd warned her that he'd have to give her anesthesia and suture her....

"I don't know," she choked out. What had he asked her?

"Then listen to me carefully. Next you're going to be accusing Jasmine—and me, as clinic paterfamilias—of something really crazy. Of stealing eggs and embryos to do experiments to produce alien beings or something. Shall we get the tabloids in here next, instead of just KALB? Is that what you want? Now, we've helped you and you've helped us and perhaps it's time to just sever our relationship, because I'd hate to lose you this way."

"I'm only warning you what she's doing..." she managed to get out when the first really brutal twist of pain wrenched her. It was so bad, she doubled over toward the table, knocking her water glass over just as the server brought the salads. He hastened off for a towel and help.

"Hale—if this is what you said I'm having—about DES, you said we only have two hours to stop it…."

"You know," Hale was saying, his voice maddeningly calm again as he glanced at his watch, "I should have thought of this. A quick change in barometric pressure, such as right before a hurricane hits, can cause women to go into premature labor. It's just a theory, but maybe this high altitude has triggered exactly what I warned you of."

"Hale, oh—it can't be. Help me, please."

"Waiter, here's my credit card. This woman's sick, but I'm a doctor, and I'm going to get her some help."

"At the hospital—E.R.," she managed to gasp as Hale helped her up and propelled her through the restaurant. "Two hours. It's closer."

"The clinic," he said, "is not much farther, just around the mountain on 556. I'm afraid by the time we got a squad down below…."

"Not the clinic. Call—ahead and—the squad—be there," she told him, but he seemed to ignore her.

She tried to tell herself it was all right. He had given the man his credit card, so there would be a record of whom she was here with. Plenty of people had seen them. Hale had announced he was her doctor. The drive to the clinic could not even take an hour. And he had warned her long ago this might happen and that she could lose the baby if he didn't help her….

"I need to call Nick—my house," she said as the waiter caught up with them to give Hale his credit card back, then opened the door for them. Hale walked her from the restaurant into the cold night air. The city looked so far down the mountainside from here. She stood on the very edge, just like Sandra, Rita. She was so high, so sick and dizzy, afraid of going over the edge even before the next wave of pain hit her. Should she time these cramps—contractions—she wondered. Less than two hours to save the baby, then ten until Bernice helped her.

"A tramcar's here, so we don't have time to waste," Hale said and pulled her toward it. "I'll take care of you. I can do this alone if I have to, but Jasmine's probably there and she can assist. Alexis, stop fighting me. You've got to trust me now, or you're going to lose that pregnancy."

"Jas—no," she cried as he helped her firmly into the cable car and sat her down on a molded plastic bench. He sat beside her, his arm around her shoulders, holding her to him while she shuddered helplessly. Someone down below—should she call to them for help, or was Hale her only help? Time...no time to waste.

The cables rattled. The car dropped away into blackness.

She opened her eyes. They were in a glass box, floating like what Jasmine hid in her drawer. She could see their black reflections, hers and Hale's. No one else—they were alone here.

She broke out in a cold sweat. She tried to look at her watch, but the numbers jumped and swam. She still felt the agony of her ticking heart, like those other times she had gone into labor early and lost her children. Her last chance now. Only one inside and time ticking, beating. She needed help fast.

And she needed Nick, but she had run out on him again.

"Call Nick," she heard herself say, her voice stronger.

"I know you're sick. Trust me. I'm going to take care of you, Alexis, you and that clinic baby."

23

Sandra surfaced slowly. One eyelid opened. The other. Light blinded her. She blinked. Blinked. Something kept beeping, humming in her head. Her vision focused. Machines. A man with his head bent over his hands. Mike.

"Mmm-ike…"

He jolted straight up in his chair. He jammed his glasses on. "Sandra! You're awake. I'll get the nurse. Nurse, nurse!" he cried, darting away.

She wanted him to come back. Hold her hand. Hold her. She remembered now. The car behind her, hitting, shoving. A great roar. Alex screaming somewhere. Then nothing but Alex talking, talking.

"Sandra, honey…" Mike murmured when he rushed back in. He took her hand, bent close to kiss her forehead. Heaven.

"Mike."

"Don't go back to sleep. The nurse is coming. It's been eleven days of hell—"

"No. Heaven. Alex?"

"She's all right. She was here earlier. She's—"

"Tell her in the car—a woman and man. Tell her to look out for both."

"But who?" Mike asked as he leaned closer, holding her hand.

"Not Jasmine, not a blonde," she said as the nurse and then a doctor rushed into the room.

"Jasmine?" Mike repeated, his voice rising. "Dr. Jasmine Stanhope? Did Alexis think it might be Jasmine? Why didn't she tell me?"

"You tell her."

"But women can change hair color. Carolyn Destin did. She's out on bond. Could it have been her?"

"I don't know. Alex—her baby?" Sandra asked, trying to squeeze his hand so he wouldn't let her go. But the doctor came close. No doctors, she wanted to scream and tried to shove at him. But she had no strength. Besides, doctors must have helped her, saved her. Eleven days, Mike said. She had come back from somewhere filled only with Alex's voice. But if Alex's voice was there, she wondered dazedly, didn't that mean she was somewhere unconscious too?

"Her baby—fine, I think," Mike was saying as he stepped to the foot of her bed. "And I'm going to be the other godparent, so you just hang on, Sandra. We'll do that—and a lot of things together."

"Hang on to you," she whispered. Godparents, she thought. Mike and I, together with a child to love. Tears squeezed from her eyes. Already she was better, but she was still afraid for Alex.

* * *

Alex began to struggle, not for her baby but against it. Against it being born too early, falling the way Sandra and Rita had. She wanted this baby. Why didn't God help her save just one of her babies?

And why didn't Hale call for help? He put her in the backseat of his car and drove fast. He had a phone here, and she begged him to call Nick, but he called only the clinic. Then he tried to call Beth, but she didn't answer.

Alex was desperate to get out of the car before they reached the clinic and Jasmine, but she didn't dare to. She kept her knees bent the way Hale told her. Maybe he would really help her, but she was so afraid. Time was ticking, so she closed her eyes tightly, but the street-lights and the TV cameras lights kept spinning into the light on Hale's head when she found herself on top of the operating table.

She was already in the transfer room at the clinic!

She screamed when the woman repositioned a needle in her arm that was attached to a dripping envelope on its own umbilical cord. It didn't hurt her arm, but it hurt her head, broke her heart. Because she knew now. Knew they would do something terrible in this place she had trusted and made other people trust. Kill her. Take back her clinic baby.

"Alexis, stop struggling." The man's voice, Hale's. "It will all be over soon."

She turned her head to see the big wall clock, but it was upside down, tilted. His face floated close above her to block it out as he pulled up his mask. It wasn't a pirate's mask, but she screamed again, quieter this time.

"All right," a woman said somewhere nearby. It was Jasmine. Jasmine. "That will put her completely under."

"Get her prepped and don't complain about having to play nurse for me. Beth's not answering her phone or beeper, but you and I have a lot to settle tonight anyway. I'll be right back. I want that baby."

Alex wanted to fight, to run. Her legs were leaden as Jasmine removed her undergarments from the waist down and lifted her legs into stirrups, strapping them in. Alex thrashed weakly as Jasmine pressed her arms to her sides and pulled velcro strips over her middle, across her flat belly.

She drifted away into a cold white fog until the man came back into the room with a crack of doors like thunder. "Ready?" he said. "Let's get this over with."

The woman washed her with some cold solution, then stepped aside to pull up a rolling machine. The man moved something over her belly. A picture came up on a TV screen. One sac, bigger than the last time she'd seen this. Her baby! Then the woman stepped closer to block out the scene as she handed the doctor a needle and held a pair of scissors.

Then Alex saw only blackness outside and inside too.

Nick was in agony, not so much from being forced to lie tied and gagged in the back of the van—but from panic about Alex coming back to her house and being harmed. And he would not be there to help her.

Beth Bradley and the man had answered none of his demands as they threw a tarp over him and the man drove the van out to park—he thought—just on the next block. Where was that police car? Why didn't someone stop them? He was too far away to limp back to the house quickly even if he did get loose. He hadn't had time to call Bernice. His only hope was that she—or his own man he'd hired to watch Alex—would somehow intervene before Alex came back. If only she could read his notes about Beth Bradley Spaulding's past he'd left on her desk before Beth saw them.

Alex awoke inside the white fog again. No, a ceiling, curtains. She darted a glance around at the familiar clinic recovery cubicle. Her brain jolted alert if not her body.

"Her blood pressure's stabilized." Dr. Jasmine's voice came to her from outside the curtain. "Thank God, because we don't need the police questioning us again. You took a big risk."

"So what's new?" Hale said. "Let me just check her heart. But first, go phone Beth again to get in here. I've got to get at least some sleep, so I'll just use Peter's bed in his office. And I gave him a bad time because he wanted it soundproofed so he could get naps during the day. But, Jasmine, we've got to come to a decision about all this. I won't have anyone pinning Sandra's or Rita's accidents on any of us."

Things came back in pieces. Jasmine and Hale—she had been having dinner with Hale, but where did Jasmine come from? Why were they here? And, she thought as he swept back the curtain and bent over her with a stethoscope, if he listened to her heart, he'd find the tape recorder with his voice on it. She could feel it taped tautly between her breasts.

She tried to raise her arms to keep him away, but they were strapped to her sides on a gurney. Her legs were down and together so she must have dreamed the rest of the nightmare—something terrible, just out of her reach. It was a strange dream because she thought she'd been talking to Sandra—and Rita had been there and told her to wake up now and fight back.

"Wha' happened?" she asked Hale, slightly slurring her words. "My baby's all right?"

"So you're back with us," he said and nodded. He put the cold sphere of the stethoscope against her skin inside the V-neck of her blouse and slid it slightly down, listening intently. The tubes to his earpieces looked like black tentacles. She held her breath. He jumped when he moved the stethoscope again, and it clicked against the tape recorder.

Ignoring the fact Hale unbuttoned her blouse and pulled out the tape recorder, she demanded louder, "Are you sure my baby's all right?"

"I told you I'd take care of things," he said, frowning at the tiny recorder. He slipped it into his pocket.

"That's mine."

"I realize that. And a lot of things," he whispered, leaning close and narrowing his eyes.

Strapped down like this and at his—their—mercy, she knew it was not the time to demand or accuse. She did not tell him that Nick probably had the police look-

ing for her long before she was due downtown at police headquarters at nine in the morning—if Nick was
really on her side. How many hours now? She expected
Nick and the police to knock down the clinic door any
minute and rescue her.

Then she remembered everything else.

"Did you suture me in time? I don't feel any more
cramps."

"We gave you a muscle relaxant," he said, then
gripped her shoulder hard and gave it a little shake.
"Now, concentrate on what I'm saying, Alexis. Jasmine's work in her lab, however risky and obsessive, is
for the benefit of women everywhere, women like you.
Galileo, Einstein, and other brilliant minds would have
been stifled or stopped if the pope or Hitler or whom-
ever had their way. You've got to get off her back. If Jasmine overstepped, we'll deal with that, but she's not evil
and she has nothing to do with your car being shoved
off that cliff. Now, I want your word I can have some
time on clearing up this misunderstanding about experimental eggs. I think you owe me. And frankly, I'd
rather send you home than keep you here…."

"Yes. Until tomorrow," she said, giving him nothing.
Nick had been right. She never should have tried this
alone. Soon she would have it in the hands of the authorities. She only prayed the police could prove Jasmine had committed the other crimes, no matter what
Hale said. But now Alex had to get out of here somehow.

"What time is it?" she asked.

"Just after two a.m.," was the last thing she remembered him saying for a long time.

She must have slept again. She dreamed voices screaming. Had Hale accused Jasmine and she was shouting back? They were arguing about Beth not being here, something about Beth. It was then Alex realized she was no longer bound. As she sat up, dizziness assailed her, but she put her legs determinedly over the side of the cart. She felt sore, loggy. She edged off and her legs almost collapsed under her. She grabbed the gurney to keep from falling, and it bumped into the wall.

"She's promised us until tomorrow to work it out." Alex heard Hale's voice coming closer. "We've got to clean up some things here and bluff it out, make sure Beth and Tom won't say the wrong thing if they're questioned. I think we can make some sort of deal with Alexis if we promise her big-time coverage when you get a breakthrough—"

"You stupid, stupid man. She's not like the rest of them. She won't make a deal like that. She's desperate to be a mother first, to save her baby, then the world. But I'll try to reason with her, promise her something, if you just give me some time alone with her. Just take a quick shower, then lie down and let me see how she's doing. And I'm going to kill your little Beth tomorrow for ditching her beeper when we needed her...."

No way, Alex thought, she was going to face down Jasmine alone. She had to get to the police, get out of here, away from this clinic and the cliffs outside.

Thank God she knew the layout here so well. However shaky she felt, despite the packing between her legs and a muscle relaxant that made her move like one drunk, she staggered out of the recovery area. Bouncing off or leaning on walls, she got down the hall. A phone hung near the back door. Should she call 911? But she'd just done a piece on how some operators stalled, asking you your name, to spell it, to explain everything, and stay on the line. And Nick and Mike would take too long to get here.

So she phoned for a taxi. She knew the number, all 4's, painted on the side of every cab. She whispered her name, telling the dispatcher the cab should come only to the far edge of the parking lot and must not leave without her. And then, feeling immensely better, she was out the door into the chill country night.

But in her panic to escape, she'd forgotten about the new motion-detector alarm system at the clinic. Blinding lights blazed on as she hobbled away barefoot, lurching at first to keep her feet. Mounted on the corbels of the roof, high-intensity lights shot her shadow ahead of her, so huge it looked distorted. A hunched monster lumbered along with her away from the clinic.

She was instantly out of breath and sweating hard in the cool night breeze. Somehow she'd pulled the muscle in her thigh again.

She forced herself to think, to stay calm. Into the shadows—she had to make it out of this light in case they looked or came out. The taxi company would send their closest car—maybe ten, fifteen minutes. She shook her head; she had her watch on. But she realized now she wore no nylons, panties, or shoes under her suit and had no purse.

Before she even made it to the parking lot, she heard the back door of the clinic open. She glanced around to see a stark rectangle of light leap out into the already bright scene.

"Alexis!"

Jasmine.

"You'll bleed to death or fall out there, you idiot," she shouted. "Come back. Hale and I can drive you into town."

Alex limped toward the shelter of the forest. It was a much longer way to the parking lot, but otherwise Jasmine would catch her. Had she seen her? Panting, her ribs aching, she leaned against a rough-barked pine. Dry needles prickled her bare feet. If she couldn't ditch Jasmine, she might miss her taxi, miss getting out of here. Why hadn't Nick sent the police? Surely the clinic would be one of the first places they would look.

From the thatched cover of pine needles, Alex watched Jasmine stand a moment, cupping one hand above her eyes to try to stare past the wall of lights. Good, she hadn't seen her, or at least not where she turned up into the dark forest fringe. But in Jasmine's free hand something glinted. Alex's legs almost buckled again. Jasmine had a gun. Feeling hunted, Alex froze like a deer before flight.

But Jasmine stepped back inside the clinic and killed the lights. Was she going to get Hale? Hadn't he seen these lights or heard the alarm? Or had Jasmine done something to him? But Alex knew her problem wasn't Hale right now.

Jasmine came back out with a big flashlight and swept the edge of the grounds, back and forth. Alex pressed to a thick tree trunk as the glare crawled by and swung back again. She didn't want to go near the edge overlooking Silver, but Jasmine had completely cut off the parking lot for now. Reluctantly, her pulse pounding, Alex picked her way toward the cliff. She still walked tipsily, and her legs felt like rubber. She'd just have to make it way around the clinic to the road and quickly, no matter what.

"Alexis!" came Jasmine's voice again. "We need to talk, to make a deal. You and me, not Hale this time. A-le-xiiis!"

Panic tinged her voice. Good. But a root or vine snagged Alex's ankle and she went down, skidding on her knees, then scrambling up. It was enough to bring Jasmine charging in that direction.

Alex darted away as best she could. She had no illusion Jasmine wouldn't shoot her. She would claim she was protecting the lab from another prowler. Or roll her off the cliff as she must have Rita, off into Nick's beloved Silver.

She heard Jasmine closing behind her, not talking now, sweeping that beam so it blinked like huge strobes among the trees. Night and light made Alex lose her way. How close was she to the cliff? How much time had passed? The taxi—if she could somehow get Jasmine's gun away from her and make it to the taxi and to Nick and the police.

Nick. She needed Nick and not just to help her now. Blind, she'd been blind to his needs for a solid, stable woman. She'd run from him like this. Surely his phone call tonight could not have been to Carolyn....

She felt bare rock without needles under her feet and stopped. The moon was a mere splinter, blurred by the sweep of Jasmine's light. Alex began to fear a bullet in her back or her belly. Running might trigger her cramps again. And what if Hale had not saved her baby? He had not exactly said he did. Wretched, exhausted, she shuffled back toward the shelter of the trees.

Jasmine turned out the light and moved in the dark. Gasping as silently as she could for breath, Alex heard Jasmine stop nearby. "Alexis, I know you're here. I just want to talk to you," she repeated, her voice deadly calm. "Hale suggests we make a deal, and I agree. Come on out or you could hemorrhage to death with that procedure Hale and I just did for you."

Alex huddled, hunched behind a clump of prickly bush. For some reason the memory of the first day she had been here with Rita, walking on this cliff, came back to her with stunning clarity, in vibrant pictures. Rita had already cut the barbed-wire fence apart so they could get through. Then later, on the day they'd trapped Carolyn here, the police had cut even more openings in the barbed wire. But why was she thinking all this now when she was trapped?

Then Alex saw what she must do. Jasmine had moved slightly away. She turned on the light again, casting the beam toward the path that descended into the valley. On her knees Alex edged out, not deeper into forest fringe but toward the edge. Praying Jasmine would never think she would be here, never shine the light here, she touched and tugged one section of fence. It was double barbed wire and pricked and cut her when she grabbed it in the wrong places, but it pulled up and away from its low wooden posts until she had a section of it, tugging it after her as she slowly crawled backward.

Still on her knees, back behind her bush, she gingerly rolled it in a huge coil. But the last length of it snagged and pulled, making a slight scraping sound. Jasmine swung around and pinned her with the light.

"I never thought you'd run out here, but you like living on the edge, don't you?" Jasmine taunted as she strode closer and shone the light full at Alex to blind her. Alex stood slowly, partway behind the bush. She wondered if Jasmine had seen the coil of barbed wire, for though it stood two feet wide, the bush hid it and the light shone through it.

"It takes a woman on the edge to recognize that," Alex said, still so furious she was fighting to sound rational. "You're the one who lives that way, at any cost to others."

"Drastic needs demand drastic measures," she said defiantly, almost smugly, not lowering the light. She held it in one hand and the raised gun in the other. The barrel pointed like a big black hole at Alex.

"In other words, Dr. Jasmine," Alex dared, "your grand cause justifies any means, any loss by others, any agony."

"How can you mock my work? You heard what I'm trying to do. It makes your attempts to help infertile women with your skimpy skills nothing," Jasmine spat out with contempt. "And how dare you suggest to Hale that you would hold him or the clinic responsible for my work? I'm responsible, and I will take the credit."

"And the blame? For attempted murder on me and Sandra, then for succeeding with Rita to protect yourself? More of your drastic means?"

"I didn't hurt either of them," she insisted vehemently. "All that is probably Destin's crazy wife again, or someone competing with the clinic or angry with your TV series, like Hale thinks. Actually, I wish I had eliminated you from the first, but you were bringing us a lot of money that I needed to build—to go on. Now I'm afraid I'm going to have to leave, start over, and someone has to pay for that—to set me up again elsewhere. You've ruined everything here."

For the first time Alex's instincts told her Jasmine might actually be innocent of the attacks on her, Sandra, and Rita. Or else she thought she was, because she was above everyone else. But then who was guilty? Some of it could be Carolyn, but she didn't believe that. Not Hale. But Beth had lied to her. And Beth did adore and guard Hale in a way Jasmine never would or could. But facing down that gun, she did know one thing clearly. She trusted Nick. Somehow she had misunderstood him on the phone and panicked, but she could not panic now.

"But with that gun," Alex went on, fighting to keep calm, "you're acting like a murderer. Are you claiming you didn't somehow get into my house those times to try to terrorize—"

Jasmine snorted derisively, but she did not lower the

gun. "I wouldn't stoop to any of that pettiness, or take the time. You just don't get it, do you? I care only about preserving women's eggs for the future, Asian, Afro-American, yes—Pueblo Native American too."

"Rita's eggs," Alex whispered. "She was right all along." Alex squinted as she tried to stare into the bright beam of Jasmine's flashlight. When she'd said Rita's name, she actually thought she'd seen her standing there in shadow, listening, angry. She'd heard that click of beads from the leather strap around her hair. She blinked again. Nothing but bright spots before her eyes, as when someone shot a photo flash at you.

"Actually, Rita doesn't matter," Jasmine was saying. "Individuals don't matter. My work is survival science for the entire human species. What if there's a nuclear war, a rampant virus, or other national or global catastrophe and we have to repopulate the earth? What if—"

"It's already a catastrophe," Alex interrupted. "There might as well have been a nuclear war with fallout or some disfiguring virus, considering the mutant, grotesque thing I saw in your lab file drawer. The one fetus was labeled as yours, so was that one too? If you're willing to turn your own babies into monsters, what will you do to other women's eggs and embryos?"

"So you were in my lab. I knew it. But so what if you saw that little failure I use to spur myself on? That one wasn't mine. It was—an early failure," she said, stumbling over her words now. The gun and the flashlight shook.

"But what if there are other failures like that—that thing? Had the egg that made that fetus been soaked in

DMSO? If you're preserving eggs for hundreds of years, what if they turn out like that and you never know it? Your work and name will be sullied for all time, and—"

"No! That failure was from a surrogate mother I paid, that's all. It was her fault. I tried it too early. Something has to help preserve those egg membranes, and DMSO does. And stop trying to change the subject. *You were in my lab!* You had no right," she shouted. "I'm sick to death of being challenged by someone who can never understand, should do nothing but support me. So let me give you a little object lesson, Alexis. Wouldn't you be glad I still had your extra eggs frozen—the ones you made me destroy—"

"The freezer tank safety lights were on when I left the lab that night. The lid was closed. You just took the chance to rob me and others of more of their eggs— ones you may turn to monster babies someday with that untested chemical DM—"

"Shut up! Don't you think I'm testing it now? I've even been rubbing it on my skin during this IVF cycle I'm in, and I'll have Hale harvest those eggs to use."

"How dare you call Rita crazy? You're the one—"

"I'm telling you," she shouted, "that you've ruined your last chance for a child—that DES baby with the terrible odds against it you still think you're carrying."

That cleared everything else from Alex's mind. "Wh—at? Hale's done what he had to tonight, and I at least trust—"

"Oh, yes, just like them all, like Beth, worship and trust Hale and hate and disdain me. Well, let me make myself clearer. You've misunderstood what happened while you were under anesthesia tonight. Since you'd never carry it to term anyway, I talked Hale into giving me your last chance for my work."

Alex's knees almost buckled. "That's not true. He just sutured—"

"You bled quite a bit, you know, a lot for a d and c. He couldn't bear to tell you himself, but you might as well face reality. Alexis, you carry no child anymore and never will. I convinced Hale this would be better for your health, better to get it over now instead of getting your hopes up and—"

"Stop it, you liar!" Alex shouted, startled by her own shrill voice. "That's not true. I can feel it. And I know I'm carrying this baby!"

Again the light wavered in her hand; the gun did too. But rage and desperation drowned her fear.

"Oh, Hale," Alex cried out and turned to stare into the darkness behind Jasmine. "Thank God you're here! Tell me I still have my baby."

She was bluffing, but she actually thought she saw Rita there nodding where she pretended to see Hale….

When Jasmine jerked toward where Alex was staring and swung her light, Alex rolled the tall coil of barbed wire at her. It could hardly knock her down, but it bounced into her. Amazingly, she went down on her knees as if someone had hit her from behind. The gun skidded across the rock face and bounced over the side.

With a physical strength and fury she didn't know she had, Alex dragged Jasmine by her hair and clothes toward the coil of wire. And though Jasmine fought and screamed and the barbs cut Alex's hands again, adrenaline and fury for her and Rita and Jing and others gave her the strength to roll her in it and away from the cliff into the trees.

When Jasmine tried to scream, Alex ripped the hem from her own skirt and jammed it through the layers of wire into her mouth. Finally, she retrieved the light and shone it right in her face.

Filthy and dishevelled, scratched and bleeding, Jasmine screwed her eyes tight shut. Alex rolled her farther back and wedged the coil between two trees.

Still breathless, Alex choked out, "You're a sorry specimen, Jasmine. For a scientist and mother—and a woman."

She limped away, dragging herself toward the back parking lot where a taxi waited, the only car in the lot besides the two Stanhope cars. Alex signaled to him with the light. No way she could face Hale right now or even see if he was all right. She'd get the police here right away. And she was heading home to settle everything with Nick.

"To town—fast," Alexis told the driver as she got in the backseat. He craned around to gape at her appearance. "We're going to have to call the police on your radio— to come out here to arrest someone. And they're going to have to go to someone's house in town. Drive, please!"

He took off while Alex huddled, relieved but exhausted in the backseat. She knew now she could have been wrong, fatally wrong. Whatever lies Jasmine had told, she could be telling the truth about not threatening her or harming Sandra or Rita. Since it wasn't Hale, Beth was next in line.

24

As the taxi pulled in her driveway, tears burned Alex's eyes at the sight of home. Nick must still be up waiting for her because downstairs lights burned. She'd ask him to explain that call, but she knew she had not misjudged him. Jasmine and maybe Beth she'd read wrong, despite her own pride in thinking she could psych out people. But Nick—no. He loved her and she could begin to return that love now. But first she needed to talk in person to the police.

She saw no police car down the block—unless they'd just moved their position or been sent to the clinic. Her clothes a mess, barefoot, she walked gingerly. Nick didn't come when she hit the doorbell. Just a minute," she called to the taxi driver, waiting with his lights on in the driveway. "I'll be right out with your fare."

Her stomach felt queasy again, but she told herself it was just nerves. How could she blame Nick for leaving after the way she'd acted? And maybe it wasn't as bad as she thought because he could have summoned the police car down the street to help him go look for her. But why hadn't he thought of trying the clinic?

She used the key she had hidden in the terra-cotta cactus crock on the patio and let herself in the front door.

"Nick?"

Exhaustion and depression swamped her strength again, but she dove at the alarm and punched in the code so it wouldn't go off. She got some money and darted back out to pay the driver, giving him a huge tip.

"Thanks for all your help," she called to him from the open front door. "I'll call the police again from here to verify everything your dispatcher told them."

"Hope they get that Beth woman arrested at her place," he called out the cab window.

"I'll call you later for an interview when all of this gets worked out."

"Can do, Ms. McCall."

"Nick?" she called inside the door again. She locked up and reset the alarm. As tight as he'd been with Bernice lately, she wouldn't be surprised if they'd gone to question Beth when she reported her to the police through the taxi dispatcher just a little while ago. Perhaps she'd barely missed him.

She scanned the kitchen counter for a note from him. Nothing but the narrow, long brown envelope with the butcher knife the police had finally returned. She tucked it under her arm, deciding it might become evidence someday. Fingerprints or not, she'd put it in her office. She had to call Bernice now, but her number was in the office too.

She hurried in, hitting on the lights. Exhausted, yet still running on adrenaline, she sank in the desk chair and spun, one-handed, through her Rolodex. Then she saw a lengthy note in Nick's handwriting next to the phone.

"Oh, thank heavens," she said, expecting an explanation of where he'd gone. But when she skimmed it, she gasped. Beth was once under suspicion for drugging and killing her ex-husband—and a pregnant woman she thought had betrayed her. And Nick had circled Hale's name. Hale, among others, had vouched for her so she was never even indicted. At least that explained what Nick had done—called Bernice, gone after Beth with her. And it explained why Beth wanted to protect and no doubt adored Hale. But surely Hale was not working with her.

Something at the corner cupboard that once held the kachinas caught her eye, and she jerked her head around. In scrubs, wearing surgical gloves, stood Beth Bradley in the flesh, just watching her with narrowed eyes.

Alex's gasp seemed to suck in all the air in the room. She thought her lungs and brain would burst. She felt light-headed, then just dizzy.

"Beth! What are you—where's Nick?"

"He'd just get in the way while we settle things. You had dinner with Hale somewhere secret tonight, didn't you, and now you run home all disheveled. Do you think I'm blind? I actually thought I might find him here with you."

"Hale. No, but Nick—"

"You never loved Nick. The moment Hale saw you were special and powerful, he wanted you and you wanted him. You're just using Nick. I know all about that, believe me."

In one terrible slash of insight, Alex saw how Beth had tried to keep Hale away from her. And after Alex had shown him gratitude or later affection, or been alone with him, something dire would happen, here in this house—or elsewhere.

"You'd better leave, Beth," Alex said, fighting to keep her voice calm and forceful when all she wanted to do was run for the door. What had Beth done with Nick? Or had she come here after he had gone? At least Beth appeared to have no gun or other weapon.

"You'd better leave," Alex repeated, speaking over her thudding heart. Beth just glared at her. "I'm going to call the police to see if they arrested Jasmine yet at the clinic. That's where I've been—"

"And Hale was there too, of course."

"He did a procedure to keep me from miscarrying. But I've finally got the goods on Jasmine for stealing eggs and embryos. I'm hoping she'll go to jail for it, so you can continue to help Hale after she's—"

"You're sending her away to get him for yourself. You've done what I couldn't, because I couldn't risk getting rid of her yet, even when I wanted to. The clinic needed her; he thought he needed her when he only needed me. But he'll know that now."

Alex began to breathe a bit easier. Hale wasn't involved. And if it came to a struggle here, she was bigger than the weaponless nurse. Still, to think of risking a physical fight in her still shaky condition scared her too.

"Beth," she went on, rising slowly and sidling a step around the desk toward the door, "I don't know how you got inside today or the other times, but you'd better get out of here."

"Not yet. This has to end, Alexis. Gill!"

The moment Alex saw him, everything else fit together. The Camelot Security man. And, as he filled the doorway, she glimpsed the silhouette of that pirate coming after that night at Reelworld while fireworks popped overhead. She saw spots before her eyes again. She grabbed the corner of the desk. Had Beth been in Miami too? Was she after Jasmine or her?

Light-headed, she tried to make it back into her desk chair, but she slid down to half sprawl across her desk. She went for the phone, hit 9-1, but Gill ripped it out of her hands and smacked it back in its cradle.

"I take it," Beth said, "you told the police you're safe at home while they look for me. Otherwise they'd be here." She came closer as Gill shoved Alex back into her big straight-backed desk chair. "I heard the taxi driver shout to you about the police looking for me at my place. We won't stay much longer, but I've got to get this IV started in you. Just think of me as finishing properly the last procedure Hale and Jasmine will ever do together. *That* will crush Hale, get his attention."

Alex gaped as Beth strode across the room and produced a rolling metal IV drip rack from Alex's own closet. Its clear, square plastic sack filled with liquid dangled a long tube. The rack rattled as she pushed it toward Alex over the Berber carpet.

"What's that?" Alex said as her body surged alert again.

"I can hardly handle you the way I did the others who were trying to betray Hale and me. Tie her down and gag her, Gill," Beth said, entirely brisk and businesslike.

Gill, Alex thought. If Beth could do all this so calmly, she had to work on Gill. She began to talk fast, before he could gag her.

"I don't know what she told you, Gill, but you're an accessory to at least one murder and possibly another if Sandra Sanchez doesn't live. You know, when a reporter is killed, it's the same as when a cop dies—no other reporter will let it rest. You'll be on the run day and night, your name and picture everywhere."

Gill frowned, but he tied Alex with cord he had looped over his shoulder. He secured her hands apart tightly to the chair back. He gaped at her filthy bare legs and feet as he tied her ankles together to the left front leg of the heavy chair.

"She's only going to use truth serum on you," he said. "To get you to tell her how you've been taking money to infiltrate the clinic to make a bigger story out of this—how you've all been trying to smear her at the clinic."

"You believe that?" Alex countered, aghast. "If she's been paying you, that's bad enough, but if you're in love with her, you've really been misled. Still, I can understand that. I didn't realize either that she worshiped Hale Stanhope at all costs—"

"Liar!" Beth shouted and backhanded her.

Alex's head snapped against the chair. Fire shot through her jaw. She tasted blood.

"Beth," Gill protested, but Alex knew she was doomed when she saw him grin and shake his head. He was enjoying all of this, somehow caught up in the game or bloodlust of it.

"Please, darling," Beth told him, "just pull her chair back away from the desk, then go out and check the guy. Here, give me that gag. I'm going to enjoy using it."

"Nick? He's here?" Alex demanded. "Is he all right?"

Gill dragged her in her chair away from the desk, then went out and closed the door.

"You're surely not going to try to kill me and Nick?" Alex brazened as Beth fussed with the IV. "You've already tried murder twice and succeeded once, so you're leaving a pattern of evidence. And now the police know you murdered your ex-husband and his pregnant wife," she bluffed. To her amazement, Beth didn't change her intent expression; nor did she stop her deft, quick movements.

Alex tried one last, desperate gamble. "Beth, do you really think Hale, who wants to create life, can love a murderess—and the destroyer of his precious DES clinic baby?"

Alex tried to turn her head away. The blow glanced off her chin. Alex rotated her jaw and flexed her wrists behind the chair. Her bonds seemed tight—excruciatingly tight. While Beth evidently decided to put the IV in her hip instead of her arms, Alex glanced at the clock on the far wall. Only four-twenty. She had to stall until the police came to check on her, or Bernice called. She wished she hadn't told the cab dispatcher to say she'd be safe at home with Nick. Keep talking, she told herself. It's what you do best.

"Is that really truth serum, Beth?" she asked, trying to speak each word forcefully.

"We were fine before you started this television probe, putting us in the spotlight. And he just ate it up, didn't he, the arrogant bastard. But he's so brilliant, so special, I forgive him and always will."

"I'll forgive you if you'll just—"

"I was already making plans to get rid of Jasmine, but then your friends threatened everything and had to go. And since you asked, this is Pitocin, pure, powerful Pitocin." She expelled a few drops from the needle attached to the tubing.

"Pitocin?" Alex repeated, wracking her brain to recall that drug. "What's that? Why?"

"I was going to use carbon monoxide on you and your friend," she explained almost patiently, "but I had to do this special for you—a message to Hale he's not always right, that he needs me." Though Alex tried to flinch away, Beth stuck the needle directly into a big vein in her thigh, then taped it in place. Slowly, she straightened and reached toward the clamp that held back the flow of the drug. Alex stared mesmerized by the clear tubing, like a snake that could bite her.

Beth hesitated. "In a way I'm sorry, Alexis, I really am, though not as sorry as I was for Destin's poor wife, Carolyn. He betrayed her just the way my husband did me—like Rita's husband did her. I regretted that—

Rita—but she wouldn't shut up, kept getting her big mouth on TV, just like you."

Alex seized the chance to talk more, though Beth was readying the gag now. "You got Carolyn Destin out on bond—you and Gill?"

"Although this usually works slowly with a lot of dilution and needs monitoring," Beth said, obviously not listening again, "I'm putting it in you fast and straight. You should go into fairly hard labor very soon but will probably die yourself before you deliver."

At that, all control slipped away. Alex went absolutely frantic. "Beth, please, please listen to me…"

But she only clicked the clamp open. With a gurgle the clear liquid swirled down the tube.

Even before it got to her, Alex felt herself go cold. Pitocin, she remembered now, was what they used to force an overdue woman into labor, and then only if there would be no complications at birth. It usually took a long time to work, and they carefully calibrated the dosage. But an overdose would kill the baby and the mother, and since they were so delicate and had been through so much already… Somehow, she seized control of her fear again.

"Beth, listen to me."

"Go ahead, I'm listening," she said, stretching the gag taut between her hands as if she meant to strangle her with it. "That's all I do some days, listen to women mooning over babies I can never have. I'm sick to death of it."

"Beth, you're an infertility nurse and a good one. Whatever you think of me, in your heart of hearts you can't harm an IVF baby, even a tiny, unborn one…."

"My heart of hearts died years ago," she said and snapped the gag before she tied it firmly around Alex's mouth. Then she went out and quietly closed the door.

Alex felt the first of the drug, cool in temperature, sting her. She had to dislodge its bite, even though Beth had put adhesive tape over it. She writhed and struggled, but her bonds held fast.

Wide-eyed, Alex stared at the dripping IV. She bucked and managed to move the heavy chair, but not the needle in her leg. How long, how long, before the pain and death? Strangely, her life did flash before her eyes—people she had loved, the babies she had lost. Nick's face blurred by, but unlike the others, she would never tell him now that she loved him too.

Despite the ungodly hour of the morning, Alex's phone rang and her answering machine clicked on. "Alexis, Mike." His voice came on to be recorded. "I wish you and Nick had checked your messages before turning in, because I called a couple of times before. Get over here first thing in the morning—to the hospital. Sandra's conscious. They think she'll be all right now and she's asking for you and about the baby."

Sandra safe, and she'd never see her again. And the baby...

Alex felt a sharp pain in her hip, as if the poison would surge out from there. She fought again, stretching, yanking, then suddenly sat still. That pain was against her buttock, not in her thigh where the needle was. The knife—that butcher knife Bernice had returned and Nick had left on the counter. She had it still clamped under her arm in its paper envelope. She had frozen up and forgotten it, and somehow Gill and Beth had not seen it. And now she was sitting on it.

She concentrated on sliding her hip hard across the knife. It sawed itself out of its own paper. But she'd never be able to grasp it tied like this, never in time.

She began to feel nauseated and her heart pounded, but she shifted until the knife's sharp edge and point protruded slightly out from the chair with her weight holding it firm. If she only had time or could reach her wrists to saw herself free. She'd never cut through the plastic tubing, but if she could only pinch it against the chair with this knife and hold it, maybe...

She snagged the tubing and fidgeted, finally pressing a coil of it against the chair. Harder, tighter. She strained to trap it, bend it. But even as she stopped the flow, she knew she'd never hold it there. She was already feeling strange, as if her body was going to kick into cramps. Betray her. Time. She was soon going to be all out of time.

Trying to hold the tubing taut, she strained and twisted her body to inch her chair closer to the desk. If she could just knock the phone receiver out of its cradle with her chin, dial 911 somehow, somehow...

But she heard feet running in the house, coming toward the office. At least two people, Beth and Gill again to finish their work. Alex hung her head and sobbed through her gag, then wailed inside with loss and rage.

But it was Nick who came through the door, limping, looking ashen, calling her name. The man behind him she didn't know. Bernice's face was next, then Hale's. Once Hale saw Nick had reached her, he turned back into the living room and screamed, "You stupid bitch! Jasmine was right. You've ruined everything after I saved you—"

"No, I did everything for you, for you!" Beth shrieked hysterically. Gill began to shout obscenities at Beth.

Over Nick's shoulder, as he pulled the needle from her leg, Alex glimpsed Bernice dragging Hale away from Beth. Nick cut her cords just as she surrendered to the dark.

Alex would rather have waked up in her own bed at home, but at least this wasn't the clinic. Nick was holding her hand, and Bernice was leaning against the far wall, looking out the window in her hospital room. Nick jolted alert when he saw her eyes open and bent to hug her. Though feeling her body wasn't quite hers, she hugged him back.

"The baby?" she whispered in his ear.

"A miracle baby, holding on."

"Thank God. Thank you, God."

"The doctors say you need a lot of bed rest, Alexis," he said, looking so spent and serious. "And I'm going to see to it one way or the other."

"I can lend you some wrist and arm shackles," Bernice said, coming to stand on the other side of the bed. "Actually, Destin, I ought to put you in them for hiring a P.I. without telling me. And then my stake-out car chases him just at the wrong time..." Bernice pointed at him like an angry schoolteacher. "And the P.I. did let Alexis slip past him when you told him she wasn't going out last night! Sorry, Alexis. Waiting for you to wake up, that just built up in me."

Alex sensed they were enjoying their sparring. "But did I really see Hale there too?" She asked as the scene from last night came back to her. She looked from one of them to the other.

"Yeah, you saw the eminent Dr. Hale Stanhope there," Bernice admitted, her voice dripping sarcasm. "He said he was worried…"

"…about his clinic baby," Alex finished for her.

"And panicked Jasmine was after you with a gun when he got out of the shower and couldn't find you or her," Bernice explained. "We started interrogating him last night, but now they've both lawyered up. I think, though, he knew basically what Jasmine was doing, but not with stolen eggs and embryos, though he did know she was using her own." The involuntary shudder which racked Bernice made Alex wonder if she had found Jasmine's two embryo experiments, but she'd ask later. She was so exhausted.

"And Beth?" Alex asked.

"She's so shattered about Hale hating her, she's told us everything—but blamed it all on Jasmine."

Alex shook her head, though even that took too much strength.

"You think she's ready for our other surprise, Destin?" Bernice asked, going to the door.

"You mean besides the fact her mother's on the way here to nurse her back to health?" Nick smiled at Alex. "Sure, I think a major dose of good news is in order— if she doesn't jump up out of bed," he said, smiling again and putting a firm hand on Alex's shoulder as if she really could get up.

When Bernice opened the door, Alex heard Mike's voice. At least he couldn't be here to fire her if it was good news. But he came in pushing a woman in a wheel-chair, a pale, thin woman with her black hair pulled straight back, whose face was all big eyes and a huge smile.

"You and me are going to make it, *chica*," Sandra said and held out her arms. Mike wheeled her closer, and Nick supported Alex's shoulders as she leaned forward to hug Sandra, so frail but so fine.

"*All* of us are going to make it," Alex promised her and patted her stomach. "But—you've lost so much weight."

"Hell of a way to diet. But I'm dying for an *empanada,* and Mike's promised to sneak some in."

Alex smiled at Mike, who looked like a kid on Christmas, his hand clasping Sandra's shoulder. "And you know what my Napoleon said," Sandra said and leaned toward Alex. She whispered in her ear, "He said lying down we'll both be the same height."

Alex laughed so loud she startled herself. And though it was a crazy thought, she pictured her unborn child wakened by that joyous noise, swimming in golden sunrise colors, safe and sound.

Afterword

"Alexis, you did it, sweetheart, you did it! She's just beautiful," Nick cried as his surgically masked face appeared around the corner of the green cloths cutting her view of her body in two. They had put up even more drapes when they decided at the last minute to go with a Caesarian section. She couldn't catch a glimpse of anything beneath her rib cage. Even with all the lights and mirrors she had not been able to see her daughter, Joy, born, though that didn't matter if she was safe.

"Is she all right?" Alex asked Nick. "How little? Count her fingers and toes."

"She's petite but perfect, barely a preemie," her ob-gyn, Dr. Jonellen Hanby, assured her, peeking around the other side. "We'll get her cleaned up and give her to you to hold, but only briefly, Alexis. All right," she announced to her assistant on the other side of the drapes, "we're going to close here."

"I wanted to go with the Lamaze all the way, but I didn't want to stress her, like you said, Dr. Hanby. She already went through enough of that before she was born." Alex couldn't help talking in her ecstasy and excitement, especially when Joy tried out her newborn lungs with a hearty wail. Alex felt she could do an entire newscast on pregnancy and childbirth right now.

But she was awed to silence when they put the pink-faced mite in her arms. The baby had her eyes screwed tightly shut, but she grabbed Alex's finger in her tiny fist the moment Alex touched it.

She cuddled her daughter while Nick hovered, his arms cradling them both. "It was worth everything," she told him. "The weeks of bed rest, all the worry. Even testifying to get Jasmine convicted."

"Worth marrying a man who keeps bossing you around?" Nick asked, but they just kissed with his mask still between them.

"You've got to go tell the others," Alex said. "The waiting room's got to be full."

"Including," he said under his breath, "telling Mike and Sandra the only shot of our daughter they're getting for the news for a few days is through the window in the preemie ward."

"Where I'm sure she won't be longer than a week or two," Dr. Hanby assured them. Her blue eyes shone with maternal as well as professional pride, which reminded Alex of something else.

"And, Nick, please tell my mother, yes, I want her to stay this week even if we can't bring Joy home quite yet."

Nick nodded. "I promised Dr. Stanhope I'd call him—though it's one in the morning in Boston." He glanced at his watch and pulled his mask off at last as Alex reluctantly gave up the baby to a nurse.

"Let's just call him together tomorrow morning," Alex said, and he nodded silently.

After the trial, Hale, who had been exonerated of criminal charges, had closed the clinic—until he could restaff it, he said—and gone home to take care of his dying mother. Jasmine had gone to jail, though only for two years, in a landmark decision case. Alex almost believed Jasmine had thought it worth prison time to give her speech on women's equality in fertility on *Court TV.*

Gill O'Fallon had plea-bargained his attempted murder indictment down to ten years in exchange for his testimony; they didn't even bother to try him for breaking and entering. It annoyed Alex that he had done a national TV interview warning people about carefully selecting a security service and updating their older systems.

Beth's first-degree murder trial had been delayed until she was adjudged competent to stand trial. It would start next month in Albuquerque, despite New York State's attempt to have her extradited to face sixteen-year-old murder charges against her ex-husband and his pregnant wife.

Only Carolyn Destin had not been accounted for or brought to justice, though Nick had received an unsigned postcard from Mexico that said only, *I won't ever be back.* Though Carolyn's capture by the police in Silver and Rita's death there had soured his passion to preserve the town, Nick had finally accepted its donation to the Living Heritage group from Hale Stanhope. But now Joy McCall Destin was their real living heritage.

"Nick, one other thing," Alex said, just as he was

going out of the delivery room. He came back and leaned over her.

"What is it, sweetheart?" he asked, looking so intent she longed to soothe his frown away.

"When you come back tomorrow—in case I forget later—would you bring that heirloom cradle from our bedroom? I meant to, but we left in such a hurry...."

"Sure. Want to see how she fits it?"

"She'll fit it," Alex said with a smile as she pressed her palm to his stubble-flecked cheek. "And fill its emptiness for good."

Author's Note

Although infertility procedures are constantly and rapidly changing, oversight and laws to regulate this growing area of medicine lag far behind, sometimes creating chaos in people's lives. Media focus on an Irvine, California, clinic scandal (the theft and switching of eggs and embryos) and the destruction of unclaimed embryos at British clinics are only two hot-button fertility topics leaping from the most recent headlines.

I read many excellent articles and books on IVF, but will not recommend any by name because they become obsolete quickly, and my novel is set in 1994. In some cases to tell the story best, I had to simplify procedures or collapse time. It is true that the cutting edge of infertility research deals with the hope to freeze eggs more successfully. But the real heart of this story, as in reality, is the courageous individual struggles of couples who fight desperately to have a biological child.

I do wish to thank the following doctors for answering my questions about reproductive medicine and the complicated field of IVF: Elizabeth A. Kennard, M.D.;

The Ohio State University, Division of Reproductive Endocrinology and Infertility (whose helpful workshop I attended); and Dr. Julianne Moledor, M.D. An emergency room nurse, my friend and fellow author, Laurie (Miller) Grant, helped with general medical questions. For informative materials, I am indebted to The Ohio State University Medical Centre and Ohio Reproductive Medicine, Columbus, Ohio. Also to the IVF patients who were kind enough to share their personal tragedies and triumphs with me in private. If I have made mistakes in presenting the problems and procedures of infertility, the errors are mine and not theirs.

For information about how a television station works behind the scenes, thanks to the hospitable and generous staff at WBNS-TV (Channel 10), a CBS affiliate in Columbus, and especially to my friend and anchorwoman Andrea Cambern for answering many questions and allowing me to shadow her. No one on the WBNS staff, including Andrea, is represented in this novel, although WBNS newsroom procedures and station layout have somewhat inspired my KALB station in Albuquerque.

Although Rita Twohorses and her Santa Cruz pueblo are fictional, they are based on a study of the Pueblo culture and people. The storyteller figures are real. The first ones were created by Helen Cordero in the 1960s, but they are made in various materials by different artists today. And, of course, the kachinas are a unique Pueblo craft.

Thanks to those known and unknown who made me fall in love with Albuquerque-Santa Fe area on our visits there. Especially to my husband, Don, for arranging and overseeing the trips that helped me get to know the starkly dramatic state of New Mexico. I appreciate the information and correspondence from Carla Ward at the Tinkertown Museum, just off the Turquoise Trail. Several silver ghost towns are resurrected along this starkly scenic drive which connects Albuquerque and Santa Fe.

As ever, the support and advice of my editor, Hilary Ross, and the best ever agent, Meg Ruley, were invaluable. Thanks for insightful advice from John Paine.

—Karen Harper
March 1997

New Times *New York Times* bestselling author

KAREN HARPER

Julie Minton thought nothing of her
fourteen-year-old daughter, Randi, leaving
home earlier that morning to go Jet Ski
riding with Thad Brockman. But now
Randi and Thad are missing—and the
hurricane that hours ago was just another
routine warning has turned toward shore.

With the help of Zack Brockman,
Thad's father, Julie begins a race against
time to find their children—but first,
they must battle not only Mother Nature,
but an enemy willing to use the danger
and devastation of the storm for
their own evil end.

HURRICANE

"Harper has a fantastic flair for creating
and sustaining suspense."
—*Publishers Weekly* on *The Falls*

*Available the first week of June 2006
wherever paperbacks are sold!*

MKH2307R

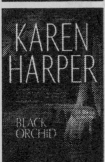

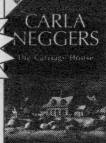